Back On Ice

IVY GLEN
BOOK ONE

NOELLE STONE

For those who crave a man who's devoted, takes control in the bedroom, and knows exactly how to make you surrender—this one's for you. Because a big puck is nothing without the perfect player who knows just how to handle it.

This book contains domestic abuse, domestic violence, mentions of gambling addiction, and light BDSM themes.

Chapter One

SOPHIE

"Aunt Fee, you're not going to believe what I just heard from one of my favorite hockey influencers!" Jordan calls through the rolled down window on the passenger side of my car as he throws the backdoor open and tosses his gear bag inside. He's a flurry of ten-year old energy as he crawls in after it, settling himself on the seat free of his stuff.

"What's that, bud?" I glance at him through the rearview mirror while he pulls on his seatbelt. His hair is damp from the locker room shower, his blue eyes shining with excitement that only someone his age can muster after a grueling hour-long hockey practice. He turns to meet my eyes in the mirror, and it's not for the first time I'm struck with just how much he looks like his dad—my older brother, Tom. Besides the smattering of freckles on his cheeks and his sandy brown hair, he is almost an exact replica of how I remember Tom when we were young.

Putting the car into drive, I let my foot off the brake to pull away from the curb.

"My favorite hockey player of all time is going back to his hometown, and that's Ivy Glen!"

It only takes me a few moments to register what he's saying.

There is only one NHL hockey player to ever come out of Ivy Glen, and that's Carter Williams.

My foot stomps the brake so hard we both lurch forward. I'm very thankful he didn't tell me this while going forty down the main street.

"Woah!" Jordan yelps, jarred from the sudden stop. "What happened?"

"Squirrel in the road," I say, smiling tightly at him through the mirror and trying not to let the emotion bubbling up inside me show. "Sorry bud. That's... super exciting about that hockey player coming to town." Pulling away from the curb completely this time, I drive us home.

"I know right? I'm so excited that I..." Jordan's voice fades in my mind as I process this absolute bombshell.

Carter fucking Williams.

Carter *motherfucking* Williams.

The boy who had been my everything.

Memories flash through me like lightning, quick and painful. Our grade school years. Romantic dates in high school, overlooking the lake in the back of his truck. Making plans for college together.

Taking each other's virginity.

A shiver runs through me remembering the morning after, when my life changed forever. I was stuck with waking up in an empty bed. His text, with the timestamp of around four-thirty in the morning, hadn't given me any indication that anything had been wrong.

> Carter: Hey, beautiful. Last night was amazing. My dad was freaking out about something, so I had to go. Lunch later? I'll text you by noon.

I hadn't heard from him all day and showed up at his house, looking for him. The look on his mother's face, with tears in her eyes, had my heart falling. Carter was gone, leaving only a letter for me behind, filled with promises of making things work, and how he wouldn't let his dad come between us.

It's you and me, Soph. The words, which he had said so many times to me over the years, signed off the end of his letter. That was nine years ago.

Then the asshole cheated on me.

Parking in the driveway of the townhome where I live with Tom and Jordan, I'm brought out of my daze. Jordan still rambles about Carter's player stats and how he might try to get an autograph. The townhouse is one of the newer additions to Ivy Glen, having been built fifteen years ago. All three of us take pride in its appearance, touching up the paint every three years or so, and keeping our small space of lawn nice and manicured. The stone-gray paint is easy enough to touch up on my own, but call Dad whenever we need to go over the white trimmings on the second floor. Painting shutters while being twenty feet above the ground is not something I'm comfortable doing myself. We head inside, and I hang my purse on the hook next to the door as Jordan drops his bag before shucking off his shoes.

"Forgetting something?" I raise a brow as he tries to bolt up the stairs. Shooting me a guilty look, he walks back toward his gear bag that he had tossed aside and hikes it back up over his shoulder.

"Sorry, Aunt Fee."

"No worries, Jordy. Thanks for picking up after yourself." I press a kiss to his hair before passing through the living room, framed photos of my nephew over the years lining the walls. There's a couple family photos too—Mom, Dad, Jordan, Tom, and me, as well as one of Tom, Sarah, and Jordan before the accident. Most of the photos are of Jordan, one for every year he's played hockey, starting at four years old in his black and burgundy "Jr. Thorns" jersey, a helmet tucked under one arm and a hockey stick clutched proudly in the other.

Turning the corner, I head to the kitchen to start dinner. My phone buzzes in my pocket, and when I look at the screen, the word "MOM" flashes at me.

"Hey." Thankful for the distraction from thoughts of Carter, I answer, tucking the phone between my ear and shoulder as I get dinner going. Warm yellow walls greet me when I enter the kitchen, making me feel slightly lighter even with the news of Carter coming back looming over my head. The white cabinets and light wood countertops keep the room bright, something I deeply appreciate right now.

"Sophie!" Mom's voice is warm in my ear. "Hi, sweetie. Listen, I need to talk to you about these floral arrangements in the front of the shop—"

"Mom!" I scold her, scowling at the pot of water I'm filling up in the sink. "What are you doing at the shop? You know working on arrangements makes your arthritis flare up."

"Oh, I'm fine," she huffs. "Besides, I'm just helping Kerry with a few things. Her eye for floral design is just impeccable." Even if I do worry about Mom working when she should be retired and letting me take care of everything, at least she couldn't be more right about Kerry.

I had been so excited when Kerry walked into the shop a year ago, fresh out of high school, and asked if we were hiring. She had brought in a binder filled with photos of different bouquets and arrangements she had made for friends and family. It was really quite cute. She had a whole pitch and presentation about why we should hire her, telling me that all her college classes are at night so she's free to work during the day. She even went as far as to say that even if Hart's Flowers wasn't the only flower shop in Ivy Glen, it would still be the best.

Hiring her had been the best thing we'd done in a long time.

Even though staying local for college wasn't what I had in mind, it was worth it to be able to help Tom take care of Jordan while he recovered from his accident. Online classes had provided so much flexibility for my schedule, allowing me to take a full load of courses while helping Tom get back on his feet.

Then, a little later, Dad asked if I had learned enough from school to help with taxes for the shop, which revealed just how much my parents had been struggling to keep the shop above water and turned into me completely changing the way they do their bookkeeping. Thank goodness I went with a business degree in accounting and financial management and not... creative writing or something. No more sticky notes left on random surfaces to keep track of expenses, or the invisible "inventory sheet" Dad kept only in his head.

Spreadsheets all the way, baby.

"I'm going to have to tell Kerry to send you home when you show up at the shop," I grumble, putting the pot on the stove. I put her on speaker, placing my phone on the counter as I tie my long auburn hair in a messy bun at the top of my head. The kitchen gets unbearably hot while I cook.

"Oh, you wouldn't dare," Mom chides, her voice echoing through the kitchen, then quickly changes the subject. "I hear they're having another town hall meeting about the rec center."

The rec center... and the twin rinks by extension. Ivy Glen Rec Center is falling apart and there's not enough money for all the repairs it needs. The owner, Benson Scott, is an 80-year-old idealist who refuses to charge for rink time for school teams and won't raise his prices for individual skaters.

His heart is in the right place, but it's leaving room for the town council to try to get rid of the rec center to put a strip mall in its place. I can't let that happen—I refuse to. I've been at every town meeting, every vote, every conversation that involves the future of the Ivy Glen Twin Rinks and Rec Center. The center means so much to the town and to the hockey community, how can they turn their back on us? On every person like me who spent their entire childhood in that rink? Who spent years forming happy memories, and have always wanted their future kids to have the same opportunity?

"Yeah, I know, I'll be there," I say, throwing some frozen meatballs and pasta sauce into my pressure cooker.

"Good. I know how much the rec center means to you. Speaking of... did you know that Carter is coming back into town?" First Jordan, now Mom? Am I the only one who was left out of this apparently widespread announcement? It's not enough that he essentially ghosted me, now I don't even get the courtesy of being told he's coming to town sooner than the day before? Not that I want to speak to him—the thought of hearing his voice fills me with such a sense of dread I'd rather go swimming in a bloody ocean full of sharks. But he could have told Tom to tell me. Or asked his mom to call. Or something.

The sound of the front door shutting snaps me from my train of thought. "Looks like Jordan is telling everyone. How nice for him. I bet his mom missed him."

"What about—" Whatever she's about to say is thankfully cut off by Tom walking into the kitchen. Mom has always loved Carter and almost took it as hard as I did when we broke up. Good thing I never told her what really happened. I'm sure whatever she's going to say, it has *something* to do with mine and Carter's past.

"Mom, Tom just walked through the door, I gotta go. Love you." I hang up as quickly as possible, hoping she doesn't get her feelings hurt, but I just *can not* do that conversation right now.

"Hey, Soph." My brother walks into the kitchen, pulling a chair out from the table in the little breakfast nook in the corner and lowering himself down gingerly. His auburn hair, the one feature we share, is in desperate need of a haircut. He pushes it out of his blue eyes as he stares down at the kitchen table.

Frowning, I study him. "What did the doctor say?" Normally, Tom would have been the one to bring Jordan home from practice since he's their off-season coach, but he had an ortho appointment today. His leg's been bothering him more than usual.

"Just to start physical therapy again. Same old shit." He runs a hand over his face, looking tired. Ever since the car accident that claimed his late wife, Sarah's, life and broke Tom's leg in four different places, leaving him with chronic pain and a limp, he's been in physical therapy on and off. The doctors did all they could in the aftermath of the accident. It seemed like things were improving the first couple of years, but the pain came back with a vengeance around four years ago. Since then, he'll go to physical therapy for three to four months, he'll stop going because his leg feels better, and then his pain comes back.

It's why I moved in with him and Jordan after the accident. Between suddenly being a single dad, as well as having to regain his ability to walk, Tom had needed more than an extra pair of hands. He needed his sister.

"I was reading up on a clinical trial for muscle regeneration—"

"Not this again, Soph. It's fine. I'm fine. I don't want to go through the whole process again just to find out I'm not qualified." Unfortunately, despite the fact that he can't walk without pain, Tom's otherwise healthy physical form disqualifies him from the majority of the trials that could be helpful to him. "Did you hear Carter's coming back to town?"

Trying not to let his dismissal get under my skin, I turn to pull the bagged Caesar salad out of the stainless steel fridge. "Yep, twice now," I say dryly into the cold air.

His silence on the matter unsettles me, and I turn to face him, bagged salad in hand. His face gives nothing away as I stalk over to him, raising my brow. "What do you know?"

"What do you mean?" he asks.

"I seem to be the only one who had no idea he was coming back. Jordan told me in the car, and then even Mom just told me over the phone." I wonder if he's still in contact with him. It would be surprising, considering Carter didn't even bother to show up after Tom and Sarah's accident, but maybe I'm the only one he ghosted after the fact. I mean, they *were* best friends.

You would think that having a boyfriend who was so close with your brother would be weird, but back then, it had worked strangely well for us. Tom had known Carter through me previously, but the year that Carter and Tom were on the high school team together they had cemented a friendship as teammates, and later as player and assistant coach. We weren't worried about what he would think when we started dating the year after Tom graduated and some of the best times we had were hanging out as a group with us, Tom, Carter's other close friend, Jake, and my best friends Abbie and Gwen.

"He's a superstar hockey player, of course I know about him." He sighs, leaning back in his chair and sticking his bad leg out in front of him. "His seven-year contract is up, so it would only make sense that he would come back home for a little bit."

I'm probably the only one in town who *doesn't* keep up with Carter's hockey career, and Tom knows this. He most likely didn't say anything out of consideration for my feelings.

He saw how broken I was when everything happened. I'm resolved to never let him have that power over me again. In a town as small as Ivy Glen, crossing paths with Carter is bound to be inevitable, but if I see him again, I'll simply treat him like a stranger. He doesn't deserve any more from me after he broke my heart and left me to pick up the pieces.

Chapter Two

CATER

Everywhere I look, I see her.

Sophie.

The sun is high in the sky as I drive down Main Street. It's just how I remember, like it got stuck in time the day I left. Of course, that comes with constant reminders of Sophie, the girl who my life revolved around the last time I was here. The thought of seeing her again makes my insides feel like they're twisting up—and not in a good way.

I'm not sure how I thought it would be, but I definitely didn't anticipate how fucking hard it would be to see Sophie in every part of Ivy Glen. The empty lot of the abandoned theater that was the prime make-out spot for teens back in the day. The town square, where I asked her to be my girlfriend when we were eight years old, and she just looked at me and said I wasn't "ready for that kind of commitment."

The bench where we would share ice cream on Thursdays after school.

Every single piece of landscape I pass is soaked in Sophie, and there was a time when I thought it would always be that way.

Until my fucking piece of shit dad took control of my life and ripped everything I loved away from me.

A sign I don't recognize on a familiar building catches my attention as I approach, but when I read the words, something twists in my chest. "Hart's Flowers". How did Sophie get her parents to replace the sign? The thing was falling apart back when we were in middle school, but Danna and Paul just kept repainting it and nailing it back up.

The new sign is one of those backlit ones, and the storefront has a little light purple awning that massively increases the curb appeal. I don't have time to read the words painted on the windows before completely passing the shop, and I fight the urge to turn back and see if all the changes are Sophie's doing.

What if she's in there? My stomach flips with a surprising amount of excitement. I could turn this car around, park in front of the store, and see her face again—

No. I shake my head as if that might dislodge my ridiculous thoughts and run a hand through my hair. I meet my eyes in the rearview mirror and give myself a stern look.

It's been nine years. Sophie is no longer interested and has moved on with her life. She might have hated me for it, but what I did back then, how I had to leave her? That was the right choice— my dad didn't give me any other option. Once he made threats against Mom, against Sophie...

Besides, I'm not here for Sophie. Tom's been keeping me updated on the status of the rec center and all the repairs it needs, and I'll be damned if I let the town replace the place that means so much to me with a strip mall.

An obnoxious ringing fills my car, dragging me away from the past. I answer my phone by pressing the button on my steering wheel. "This is Williams."

"Williams! My man! It's Lenny." The irritating, trying-too-hard-to-be-charismatic voice reverberates through my speakers.

Fuck, I should have looked at who was calling before answering the damn phone.

Lenny, the team manager for the Vancouver Vultures. No doubt to talk about the contract they're trying to offer me. I played the last seven seasons with them, ever since I was drafted, and he's been trying to renew my contract. For the third time this week. "Lenny. Come on, I told you—"

"Yeah, yeah, that you don't know, that you want to consider other offers, and you need some time to think. There must be some fine pieces of ass in that middle of nowhere town you're from if you're willing to leave the big city."

A sensation of fierce protectiveness rises in my chest at his words. He knows nothing about this town or what it means to me. Fuck this guy.

"Fuck off, Lenny. Send the proposal over and I'll take a look. But stop calling me."

"Sure, sure." He brushes off my harsh words. He's used to it, working with hockey players. "But I need that answer soon, Williams."

Hanging up without acknowledging that, I pull into the driveway at my mom's house, parking and running my hands over my face. The house looks just like I remember. Two-story colonial houses are not rare in our neighborhood, but the stacked front porches and large white pillars in the front make it obvious how much Dad was obsessed with appearing better off than others. I've always loved the blue paint though.

As for landscaping, there's not a leaf or blade of grass out of place. I've been sending her money since I was drafted, to keep the house in order and pay her bills, since Dad essentially abandoned all sense of responsibility at that point.

Staying with my mom had seemed like a no-brainer, but now I'm second guessing myself. I haven't seen her since I left town, Dad made sure of that. He didn't allow her to come to any of my games over the last seven years, spinning some story to the media about how she has anxiety in large crowds and "prefers to cheer her son on from the flatscreen at home."

Even though we've talked on the phone plenty, it's so easy to pretend everything is alright when you can't see the other person's face. As I pull my bags out of my trunk, I resolve to make sure she knows Dad isn't a threat anymore.

It feels strange knocking on my front door, and when Mom answers, she looks more run-down than the last time I saw her. She's still in her robe and slippers despite it being afternoon, her blue eyes glassy and her black hair spilling onto her shoulders and streaked with considerably more gray.

Back when I was young and naïve enough to look up to Dad, I wished I resembled him more. Now, I count myself lucky that I favor Mom's side of the family. Having gotten her blue eyes and black hair, I've been told how much I look like my grandpa, who passed away when I was a baby.

Guilt eats at me for leaving Mom alone like this, but it could have been so much worse if Dad had been here instead of with me.

"Oh, Carter!" Her eyes light up and she hugs me around my waist. With me at 6'3, her head only comes up to my shoulder. My bags drop to the floor when I wrap my arms around her back.

"Hi, Mom." A heavy sigh escapes me as I rest my chin atop her head. I don't think I realized just how worried I had been that she would be upset or angry with me for staying away.

Because it doesn't really matter that I stayed away for her own good. Keeping my dad happy by becoming his ATM machine and drafting to a team on the other side of the country had kept my mom physically safe from him, but it had clearly done a number on her mental state. I still can't shake the guilt, even though I know if I had tried to go against him, he would have just come home and made Mom's life a living hell.

She backs away, peering around me with wide eyes. "You're sure it's okay that you're here?"

"I told you, Mom," I grab her gently by the arms and look into her eyes, "Dad is gone. I haven't heard from him in over a year. Whatever he got mixed up in, it looks like maybe it caught up to him. He can't control us anymore." She nods tightly, and I let go, following her with my bags as she steps into the house.

"When's the last time you went outside?" I keep my tone as light as possible as I take my shoes off by the front door, then walk through the entryway behind her. I'm convinced that Dad is gone, that his shitty lifestyle of gambling and worse, and his even shittier "associates" have finally been the end of him.

Even knowing that, simply walking into my childhood home gave him more power over me than I thought possible.

My stomach clenches involuntarily as my eyes dart around the front entryway. Literally nothing has changed. I might as well be seventeen again, Dad screaming at me over a shot I missed during hockey practice.

"I went outside a couple of days ago." She waves me off, turning to face me in front of the bottom of the stairs. "I had to go to the grocery store and Bertha was at a doctor's appointment. So I figured a little grocery shopping never hurt anyone."

"Good." I force a smile, trying to push the memories of my dad out of my mind. Mom has become more... hesitant to leave the shelter of home. Bertha, the woman I hired to help Mom out around the house and keep her company, has been a huge help for her mental health, but now I'm worried that she's too comfortable staying inside all day. "Now that Dad is gone, you should get out more, Mom. Join a book club... or just meet one of your friends for coffee. I don't like the idea of you cooped up in this house all day."

"I'm fine, my sweet boy." Mom smiles sadly at me and reaches to squeeze my arm. "I'm just glad you're back. Are you okay with staying in your old room?"

"More than okay. I'm glad to be back." After I press a kiss to her head, I head upstairs with my bags to get settled. Halfway up, I pause. "Mom?"

"Hm?" She looks up at me absentmindedly from the spot on her sleeve that she apparently found very interesting.

"You know… you don't have to stay here. I can buy you another house. One that he hasn't tainted with—"

"No." She shakes her head. "Thank you, but no. I'm enough of a burden on you already, between you paying the bills and taking care of our home. You don't need to buy me a house."

Nodding lamely, I say, "You're not a burden, Mom. But I get it. Just let me know if you change your mind."

"I know, sweet boy. Thank you for looking out for me." She turns and walks towards the kitchen, leaving me to climb up the rest of the stairs.

My feet sink into the plush carpet of the hallway, muffling the sound of my steps. My heart quickens like Dad is going to come around the corner and berate me for something trivial like forgetting to turn a light off.

My door, the last one on the left of the hallway, creaks open as I turn the handle. Not one thing has changed. It's like nobody has taken a single step into my room the last nine years. Well, except to clean, I think as I note the lack of dust on the surface of my furniture.

The queen sized bed in the corner still has my navy blue comforter folded nice and tight around the mattress. The pillows look as though they were fluffed this morning. My gray walls are still covered with as many hockey posters as I could fit, and the shelves on my walls are lined with every hockey trophy and medal I've ever gotten. There's a new one at the end though…

Upon closer inspection, I see that it's the trophy for the championship we won the day before Dad dragged me to Notre Dame. They must have brought it to me after I left. Closing my eyes, flashes from the game that day invade my mind, and all I can remember is the way Sophie felt in my arms when she ran up to me for a kiss after I shot the winning goal. The way we danced at the after party before she brought me back to her empty house.

My eyes snap open, and now all I can see is Sophie.

In the corner, helping me hold a poster in place so I could hang it straight.

Laying on my bed on her stomach, feet kicking and an open textbook in front of her while she helps me study for a biology test.

Her rubbing comforting circles on my back after she overheard my dad berating me for my performance after a game.

Our first kiss, in this very room after I confessed how I felt about her when we were fifteen years old.

Staying in this room is going to be torture. There has to be something that doesn't remind me of her.

Flopping on the bed, I groan, looking at the ceiling. The poster right above my bed is an image of a full moon in the night sky. Sophie helped me pick it out. After we got it up, we spent the afternoon making out in my bed.

A grunt of frustration leaves me when I feel my cock pulse in my jeans at the memory. It must be some Pavlovian response to the bed or something because there's no fucking way that I just got hard as a rock from a memory of kissing.

Needing to focus my mind on absolutely anything else, I hop off the bed and move to unpack my bags. I promised Tom I'd swing by the rec center later before the council meeting, but I can be a bit early. Before I can dwell anymore on the past or how Sophie used to feel in my arms, I shoot him a text to let him know I'll be there early, and give Mom a kiss goodbye on the cheek.

It's not until I pull up to the rec center that I realize this place might hold just as many memories as my bedroom.

Chapter Three

CARTER

TOM'S TEXT COMES THROUGH RIGHT AS I SHUT THE door to my car in the rec center parking lot, and I respond with a thumbs up before shoving the phone back in my pocket.

The deterioration becomes clearer the closer I get to the building. Damn.

Tom might have *under* sold how much help the center needs.

The white paint on the large, rectangular building has yellowed, chipped, and is flaking off in some places on the exterior. The "Twin Rinks Rec Center" sign's light is out on half the letters, so it just spells "T i Ri s R c nt r", and half of those are blinking furiously like they could go out any second. If not for the sign, someone might mistake the building for a large warehouse.

I make it to the doors, where the privacy film is peeling from the corners of glass. The door makes an embarrassingly loud groan when I open them, and I cringe, surprised that no one has filed a noise complaint yet.

Inside isn't much better. The lobby needs more than just a new coat of paint, and when I look above, the ceiling tiles are water-stained and warped. In the hallway is more of the same, including some cracks in the concrete that must have come from frost heaves. The handrails are falling down in some places, leaving them bolted to the wall on only one end, and *that* is a safety hazard.

I finally approach the southside entrance to the actual rink and push the doors open, pleased that these ones don't screech like nails on a chalkboard. Leaning back against the wall just inside the doorway, I shoot Tom a text.

Me: I'm here

"Jr. Thorns, I'd like you to meet a very old friend of mine. Some of you might recognize him from the NHL, but before he did that, he played in the rink here, just like you."

That's my cue.

The fervent whispers of adolescent boys meet me as I round the corner, and I see Tom in all of his coaching glory, complete with a black and burgundy "Jr. Thorns" hoodie, a matching hat, and jeans. He taps the clipboard as his eyes meet mine. The team is in a huddle facing him, so they don't see me right away.

Before they spot me, I take the rink in. It's strange being here again, State championship banners line the rafters, including the one I won for my own team nine years ago. It's more rundown than I remember, but that same feeling of... home fills my chest when I look at it.

The small gasps of parents in the bleachers have my attention snapping back towards the kids as they turn their heads towards me. Red, sweaty faces meet mine, their expressions turning from exhausted to excited in a split second.

We hadn't planned on me meeting the team today, but when I told Tom that I was coming early, the timing worked out perfectly. He just asked that I let him go through his post-practice notes with the boys before introducing me.

"Carter Williams." Tom grins, and kids rush me.

"Mr. Williams! Do you have a pre-game ritual?"

"Is it true you used to play here?"

"Jordan says that you knew him as a baby but I think he's lying."

"Woah, woah, woah!" My voice rings out as I put my hands up. "Hold your horses there, Jr. Thorns." I take a deep breath, readying myself to answer their questions in rapid-fire. Each kid gets my attention as I supply them with the answer to their questions. "No real ritual, just meditation and hydration." Pointing to the next kid, I follow up, "I did play here. I started when I was younger than you, and played every season up until I left for college." My attention moves to the last one. "And yes, I most definitely did know Jordan as a baby—since he was born, in fact, and we used to hang out all the time."

I easily pick Jordan out among his teammates and shoot him a wink. Even if I hadn't been sent an image of Jordan in his Jr. Thorns uniform, a hockey stick in one hand, and his helmet tucked under his other arm just last week, I still would have recognized him. The kid is the spitting image of his dad, from his eyes to the shape of his nose. The only thing different is his sandy brown hair and freckles.

I can't suppress my grin when his teammates all turn and gape at him. Jordan's chest puffs up and he gives a smirk that straight up says "I told you so", and I'm so glad to set the record straight. I stand up, pulling myself to my full height. "Three more questions." After answering their random inquiries, like what's my favorite food and have I ever been to Australia, they ask for autographs.

Parents rummage through bags trying to find something that I can sign, but I mostly end up inking up some jerseys, helmets, and hockey sticks. Everyone disperses, parents ready to go home and get dinner started, and I'm left with Tom, Jordan, and two other boys from the team.

My eyes catch on Tom's gait as he limps his way to one of the bleachers. Fucking hell. He told me it was a bad injury but I haven't seen the guy in nine years... that shit looks painful. He catches my stare and slightly shakes his head, telling me he doesn't want to talk about it right now.

Respecting his wishes, I join him on the bleacher, and focus my attention on the three small hockey players in front of me. "You don't have any questions for me, Jordan?"

His eyes—Tom's eyes—stare back at me and widen as if he can't believe I'm actually talking to him even though I just told his whole team I've known him since he was born. He looks to his dad for reassurance, and Tom just laughs. "Come on, Jord. I told you, I've known him a long time. You can ask him anything."

Jordan's cheeks flush, and he chews on his lip nervously. I'm not sure why he's so nervous, Tom told me that the kid is even more outgoing than *I* used to be.

"It's true." I smile gently, trying to put him at ease. "Ask me anything."

He screws his eyes shut tight before he blurts out in one unintelligible sentence, "Wouldyoumaybeeverbeabletoworkwithmeontheiceyou'remyfavoritepalyerofalltime!"

Tom and I exchange a glance. "Do you want to try that again, bud? Maybe a little slower?" Tom's trying to hold his laughter in, and I do my best to keep a straight face as Jordan's face flushes an even deeper red.

He nods, taking a deep breath, and looks down, starting over. "I was wondering, Mr. Williams, sir, if you would ever be able to, maybe work with me on the ice? You're my favorite player of all time."

A grin splits my face, knowing the kid who I thought would be my nephew the first year of his life, my best friend's son, sees me as some sort of hero. "Jordan, look at me." He looks up hesitantly, and I say in a dead serious voice, "Number one, call me Carter. Number two... we're going to be on that ice so much that you're going to have to get your dad to get rid of me."

His eyes light up and he turns to look at his friends before looking back at me, "Can Bodhi and Theo come too?" The two boys standing behind Jordan look at me with vastly different expressions.

The one on the left only runs a hand through his sweaty hair—hair that's so blonde it's almost white. His brown eyes are pointed downward like he doesn't want anyone to think he's too excited.

The one on the right has hair almost as black as mine, and bright green eyes that shine with hope.

"I would love that," I say, and find that I actually mean it.

The three boys all hiss out some variation of "Yesss!" and turn to face each other, doing some ridiculously complicated three-way handshake that I couldn't replicate even if I wanted to.

"You boys ready to go?" a woman calls out by the door, who I notice has the same bronze skin and black hair as the friend who had been standing on Jordan's right. This must be his mom. "Why don't you guys go rinse off in the locker room so my car doesn't smell like sweaty hockey players."

The boys nod, and Jordan gives his dad a quick hug before he and his friends rush to the locker room with their bags. "Bye, Dad! Bye, Carter!"

"Thanks again, Selma." Tom nods to the woman, who waves back before heading out the door. "That's Theo's mom," he explains. Ah. So the one with the white hair is Bodhi, and the other one is Theo. "They're doing their Friday sleepover. We rotate whose house it's at every week."

"They seem close." I smile after them, remembering how tight-knit my high school team and I used to be.

"They are. Selma and Bodhi's mom, Tara, were all in the same mommy and me group with Sarah, so they've known each other their whole lives. We tried to make sure they kept seeing each other... after everything."

After the accident where his wife Sarah died, he means.

He stares into space before he blinks himself out of it. "Shit, it's good to see you, Carter." Tom's expression changes to a broad smile as he takes a step and squeezes me in a quick hug. "It's been too long."

Guilt pangs in my gut as I return the embrace. "I know, man. I'm sorry, my dad—"

He cuts me off, shaking his head. "Don't. You told me all about what that bastard had been doing. I get it. I'm just glad he's gone now."

"Fuck, me too." I let out a shaky laugh. "He's finally gone, and I'm free to come back home and save this place."

Sighing, Tom shakes his head. "I hope so. Let's go for a walk. I can show you what needs fixing so you can walk into the council meeting with a clear picture of what we need."

We walk around the rinks, Tom pointing out all the things that need repair and the walls that need repainting. "There's air vents there, there, and there," Tom points to three different places on the ceiling, "that need to be replaced. Wiring hasn't been up to code in about eight years. If you look *inside* the rinks, you'll see half the boards are beat to hell, and the other half are two hits away from being destroyed completely..."

Tom goes on to list so many other things it's hard to keep up. I've been trying to figure out how I can help the place, but after seeing how much work it needs, I'm wondering if I just need to offer to pay for everything. It's not like I can't swing it after a sensational seven years in the NHL.

There's no way we can raise the amount we would need in a decent amount of time. We're about halfway around when we're approached by an older gentleman that I recognize back from my high school days. Benson Scott, the owner and founder of the rec center and Twin Rinks.

"Tom! And is that Carter Williams?!" I try not to wince at the volume, but it's much louder than I was expecting. Tom *did* mention that Benson is hard of hearing, but failed to mention how he apparently yells to compensate for it.

He looks between us through the large glasses on his nose, his weathered face smiling broadly at us. He has a surprisingly full head of hair for a man that must be at least eighty by now. It's not hard to see the man from ten years ago. I remember him being slimmer then, but has rounded out quite a bit since.

"It's nice to see you, Mr. Scott." I raise the volume of my voice, reaching my hand out for a handshake. He grabs it with gusto.

"Oh, please, Carter! Call me Benson! Everybody else does!" His voice echoes in the empty area, but I can't help but match the smile on his face. The man exudes "happy".

"Got it. It's nice to see you, *Benson*." I enunciate the last word in a teasing matter, and he chuckles. "It looks like you could use some help around here. I'd love to talk to you about a financial contribution—"

"That's very kind of you. I won't turn down more help. I've been working with our Sophie on drumming up some exposure for the place! Maybe then she can raise the money we need to save it! But maybe I should let you talk to Sophie and see what she thinks."

Before I can open my mouth to ask him exactly what he means about Sophie, a loud ringing comes from Benson's pocket. He pulls it out, and shakes his head before turning to us. "Sorry, boys! I'll catch you later, I have to take this!"

He walks away with the phone pressed to his ear, yelling loudly into the microphone.

Narrowing my eyes, I turn to Tom. "What the fuck did he mean about Sophie saving it? You never said anything about that during our *numerous* phone conversations about saving the rec center."

Tom shrugs. "She's been attending all the council meetings, trying to figure out ways to keep the rec center from shutting down. She manages the whole thing now, you know."

Shit. Part of me was hoping to see her again, but for it to be smack dab in the middle of all of... this?

"Why..." I run a hand over my face as I try to process, "why didn't you say anything?"

"Listen, man," Tom claps a hand on my shoulder, "I know how hard it was for you to leave her behind. You had your reasons and I respect that. I was just trying to not reopen old wounds. Keep our conversations a "Sophie-Free" zone."

He's right. At one point, years ago, I had asked him to not mention her to me if he could help it. It was just too painful. He knew all about the situation with my dad, so he understood, and I was so thankful to him for not giving me a hard time about it.

"But you should know, Carter..." Tom trails off, looking unsure.

"What is it?" I ask, my curiosity piqued.

"She's not the same Sophie you remember."

"What's that supposed to mean?" Not the same Sophie? I can't imagine her any differently than she used to be.

He shakes his head. "You'll see later. Now, come on, Mr. Superstar, you're coming to this meeting with me."

We take my car to town hall, and I follow his lead to the meeting room. He stops us in front of a set of double doors, and I can hear the unmistakable timbre of Sophie's voice through the wall. This is the first time I've heard her voice in nine years. Despite the fact that we can't really make out her words and she sounds absolutely pissed, my cock perks up at the sound of her voice. I vaguely make out her saying something about reallocating some of the town's funds to the rec center. I don't think I ever heard her sound so determined in all the years we were together.

I try to subtly adjust myself, and Tom glances at me and shrugs. "She's very... passionate." He winces when the pitch of her voice goes higher. A deeper voice sounds, and hers picks up again, lower, calm sounding.

Tom shakes his head and smiles. "You ready for this, Carter Williams?"

I don't have time to answer before he opens up the doors to the meeting room.

Chapter Four

SOPHIE

"M R. S COTT AND HIS WIFE BUILT THIS PLACE, AND IT has been a staple in the community for the last fifty years. Why should we spend years benefitting from their generosity and then turn our backs on them when they need it most?" My voice rings with conviction in the council chambers of the historic town hall building. Small murmurs of agreement surround me as I stare at the councilmen from my spot standing in front of my seat, giving me the courage to continue.

"Who has benefitted the most from this rec center? Certainly not Mr. Scott and his wife, who have the financial records to prove that they've only taken enough of a cut to pay their bills and raise their kids. Every dollar outside of that went back into the rec center. The people of this town have been benefiting from the Scott family for fifty years, and it's time we take on some of the burden."

Glancing around my fellow townspeople in the audience, their nods and looks of agreement spur me further. Everyone seems to be receptive to my words, from the suit-and-tie businessman on my left, to the elementary school nurse on my right. "I say we start with the schools. Mr. Scott does not charge a single dime to schools for practice time on the rink. How much money has that saved them over the years? We can redirect funds meant to upgrade the bleachers in the football stadium for the what... third time in ten years? We use that money and direct it to the rec center, which should be treated as an extension of the school in that regard, since practice is free for the team." A small burst of chatter erupts from the townspeople surrounding me, and I hold back a smile as I make eye contact with each member of the council sitting at the long head-table at the front of the room..

"Hold on just a second there, Ms. Hartwell." Mr. Gibbons, the middle-aged councilman at the far left of the table, holds up his hands. He took over Carter's dad's seat when they left town, and he's been nothing but a money-grabbing pain in the ass.

This whole thing with the rec center started about two months ago when some busy-body reported the light-up building sign being out to the town instead of talking to myself or Benson. This brought unwanted attention to the center and made the council bring up the question of its "curb appeal", which *then* invited further speculation on what repairs are needed. Now we're faced with a fight to the death with the council because someone said we'd be better off knocking it down and building a strip mall if we couldn't get the center in "acceptable condition".

"That's a lot of pretty talk, but let's be realistic. It's a lot of work to reallocate all of those funds, and I'm not even sure Ivy Glen needs a hockey team anymore..." He trails off, looking down the table at his fellow council members, clearly seeking backup.

Abbie's dad, Michael Wixx, is one of the only two faces who don't seem convinced. He meets my eyes with a grimace. The only other member of the council who doesn't look to be in agreement with Gibbons is Oscar Davis, but I have a feeling that's because he's ogling my chest instead. Damn guy can't take a hint—I've been shooting down his attempts to go out again for months.

Suppressing the disgusted shiver that threatens to erupt at Oscar's scrutiny, I steel myself, remaining focused. The council will really just do anything to screw us over. My voice is low as I try to keep my temper controlled. "It's not 'a lot work', it's all part of the athletics department funds—"

"Paul is right," Ms. Sinclair says from a few seats down, nodding towards Mr. Gibbons. "Football seems to be the star of the show now, hence the constant bleacher upgrades. People will donate more to a sport that produces star players." She shrugs. "We haven't had a famous hockey player come out of Ivy Glen in ages. Not since Carter Williams."

I'm just about to tell Sinclair exactly what I think of the fact she only thinks hockey is worth something if we get a famous player out of it when the doors behind us fly open, and a familiar, heart-stopping voice rings out, "I think I have a solution."

My entire body freezes and my words die in my throat. Chills skate down my spine, and I'm not sure if the roiling in my stomach is because I'm actually going to be sick or if my fight-or-flight response is kicking in.

I knew he was coming, but nothing could have prepared me for this. To know that he's in the same room. That if I just turned around, I'd see his face, and most likely get lost in his ocean blue eyes like I have so many times before. Eyes that used to solely be for me. Carter is here, and while waves of murmurs take over the crowd, I stand there frozen.

"...all-star hockey player..."

"...son went to school with him..."

"...he was always such a kind young man..."

Shit. I can't bring myself to look at him. If I do... I don't know if I'll run into his arms like a pathetic love-struck idiot, or punch him in the face. Instead, I focus on the front of the room.

I swear the entire council now has hearts for eyes as they look at him. "Of course, Mr. Williams," Ms. Sinclair purrs at him.

Thirsty bitch. "Please, the floor is all yours. Ms. Hartwell's time had *just* run out."

All of my panic turns to annoyance.

Of course. I don't look at him out of spite as his footsteps sound across the now silent room. There's probably a vein popping out of my head right now. Where the hell does he get off coming in here and interrupting me?

Huffing, I cross my arms, still staring at the council as they all stare star-struck at Carter. Well, besides Oscar and Mr. Wixx. I can feel Carter's gaze burning the side of my head, but it takes all of my self-control not to turn my head. I wonder if he looks the same. If there's any trace of the small-town boy who loved me then left me high and dry, or if that's all been washed away by fame and fortune. If there's any justice in the world, he'll be missing a few teeth and had his nose broken one too many times to be as gorgeous as he'd been back then.

He clears his throat before speaking. "I've offered to work with Benson Scott on the repairs for the rec center. If it all works out, I'll be donating whatever funds are required for reconstruction. The rec center is a staple for the community of Ivy Glen, and we shouldn't give it up if there's something we can do about it. That being said, its structure and layout are completely outdated, and I believe it would benefit from a major transformation."

"I completely agree," Mr. Gibbons nods like a fucking bobble-head, and the rest of the council sounds their agreement.

This is ridiculous.

I have been fucking trying for *months* to save the rec center, and Carter 'NHL Star' Williams just shows up, throws his money at the problem, and everything is fixed.

This has to be some sort of PR stunt or something. The guy hasn't come into town in nine years, and suddenly wants to play the hero? I can just see the headline now, "HOMETOWN HERO: Hockey Legend Selflessly Saves Town Ice Rinks from Utter Destruction!"

Has to be because he'll be signing a new contract, then use this to up his value to potential teams, get a higher paying contract, then we'll never hear from him. I'd bet he'd probably convince everyone to name the new project after him. "The Carter Williams Rec Center."

Hell no.

Putting on my best "fuck you" customer service voice, extra polite and saccharine, I address Carter, but keep my eyes on the council. "That's very kind of you, Mr. Williams. However, you can't just throw money at the problem and have it solved overnight. The town has to *want* to keep the ice rink afloat, or else we'll be facing this exact same problem in another twenty years, in which case you won't be around to fix it."

"I understand that, Sophie." His voice is placating, smooth like velvet, and I have to suppress a shudder at the sound of my name on his lips. "But it's more than just throwing money around. I have ideas to make hockey relevant to the town again. I mean, I've played in enough hockey rinks to know what the rec center is missing." The council all chatters their agreement, and the townspeople murmur with far more enthusiasm than they did when I was speaking. He talks more about how his experience makes him singularly qualified to oversee the reconstruction of the rinks. Some bullshit about state-of-the-art locker rooms and self-serving concession stands, and the council is just eating it up, telling him yes to everything and offering to have some new plans for the rinks drawn up.

My brain tunes them out. The fucking gall. I have been working my ass for the last two months trying to come up with new fundraising ideas. I've snagged sponsors, publicity spots, and spent countless sleepless nights trying to come up with ways to save the piece of my heart that lies within these rinks.

Then Carter comes in for less than ten minutes and convinces the council to let him take over and basically tear down the rink. Un-fucking-believeable.

My mind only registers that the meeting has ended when the people around me stand and chatter with excitement. I need to get out of here. Exiting my row of seats, Carter's voice calls after me. "Hey! Sophie, wait!" Ignoring him, I move through the townsfolk who are not moving towards the exit, but toward...

I whip my head around and see Carter surrounded by the majority of the council, as well as at least twenty other people.

Holy shit.

Black hair, shorter on the sides and longer on top, is styled in an artfully messy way. His broad shoulders pull his button-up shirt tight across his chest, teasing at the built muscle underneath. His body has filled out since I saw him last, but his face...

His jawline is sharper, his features more defined. I had thought he was hot before, but damn, the years have been kind to him.

Yet, underneath it all, I still see the boy I loved. *My* Carter.

Our eyes meet briefly, his torturingly familiar, ocean-blue eyes attempting to pierce through my very soul.

They hit me like a kick to the chest, almost making me lose my breath before I turn away from him.

Nice try, but I learned my lesson nine years ago. I won't be looking into those eyes any longer than necessary.

Unlike the rest of the town, I am not dumbstruck by the man-turned-apparent-legend that is Carter Williams, and take the opportunity to make my exit. I nearly freeze when I see Tom leaning against the wall, frowning. My eyes narrow and I gesture violently towards Carter with a look that says *"Did you do this?"*

He shrugs, which only further stokes the anger rising inside of me.

Rolling my eyes, I stalk past my traitor of a brother, barging through the door and letting it slam shut behind me.

I make it halfway down the hallway before I hear his voice again. "Sophie! Sophie, wait!" Increasing my speed as much as I can in these damn heels without tripping and breaking my neck, I try to escape before he catches up with me. The last thing I want to do is face him right now.

The clack of shoes speeds up and I keep my head forward, pretending that I don't hear the voice calling after me. I've just exited the building when the door opens behind me. I can't take it anymore—the running, the urge to look at him, the pain in my chest. It's all too much.

"Can we talk? Please?" He has no right to sound sincere.

Whirling, I take the two steps separating us and jam my finger into his chest.

His very hard, sculpted chest.

"You want to talk?!" I can't help but shout. Doing my best to ignore how good he looks in his button down shirt with the sleeves rolled up and fitted slacks, I poke further into his chest so hard he winces. "Let's talk, big shot. Should we start with how you left everyone for nine years and have no right to waltz back in like you own the place? Or how I have spent every spare minute for two fucking months fighting that council tooth and nail, showing up with fiscal schedules, lists of way to minimize the cost of the repairs, bids from contractors, and you just swoop in like some kind of goddamn knight in shining armor and steamroll that. You've practically convinced them to tear it down so you can have some sort of self-important monument to yourself!"

He looks at me with surprise, his mouth opening and closing like a fish. All that and he has nothing to say for himself? "Soph, I—"

"You know what? No." I take a step back, shaking my head and throwing my hands up in exasperation. Not hearing from or seeing him for nine years is one thing. But for him to come back to town and try to destroy the rinks, the place we spent the most time together? We grew up on that ice and he knows how much it means to me. Implying we should just tear the whole thing down because it's "outdated" is a whole different kind of betrayal. "This is low, even for you." He says nothing as I turn and walk away. Behind me, I hear the door of the building open again.

I barely hear Tom's voice when he says, "Can't say I didn't warn you."

Carter sighs. "Yeah. Yeah, you did."

Whatever the fuck that means.

"I come bearing the holy offerings! Let me in!" I use the hand not holding the bag of Chinese food to knock on the door again. The doorknob turns and my best friend peeks her head out, raising an eyebrow at me when I lift a wine bottle with a grin.

Abbie, BFF since high school, moved away for college and only came back to Ivy Glen a couple of years ago after graduating from nursing school. We try to get together at least once every few weeks for girls' night, and we've already had ours this week, but I really need this.

Abbie's shoulder-length brown hair swishes as she moves to open the door the rest of the way. She gives me a look when I walk right past her, beelining straight through her living room to go to the kitchen, her freckles crinkling on her nose. Once there, I pull a corkscrew out of the drawer and uncork the bottle. The liquid makes a chugging sound as I take a swig straight from the bottle.

Her kitchen is stacked with odds and ends, cute little wooden signs fixed to the walls with little sayings like "But first, coffee," "Oh for forks sake," and "Let's make pour decisions".

"Rough day?" She laughs, walking in after me.

"You don't know the half of it." I turn toward her as she takes down two glasses, presumably to stop me from guzzling the whole bottle. As I grudgingly pour some in each, she gets plates so we can dish out the food.

"It's like, how does he think he can just waltz back into town after disappearing for almost a decade?" I ask once we're settled on the couch with dinner. Her style is evident in this room as well, with cream walls, a lavender couch and throw rug, and a giant sign on the wall that reads "Sassy, classy, and a bit smart-assy".

Abbie's clearly not surprised I'm immediately complaining about Carter. I've called her twice already since I found out about his return.

I take a bite of an eggroll, talking around it. "Then, he has the nerve to *demand* to talk to me? After he fucking cheated on me? I don't fucking think so."

"Oh shit," Abbie leans forward, eyes wide. "What happened?"

"What happened is he showed up to the council meeting and told everyone he's paying to redo the rec center. Like, completely redo, tearing the existing building down. I don't know how I can stop him without having to talk to him."

"Is that what you want?" Abbie eyes me knowingly.

What I want is to be able to live the rest of my life without having to think about Carter or how he demolished my heart ever again. What I *want* is for him to be ugly so my mind isn't warring with my body over how attracted I still am to him after he destroyed me. He's only gotten better looking since high school, which I wouldn't have thought possible, but it's marred by the fact that all I feel is betrayal when I see his stupidly handsome face.

"I want a lot of things, Abbs, but that's definitely at the top of the list."

"Well..." Abbie says slowly, plucking a piece of chicken off her plate with a pair of chopsticks. "You can't avoid him forever, especially if he's going to be working on the rec center. Maybe you can finally get the closure you need and move on with your life."

I nearly choke on my food. "Excuse me! I've already moved on with my life, thank-you-very-much."

Abbie just rolls her eyes, which makes me want to toss an eggroll at her. "Sure. Soph. If you say so."

Not wanting to be under her scrutiny regarding Carter any longer, I switch the topic to work at the flower shop. From there it's on to her day with wacky fellow nurses, and after an evening of doing our nails and watching movies, I make my bed on her couch, ready to crash for the night. It may not officially be a "girls night', but being here is definitely better than going home and having to deal with my brother.

Logically, I know that I'll have to talk to Carter at some point to get closure, but that's a problem for future me.

Chapter Five

CARTER

IT'S WEIRD GOING TO A BAR IN YOUR HOMETOWN WHEN you weren't old enough to drink the last time you were there. The bar that Tom and I walk into, Danny's Place, is where we always talked about going when I turned twenty-one.

Better late than never, I suppose.

It's seven p.m. on a Friday so the night life hasn't quite picked up yet. I feel a little overdressed for the location; most everyone here is in jeans and t-shirts like Tom, and I'm over here in slacks and button up dress shirt. I've never actually been inside the bar before, but from what I heard growing up, it's the go-to bar for locals. The interior is well-maintained and gives off a friendly vibe. Maroon leather booths line the walls, and there are various round tables in the middle that seem like they may be cleared out on the weekend for dancing.

"Hey, Danny," Tom greets as we approach the bar.

"Tom," Danny says gruffly, using a rag to dry off a glass behind the counter. Even though he's probably a couple of inches shorter than me, he's pretty intimidating. He's built like a lumberjack and looks the part with his blue plaid shirt, white t-shirt underneath, and neatly trimmed beard. He's probably in his mid-forties, if the faint streaks of gray in his black hair are any indication.

His eyes land on me, but the only acknowledgement I get is a split second look up and down before he nods and turns to the bar.

Shooting Tom a questioning look, I slide onto an open barstool.

"Don't take it personally. It took me five years to get to a first name basis with him. He's just getting our drinks," Tom says, joining me at the bar.

My brow furrows. "We haven't given him our order."

Tom chuckles. "Yeah, and don't try to give him one either. The man has his ways. Knows just what you need by looking at you."

This could be interesting.

A moment later, Danny returns to us, one drink in each hand. He slides what looks like a scotch on the rocks toward Tom, and a short glass with some sort of cocktail over to me. The slice of orange peel used as a garnish has me raising my brow. "Old Fashioned," he grunts at me, then walks to the other side of the bar.

I've never had an Old Fashioned, despite knowing it's a classic. My grandpa used to drink them all the time before he died. I take a tentative sip, the sweet vanilla and caramel notes of the whiskey mix nicely with the citrus of the orange peel.

The slight burn in my throat as it moves down turns to warmth, and I close my eyes a moment, savoring the taste.

Meeting Danny's eyes across the bar, I raise my glass and nod with a grin. He grunts in approval before moving his attention elsewhere.

Tom takes a sip of his scotch with a smug look. "See? Just what you need."

"Yeah, yeah," I grumble, but grin as I take a proper drink of my Old Fashioned. I can't help but think of Sophie, and how if things had been different, if I had gotten an offer from Boston, maybe this would be a regular Friday night thing the three of us did in the off season. The thought causes me to unload what's been on my mind since we left Town Hall. "I didn't expect to see Sophie like that."

"I told you she was passionate," he mutters, nursing his drink.

"That's not..." I run a hand through my hair. "It was just... fuck." A sigh leaves me. I'm not really sure what I'm trying to accomplish here. The Sophie I left behind nine years ago and the Sophie I met tonight are two completely different people. She always had this confidence about her, but in high school, she was quiet, shy, and just radiated happiness. Now, I don't know what she is, but she's certainly not quiet and she certainly didn't look happy. It's strange to think that she's grown up just as much as I have, and that I am completely unaware of what her life looks like. What her day-to-day is.

I really have no one to blame but myself for that, but it's an unexpected punch in the gut just the same.

But fuck, did she look good. Looking at her across the room in that meeting had been torture. She had been so athletically built in high school from years of playing hockey, which, obviously, I found sexy as hell, but in the last nine years, she's made this transition into a full-fledged *woman*. She's still built the same, but now there's the slightest of curves where there weren't really before. Her long legs had looked even longer because of the heels she was wearing, and that button-up top she had on gave me just the slightest glimpse of the top curve of her breasts.

Fuck.

And then she started yelling at me, and all thoughts of how fuckable her body looked flew out the window. Instead, I was left to look into the pain of her face and know that *I* was the one that put it there.

"Just... can you tell me about her?"

Tom looks at me skeptically, probably because I made him swear to never bring her up unless it was absolutely necessary, but I want to know. My brain is trying so hard to correlate the Sophie I knew to the one I just saw, and it's driving me crazy.

"You sure?" he asks knowingly. After I give a nod of confirmation, he sighs. "After Sarah passed, Soph moved in with me full time. She's been helping me with Jordan ever since. Which is great, because Jordan loves his Aunt Fee."

A smile ghosts my lips when I remember all of us eating at Sal's, our old hangout, and Sophie bragging about how one of Jordan's first word was "Fee-fee". While not her name, it's the sound that came out of the little guy when she repeatedly sat in front of him saying "Sooo-feee".

"What's she been up to all these years? Has she met anyone?"

Tom's voice lets out a little raspy chuckle. "No, but I wish she would do something for herself for once. She's been living with me, which is great. But she also manages our parents' flower shop and the Twin Rinks."

I ignore the hope that fills my chest at the mention of her not seeing anyone. I have no business thinking of any kind of future with her... no matter how much I might want it. I'm clearly the last person she wants to see and for good reason. For years I promised her it was the two of us, together always.

I broke that promise.

Even if she *did* want to see me, I don't think it would work. As much as I want another chance with her, reality bites. As soon as this rec center project is finalized and I have my new contract, I'll be off to training camp and out of her life again.

"Not to mention," he continues, "she's been doing all this since she was still in college, getting her business degree in accounting. Now, instead of charging for any financial services, she does it for free on top of everything else. I don't know how she does it all."

She's stretching herself thin. One of these jobs would be enough to fill anyone's time completely, but she's doing so much. I want to know what drives her, why she's spending so much time doing everything for everyone else, and nothing for herself.

"So Carter..." His voice is hesitant as he looks over at me. "What's going on with your dad?"

Sighing, I run a hand over my face. "I'm pretty sure he's dead in a ditch somewhere. Usually, he's on my ass about money, threatening Mom, spouting all kinds of bullshit. And then a little over a year ago, it all completely stopped. He had been disappearing for longer stretches at a time. His gambling was out of control, and I'm thinking maybe he pissed off the wrong person. If the bastard was still kicking, you know he would've resurfaced to get his fingers into my next contract. There's nothing he likes better than exercising control over decisions that should be mine."

Tom knows all about how Dad essentially blackmailed me into signing with the team he wanted me to, holding Mom's safety over my head. He was one of the few people I talked to about everything when it was happening.

Tom nods somberly. "Speaking of next season... do you know what team you want to sign with?"

I shrug. "I have a couple of offers on the table, but I'm not in a rush to make a decision."

"Did you get any offers from New Jersey or New York? Between injuries and Sullivan's retirement, Boston's got room for a winger on their first line." Tom mentions it casually, but I know he would love for me to be local again. Hell, I can't deny the thought of living close to Tom is pretty appealing, but is it really what I want?

"Yeah, but I don't know, man. For so long, I stayed away from home just to keep Mom safe. To keep Sophie safe. But now that they *are* safe, it's like I don't know what to do with myself. My piece of shit dad had me looking over my shoulder for years. Now that I'm free of all of that, I just want to take my time and figure things out."

Tom claps a hand on my shoulder. "I'm here, Cart. Whatever

you need. A sounding board, a non-biased opinion, or just someone to keep an eye out for your mom, I'll help you in any way I can."

"Just a single bed is fine," I tell the concierge, hiking my bag further on my shoulder. I had thought staying with Mom during my visit was the best idea, but after getting home from the bar, the earlier visions in my room assaulted me, and all I could see was Sophie. Again.

Then the memories of Dad and all of his abusive shit hit me like a ton of bricks. That, on top of the memories of Sophie, made me feel like I couldn't breathe. Getting out of there was a no brainer.

Mom seemed put out, but understood when I told her there are just too many memories in that house. I don't know how she stands staying there. Hoping that staying in a room that doesn't constantly remind me of my high school girlfriend would keep me from thinking of her, I drove my car to the only place to stay in town. Ivy Glen Inn. It's rustic, but in that homey-way that most everything in Ivy Glen is. The building is only two stories, the brick exterior giving away its age. It's not what I'm used to staying in, considering the Vultures always housed us in upscale hotels for away games, but I'm not so far up my ass that I can't stay in a three-star establishment.

After running my credit card at the terminal, the concierge in the lobby smiles and hands me my key. As I unlock and open the door to my room, I'm hit with the standard "hotel room" smell that I grew accustomed to after seven years of traveling. A queen sized bed with a maroon comforter fills most of the space, with two nightstands on either side.

I throw my bags on the bed, then pull out some boxers and sleep shorts. Steam fills the small bathroom once I start the shower and step under the hot spray of water, closing my eyes.

Despite all my attempts to remove her from my mind, thoughts of Sophie return. Even with how pissed she was at me, she looked beautiful. The angles of her face are a little sharper, but her eyes are the same. Honey brown and expressive as hell. The way her long, auburn hair was curled slightly, falling down her back.

I had spent our entire childhood knowing how she was feeling based on her eyes. They were joyful, or full of love. Sometimes mischievous. Occasionally sad. But I had always known how to fix that last one. When we were kids, I'd tell stupid jokes until she laughed, and when we got older, I'd be able to just hold her and be a comfort.

Tonight, reading the emotions in Sophie's eyes was like picking up my favorite book only to see that someone had changed all the words. And then recognizing my own handwriting on the pages.

Fucking fire and pain was all she had as she unleashed her fury on me, and I deserved it.

I *hate* that I have something to do with that pain.

I *hate* what Dad did. What I had to do because of *him*.

And I *fucking hate* how I ghosted her. How it made me feel like I was exactly like *him*.

Because Dad? He's a selfish bastard who couldn't even treat his own wife right.

But me? I loved Sophie, more than the air I breathe, and I *still* hurt her.

Maybe she's changed, but so have I.

Back then, a part of me loved how it felt like she needed me. How she would stick close to me during parties and get togethers, letting me take care of her. She clearly doesn't *need* me anymore. Or, more likely, she doesn't want to need anyone.

But it's becoming equally clear that I *want* her. That I never stopped wanting her. I want to know her again, everything that she's been through and who she's become. I want to run my hands over the slight, soft curves of her body that weren't there nine years go, peel her clothes off and—

My cock grows hard thinking of her, and I grasp it in my hand, pumping up and down. Sophie. *My* Sophie. Fuck, what I wouldn't give to watch the look her eyes turn from hate into need, and then, surrender.

Thoughts of how I'd gently grab her neck and kiss her breathless, dominating her mouth with my tongue fill my mind. How the lipstick she wore tonight would look wrapped around my cock, my fingers fisting in her hair as I guide her up and down. I can already tell she'll need someone to get her out of her own head. She may not want my help now, but if she'll let me, I can give her exactly what she needs.

Fuck. My free hand braces against the shower wall as I lean forward, the hot water running over my back as I stroke faster, picturing her perfect tits bouncing underneath me as I thrust into her, holding her legs over my shoulders.

My hand tightens as I imagine flipping her onto her hands and knees, fucking owning her pussy, pounding into it until she screams my name. If she's good, I'll reach around and rub her clit until she comes undone around me—

I gasp her name as hot ropes of cum paint the tile of the shower wall.

Being away, it was easy to pretend that I no longer had feelings for Sophie Hartwell. I admit, when I first planned on coming back to town, the prospect of seeing her again had my stomach flipping. Then, simply being in Ivy Glen and being reminded of her at every turn was hard. But having her in front of me, breathing the same air as her and not being able to take her into arms had been fucking torture.

I need to make her mine again.

Catching my breath, I make a promise to myself. I'm going to apologize and explain everything to her. I'm going to get on my fucking hands and knees if have to.

I know I fucked up. She deserves so much more than what I gave her.

But maybe... if she hears me out, I can have a second chance.

Chapter Six

SOPHIE

My alarm blares, and as my eyes crack open, rapidly blinking away the grittiness from my makeup the night before, one thing occurs to me.

I'm officially too fucking old to sleep on Abbie's couch.

My back groans as I sit up, reaching my fists above my head in a stretch that makes my shoulders crack in ways I didn't think possible.

Yep, too fucking old.

"Turn that thing off!" Abbie grumbles, half asleep, from her bed in the other room. I find my phone where it fell on the floor last night, and turn off the alarm.

Crawling into bed with Abbie, I prod her with my finger. "Hey." Despite the fact that there's plenty of room in her queen sized bed for the two of us, no amount of alcohol can make me sleep through the way she tosses and turns all night. More often than not, she would end up laying half on top of me, spread out like some sort of restless starfish.

"What?" She cracks one eye open, glaring at me for interrupting her sleep.

"Thanks for being a good friend. I'm going to go home to get ready for work."

"Yeah, yeah. I love you too. Leave me alone so I can go back to sleep."

Chuckling, I leave her room to grab my clothes from yesterday. Abbie let me borrow some sweats to wear to bed last night, and once I change out of them, I throw them in the hamper on my way out the door. I'll run home really quick and get changed before heading to Hart's Flowers.

Saturdays are full days at the flower shop, and something I look forward to every week. Ever since I picked up managing the Twin Rinks, I don't get nearly as much time in the shop as I used to. While part of me loves the fact that I get to do both jobs, the other part feels guilty for letting someone else help so much with the shop that my parents spent years growing from the ground up. During the week, I'm at the shop from open to till noon, then head to the rec center. On Saturdays, the assistant manager, Brandon, opens Twin Rinks, so I can stay at the flower shop until three, then grab Jordan and his two best friends for his hockey practice while I coach my own junior high rec team. The busyness of the flower shop on a Saturday should be enough to keep Carter far, far away from my thoughts—where he belongs.

When I arrive home at 8:30, the house is quiet. Tom's truck is in the driveway, so I'm assuming he's getting as much sleep as he can before heading down to the rec center to coach the younger hockey teams.

Twenty minutes and a hot shower later, I'm running out the front door in my pink Hart's Flower Shop t-shirt, jeans, and my tennis shoes. I grab a Twin Rinks hoodie for the practice later and throw it in the back seat as I slide into the car. I'll *just* make it in time. Last thing I need is to show up late and get a talk from my parents about how I'm "doing too much" and I need to "take a break and focus on myself."

I pull up to the shop at 8:59, right as Kerry is flipping the "closed" sign to "open", and she unlocks the door, smiling at me.

"Hey, Sophie!" she says as I approach, and grin back at her.

"Good morning, Kerry." I walk through the door she's holding open for me.

One of my favorite things about the flower shop is how it's always bursting with color. I'd probably feel that way about any flower shop, but Hart's Flowers is filled with so many childhood memories that every morning, the sight of it settles something within me. This place is safe. Predictable.

I do a quick inspection of the floral coolers that line the painted light-blue walls. One is filled with pre-made arrangements, and the others have tall, rustic metal buckets filled with specific flowers, separated by color. As always, Kerry has everything for the day ready to go.

After tucking my purse under the counter, I move to the tablet we use as a POS system, clocking in for the day.

My stomach rumbles, and I realize that I didn't have any time for breakfast.

"I come bearing gifts." Kerry's voice is chipper, and she's holding a cup of iced coffee and a pastry bag out towards me. Her bright green eyes sparkle, and I know she just heard my stomach as loudly as I did. She's wearing the lavender version of our Hart's Flower Shop staff shirts, making her eyes pop and her bronze skin glow. Her long, black hair is in a braid that drapes over her shoulder while curled tendrils frame her face, only adding to her angelic appearance.

"Oh, sweet Kerry, you're a lifesaver." I gratefully take the treats from her and immediately chug a third of the coffee. A moan escapes me at the taste of the salted caramel goodness. She always knows just what to get me.

Kerry laughs at my theatrics. "There's a chocolate croissant in there too."

"I knew I liked you." I wink at her, and she chuckles.

"How much do I owe you?" She waves me off.

"You bought lunch last week, remember?" She's right. I sigh, knowing that arguing that I *should* be buying her lunch for all of her hard work and she doesn't owe me anything is an argument neither of us will win.

The bell over the front door chimes, indicating we have our first customer. "Greg!" Kerry exclaims, a smile lighting up her face. "How are you? What can I help you with?"

"Hey, Kerry." The customer, a young man who looks to be about Kerry's age, smiles nervously. "I need some help. I'm meeting my girlfriend's parents for the first time at dinner tonight, and I want to make a good impression. Do you have any ideas?"

"You bet I do," she winks, and leads him to the display coolers, showing him the different flower combinations they could go with. Once he makes his choices, they come back to the front register and Kerry tells me to ring him up for a custom bouquet of white and pink lilies, dark pink carnations, and some babies' breath. He pays, and can't seem to stop staring at me. Before I can ask if I have something on my face, Greg speaks up.

"You're... you're the Sophie from the Town Council meeting last night, right?" he asks, somewhat cautiously, no doubt remembering how worked up I got.

"Yep, that's me," I say with a tight smile just as Kerry comes out with the full arrangement.

"I bet you're excited Carter Williams showed up and saved the day." He nods, like he's agreeing with himself. "He's gonna do great things for this town, I can tell."

Forcing myself to smile politely and ignore the anger at Greg's words, I watch as Kerry hands the arrangement over, wishing him luck at dinner tonight.

It's not Greg's fault. If I hadn't been trying to save the damn place myself for two months, and didn't personally know Carter, I'd probably think the same thing.

But I *do* know better.

Shit, I had been so determined to not think of Carter, but of course, he's going to be talked about. Having an NHL star come to Ivy Glen is the most exciting thing to happen in this town since... well, since he was drafted.

Kerry, sensing my shift in mood, wisely doesn't comment on what Greg said. Instead, she turns to me after the bell rings at his exit. "I'll send you the picture I took so we can add that to our menu. We can call it, 'Meet the Parents.'"

The look-book is a menu of sorts, displaying all the arrangements we have and what occasions they might suit.

"Let's wait until the end of the day, and I'll add all the new ones at the same time," I tell her, writing myself a sticky note so I don't forget.

She nods, biting her lip. "I've been thinking, Sophie, what if we start marketing outside Ivy Glen? Like Oakdale, Willow Creek, or one of the other bigger cities nearby? I have some ideas."

It's not something I haven't thought of before, and it would be a great opportunity for the shop. But heading up a marketing campaign to an entirely new demographic of people does not feel like something I can manage on top of the rec center, helping with Jordan, and not only handling the finances for the shop, but also manning the storefront.

If Kerry felt like she could be the driving force behind the marketing, it would be a fantastic business opportunity.

"That's a great idea, Kerry," I admit, turning to face her, "but it's not something that I can head up right now. If you want to take it on though, I'll fully support you."

Her face lights up and she nods again, heading to the back to ready arrangements for some of our weekly orders while I man the register. Saturday is our busy day, and we hardly have a moment to breathe between consultations on baby showers, anniversaries, weddings, and checking out customers. Gladys Mitchell comes in around noon, her equally elderly Yorkie in her arms.

"Hi there, Monty!" I coo, giving the canine a small treat from the bowl on the counter, "how's my favorite puppy?"

"Calling him a puppy is like calling me a teenager," Gladys chuckles, then shakes her head, sighing. "I had to take him to the vet this week, it looks like he's going deaf now."

"Poor guy." I frown, scratching him under the chin as his little tail wags.

Gladys places an order for some flowers to send to her friend whose husband passed away, and as I print her receipt, reminding her, "Don't forget to send me over those financial statements for your taxes so I can get started."

"You're too good for this world, Sophie Hartwell." Gladys sighs, tucking the receipt into purse. "I don't suppose you'll let me pay you this year? Or I could set you up with my grandson?" She arches a brow at me and I stifle a chuckle.

"Not a chance on the payment, Gladys. You've been a loyal customer of the flower shop for years, it's the least I can do. I'll let you know on the grandson, though." I wink conspiratorially at her, and she tuts out of the shop, a self satisfied smile on her face.

A while later, after Kerry and I have each taken a thirty minute lunch break, I'm handing Mrs. Donahue her once-a-year order of a massive bouquet of red orchids, which she'll bring to her husband's grave.

"Thank you, Sophie, dear." She smiles kindly at me, her wrinkles deepening at the expression. "What do I owe you?" She asks this question every year, even though the answer is the same.

"It's taken care of, Mrs. Donahue. Give Mr. Donahue our best." Same as every year on her and her late husband's anniversary, she takes me in a frail hug, pressing a pink-lipstick kiss to my cheek.

"You're a good girl, Sophie." My heart breaks a little at the words, imagining how much she must hurt every day that my small action once a year fills her with such gratitude. She shuffles out of the store, on her way to the cemetery. Mr. and Mrs. Donahue were together for sixty years before he passed away from a stroke six years ago. I can't imagine having to live without someone I was with for that many years.

Carter had been in my life for twelve years, and I was absolutely devastated when things ended. And it wasn't even like he died or anything.

Enough of that, Sophie. No thinking about Carter.

He doesn't deserve to take up even an inch of space in my mind. My brain is officially a "cheating, arrogant, rec center ruining, asshole free" zone.

Three o'clock hits, and I call back to Kerry, "I gotta go pick up the boys for hockey practice!"

She comes up from the back of the shop, rolling her eyes at me. "Any chance you can *keep* Theo while you're at it?" I laugh at the jab at her younger brother, who has a particular talent for driving her crazy. She tells me she loved having a baby brother when he was born, since she was ten, and it was like having a live baby doll, but his pre-teen days are kicking in hard now and she could do without the attitude. "I'll be fine by myself for the last hour until closing. You have a good rest of your day."

"You too, Kerry. Thank you."

I still need to find a new supplier for succulents since our last place increased their prices, and the delivery schedule for next week needs to be finalized, but I can take care of that later.

It's time for the best part of my week: Hockey practice.

Chapter Seven

SOPHIE

Forty-five minutes later, the boys and I get to the rink. I throw my Ivy Glen Twin Rinks zip-up hoodie over my shoulder and follow my three charges into the rec center. I'm supposed to coach my team in less than a half hour, so there is just enough time to sit and relax for a few minutes beforehand.

I enter the rink, ready to have fifteen minutes to clear my head before coaching my rowdy team of fifteen teenage girls. All plans of relaxation die when I see Carter standing next to the rink, talking to Benson.

It's been less than twenty-four hours since I jammed a finger into Carter William's chest and yelled at him for hijacking the project to save the rec center.

In my head, I had this grand speech for the next time we'd see each other, condemning him for how he left me behind after he promised me forever. I'd demand an answer from him; Why did he leave me behind? He'd have to face nine years of pent-up anger and hurt.

But I thought I'd have at least a few more days before seeing him again. As much as I want answers, I'm not mentally prepared to face them yet. Before I can backtrack and hightail it out of there, Benson calls over to me, "Sophie! Just the girl I wanted to see."

Making way over to them, I realize with how Carter is looking right now, I probably wouldn't have been able to air my grievances, anyway.

Because. Hot. Damn.

It is absolutely criminal how hot he is. His black hair is messily styled in a way that is just begging my fingers to run through it. His black shirt under his flannel is tight across his muscles, and he's wearing these dark wash jeans that I'm sure do wonderful things for his ass. And I don't miss the way his piercing blue eyes move up my body.

My cheeks flush and it takes all my self control to not smack myself across the face. Instead, I hastily zip up my sweatshirt, acting as if it's Carter-proof armor. I hate that after all these years, he still has this effect on me.

"What's up, Benson?" I ask, ignoring the way Carter's eyes darken at my flushed cheeks.

"Sophie, I was just talking to Carter here about his plans for the rink, and I would like it if you two worked together on the PR and rebuild. I don't want a single thing done without your consent."

Work... together?

No, no, no. That's the absolute last thing I need to be doing with Carter right now.

Nuh uh. No way.

"I don't think that's the best idea—"

He interrupts me with the click of his tongue. "Nonsense. You've been here a long time, you know what this place needs more than anyone. And most importantly, I trust you. Besides, I still remember how you and Carter used to spend hours on this ice."

"I—"

"The two of you together will make Ivy Glen Twin Rinks

great." He looks at me pointedly. "It's either that, or I'll refuse the rebuild and let a developer turn this place into a strip mall. I'm not getting any younger, Sophie, and I want my legacy left in the right hands, or no hands at all."

My eyes dart to Carter, who is looking at me with such intensity I have to look away. "Well?" Benson asks, looking between the two of us. "What's it going to be?"

Carter speaks before I can say a word. "I'm in. Soph?"

Fucking hell. Talk about being backed into a corner.

"That sounds great," I say through gritted teeth, my smile tight.

Dammit. I can't believe that not only has he wormed his way into this project, but now I have to work directly with him. Nine years I waited to confront him so I can finally move on with my life. How am I supposed to move on if I have to see him all the time?

Benson claps us both on the shoulders, tells us to let him know when we've got anything he needs to sign off on, and leaves the two of us standing there.

My skin prickles in awareness, leaving goosebumps behind. It's like my body is having some kind of pavlovian response to being alone with him.

I need to get away. Turning my attention to practice, I don't say a word as I look toward the rink where Jordan's practicing to check in on him. They're doing warm-ups as Tom barks directions. "Sophie, wait!" Carter's voice calls out from behind me.

Man, am I getting tired of hearing those words.

Ignoring him, I continue my walk to the rink. He calls my name again, and I keep my gaze ahead, giving no indication that I even hear him. I can't believe he's pushing me so hard. He's already won. What more does he want? For me to be happy he came in and stole the spotlight, playing the hero? He gets to throw his money at the problem, collect on the good press, then disappear after he gets what he wants all over again. There's nothing heroic about it.

A sigh sounds behind me, followed by a hand grabbing my arm and turning me around. "For fuck's sake, Sophie, talk to me!"

"Leave me alone, Carter," I spit, wrenching my arm out of his grip. He releases me easily.

He runs a hand through his hair, his eyes tired. "Look, can't we just have a mature conversation—"

"A mature conversation? You mean like the one we had before you waltzed into that town meeting, throwing your weight around like a big-shot rich boy hockey star? Oh wait! Your head was too far up your ass to accomplish that." Two points to me for the fantastic imagery.

"I'm not 'throwing my weight around,' I'm trying to help! And you won't even talk to me!" he says angrily.

"Maybe I wouldn't have to try so hard to ignore you if you would just leave me alone! You've been doing a great job at it for the last nine years. I don't know what's changed now."

"You don't know what you're talking about."

"You fucking ghosted me, Carter!" My voice almost cracks. "You completely fell off the face of the earth, and it wasn't because you were dead in a ditch somewhere! I know, because I saw pictures of you plastered online everywhere!" My chin lifts, daring him to deny it. It's out there now. Now is his chance to tell me what happened. If it was all a misunderstanding...

His face has paled, and he looks like he might be sick. Well, join the club, buddy.

Of course. Betrayal hits me all over again when he says nothing to deny what happened. My insides twist, his silence bringing back emotions I've been pushing down for nine years. "You know what? Forget it. Just text me when you want to meet up about the rink. Otherwise... fuck. Off."

This time he doesn't follow me as I head to the other rink where my girls are arriving for practice, entering the locker room.

"Was that Carter Williams? Oh my god, he's so hot." The girls are in a tizzy, giggling and peeking at Carter, who is still staring at me with intensity in his eyes. Despite everything, his stare still sends heat down to my core.

I swallow roughly. "Yeah, and infuriating." Shaking my head to clear my thoughts, I call out, "Okay ladies, go get changed and start your warm-ups!"

That night, I toss and turn in bed, unable to get Carter out of my head. How is it that even when he's not here, he's torturing me? You'd think I'd be used to it by now.

The memory of the last time I saw him before yesterday is still clear in my head... it was the night of the hockey championships. I'd just played the best game of my life, my rec team dominating as we took the championship. I remember it so clearly, rushing from my rink to catch the fourth period of Carter's final game. The way he met my eyes after shooting the winning goal in the state championship, sharing his moment of victory with me. I had been in the stands as we made our way towards each other, two magnets drawn together. The way he claimed my mouth so thoroughly that the crowd behind us sent out cheers and wolf whistles.

Then we drove to dinner, pulling over briefly to talk because I had seen a scout from Notre Dame at the game. He kissed me then too, excitement and wonder flooding him when I shared what I had heard. The scout told someone on the phone that Carter had "serious talent". He always shared his victories with me, like I was partly responsible for them. We had talked about college a lot, and he knew I was ready to follow him wherever his hockey career took him. He made sure to tell me it'd always be me and him, no matter what. That he'd never leave me behind.

Laughing and talking over burgers and fries with Carter, Tom, Abbie, Gwen, and Jake at Sal's that night made me think we'd have so many more evenings like that. Carefree and full of joy, always the two of us together.

That whole evening… when he declined a drink because he was the one driving, pulling me close and calling me "precious cargo". The way we danced together like we were the only two people in the world. And that night, I remember more than anything. How I had finally been ready to give myself to him for the first time, and him to me in return. I was so nervous laying myself bare, but all that fear disappeared when I looked into his eyes and saw how much he wanted me. How his lips moved down my body—

The chime of my phone knocks me out of my reminiscing, and I pick it up off the nightstand, scowling at the text from Carter.

> Carter: Sophie, can you meet tomorrow at 5? Contractor I'm interviewing wants to do a full uninterrupted walkthrough.

He's just doing what I told him to, but I wasn't expecting him to be so on top of it. I reply with nothing more than a thumbs up emoji. That'll drive him crazy.

Just like he's driving me crazy. Because really, where does he get off looking so damn delectable? After all these years, and all he's done, my body still reacts to him just like we're eighteen again.

Actually, even more, if possible.

It's going to make it ten times harder to stay mad at him when I need my anger just to get through one conversation with him without wondering what it would be like if the last nine years had never happened.

Chapter Eight

CARTER

My phone rings, ejecting me from my Sophie-filled dreams. I'm not sure if I'm thankful for that or not.

The combined effects of being in an unfamiliar bed and having Sophie on the brain has my heart pounding, bringing me back to the night that my dad had angrily ordered me home, leaving Sophie alone in her bed.

The night that led to me being forced to leave Ivy Glen and changing the course of my life forever.

Even though it's most likely not my dad calling me, I let out a sigh of relief when I grab the phone and see Jake's name flashing on the screen. The time makes me cringe a little when I see it's ten forty-five in the morning. I can't believe I slept so late.

"Hey, asshole," I say affectionately, holding the phone to my ear as I flop back onto the bed, my heart still pounding from the adrenaline pumping through my veins. Jake and I had played on the Ivy Glen High School hockey team together, and we both got drafted to the NHL at the same time. We kept in touch through the phone until last season, when he was traded to the same team as me, allowing us to play together again.

"Hey, dickhead," Jake's voice sounds through the speaker. "How's the life of a free agent treating you?"

"You tell me." I grin, knowing we had both talked about the day when we wouldn't be bound by our contracts anymore, free to play for a different team. "You're one now too."

"Fucking finally, man." He chuckles. "You back in town? I was thinking of going out for a drink tonight."

"Nah, I'm still down in Ivy Glen right now. You know how Tom said the rec center was in trouble? Turns out it's worse than we thought. I'm funding a total reconstruction to keep it in business. You should come down."

A low whistle echoes through the phone. "Damn. I'll think about it, except I don't really want to share the top bunk with one of the twins."

Jake's mom divorced and remarried after having him, leaving Jake the oldest of nine half-siblings. He adores them, but has confessed to me on more than one drunken occasion that he feels like a wrench thrown into the cogs of his mom and step dad's family.

Like his mom was the "buy one", and he was the "get one free" that nobody actually wanted.

"I'm staying down at the Ivy Glen Inn, and I think they've remodeled recently. I'm sure there's plenty of rooms available. We could go out with Tom and catch up with him as well."

"Yeah, man. Let's do it. It'll give me time to check out some state-side teams since I'm not really feeling the offers from Canada. I'll plan on being there next weekend."

We hang up and I toss my phone back on the nightstand, not moving from my place on the bed. The dream about Sophie last night was... intense. She finally let me explain myself, and forgave me. She let me kiss her. Things had just got hot and heavy when my phone rang. With the way I had been reacting to Sophie since I got back, it probably saved me from having a wet dream like some teenager.

I need to get my mind off Sophie. Maybe checking in with Mom and seeing how she's doing will do that. The day after I got here, I called the locksmith and had the locks to the house changed, so hopefully she's feeling more secure now.

It's nearly noon when I pull up at Mom's house and let myself in with one of the new keys. "Mom?" I call out, shutting the door behind me.

"In here, sweetie! You're just in time for lunch!" Her voice calls from deeper inside the house. She sounds happier than she did the day I got here, and maybe that means that it's finally sunk in that Dad is gone.

"Do you want some grilled cheese and tomato soup?" she asks when I find her in the kitchen, standing in front of the stove with an apron on. Her black hair is smooth and brushed, and she's in actual clothes, instead of the bathrobe she wore the last time I was here.

The kitchen looks the same as always, dark and gloomy. Dad's always been big on image though, and refused to let Mom change it, stating that it made the house seem more refined. Despite the way the room is decorated, it's hard to feel gloomy when Mom hums happily in front of the stove. It's been well maintained over the years, Mom clearly diverting some of the money I send her for that purpose. I wonder if it's because she's afraid that Dad could come back at any moment and she wants to make sure nothing sets him off.

"That sounds amazing, Mom. Thanks." Sitting at the table, I watch as she hums along with the song that's playing from the small radio on the counter. A minute later, she's placing two meals in front of us.

"I'm feeling... nostalgic today," she admits, sitting at the table across from me. "Bertha left the door to your old room open after she cleaned, and I found myself looking through your old stuff. Photos, trophies... the posters on the wall." She gives a small smile.

"Remember how you, Jake, and Tom used to come over and hang out here? It made the house feel so alive."

"I do," I tell her, then take a bite of grilled cheese. "You used to make us snacks and let us take over the TV with our video games."

The lines around her eyes crease in a bigger smile. "Yes, and those boys always had such sweet things to say about my cooking. It was nice... before your father..." Her eyes get this far off, glassy look, and it's clear what she's remembering.

How everything with Dad was fine until one day, it wasn't. He had always been a little nagging, a little controlling, but nothing too crazy. Then comments he made towards her started getting worse. More aggressive. Adamant that she made sure dinner was on the table when he got home. That the house needed to be spotless. One day, when I was a sophomore in high school, Mom burned dinner. He blew up in a rage. I realize that the abuse had been happening behind closed doors for much longer than I was aware, but as a kid, I was blissfully ignorant.

The meatloaf only burned because I had broken my arm at school and she had to rush to the hospital, completely forgetting about the food. Dad had come home to a burned dinner and an empty house, and ever since that night, things were different. We got home from the hospital to see a trashed kitchen. Broken plates on the floor, all the chairs at the table flipped over except for one, which he was sitting on, waiting for us.

The burned meatloaf was on the table and he was drumming his fingers on the wooden surface, staring us down. That was the first night he ever raised a hand to Mom in front of me. He stopped himself before he hit her. I learned what could happen if we stepped out of line.

It was like the mask came off. He no longer tried to hide what he was capable of from me, realizing that I was less likely to stand up to him if I knew Mom would pay for it if I did.

In response to my broken arm, he only told me I was lucky it was off season for hockey, otherwise he'd have made damn sure a broken arm was the least of my worries.

"Mom..." My voice is rough as she withdraws further into herself, the memories of Dad's abuse resurfacing. "You don't need to be scared anymore. He's gone." I reach across the table and grasp one of her hands in mine. "Dad... he can't hurt you anymore."

"You don't know that," she shakes her head frantically, "he could be out there, waiting for me to show my face."

"Mom, we talked about this. He hasn't demanded money from me in over a year. He would never let me go so easily unless he was truly gone."

Her brows furrow as my words sink in. "He hasn't... he hasn't asked for money in that long?" At my nod, a whoosh of air leaves her. "That's... that's good."

"I want you to go out and live your life, Mom. Maybe enroll in an art class. Remember how much you used to love painting? You could catch up with your friends. You know Tom's son, Jordan? He's ten now, and I'm working with him on the ice. You should come to some games."

Her eyes light up at the mention of Jordan. "Oh, I remember Jordan! He was such an adorable baby, and you and Sophie were both so sweet with him." She seems to have instantly snapped out of her funk about Dad because she gives me a sly smile. "Have you seen her since you've been back? She's only gotten more beautiful over the last nine years. Remember how I said I went to the grocery store the other day? I was leaving, but I glimpsed her walking into the store when I was pulling out of my parking spot."

"I—" I shake my head, opting not to tell her just how horribly our last two encounters have gone. Nevermind not wanting to relive having my balls handed to me on a silver platter courtesy of a verbal lashing delivered by Sophie. "It doesn't matter, Mom. She's probably moved on, and that is for the best."

"It is not for the best, Carter Joseph Williams!" Mom looks at me with a spark in her eyes I haven't seen before. "What you two had back then, that was true love, I know it was. You never give up on true love."

Mom's not wrong. What Sophie and I had... I don't know if I could ever find something like that with anyone else. Or that I would want to.

The parking lot of the rec center is empty when I pull up at four fifty, save for a white pickup truck and rust red, beat up sedan. Sophie and the contractor must already be here. The rink closes at four on Sundays, giving us the perfect opportunity to do a walk-through without having to dodge the rec center patrons.

The contractor, a middle-aged and balding man with a bit of a belly, is standing in front of the doors to the center, shaking hands with Sophie.

"...The manager of the rinks. Nice to meet you, Mr. Henderson." Her voice is calm and a professional smile is plastered on her face.

"Please, call me George," he says, then glances at me as I approach, quickly dropping Sophie's hand. "Mr. Williams! It really is you! I'm a huge fan." Sophie rolls her eyes and glares in my direction.

"Carter," I reach out my hand to shake his, "a pleasure to meet you in person, George. Shall we?" I motion to the building, and the three of us make our way to the rinks. On the way over, I go over the scope of the project while Sophie is eerily silent. The walk-thru is... awkward, to say the least. Not that George notices. He has his clipboard out, making notes of what needs repairs, then offers suggestions for remodeling.

Sophie and I walk behind him, answering questions and

pointing out things that need updating. Despite the fact that she keeps as much space between us as possible, I can practically feel the heat radiating off her.

Sometimes I sense her eyes on me, but when I turn, she's looking somewhere else.

"How long has it been since the wirings been updated?" George asks, tapping his clipboard. His eyes are on me, but I have no idea.

"1976," Sophie clips out, "which we didn't know until recently."

George lets out a surprised sound, then jots something down on his board. "You mentioned issues with the cooling system under the rinks as well?"

Again, I have no idea what the answer to that is. Thank goodness I have Sophie here with me. "Yes," she says, not looking at me. "We have to set the temp to around five degrees, even though the ice itself is around twenty. It uses way more power than if we had a system that works, and it runs up the electric bill."

"Might be the out of date wiring..." George muses. "Though I'm going to take a guess and say that the cooling system hasn't been replaced since—"

"1976," he and Sophie say at the same time, then both chuckle.

George puts his pen at the top of his clipboard and looks between the two of us, rubbing his jaw in thought. "We're tearing down the building to rebuild, right?"

I'm just about to nod my agreement when a small sound comes from Sophie. Her expression stops me cold. Furrowed brows, a down turned mouth, and eyes full of despair meet me. George noticed her face as well and quickly backpedals. "Or, we could preserve it. Use the foundation and rebuild what needs to be while modernizing it. I'll draw up the bid and email it to you, Mr. Williams."

"You'll have to send those suggestions to Sophie." I nod my

head towards her, "Per Mr. Scott, she gets the final say on everything."

"Thank you for your deference, Mr. Williams," Sophie says, an undertone of venom in her voice. "I honestly thought your ego would have a hard time accepting Mr. Benson's words on that."

Mr. Henderson shakes his head. "I'll just send it to both of you so everyone's on the same page. I'll follow up in a couple of days."

With that, he exits out the front doors, wishing us a pleasant rest of our evening. Without another look at me, Sophie follows after him.

"Sophie, come on. I feel like we could do really great things for the rink if we work together, but that's impossible if you won't talk to me." My words have a tired, desperate edge to them, and she turns around. I think maybe she'll finally listen.

"You're right." She sighs, running a hand through her hair. "If we're going to work together, we should establish some boundaries."

Boundaries? She wants more ways to keep us apart?

"We don't need boundaries, Soph, we need to fix what's between us."

"How can you even say that, Carter?!" Her eyes are hard as steel, but I see the fucking tortured look behind them. "You have the gall to demand we fix it, fix 'us,' when you're the one who broke it? Broke me?" Dammit. She's not even wrong, but how can I explain to her what happened?

"Sophie, I swear, I never meant to do any of that."

"You're the only one in control of your actions." She shakes her head. "You could have called. Gotten whatever was on your mind out into the open. Broken up with me and let me know where we went wrong. But no, you just... left me on read. Even after you got a new phone. You barely answered me on anything, and strung me along, making me worry about you! When clearly you were doing just fine without me."

My hands shake, trying to hold back from pulling her into my arms and apologizing for every hurt I've ever caused her. Because I can't even tell her it didn't happen like that, or that she's wrong. "I—"

She doesn't let me speak. It's like a dam's been broken and all of her words are tumbling out so quickly she can't stop them.

"I finally moved on. I have a life, Carter. It may not be perfect, but it's mine and I love it. Then you come back to town swinging, getting involved in the rec center, the place that we loved—"

"I still love it!" My voice comes out louder than I intended. "I'm only doing what needs to be done—"

"You just waltzed in here, throwing money at everything, thinking that gives you the right to take over and make all the decisions! If I weren't here, you would have agreed to tear the building down!" Her face is twisted up in rage.

"I'm just trying to fucking saving it, Soph! Why can't you see that?"

"Because I don't believe that you care! You fucking left, Carter! You decided you didn't want this town. That you didn't want... me." Her voice breaks at the last word, and just when I think I'm going to jump in and explain everything, she keeps going. "You wanted something new and exciting, so you left. Fuck everyone else and their feelings. Nobody heard from you for years. You became a damn ghost."

I didn't want to leave. I told her my dad made me the day it happened. "What the hell are you talking about?!" My voice echoes in the empty rink. "I didn't leave because I fucking wanted to, you know that! Now I'm here and I want to help."

What can I tell her to convince her I'm not here to destroy anything? That she's been doing a damn good job managing the rink with what she has, but we're past the point of tape and glue on this place?

"Sophie, there are things that you don't—"

She shakes her head, throwing her arms up. "No, I'm done. I'm an idiot for ever thinking what we had was real."

Fuck that, I'm done with her shutting me down. She thinks I wanted to leave? That I didn't want her anymore? That anything besides the threat of her safety could keep me from her? She couldn't be more wrong. There's only one way to show her.

She's about to turn away from me again when I grab her by the back of the neck and slam my lips on hers.

Chapter Nine

SOPHIE

MY WORDS, NOW FORGOTTEN, DIE IN MY THROAT. THE kiss burns, and I'm not even in control of my hands as they fist the front of his shirt, pulling him impossibly closer to me. His hand is hot on the back of my neck, his grip firm but gentle as his thumb presses right under my ear.

I haven't been kissed like this since... fuck. I don't think I've ever been kissed like this. His mouth dominates mine, his tongue demanding immediate entrance. I comply, sinking into the warmth his touch brings, awakening feelings within me that have been long dormant.

His other hand moves to wrap around my waist, and his hard length presses into my stomach as he pulls me closer. I'm being claimed and consumed. So much so, it isn't until he breathes "Sophie" against my lips that I snap out of it.

What the fuck am I doing? This is Carter. The man who ripped my heart out and stepped on it. I can't let myself forget that.

My fists in his shirt turn to palms against his chest as I push away from him, breaking our kiss. He lets me go easily, his eyes a little glassy as he looks at me.

This can't happen.

With our history, this can only end badly.

Shaking my head, I take a couple of steps back before turning around completely and leaving the rink.

It's not until I'm driving home in my car that the reality of what just happened hits me.

Carter kissed me.

He didn't just kiss me. He kissed me like his life depended on it. Like I was the air he needed to breathe. I remember it being good... but had it always been *that* good?

My fingers brush over my lips, still tingling from the force of the way he claimed me.

It's not like I haven't been with anyone since Carter left. I've been on a few dates and had a handful of hookups over the last nine years, the latter were always people passing through town. I couldn't risk having a one night stand with someone I already knew. This town is too small and word gets around too quickly. Instead, when the need to relieve tension would arise, I'd hit Danny's, hoping to find someone who would be gone the next day.

The encounters were often fumbled, awkward, or unsatisfying. Who am I kidding? They were all of those things, every time.

None of them ever elicited this kind of response from me. This burning coil of *need*—

Shit, I need a distraction. Any distraction. And possibly a cold shower.

But first, the distraction. Problem is it's Sunday evening, and everything is closing. I can't even stop anywhere for... shit. Dinner.

I completely forgot I'm supposed to have dinner with Tom and Jordan at my parents' house. That's something that I am *not* in the mood to deal with right now. I'd have to hear more about Carter. Mom would ask me questions, no doubt with an elbow jab and a wink. Jordan would talk about how cool it is he's staying here, and I would be left red-faced, with the memory of that sinful kiss locked in my mind.

No, thank you.

Opting to head home, I shoot off a text when I park:

> Me: Hey guys, sorry to miss dinner, but I have a pounding headache. I'm going to just stay home tonight.

> Mom: Feel better, sweetie! Are you drinking enough water?

> Dad: Love you, champ. Feel better.

> Tom: *eye roll emoji*

Scowling at my brother's text, I leave the group chat and send him a private message:

> Me: *middle finger emoji*

> Tom: *laughing emoji*

There's no way Tom knows about Carter kissing me... right? No, he's just being an ass. I haven't directly asked him if he's the one who told Carter about the rinks being in trouble, but I can fucking tell. He apparently kept in contact with Carter and never told me.

Tom's so on my shit list for now.

Damn traitor.

My shoulders finally deflate when I walk into my house. At least with Tom and Jordan at my parents', I'll be home alone for a while.

Takeout sounds heavenly, so I go through the menus stuffed into a drawer in the kitchen. Almost every place I've eaten with Carter at some point. Normally, it wouldn't be a problem, but his close proximity and the memory of his kiss fresh on my mind has me flighty. None of these places will work. But at the very bottom of the stack... yes!

Pad Thai.

I only got into it a couple of years ago, so there are no Carter-related memories of Pad Thai Express. By the time the food arrives, I've flopped on the couch and have flipped through the channels on the TV at least ten times. Everything reminds me of that damn kiss. Rom-coms. Sitcoms. Even the documentary I found was on the relationship of Cleopatra and Mark Antony. Everything has some sort of love-story plotline in it.

A half hour later, the takeout container is empty, and I didn't get to watch more than five minutes of one show or movie before something vaguely romantic happened or was mentioned.

Thinking of reading a book, I go through my bookshelf and curse myself for how many romance novels I have. Don't I own anything more... platonic?

Checking Tom's room, I can only find books on hockey. That's equally unhelpful.

Maybe something... younger would be good. Does Jordan have like... Hardy Boys or Nancy Drew novels? I crack his door open, but immediately slam it shut when I'm met with a giant poster of Carter's face.

Well, that's new. But, of course. Favorite hockey player of all time and all that.

By the time eight thirty hits, my quest for reading material ends, and I decide to take a nice, hot, relaxing shower. I'll go to bed early, and by the time I wake up tomorrow, all thoughts of Carter's soft, demanding lips will be out the window and I can pretend like it never happened.

When Tom, Jordan, and I moved into this house, Tom gave me the master bedroom so I could have my own bathroom. While I protested, I'm especially grateful for it now since Jordan is at the age where clothes are all over the floor and their tub is lined with ten different body washes. I don't think I'd have room for any of my stuff if I had to share.

The hot water envelops me like a steamy embrace, and I realize there's no getting rid of the memory of that kiss. Not tonight, at least.

As I wash my hair, my mind goes back to the night we had sex for the first time. The way we danced at the championship game afterparty, then made out behind one of the lake cabins.

Then at my house, empty since my parents were out of town, he pushed me against the door once we were inside and kissed me. My hands move across my body as the memory overtakes me.

A moan escapes me as his tongue plunders into my mouth, allowing me to taste him fully. His responding growl sends heat down to my pussy, which is already clenching in anticipation. He shoves a knee between my legs, allowing me to grind my pulsing clit down on his clothed leg.

One of my hands dips down into my folds while the other grasps my breast. My fingers circle my clit, feeding the spark that's been burning since Carter kissed me. Remembering the way he carried me up to my bed, slowly undressed me, and made me come on his fingers and tongue have me writhing.

"Oh, Carter." My voice is breathless as he dips his fingers past my underwear, swiping through my folds. They swirl and tease over my clit at the same tempo as his tongue twirls over my nipple.

A moan escapes me as he delves two fingers into me, his thumb taking over my clit. The sensations build, sending me higher and higher until —

He withdraws his fingers and mouth from me.

"What are you —?"

"I want you to come in my mouth."

Wordlessly, I nod as he pulls off my thong, settling in between my thighs.

"So pretty," he breathes, staring at my pussy in wonder, "I've never seen it so close before."

My cheeks redden at the compliment, suddenly feeling self-conscious.

He places a gentle, open-mouthed kiss on my folds, and it's easily the most intense pleasure I've ever experienced. I inhale sharply, and he rumbles in satisfaction, his tongue taking over as he slowly circles my clit. I writhe on the bed, desperate for him to make contact with that one spot. Finally, he pulls my clit into his mouth, eliciting a deep moan from me.

Slipping two fingers inside of me, I lean back against the tile of the shower and rub the heel of my palm against my clit. I've tried so hard to not think of that night, but Carter's kiss has brought back every memory. Every touch, the way he looked at me as he slid inside me for the first time. How sweet he was.

"If you want me to stop, just tell me."

"I won't want you to stop." My voice is barely a whisper.

He pushes forward, and I gasp at the intrusion, his thick length stretching me painfully. He stops when he hears me, breathing hard himself, "Is it too much?" I shake my head fervently.

"Just breathe," he says, his arms trembling slightly as he continues to press into me. Once he's fully seated, I take a few measured breaths until the burning sensation fades. I meet his eyes and nod, and he moves slowly, both of us letting out a low groan.

The burning sensation quickly fades, and he picks up his paces, his face burrowing into my neck. "You're amazing, Sophie," he pants, his breath hot on my skin. "So beautiful, so perfect."

I come with a small cry, my core clenching around my fingers as I ride the friction of my palm through the waves of my orgasm.

The memories don't stop; they keep flooding in, reminding me of why I'm not going to let him back into my life.

I wake up to a glorious morning glow and a smile plastered on my face, despite the slight ache between my legs.

When I reach for him, hoping for a morning cuddle, all I find are cold sheets. Hm. He shouldn't have had to leave yet. He said he would tell his parents he was sleeping at Jake's.

"Cart?" My voice echoes the empty room. No answer. I sit up, rubbing my eyes and looking around, already missing the warmth of him next to me.

With a heavy sigh, I roll out of bed and throw on my panties and oversized sleeping shirt. I take a peek out the window and frown, noting his car missing from the driveway. Maybe he was worried about my parents coming home early?

I snatch my phone from the nightstand and see a text from him, relief washing over me.

> Carter: Hey, beautiful. Last night was amazing. My dad was freaking out about something, so I had to go. Lunch later? I'll text you by noon.

My thumbs work quickly as I reply:

> Me: Sounds great. Can't wait.

I watch the screen, half expecting it to buzz immediately, but nope, it just sits there, silent.

As the minutes tick by without a peep, my post-bliss buzz cools off, and I'm left with a growing list of questions. This isn't how I thought I would wake up the morning after losing my virginity.

I had waited all day for a response, even going so far as to text Tom and see if he'd heard from him. It wasn't until an hour after he was supposed to reach out that I took action. Something wasn't right. Carter would never stand me up. The memory of when I got to his house is still imprinted on me like it was yesterday.

"Hey, Mrs. Williams," I start, trying to sound casual. "Is Carter around?"

Her face falls, and I notice her eyes are red and puffy like she's been crying, and she's still in her robe.

"Mrs. Williams," concern lines my voice, "is everything okay?"

Between the crying and Carter going MIA... something is seriously wrong.

"Sophie, sweetie, come inside." She steps aside, allowing me through the front door.

"What's going on?" I swallow, my nerves getting the best of me as I walk through the foyer and family room, and into their kitchen, a place where Carter and I have spent so many afternoons doing homework together.

Mrs. Williams sighs as she sits at the table, motioning to the seat next to her. Numbly, I sit, waiting for an explanation.

"Carter's dad made him apply to Notre Dame last year. Carter didn't think he'd get in. Last week, his acceptance came. His dad wanted to wait to tell him until after the championship game."

"So... where is he?" My voice breaks, not fully understanding what she is saying. If he got into Notre Dame, wouldn't he tell me? We were just talking about it last night.

"He technically has enough credits to graduate," his mom says, her eyes tearing up. "Carter's dad... he wanted him to start now. I'm so sorry, Sophie. He thinks that if Carter waits, he won't decide on Notre Dame because of his... well, his ties here."

She doesn't need to put a fine point on it. "You mean me. I'm the ties?"

And by ties, he means small-town girl who could supposedly derail Carter's fast track to the big leagues.

Mrs. Williams leans closer, lowering her voice even though we're alone. "He forced Carter to leave weeks before he needed to, hoping the distance would... help him forget, I guess. Or at least not do anything rash like, I don't know, follow his heart instead of a hockey scholarship."

I'm trying to process this, the idea that someone's dad would think I'm a distraction big enough to take his son across a quarter of the way across the country. Mr. Williams is not a warm man. I used to try to do everything in my power to break through his icy demeanor, but now I realize I never had a chance.

"I thought..." I can't stop the words from leaving me, even though *it's the least of my worries,* "I didn't think Mr. Williams... hated me so much."

"Oh, honey." *Her hand grapes mine on the table.* "He doesn't hate you. He just has... plans for Carter."

"Plans that don't include me." *My voice is quiet.*

When she gave me the note Carter left me explaining what had happened, I had thought we still had a chance. He promised to make it work. "It's you and me, Soph," he had said.

What a load of shit.

What was supposed to be one of the best nights of our lives had turned into one of the worst.

Once I've dried my hair and got dressed, I crawl into bed. Tomorrow is a new day, and soon the rink will be rebuilt, and he'll ride off into the sunset with whatever team he's signing with this season.

We can meet occasionally to go over stuff for the Twin Rinks, but that's it. We will have platonic meetings, and absolutely under no circumstances will I let him kiss me again.

Even if I really, *really* want him to.

Chapter Ten

CARTER

"Are you sure it's okay for me to be here?" My question is directed at Tom when I slide into the booth across from him and Jordan.

"Yeah, man, it's fine. Sophie has to be at the flower shop this morning anyway." He brushes my concern off and flags down a waitress for a couple of coffees and a juice.

It's Monday morning, and that means breakfast at the cafe, the New England Nook. It's a tradition that Tom, Sophie, and I had throughout high school, and continued even after Tom graduated. Clearly, they kept it going after I left, bringing little Jordan into the mix.

It hasn't changed a bit since I was here last, the round tables in the same position, memorabilia lining the walls from various state sports teams. For hockey, it's the Boston Reapers, football has the New England Blue Coats, and baseball, it's the Boston Pioneers. The tan leather booths along the windows, the same little carafes for syrup lining the end of the tables. It's well loved, but not shabby by any means.

If Sophie had been here, I would have kept my distance, if only to give her some room to breathe after last night.

I can't believe I kissed her. One moment, we were screaming at each other, and the next, my mouth was on hers, desperate for her touch. I hadn't even planned on kissing her, but now that I have, she's on my mind even more than she was before, if that's even possible. All I know is no other woman has made me feel the way she makes me feel.

I want her back.

"How was the contractor meeting?" Tom asks once the waitress comes over with the coffee.

"Surprisingly well," I say, almost laughing at the unintentional double entendre, "he's drawing up plans and really, I think he's the guy for the job. It looked like Sophie liked him, and he seemed to have an innate sense of what we're looking for, and as long as his plans line up with that, I think we'll hire him."

"How come I didn't know you were working with Aunt Fee?" Jordan asks, bewildered. I can imagine it would be hard to reconcile an NHL hockey player knowing your aunt. I love seeing the excited look in his eye when he discovers something new.

Tom grins and elbows him. "They're going to save the rec center. *And*, did you know that Carter and Aunt Sophie used to date in high school?"

Jordan's whole face lights up. "No way! Are you kidding? How cool would it have been to have Carter as an uncle?"

I can't help my chuckle at his excitement. "Yeah, she's always been pretty amazing. Ever since we met when we were seven. You never know," I shoot him a wink, "I may still become your uncle."

A throat clears behind me, causing Tom and Jordan's eyes to jump up to the source of the noise. I can tell by Tom's semi-guilty face that Sophie has decided to join us. Who knows how much she just heard.

Despite my light hearted tone, I almost hope she *did* hear me. Maybe she'll realize how much that kiss we shared meant to me.

I turn around and give a slight wave. Based on the bright red hue of her face, I'm assuming she heard at least the last thirty seconds.

Welp, I guess I'm done tip-toeing. Not like that was going to be an option for much longer anyway, seeing how my old, long-buried feelings for Sophie Hartwell are coming back from the dead with a vengeance.

If only I could get her to listen to me for more than two seconds without her losing it.

"Hey, Soph." Tom tries to sound nonchalant, but I hear the guilt underneath. "I thought you had to be at the shop this morning to get the morning orders done before it opened."

"I did," she says, playing with the strap of the bag on her shoulder, "but Kerry's appointment got rescheduled and she was able to come in so I thought I'd try to catch you guys."

"Come sit, Aunt Fee!" Jordan says cheerily, "We haven't ordered yet."

Sophie smiles tightly at Jordan, and awkwardly slides into the seat next to me. The close proximity gives me a prime view of the blush on her cheeks. She's in a purple work shirt today, her deep auburn hair pulled half-up.

The waitress comes by and takes our orders, and Tom turns to Sophie. "We missed you at dinner last night. Mom wouldn't stop going on about how you work too much and that's why you had a headache."

She had a headache last night? Was that... after? I turn my head slightly towards her and can tell immediately that there had never been a headache. Based on the way her eyes keep darting to me and the way she taps her fingers on the table like she's anxious, she had faked it the night before.

I'm a master of Sophie-ology.

"Yeah, well, she's the one who can't stay out of the flower shop long enough for her arthritis flare-up to go down," she mutters, and I wonder just how much Sophie has on her plate. She manages the Twin Rinks and helps at the flower shop, but I'm sure there's more than even Tom knows. Sophie's always been about helping people.

Sometimes it's because she can't tell anyone "no", but most of the time it's just her big, gentle heart calling the shots. Though based on our interactions, I don't doubt she no longer has any issues telling people "no" if she needs to.

Jordan jumps in, "Aunt Fee, why didn't you tell me you used to date Carter Williams? That would have made you my favorite aunt!"

"I'm your only aunt." She scowls at him playfully, and then when he looks at her, still expecting an answer, she tosses her hair back over her shoulder. "I... forgot. Yep. I forgot I even went to the same school as him. So weird."

Tom and I look at her blankly. "You forgot?" Tom's tone is amused, and she just shrugs, a smirk appearing on her lips. Even though I know it's not true, that she didn't really forget about me, something primal rises within me, bristling at her words.

Just then, our food comes, and we all eat in silence before I feel like getting a little payback.

"It's good to see you again today, after our meeting yesterday. You know, I think it went great. I'm convinced this contractor can really give this place the *kiss* of life. What are your thoughts, Sophie?"

I watch, barely holding back my shit-eating grin as Sophie turns so red, I might have thought she was choking if she didn't take a deep, measured breath. Even her ears are burning as she finishes chewing the bite she had brought to her mouth. *I'm not so easily forgettable after all, am I Sophie?*

Is she remembering how I explored her mouth with my tongue? Or the little noise she made when I gripped the back of her neck?

I know my dick's been remembering it.

Repeatedly.

Finally, she swallows the bite, and clears her throat. "It was solid. Don't get me wrong, it was really lacking in certain areas, but nothing that can't be fixed with some coaching later on." She takes another bite of food, while maintaining a calm facade and completely avoiding eye contact.

Well, bend me over and fuck me sideways. The girl's got bite. I think I'm really going to enjoy this different side of her.

The silence is charged with tension as we all finish eating. Sophie keeps her eyes on her plate, and I can't stop mine from constantly wandering over to her.

"So... um." Tom looks between the two of us, trying to figure something out before he ushers Jordan out of the booth. "Jordan, I think it's time to head out and leave these two to their, uh... business discussion."

"Bye, Carter! Bye, Aunt Fee!" Jordan calls, scooting out of the booth.

"Bye, Jordy," Sophie says, smiling fondly at her nephew.

"Cya, bud." I wave a hand.

As soon as they round the corner, Sophie whirls on me. "What are you doing here?" she snaps, narrowing her eyes.

"Um..." I look between her and my plate, "eating breakfast?"

"No, you know that's not what I'm asking. Why are you *here*, with my brother and my nephew on Breakfast Diner Monday?" Her voice is a half whisper, but harsh all the same. Almost as harsh as the finger she jams in my chest. "And *don't* think what happened last night is going to happen again."

A dopey grin appears on my face. "Do tell, Angel. What happened last night?" Her nostrils flare at the mention of her old pet name. The one I gave her when we were in first grade because in her pristine white dress on the first day of school, she looked just like an angel.

Instead of answering me, she flags down the waitress.

"Can I get the check, please?" Her voice is ten times more polite than it was a second ago.

"Mr. Williams picked it up when he got here, honey," the waitress smiles at me and I give her a small salute as she heads to her other tables.

A feral noise leaves Sophie as she turns back to me. "You know, it's too late for you to come in here, trying to save all the relationships you left behind. You had your chance after the accident, and you made it perfectly clear where your priorities lie. We needed you. *Tom* needed you. I mean, I get that you couldn't make it out here right away, but you didn't even show up for the *god damned funeral*." Her last words have me flinching back. "You're acting like you suddenly care, but you're going to pick up and leave the second whatever PR you're hoping to get from this comes through. You chose to leave us, and we were doing just fine without you."

With that, she moves her napkin from her lap to her now empty plate, gives me the coldest look I've ever seen from her, and scoots out of the booth. Cool, calm, and collected, she walks gracefully towards the door of the cafe and leaves me behind, dumbstruck.

Obviously, I broke up with her all those years ago. I had to. My dad... I had to keep her safe. The only way I could do that was to make my dad think I wasn't interested anymore.

This anger that I'm seeing in her though, it's more than that. Doesn't she understand I did what I had to do for *her*?

Fuck. She *doesn't* realize that.

I told her Dad dragged me away that day, but I never told her why I *stayed* away. I hadn't wanted her to know just how bad things got with him. How much he controlled me. Scared me. He used the threat of her parent's livelihood—the shop—like a knife in the side, forcing me to stay in line. He was powerful in town, he had the means to get them closed down. More than that, he threatened *her*.

Tom knew. I had to tell him after the accident. He had to know why I never showed up. We both knew that Sophie finding out what my dad was capable of was not safe for her back then. She would try some way to go against him, and lose. Instead, the secrets just piled up... and I almost forgot just how badly.

From her point of view, I'm an asshole who just up and left the second bigger and better things came along.

When I came to town, I didn't think it would be easy for things to just go back to the way they were, but I never anticipated it would be this difficult either. It's not that way for her. Not when there's so many unresolved issues and unanswered questions.

There's only one thing to do. I need to tell her everything. Every threat, every extortion, every reason. And maybe, just maybe, I might stand a chance to win her back at the end of it.

Chapter Eleven

SOPHIE

GETTING INTO THE CAR IN THE PARKING LOT OF THE diner, my hands still shake from the adrenaline of my confrontation with Carter. I type out a text to Abbie.

> Me: SOS. Carter drama. Come for lunch?

Hitting send, I watch as the message is marked "delivered", then make the drive back to the flower shop. I'm fuming, and I need someone to vent to.

The nerve of him.

Showing up to *my* weekly breakfast with Tom and Jordan, and telling Jordan he might still end up being his uncle? What the hell is that about?

Can he honestly think that's still a possibility? After he ghosted me? *Left* me? *Cheated* on me?

Does he believe one earth-shattering, time-stopping, panty-melting kiss is enough to erase all the damage he's done?

Yet when I left, the look on his face was one of genuine confusion. I've known him almost all our lives, I can tell when an expression is genuine.

When I park at the shop, I'm all out of sorts. Irritated by my conversation with Carter but feeling a seed of doubt about what happened so long ago, I slam my car door harder than I mean to.

My voice is unintentionally harsh when I walk in and see Kerry tending to some arrangements. "Any customers?"

She shakes her head, her brow furrowed. "Only one. Are you okay Sophie? You seem... on edge."

Sighing, I walk to the register and toss my bag under the counter. "I'm fine, just some personal stuff going on."

She gives me a small, understanding smile. "Okay, well if you if you need anything—"

Her words are cut off by the sharp ring of a bell, closely followed by the bang of the door as it hits the wall behind it.

Kerry jumps in surprise, and I only roll my eyes at the figure in the doorway.

"You're over an hour early, Abbs."

"Sophie Hartwell. You cannot send me an SOS text about Carter and expect me to wait until lunch. Plus, I didn't have any patients scheduled anyway."

"Kerry, we're going to go into the back." I peer around Abbie, who is looking at me with an impatient expression. Her brown hair is in two short French braids, her blue scrubs making her honey-brown eyes pop.

Kerry waves me off from her space near the arrangements. "I've got it."

When we reach the back, I flop into the seat at the desk that holds the office computer, and Abbie stands across from me, leaning against the table where we work on our flower arrangements.

She crosses her arm and raises an eyebrow. "Spill. Now."

So I do. The arguments, the tension, and that kiss...

"Was it good?" Her expression tells me she thinks she already knows the answer.

"I—was it... what?" I sputter. Of course I fucking enjoyed it.

But I'll be damned if I give that information up willingly. "What do you mean, was it good? It's not like I *told* him to kiss me, he just... grabbed me, and things got out of hand. Nothing else happened. I left after."

She doesn't need to know that one kiss was enough to get me so hot and bothered that I came in the shower with his name on my lips.

The skeptical look on her face says she already knows more than I'm saying out loud. "So you're telling me that Carter Williams—your first love, high school sweetheart, and hottie hockey god—kissed you... and not just kissed you, but grabbed you and all but claimed your mouth with the burning, pent up passion of nine years of longing, and you didn't enjoy it?"

Well, fuck, when she puts it like that...

Nuh uh.

No way.

Denial may be a river in Egypt, but I'm going to stay for as long as possible. "Nope." I pop the "p" and stand up from my chair, crossing my arms to match her stance. "I would never enjoy anything with Carter. He had his chance, and he blew it."

Abbie rolls her eyes at me. Her silence is unsettling, and I keep talking just to fill it, reminding myself why what I just said is true.

"I mean, the nerve of him! I tell him what's bothering me, and he acts like he doesn't even know what I'm talking about! Like he *didn't* leave me for Notre Dame without telling me, cheat on me, and then not even bother to show up for Sarah's funeral. Tom needed him, and is somehow still friends with the guy after it all, and acts like it's no big deal. How can he think things can just... go back to the way they were?"

Abbie frowns, tapping her fingers on her arm like she's thinking. "You're right. You would think Tom would be just as upset that Carter didn't come back to town after the accident... maybe things aren't as they seem. Have you talked to Tom? I can't help but think..." She sighs, shaking her head. "It was obvious how in love the two of you were. How happy. The love and adoration in his eyes when he would look at you was almost nauseating. I just don't think he would have hurt you like that without a good reason."

I hadn't thought so either. "Yeah, well, he did," I say bitterly.

"That's why I think something happened. Or changed, or... something."

"Something changed alright..." I murmur, remembering vividly the way my heart was ripped out of my chest on the day of graduation.

"Oh my god, is that Carter? I thought he was still with Sophie."

The words from the girl sitting in front of me have my heart pounding in my chest.

Just a moment ago, I had been close to tears, thinking about how utterly wrong it was that we were having a graduation ceremony without Carter. Sure, I'd hardly heard from him the last two months, and there had been complete silence the last two weeks, but he was so busy at Notre Dame and his dad was there, making sure he stayed focused.

Even though he'd graduated early, it was still Carter's official graduation ceremony too. I had really thought he'd fly out here for it. We had always talked about finally graduating high school together. I had planned to take a picture of us kissing in our caps and gowns so we would always remember the day.

"I didn't know he'd ditched Sophie. I can't believe he would let this new chick tag him like that." The girl passes her phone to the person next to her, heads close together as they gossip.

Heart pounding, I lift my graduation gown enough to pull my phone out and look up Carter's socials. He's been tagged in four different pictures. The first one, the one that makes me feel like I'm going to throw up in the middle of the administration calling students to the stage for their diplomas, is the most damning.

It's a shot of him immediately following a practice, if his red face and sweaty hair are any indication. There's a girl, dressed in a jersey with his number on it and leggings, leaning up and kissing the corner of his mouth.

The mouth that would say such sweet things to me and kiss me until I couldn't breathe.

My heartbeat pounds in my ears as I scroll through the other pictures.

This can't be happening.

The rest of the photos are of a party, and Carter is in the background, surrounded by not only the puck bunny from the first picture but multiple others.

They were all uploaded today. My vision blurs and tears hit my phone screen. How many times had he told me, "It's you and me, Soph." or said that we would always be together?

Why would he do this to us?

"Look, Carter was loyal." Abbie's words snap me out of the memory. "All throughout high school, girls tried to get his attention, and he only had eyes for you. I don't think that just... changed. A picture is worth a thousand words, but they aren't always the words we believe they are. Just... think about it, okay?"

"Yeah, okay. Fine," I say tightly, not wanting to admit she was right. Of course, that didn't stop everyone at school from asking me what happened with Carter and me. If we had broken up before or after the pictures were posted. Seeing a way to escape with a little less embarrassment, I told them we had broken up a month before. Nobody except Abbie and Gwen knows the truth.

Even my parents don't know the whole story, which is probably why they still love him. I've fielded no less than twelve texts since he got back into town from Mom, asking me if I've seen him yet.

Abbie left shortly after since she got here too early for lunch and only gets an hour break, and I spent the rest of the workday in a haze, running our conversation through my mind. At some point Kerry had brought me something from the cafe a few doors down, and I ate it absently, mulling over our conversation.

Is it possible I've had it wrong the last nine years? My thoughts ping-pong between *Carter was just as in love with me as I was with him,* and *absolutely not. Even if the pictures were misleading, he never had allowed anything like that to happen before.*

After graduation, I questioned everything about our relationship. Could he have been unhappy the entire time we were together? Did I imagine how deep our connection went? Did *I* do something wrong?

So many hours were spent agonizing over it, but a year later, I pushed it all to the back of my mind, determined to never speak to or see Carter's face again.

Things with Carter *had* been good. After all this time, after all of the years of wondering in the back of my mind where we went wrong... what if there's a *reason?*

The thought runs repeatedly through my mind for the rest of the day, even as I leave Kerry to close up the shop and drive to pick Jordan up from Theo's house since Tom was still busy at the rink. Grabbing pizzas on the way home—one Hawaiian and one pepperoni pizza as always—since there is no way I'm cooking after the day I've had, we hang out and wait for Tom to get home shortly after.

While I enjoy the comfort of our routine, Abbie's words never leave my head. Once dinner and homework are done, and Jordan heads upstairs to get ready for bed, the words spill out of me.

"Tom?"

"Yeah, Soph?" Tom looks up to meet my eyes.

How am I going to word this? I want to be sensitive, but I also can't tiptoe around this subject any longer.

"How..." I sigh, shaking my head. This is harder than I thought. "How can you be friends with Carter after everything? He never even showed when everything happened. I thought at least if he didn't show up for me, he'd come for you."

"Hmm." Tom's mouth forms a tight line as he drums his fingers on the table. He seems lost in thought. I'm about to tell him never mind when he finally speaks, not meeting my eyes. "Things were hard... back then. For everyone. Your eyes were red on that graduation stage, and then the accident happened, but we weren't the only ones having shit hit the fan. I get where you're coming from, Sophie. I really do. But..."

He takes a breath and looks at me from across the table, his blue eyes swirling with emotion. "Listen, it's not my story to tell. But you should talk to Carter. It may not fix everything, or anything, really. But it won't hurt."

My mouth opens to demand an explanation, but before anything comes out, he continues, "Above all else, I want you to be happy. Trust me, if Carter was truly a bad guy, I wouldn't still be friends with him."

He had his reasons? Reasons legitimate enough that Tom understands?

I consider a moment, resisting the urge to smother the spark of hope in my chest. Is it possible that he didn't rip out my heart because he's an asshole? He's been the villain in my mind for so long, but Tom wouldn't lie to me. He's always come through for me. Maybe I need to listen to him now.

Once in my room, I open my desk drawer, reaching all the way into the back. There, folded so small, it's the size of a silver dollar, is the note that Carter left for me after his dad forced him to leave early for Notre Dame.

I had reread this letter so many times the first month he was gone, the ink splotched out where the creases of the folds are. I remember sitting across from Carter's mom at their kitchen table, and she handed me the note. The first few lines jump out at me now:

Hey Soph,

If you're reading this, it means I didn't get a chance to tell you all this in person, and for that, I'm really sorry. First up, I need you to know that I love you.

My dad made me come home last night, and dropped the bomb

that not only am I admitted to Notre Dame, but I'm being pre-drafted for the NHL, which is huge. I'm really sorry I didn't straight up tell you about Notre Dame. I didn't think I'd even get in.

I also didn't think my dad would drag me out to Indiana months before school starts, so maybe we can't trust my judgment anymore. He took my phone so I'm not "distracted", though I'm not sure what there is to focus on during a thirteen hour drive besides my phone. You know how my dad can be.

I'm going to look into local colleges for you while I'm here, and see if there's a place where they post summer jobs for both of us. He can't keep us apart, Sophie, I won't let him. No matter what he says, I'm my own man, and I want what I want—and I want you. Always.

Hang tight, Soph. I'll figure this out. I don't care if I have to use an office phone or borrow one of my teammates phones, I'll be in touch. I need to hear your voice.

Remember, it's you and me, Soph.

Love,

Carter

We had been so in love.

I had been *so* fucking sure I was going to spend the rest of my life with him.

Abbie's on to something. Between this letter, the nature of our entire relationship, and his actions following his move to Notre Dame, it doesn't all add up.

The more I think about it, the more it seems something must have happened.

What will it mean for us, if it turns out Abbie and Tom *are* right? Part of me is afraid to find out and put my heart on the line again.

Regardless, I have to talk to Carter. I'll just have to guard my heart until I know the truth.

Chapter Twelve

CARTER

Sleep is for losers.

That's what I tell myself to feel better about the way my eyelids droop against my will as my feet hit the pavement. After tossing and turning all night with visions of Sophie and our one night together so many years ago plaguing my mind, I did the only thing I could think to do.

Got out of bed at five in the morning to go for a jog.

Seeing Sophie at breakfast yesterday had made it impossible to think about anything but the way she blushed when I alluded to our kiss.

So I threw myself into work, spending hours on the phone with Rob, my sports attorney, and looking over all the offers I received from teams. There are plenty that I'm excited about, but I'm not really feeling the urge to sign yet. Plus, Jake and I agreed to collaborate on what teams we can get on together. Then I spent half the day on the phone with the contractor for the Twin Rinks.

When I still wondered how deep she would blush if I were to remind her of the night we actually had sex, I decided that my testosterone and I needed a good, long workout.

I thought running five miles on the treadmill and pushing my weight limit on the bench press would make me pass out as soon as I got into bed.

No such luck.

Which is why I'm pushing my fatigue to the back of my mind, determined to convince myself that *sleep* is for losers.

The glow of the sun slowly rises over the horizon, illuminating the houses I pass by. Brisk air electrifies my nerves, the burn behind my eyes fading the longer I push myself.

My watch shows six thirty when I open the door to my hotel room, desperate for a shower. At least my run did what it was supposed to do. I'm now wide awake.

I take my time in the shower, then make myself a pot of the crappy hotel coffee. I haven't seen or talked to Mom since Sunday morning, and now it's Wednesday. Fuck, I'm the shittiest son ever. Maybe she'll be up for having breakfast with me.

> Me: Hey Mom, do you have any breakfast plans?

> Mom: No, but I have stuff to make French toast if you want to come over?

> Me: I'll be there in twenty.

When I get to Mom's house for breakfast, we sit down to eat the French toast and bacon she made for us. I'm telling her about the different offers I'm looking through for next season and all about the Twin Rinks project, when I let it slip how frustrated Sophie seems to be with me.

"You've seen Sophie?" Mom glows like I just told her I'm giving her grandchildren.

"Yeah, um." I rub the back of my neck. "She's the manager of the Rinks, so Mr. Benson wants her approval on everything. Then I saw her Monday morning when I met up with Tom and Jordan for breakfast."

"So..." she looks at me knowingly, "what's going on with you two?"

What's...going on? Besides laying awake at night, remembering the feel of her in my arms, her body against mine... or the way she melted under my touch when I kissed her, only to step away when reality seeped in.

And how we can't go more than two minutes without erupting into a fight of some sort?

"Nothing," I say, then take a sip of water before clearing my throat. "Nothing's going on between us." Even if I tell her everything, there might never be anything again. "Just another thing Dad ruined..."

My relationship with Sophie, my choice of what team to sign with when I was first drafted to the NHL, my faith in humanity in general... what *hasn't* he ruined? One of the many good things about him dropping off the face of the earth is he can't ruin anything else.

"Carter..." At the sound of Mom's choked voice, I meet her gaze, my heart nearly breaking at the unshed tears in her eyes. "I should have done more when you were younger. I should have stood up to him, told him that he couldn't treat us that way..."

My anger spikes. He's not even *here*, and he's still making her miserable. How can she blame herself for his actions?

"Mom, it is *not* your fault." She just shakes her head, her eyes glistening with unshed tears.

She won't believe me.

She *can't*.

He spent years drilling into her that she was responsible for every mood swing, every outburst, every bad day he ever had. For every time his fist made contact with her. The fury in my chest takes a back seat, and I remind myself how important it is to me, to her happiness, to unravel the hold he *still* has on her.

"Hey," I say softly, standing up and walking around the table to her. "We did the best we could." She stands when I pull on her hand, and sinks into my arms when I wrap them around her. I say "we" because I *know I* could have done more. "Dad... he was terrifying when he was violent. You were just trying to survive."

I put my hands on her shoulders and take a step back to look her in the eyes. "It's over. We never should have had to deal with that, but we survived. We can take our futures into our own hands now. I'm here, Dad is gone. I don't want you to be scared to live your life."

She lets out a shaky sigh. "I know, but what if—"

"We've changed the locks. I have Tom helping keep an eye out in case he pops back up, but I really don't think he's coming back. Even if he does, I'll always protect you. Take care of you. It's okay for you to live your life how *you* want to. We can get you into therapy, or find a support group. All I want is for you to be happy."

"I appreciate that, Carter, I really do. And..." She takes a step back, seeming less upset than she was a moment ago. "If I'm making an effort to do what I want with my life, I want you to do the same thing. I think Sophie could be a part of that."

"I'll make you a deal," I tell her, grabbing the dishes from the table and walking to the sink. "You start going out more, maybe look into a therapist, and I'll do my best with Sophie."

Mom smiles, unaware of the turmoil now raging in my mind as I move to wash the dishes.

I told her I'd do my best with Sophie, and I want to. I want her. She feels *right*.

I also want to keep playing hockey.

If one of the Northeast teams doesn't offer a contract, there's no way I can keep both. That is, if I can ever get her to listen to my side of the story.

Mom dries the dishes after I wash them, and she looks so happy, having me here. How she can stand to still live in this house, I'll never know. It has to weigh on her, even if it's just a little bit. The color of the paint on the wall behind the sink catches my eye. A reminder of how much control Dad has exerted over Mom and still continues to do so, even when he's not here.

"Hey, Mom? Didn't you hate the color of these walls?"

"Oh yes, it's horrible."

"Why don't we paint it?"

"...What?" she stutters, as if she can't quite believe what I'm suggesting.

"Let's paint the walls, Mom. This house is *yours*. Legally. Dad may have held paying the mortgage over your head for years, but he's gone, and I've paid it off the house. His credit was too poor to be on the loan, remember? Let's make all the changes you've always wanted to make, but Dad wouldn't let you."

"I..." She trails off, looking around the room. "I hate that wall sconce." She points across the room, to the wall next to the doorway that leads to the foyer. It's gaudy, that's for sure. A wrought iron design that darkens the room and adds a trying-too-hard-to-seem-expensive tone to the room.

Without a word, I walk over, wrap my hand around the neck, and rip it off the wall. A small gasp leaves Mom, and I whip my head around just in time to see her look of absolute shock transform into a blinding smile.

"What else?" I ask, tossing the sconce onto the table.

Two hours and a 3-page supply list later, I'm planning the first project to remodel the house when my phone rings. Jake's name lights up the screen, and I snatch it up quickly.

"Hey, asshole," I answer, holding it between my ear and shoulder as Mom brings me a torn piece of wallpaper from the downstairs bathroom before disappearing upstairs to get ready so we can go to the store. Seems like we'll be replacing that too. I had thought she might enjoy redecorating, but I didn't foresee how therapeutic it would be to renovate the home that she had no control over.

"Hey, dickhead," Jake says, chuckling. "I'm coming out on Friday. Are you and Tom free to meet up?"

"We should be," I tell him, making the note "new wallpaper or paint?" on my list.

"Cool. I'll start a group chat. Are you considering the Las Vegas offer?"

"I did, but now I think… part of me wants to make sure we stay close to home."

A beat of silence, followed by a low chuckle. "It's Sophie, isn't it?"

How the hell does he figure that? I mean, he's right, but I'm mildly disconcerted that he can read me so easily.

"Yeah, it is."

"Is she talking to you? After the way things ended between you both?"

"Kind of. Mostly yelling, which I definitely deserve. I may have burned that bridge, but fuck, man… she's still just fucking *everything*."

"Seems kinda risky planning your hockey career around a girl who sort of hates you."

Yeah, but so fucking worth it.

We chat a bit more before we hang up and I wander to my childhood bedroom. This time, the visions of Sophie that assault me are accompanied by a bitter edge. The memory of what happened when my dad forced me to leave her behind.

"We need to talk, Carter." Dad's voice is harsh and his knuckles turn white from his grip on the steering wheel as he drives me away from the only home I've ever known.

"What's wrong?" I ask, my gut sinking. What more could he possibly do?

"Starting now, I'm going to be managing your career. I'll be

your agent." His tone has that no-nonsense, what-I-say-is-final quality to it, so I'm silent as he continues. "You cannot *blow this, son. Your success is my success. I've gotten an apartment close to campus to live in while you're in school."*

"What? No, Dad, I don't need an agent, I'm doing fine on my own—"

"Listen here, Carter. You really don't want to argue with me. If you don't accept the fact that I'll be living nearby and overseeing your success, I'll move back home and make sure your mother pays the price for every day I have to live with her instead."

Shit. He's been keeping a tighter leash on his temper in front of me lately, but I've seen the bruises.The ones she'd hastily pull her sleeves down to hide. What could he do if I'm not there?

"What about Sophie? I can't just leave her behind!" I won't let him see the tears that sting my eyes. Crying is weakness in his eyes, and I don't need to give him more ammunition against me.

"That girl is nothing but a distraction. You will **not** *contact her. If you do, I'll make sure that disgusting little flower shop her parents own is ruined. I'll make sure every college acceptance she gets is revoked, and she'll never work anywhere in our town." He takes his eyes off the road for a moment to level me with a glare. "Do. Not. Test. Me."*

I don't dare say another word. Fighting him on this will just make him double down and come up with more creative ways to ruin Sophie's life. I don't doubt he can do exactly as he's threatened, he has so many connections I'm sure it would only take a handful of phone calls to achieve the total destruction of the Hartwell name.

I'll have to find a way to get in contact with her without him knowing.

"Yes, sir." My voice is quiet. Defeated. I don't say much of anything for the rest of the drive, but that doesn't bother Dad one bit. He talks of his plans and how much money I'm going to make him, and how he'll be set for the rest of his life.

What the hell am I going to do? If I tell Sophie everything that's going on, she'll try to help. If she does that, Dad will ruin everything for her and her family. I don't want to leave her... but what if that's the only way to keep her safe?

Leaving was never part of the plan, but I was a stupid kid who had thought just disappearing from her life would hurt less than telling her we couldn't be together. What a stupid thought. It's clear to me now more than ever that ghosting her was just as big of a mistake as not telling her the truth of why I was leaving.

"Are you ready, sweetie?" Mom's voice snaps me out of my thoughts, and I see her leaning against my doorway, smiling softly.

I am ready.

Ready to help her erase every memory of Dad from this place that she can.

Ready to do the same for myself—to fix all the things he's ruined. I may not have my own house to remodel, but Dad left plenty of invisible scars the day he kidnapped me to Notre Dame.

Sophie's had enough time to cool down. I'm going to repair what Dad broke, and I'm going to do whatever it takes to make sure Sophie gets *my* side of the story.

Chapter Thirteen

SOPHIE

Saturdays are always my favorite.

The flower shop is busier since the nine-to-fivers can come in, and it's the day my rec team practices. This week it's especially exciting since I'm supposed to help with a delivery for a large birthday party, and I love helping arrange where all the flowers go. Nothing sounds better right now than losing myself in the comfortably predictable hustle and bustle of the shop and getting Carter out of my head for the day.

My keys are in my hand and I have one foot out the door, ready to bury myself in work.

Until my phone rings.

Mom never calls me before work, especially not on a Saturday. Not since she started listening to her body and sleeping until nine every morning. It's currently eight, a full hour before she would normally be up.

"Mom?" My voice is slightly panicked as I answer. Has something happened?

"Sophie! Hi, honey, have you left the house yet?"

"No?" My tone rings in confusion when she sounds perfectly

happy and not worried about anything. This is so bizarre. "Is everything okay? I—"

"I'm glad I caught you before you left. Listen, sweetie," Mom cuts me off, the "no-nonsense" tone of her words confusing me further. It's not a tone I've heard often in my life, even as a teenager. "I'm putting my foot down. When was the last time you had a day off?"

"Um..." I don't think I like where she's going with this.

"And I mean no flower shop, no Twin Rinks, and no working from home on financials."

I've had a full day off recently... right? Though as much as I wrack my brain, I can't think of the last time I had *no* work.

But I *like* work.

"I'm sure there's been... I mean, that one time—

At my nonanswer, Mom clicks her tongue. "That's what I thought. So I've taken care of things for you this weekend."

My thoughts come to a screeching halt. She did *what*?

"Mom," I say slowly, keeping my voice calm as I step back into my house and shut the front door, "what do you mean you've 'taken care of things'?"

"You have the weekend off!" She sounds so excited, like she's just given me the best gift ever.

"I—what? No, Mom, I have to get to the shop. I'm supposed to be at the rink this afternoon—"

"I've handled it," Mom says with finality. "Kerry is manning the shop, I'm going to direct delivery and set-up of the arrangements for that birthday party, Tom is taking Jordan camping, and I already spoke to Benson and he's going to have Brandon cover this weekend."

She did... everything? Does she not understand that I *want* to work?

"Mom, is this really all necessary?"

"Yes," she says, her no-nonsense tone back in place. "You didn't even take off last month on your birthday weekend because you were taking care of Jordan while Tom was out of town at an education conference."

"Taking care of Jordan isn't work to me," I defend myself weakly.

"I know, sweetie." Mom tells me softly, "but you need time for yourself. And as much as you love Jordan, you can't get that time if you're taking care of someone else. Which you're *always* doing."

I... I guess she's right. Which I hate.

"Alright." Sighing, I drop my keys on the table next to the door. "I get it. You win."

"I know I do." Mom preens. "Now, I mean it. You are to have a completely work-free weekend. You're not even going to open your laptop to work on finances of any kind."

I try to protest, but my mom is relentless. She has to bully it out of me, but eventually I agree, and she hangs up the phone, leaving me to my work-free weekend.

Just great.

What the hell am I even supposed to do?

I need to work. If I'm not working, what's going to stop me from remembering the way Carter's hand gripped my neck when he pulled me in for that kiss? Or the way his eyes twinkled when I tossed some of his own attitude back at him at breakfast this week?

Or imagining what those hands might feel like as he strips me naked?

Shit. See?

Frustrated, I scroll to Abbie's name in my phone.

She answers on the third ring. "Hey babe, what's up?"

"I got grounded," I pout, causing Abbie to burst into laughter.

"You're twenty-seven years old, Soph. How did you get grounded?"

"My mom... she called both my jobs and sent Tom and Jordan away for the weekend so I can have a 'weekend off'." I find myself doing air quotes even though Abbie can't see me.

"Did she say no friends?" Abbie teases, getting her laughter under control.

"She didn't." I play along. "You wanna come over?"

I hear her smile through the phone. "I'll be there in an hour."

An hour later, I open the door after the doorbell rings to find Abbie balancing a box of donuts in one hand and carrying a little cardboard drink caddy in the other.

"Have I told you how much I love you?" I ask, taking the drinks from her and almost drooling at the iced coffees inside.

"Not today." She winks as she walks past me into the house.

"Then... I love you." I glance down and see the caramel drizzle on my coffee. "A lot."

She only cackles as she walks inside, setting the box of donuts on the table.

We sit on the couch, and I take a long sip of the salted caramel goodness in my iced coffee.

"So..." Abbie starts, flipping open the box and taking out a chocolate long john. "Have you given any more thought about talking to Carter?"

Damn, straight to the point.

"Yeah, I mean, I talked to Tom on Monday night about everything and you've both made some very... valid points. I know I need to clear the air, but I've been so busy..."

Abbie levels me with a look that says *do you really think I'm that stupid?* "Uh huh. Yeah, sure. I call bullshit. You're stalling, and you know it."

"I guess I'm nervous about what he might say," I admit, holding on to my coffee tightly. What if we talk and I still can't forgive him? Or... what if I *can*? What would that mean for us?

"I mean, even if you're not going to talk to him," she grins and takes a sip of her drink, "you should totally get laid because you can't just be celibate forever. I'm always in a better mood after a good fuck."

I can't help the quick flush of my cheeks and the thought that, at the very least, my body still likes him. "That's why they've made technological advancements that allow me to have an orgasm without having sex with my cheating, ghosting ex."

"Oh sure," Abbie nods sarcastically, "that's why you agreed to go on a date with Oscar."

A shudder practically overtakes me at the thought of my short-lived fling with Oscar Davis. I had known he had a crush on me in high school, and he had always been as sweet as he was dorky, even if the attention was unwanted. Not that he was a bad guy, he just never seemed to get the picture that I wasn't interested in him. He seemed to have it in his head that if Carter and I ever broke up, he would be "next in line". And while he never did anything directly disrespectful of our relationship, his expectation gave me a weird feeling.

He went through a major transformation after graduation. Hit the gym and switched his glasses for contacts, and as a result, seemed to gain a bit of confidence. Thinking back, it might have been because Carter wasn't around, so he didn't have any "competition".

Two years ago, he asked me out, and I finally gave him a shot. We went on a few dates, but there wasn't any chemistry, at least not on my end. He's a sweet guy, and I enjoyed his company well enough, but eh.

He was upset, but understanding when I told him we shouldn't see each other again. About six months ago, he started trying again, asking me out every couple of weeks. It's exhausting.

"Okay, no more sulking about men!" Abbie announces, jolting me out of my daze. I didn't realize I was staring off into space until she had raised her eyebrow at me. "Let's have a girl day. We'll watch movies, do our nails, and tonight, we'll go out and meet some new guys."

I roll my eyes, but deep down... way deep down, I wonder if that's exactly what I need.

So, we spend the day in the living room watching romantic

comedies, doing each other's nails, trying different face masks, and lazing on the couch.

When the evening hits, we move upstairs to my room to get ready for a night out. I hop in the shower while Abbie does her hair and makeup. I come out in my towel, my hair dripping wet, to find what looks like a closet explosion. There are clothes everywhere.

"Abbie!" I cry, picking up a pair of ripped jeans that I haven't worn in six years from the bed. "What did you do?"

"I'm finding something suitable for you to wear!" she shouts from my walk-in closet, and I go over only to find her rifling through the hangers in the back.

"Those are—"

"Sexy as hell?" Abbie raises a brow while tossing a black wad of fabric at me.

The dress I catch is a classic little black dress, which stops mid-thigh and has a sweetheart neckline with capped sleeves. The material is stretchy enough that it forgives the curves I developed after I stopped playing hockey. I bought it the year after Carter left, when I was determined to move on and start dating again.

It hasn't seen much action.

"I haven't worn this in years." I sigh, holding the dress in front of me.

"You're wearing it," Abbie says with finality, and leaves the closet to let me get dressed. Sometimes I don't know whether to love or hate how bossy she is.

When I come out of the closet five minutes later, dressed and toweling off my hair, Abbie gathers the mess of clothes from my bed and tosses everything back into the closet, leaving me to deal with the mess later. It's not until she gets back that I get a look at her.

"Where did you get that?" My jaw drops. She's wearing a black jumpsuit with a corset top and wide legs. Between the outfit, her sheet of glossy straight hair, and the sultry makeup with red lipstick, my friend looks *fierce*.

"I brought it." She shrugs, then points to the bathroom where she's pulled a chair in front of the mirror. "Let's get your hair and makeup done."

"I—you brought it? You mean you *planned* to get me out tonight?" I wonder if she plotted with my mom about taking this weekend off as well. That scheming little—

"Of course I did," she rolls her eyes, "now come on, we don't have all night."

I can't even be mad. Abbie always somehow knows exactly what I need.

An hour later, she has my hair dried and curled in soft waves that hit my shoulders, and smokey eye makeup that compliments my dark-nude lip gloss perfectly.

Part of me hopes I do run into Carter because I look damn good.

The other, more sensible part of me wants to forget about guys entirely for the evening, dancing and drinking until all thoughts of a certain tall, sexy, mouth-watering, left wing hockey player disappear.

"You're a miracle worker, Abbs."

"I'll add it to my resume." She winks at me in the mirror.

I settle on a pair of black pumps and some crescent moon earrings, twirling in front of the mirror with Abbie, excitement thrumming in my veins. Getting ready is always the worst part. Now that we're actually about to leave, I'm giddy with the thought of letting loose for the night.

We take an Uber to the only popular bar in town, Danny's, the bouncer nodding at us as we step out of the car. "Sophie. Abbie."

"Hey, Henry," I say, grinning, "turn away any high schoolers yet?"

"Not yet, but the night is still young." He smirks.

Normally, Danny's doesn't have anyone checking ID's at the

entrance, but Saturdays can get crazy with high schoolers trying to pass for the legal drinking age. Stopping them at the door keeps the inside less chaotic.

"Let me know if you need backup," Abbie calls over her shoulder as we pass by, and Henry barks a laugh.

Hanging our coats on the rack by the door, we make our way towards the bar. The music pumps through the speakers inside, so I barely hear Abbie when she mutters under her breath, "I swear I didn't plan this."

"What?" I whip my head around only to see Carter across the room at one of those tall standing tables with Jake Ashford, who I didn't realize was also back in town. They both look good, but the sight of Carter almost makes my mouth water.

He's wearing a gray button-up shirt with the top two buttons undone, and his sleeves are rolled up, showing off his corded forearms. Deliciously snug black jeans hug his muscular thighs, and his black hair is styled like he just rolled out of bed, and holy fuck, I want to run my fingers through it.

Before I can get my hormones under control, my eyes fall to his, and find that he's already looking right at me. Shit. I totally just got caught eye-fucking my ex.

But damn if he isn't returning the favor. His attention is on the way the dress clings to my curves. My cheeks heat under his gaze, and when his eyes finally meet mine, there's a darkness and intensity that tells me my original plan for tonight of not thinking a single thought about Carter Williams just went out the window.

Chapter Fourteen

SOPHIE

Carter's blue eyes pierce mine from across the room, and before I can blink, he's moving. Shit. He's coming over here, walking straight towards me and—

"Sophie, Abbie. The two of you look beautiful tonight." Carter's smile is all charm.

"Hey, Carter," Abbie says lightly, and when I don't immediately say something, she elbows me.

I can't help it. He looks so fucking delicious, and if I open my mouth at this very second, I might end up inviting him back to my bed here and now.

"Do you guys want to come over and have a couple of drinks with us? My treat."

My eyes dart behind him to see Jake rooted to his spot at their table, his eyes locked on Abbie. She notices his stare and bites her lower lip, looking him up and down. I can't blame her, he looks almost as good as Carter with his tight black shirt that shows off his muscles. She used to tell me how much she wished she could run her hands through his mess of brown hair. He's not as broad as Carter, but is still as toned as any player in the NHL.

Abbie always had a huge crush on Jake all throughout high

school, but she was shy and he was popular. Carter, Jake, Abbie, and I would often hang out in a group setting though, along with my friend Gwen, who moved away after graduation.

Abbie had come out of her shell with him around the end of senior year, but then he left for college after graduation and so did she.

"That sounds great." Abbie turns her attention back to Carter and loops her arm through mine. Although having drinks with two NHL hotties we already know seems counterproductive to the whole idea of going out to meet *new* guys. It looks like Abbie won't back down from this one. I'll just have to keep my cool and *not* climb Carter like a damn tree.

"Danny!" Carter calls over our heads, "whatever these two want tonight, put it on my tab!"

I turn just in time to catch Danny's curt nod. He glances at me and raises his eyebrows in question, and I only shrug in response. The corner of his mouth tilts up ever so slightly, and that's as close to a smile anyone will ever get out of him.

Tom thinks that getting to a first name basis with Danny is the height of friendship with the surly bartender, and maybe he's right because that little mouth quirk took me four years and a couple of drunken tirades about my love life.

Embarrassing? Yes.

Worth the look of surprise in Carter's eyes when I turn back to face him? Also yes.

My own smirk teases my lips as Abbie and I follow Carter back to the table where Jake is waiting, still slightly slack jawed and staring at Abbie.

"Hey, Jake!" I smile, pulling him into a hug and breaking his one sided staring contest. I sense Carter bristle at my familiarity with Jake, especially considering I haven't offered *him* a hug since he's been back. "You remember Abbie, right?"

"I remember the Abbie we used to hang out with, but damn."

He makes no attempt to hide the way his eyes look her up and down. "I'm feeling like an idiot right now."

"Oh, yeah?" Her tone is flirty. "Why's that?"

"I must have been an idiot or an asshole to not realize how absolutely *stunning* you are."

"Maybe it's both," she says coyly, her eyes sparkling, and he barks out a laugh.

"It might be," he concedes right as a waitress comes by and drops a tray of drinks in front of us. Eight shots of tequila, two margaritas, and two whisky-looking drinks.

Danny *does* always know what we need.

Abbie immediately grabs two of the shots and shoves them at Carter and Jake before taking two more and handing one to me. We all look around our little group before downing the shots. The tequila burns as it goes down, but warmth immediately fills my chest, causing me to relax a little bit.

We slam our glasses back down on the table, and Abbie turns towards Jake. "So, hotshot, what are you doing back in town?"

Jake grins in a way that I'm sure has all the puck bunnies dropping their panties. "I just thought I'd come back for a visit when I heard my buddy was back in town." He claps Carter on the shoulder. "Though now I'm kicking myself for not coming back sooner." Abbie's cheeks flush slightly under Jake's gaze. "Didn't you go away for college as well? What are you doing now?"

"I'm an RN," Abbie says, picking up one of the margaritas. "I'm working at my uncle's medical practice."

"Does that mean if I hurt myself playing hockey or... dancing, you can patch me up?"

"Only one way to find out." Abbie puts her margarita down and grins mischievously, taking Jake's hand and dragging him to the dance floor.

I can't help but smile as I watch the two of them dance together.

"So... how has your week been?" Carter's question catches me off guard, but I keep my eyes on my friend. It's an effort to bite back my knee-jerk reaction to be snarky, but I'm supposed to be giving him the benefit of the doubt. When I do turn my head, he's looking at me intently. It's a look full of promise, one I remember from high school, but on his older, more mature face, it is somehow hotter. It's possible this isn't the first time he's looked at me like this since he's been back, and I've just been too angry to see it.

"Same old..." I shrug, picking up the margarita from the tray and sipping. "Flower shop, Twin Rinks, go home, rinse, repeat until the end of time."

"Do you enjoy it? Working at your parent's shop, I mean."

"They need me," I say nonchalantly, "and I want to help. I enjoy making my parents's lives easier."

"It seems like you're making everyone's lives easier except your own." Carter looks at me with a raised brow and takes a sip of the whiskey-looking drink Danny sent over. "You work two jobs, and then you still meet for Monday breakfasts and take care of Jordan."

"You sound like my mom," I almost snort. "Actually, about Monday, Carter... I'm sorry. I shouldn't have stormed out like that, especially when you were just trying to do something nice."

Carter frowns. "You don't need to apologize to me, Soph. But I need to tell you... there are some things that you don't know about what happened. My dad... he isn't a good guy. It's a long story, but just ... I wanted to come back. Not just for graduation, or after the accident, but all of it. For your birthday, every Christmas, every summer. I really did, but I couldn't. Hell, I never wanted to leave you in the first place." He sighs and runs a hand through his hair. "I was waiting to talk to you in person and explain. It doesn't excuse ghosting you, but please, just know that everything I've done is to keep you safe."

Despite the old hurt, I believe his words. He's right, it doesn't excuse how he handled it, but hearing him say that he didn't have a choice, that he didn't want to leave me behind puts a balm on my soul that soothes the jagged edges I didn't realize were still there. It doesn't explain the cheating, but... I'm willing to hear his side of things on that.

"Will you... will you tell me everything? Not tonight, obviously, but... soon?" His gaze pierces my soul, and I'm leaning towards him. His eyes rove my face, searching my expression.

He gives me a soft smile. "Of course." Then he leans in close so his mouth is next to my ear, "Will you dance with me?"

His lips ghost the shell of my ear, sending bolts of need straight through me. Biting my lip, I nod as he pulls back, before taking my hand and leading me to the dance floor. He pulls my back flush against his chest, his hands settling on my hips as we sway to the music. His thighs press to mine, and I can feel the evidence of his attraction against my lower back. Fire burns low within me. I want him *so badly*.

While I need to know what happened all those years ago, for tonight... for tonight, the fact that I'm going to get answers is enough. I want to let go and enjoy the feel of him.

The way his hands feel as they roam from my hips to my stomach and back again, like he's trying to commit every inch to memory.

The heat of his body against my back.

I reach my arm up behind me, draping it around his neck. His hold tightens briefly, and I wonder if he's remembering the last time we danced like this.

Our last night together. Could this night end in the same way? With him in my bed?

At the start of the next song, he spins me around to face him, and I put one hand on his shoulder, staring up into his ocean-blue eyes. His gaze flicks to my lips briefly, and I hold my breath.

He doesn't kiss me, but his hands slowly explore my back as we sway to the music, and one of his thighs finds its way between mine, keeping us locked together as we move to the beat.

I'm not sure how much time we spend like that, lost in each

other's arms, my fingers running up and down the muscles of his arms and chest, and his hands continuing their movements just above my ass.

His touch... it's both familiar and new at the same time. Exhilarating and comforting. Lights every single nerve ending on fire while simultaneously feeling like the safest place I could possibly be.

And that's with my dress in the way. How intense would the feeling be if there was nothing separating us?

Just past Carter, a wave by the door catches my attention. Abbie and Jake are putting their coats on before heading out of the bar.

"Oh my god." I laugh softly, causing Carter to release me and turn to see what I'm looking about. Abbie winks at me and Jake is looking at Carter, eyes wide and jerking his head toward Abbie in a *can you believe this?* motion. They disappear out the door, and Carter lowers his head to be heard over the sound of the music.

"Who would have thought?" He chuckles. "I didn't think she would go along with his terrible pickup lines." His warm breath blows on my ear and I want to feel that breath all over my skin. On my stomach, my nipples, between my legs...

"Must be the magic of the evening," I say, and wink. "I think I'm ready to get out of here."

"Do you want to ride together?" His voice is husky, sending a shiver down my spine. "I'm at the inn, your house is on the way."

I agree, and we walk to the coat rack. "Why aren't you staying with your mom?"

"Oh... it's just easier for her this way." He rubs the back of his neck and won't meet my eyes, but I let it go. Maybe it has to do with everything else he hasn't told me yet.

Chapter Fifteen

SOPHIE

WE GET AN UBER AND RIDE BACK TO MY PLACE IN silence. The space between us is charged with so much heat, I'm afraid one look at his face will have me going up in flames. My heart pounds in anticipation. If he makes a move... what will I do? A shiver runs through me at the memory of the way we danced together, and in response, his hand slides on to my bare knee.

"Cold?" His voice is slightly husky.

Before I have to answer, we pull up to the curb in front of my house. Carter rushes out of his side of the car to get to my door, and then walks me up the steps of the front porch as the driver idles on the curb.

"Just want to make sure you get inside okay," he murmurs.

I unlock the door. It pushes open easily, and I turn to face Carter, who is looking at me intensely.

"I—" My words catch in my throat as his hand moves to cup the back of my head. He moves slowly, giving me every chance to back away.

I don't want to. I want to give in, even if it's just for the night.

When I don't move, he leans down, capturing my lips with his. The kiss is nothing like the one at the Twin Rinks.

That one was urgent—desperate, even. I had gotten swept away in the intensity.

This one is slow and deliberate, claiming.

He tastes like whiskey and oranges.

Like stargazing and late-night phone calls.

Like holding hands while you watch the first snow of the year and sneaking kisses behind a lake house.

But he also tastes like jumping into the deep end.

Skydiving.

Something familiar yet new at the same time, and damn, I need to learn it all.

His tongue explores my mouth with intention, and I welcome him in, heat pooling low in my belly.

When he pulls back, both of us breathing hard, I turn my head to look at the Uber driver waiting, and wave him off. With a rev of the engine, the car drives off, and Carter and I move into the house, shutting the door behind us.

"Tom and Jordan?" he asks breathlessly

"Camping for the weekend. We have the house to ourselves."

The door shuts, and Carter is immediately on me again, my back against the wall as both his hands cup both sides of my face. He tilts it up for better access, and I grip his shirt roughly.

"Do you want this, Angel?" His hips grind into mine.

Do I want this? Hell yes, I want this.

"I do." My voice is husky, my breathing heavy as I hold onto his shirt for dear life.

With that, he moves his hands, putting both of them under my ass and lifting me against him as he continues to dominate my mouth. My dress rides up as I wrap my legs around him, causing my center to press directly against his stomach, my thong the only thing separating us.

"Up the stairs, last door on the left," I groan into the kiss.

I'm so lost in the feel and taste of him that it doesn't register that we've arrived in my room until he's laying me gently on the bed. He briefly backs away to shuck off his pants, then continues our kiss, propping himself up on an elbow and letting his free hand roam all over my body.

Why does he feel so good? It's not like I've been with a lot of guys, but it's never like *this*.

His touch lights my skin on fire and I arch towards him, wishing for about a million less layers between us.

As if reading my mind, his fingers find the rolled-up hem of my dress at waist, and he moves to help me take it the rest of the way off.

I scramble to my knees on the bed and he mirrors my movements, pulling it up over my head. We're a foot apart, staring at one another. My cheeks heat when his eyes linger on my body, his hands reaching out to run reverently over my skin. I've never been self-conscious of the way I look, but I've also never had anyone else look at me like *that* either. Like I'm a freaking goddess or something.

His eyes fly to mine, and he leans forward, cupping the side of my face again. "You're so fucking beautiful, Soph. Nobody has ever compared to you." Then he kisses me again.

Carter's words send a pang of jealousy through me. Thoughts of him with anyone else make my stomach turn, but I can't help but hope his words are true. Some part of me is wickedly satisfied with the idea that none of his other partners measured up.

His kisses move from my mouth down my neck. Instead of going for my breasts like I had expected, his lips move down to my shoulder. Then he holds out my arm, kissing the sensitive flesh of the inside. His mouth grazes my wrist, then the palm of my hand. Each kiss is a tease, a tiny bolt of electricity shooting straight to my clit.

By the time he repeats the process on the other side, I'm a writhing mess of need. Low whine escapes me, and Carter gently pushes me so my back is on the bed again. "Shhh. I'll give you what you need, Angel. Let me worship you."

And worship me he does.

His mouth licks and sucks and nibbles its way down my body, unclasping my bra and pulling off my thong. A shudder overtakes me when he runs his tongue across my stomach, and my eyes close as his hot, wet, mouth nears my pussy, but he doesn't go there yet. Instead, he ignores the mess he's created between my legs and works down my thighs, my calves, before finally brushing his lips over the tops of my feet. Each touch heightens the sensation until a single kiss feels like caress over my entire being.

When he's done, he sits up briefly, removing his clothes. His body is a work of art. I knew his chest is broader than it used to be, but the fact is only made more apparent by his lack of clothing. His hard cock stands at attention, nearly making my mouth water. Now that nothing else stands between us, he crawls onto the bed and on top of me.

When my hands reach for him, he grabs them, holding them above my head.

"Tonight is about you. I'm going to worship this fucking sinful body," he repeats in a whisper. "Let go."

A gasp escapes me when his hand reaches down to skim across my soaking wet folds. If I thought his touch was electric before, that was nothing compared to now.

"Look at you, so wet and ready for me," he rumbles before claiming my mouth, his fingers circling my clit. He swallows my whimpers as his pace picks up, my hips bucking up into his touch. His kisses from before have set every nerve ending on fire, and everything is impossibly *more*. His hand holds both of mine above my head, leaving me helpless to do anything but *feel* as he brings me closer to the edge.

I'm so close. So, so, close, that when his circles become smaller and he increases his pressure slightly, I erupt. Stars explode in my vision. All I feel is his body on mine as his fingers coax me through the end of my orgasm. "Fucking hell, Angel. You're a goddamn vision when you come undone for me."

My chest rises and falls rapidly, his praise turning me on even more. He sits back and brings his fingers up to his lips. His eyes never leave mine as he sticks those two digits into his mouth and sucks my wetness off of them.

Holy shit, that's hot.

"Oh, fuck," he moans as his eyes practically roll into the back of his head. "I've gotta taste you, Angel."

He moves down my body until his mouth covers my pussy, his tongue immediately licking at my core. Again, everything is heightened, and Carter presses down on my lower stomach, holding me in place while he ravages my clit with his tongue.

"Carter," I whimper, fisting the sheets next to me and doing my best to just submit to the way he plays my body, like an instrument he's been practicing for years. It's like I'm on fire as he tastes me, swirling his tongue where his fingers were only moments before.

All too soon, he pulls his perfect mouth away from me, and my hips arch in protest.

"I promise I'll taste you again later, but for now, I need to be inside you." Biting my lip, I nod, but he falters. "I... I don't have a condom. Do you?"

Shit. "No, but I'm on the pill. Are you clean?"

He nods. "I've never had sex without one, and I just had my postseason physical. They test for everything."

"I've never done it without a condom either," I admit, pulling him close to me. "Are we about to take another type of virginity from each other?"

He rumbles a laugh before kissing me again. "I guess I save all my firsts for you."

Once he's positioned himself at my soaking entrance, he lifts my knee before he pushes in. We both groan as he slides in to the hilt, and he stills to let me *feel* him. With nothing between us, I feel every single dip and ridge of his perfect dick. "Focus on the way my cock stretches you open," he whispers in my ear, "close your eyes and only think about how we fit together so perfectly."

I close my eyes and fixate on the slight burn that morphs into pure, intense pleasure as he moves his hips back and forth, thrusting into me at a slow, deliberate pace.

His hand touches my cheek, and my eyes flutter open. I'm staring into the eyes of *my* Carter. My sweet, attentive, loving Carter. I tilt my face into his touch, and his lips capture mine in an all-consuming kiss.

Our lips move together slowly, matching the pace of his thrusts as Carter rolls into me.

"Angel," he gasps against my mouth. "Fuck, you're gripping me tight. I can't hold back."

"I don't want you to," I gasp on a cry, the sensations too much and not enough at the same time.

He sits back on his knees, pulling me with him so I'm straddling his lap, with my legs wrapped around his waist, and his palms hold me up by my ass.

A keening sound escapes me as he ups the pace, his agonizingly slow thrusts becoming almost frantic. My arms fling around his neck, holding on for dear life as he bucks up into me, his bare cock running along my sensitive walls.

"You feel so fucking good," his voice is raspy as he breathes hard, holding me to him so tightly it's like he's afraid I'll disappear, "I want to live in this perfect pussy for the rest of my life."

His words fuel the fire growing in my body, and I'm approaching the edge of bliss as he repeatedly hits my g-spot. I can't stop the sounds that escape me every time he buries himself completely inside me.

He presses his forehead against mine, and one hand moves from my ass to grip the back of my neck. With anyone else, the touch might feel controlling or stifling. With Carter though, I just feel *safe*. Grounded.

His moans and gasps are enough to send me straight over the

edge and my orgasm tears me apart, starting in the very base of my stomach and stretching outward until all I feel is pleasure..

"So—phie," he grunts as he thrusts, then slows, a low groan leaving him as he empties himself inside me. We stay there, foreheads pressed together, breathing hard, before he

I'm a goner. I'm dead—this is how I die. Death by the best sex of my life.

His dick slides out of me as he moves to lay me on the bed before getting up. Is he... leaving? Shit. It's not like I thought we'd be *together* after this, but with his intensity, I thought he would at least stay to cuddle. My thoughts don't have time to spiral any further because he disappears into the bathroom and reappears with a wet washcloth, positioning himself in between my legs.

"What are you...?" My words trail off as he stares at the cum dripping out of me, looking fascinated. With a small shake of his head, he wipes away the remains of our releases from my pussy, gentle in his touch.

With a small kiss to my mound, he tosses the washcloth into my hamper by the door, and crawls back into bed with me, settling us both under the covers.

Pulling me close and laying a gentle kiss to my forehead, I drift off to sleep. Me in his arms, and him, possibly worming his way back into my heart.

"You're still here." Sophie's voice comes from behind me, and I look over my shoulder at her. She's adorably sleep-rumpled in a giant t-shirt and small sleep shorts, her hair a little crazy.

"I am," I say with a raised brow, then turn back to fiddle with the coffee maker. I had thrown on the clothes I wore to the club last night, on the slim chance that Tom and Jordan came home earlier than expected. "Did you think I wouldn't be?"

"I don't know..."

I pour two mugs, then move to the fridge to pull out the coffee creamer.

Salted caramel cream. Of course.

I pour creamer in the mug until the coffee is the correct color, and make a matching one for myself. "When I woke up and saw you weren't in bed, I just thought..." She trails off, uncertain, and it hits me. Her hesitation.

The last time we slept together, I was gone in the morning, and she didn't see me for nine years. I imagine her waking up a few minutes ago to an empty bed, thinking the worst of me again.

I'm such an idiot. I should have stayed in bed until she woke up. Or woken her up with my head between her legs, giving her a taste of what life could be like for us now.

Last night was... amazing. Better than I had even dreamed. We've both grown and matured in the last decade, especially with our sexuality. As much as we've changed, we're still *very* compatible in that category. Bringing her pleasure gave me more satisfaction than I had thought possible.

Before I can tell her I have no desire to leave her feeling alone again, she sits at the kitchen table, pulling the laptop there towards her. She's acting a little fidgety, like she isn't sure what to do with me here. Her eyes dart over to me, and she fiddles with the ends of her hair. The last thing that I want is to make her uncomfortable, but if me being here the morning after sex pushes her out of her comfort zone, well, maybe it's just something she needs to get used to.

"Work?" I ask, tilting my head towards her laptop as I bring the mugs over to the table and sit across from her. The t-shirt she's swimming in catches my eye. "Is that... is that one of my old shirts?"

I don't know why I ask, it obviously is. It's an Ivy Glen High Wolverines hockey shirt. Regardless, her cheeks turn a deep red as she flips her laptop open.

"I just grabbed the first sleep shirt I could find," she says defensively.

"But you kept it. All these years, even with what I did, you kept my hockey shirt."

"It's... it's a really soft shirt." She smiles a little, the awkwardness between us fading a bit. I'll let the shirt thing go, but seeing her wearing it... well, it gives me almost as much hope as last night did.

Sophie turns her attention to her computer and I settle in, happy to be in the moment with her. She starts typing and it's clear her focus has shifted from us to something else. *Has to be work.* I sip my coffee contentedly. She glances up with a quirk to her lips. "Don't tell my mom I'm working."

A chuckle escapes me. "Your secret's safe." Sophie deflates, a faux sigh of relief escaping her, so I ask, "But... why can't she know?"

Sophie takes a sip of the coffee I made her and moans. "You made that *perfectly*." She takes another sip before putting it down. "Mom banned me from working this weekend. She says that I don't take any days off." She rolls her eyes even though I'm pretty sure her mom is correct on that front. "They can keep me from entering the Twin Rinks and the flower shop, but they can't stop me from going over their finances."

"What a rebel." I smile over the rim of my mug.

Damn.

That *is* some good shit.

"It's like a puzzle." She's so entranced by the numbers on the screen, she doesn't even look at me when she talks. "It's my favorite part of any of my jobs. Numbers make sense. I don't have to decide if two plus two equals four—it just is. The correct answer always comes through, you just have to find it."

I've never heard anyone so enthusiastic about... accounting.

It's soothing watching her work. When she bites her lip and scrolls, I can tell she's looking for something specific. Then her eyes widen just the slightest bit before a triumphant smile lights up her face, and she's typing away again.

She always loved math in high school. It brings me back to watching her across one of our parents' kitchen tables as we worked on homework together. She would catch me staring and turn the cutest pink color.

After a while of watching and guessing what's going on with the numbers based on her facial expressions, I say, "Do you want to come with me to meet with the developer?"

"Hmm, I think I'll get in trouble with my mom if I do that." She shoots me a wink before turning her attention back to the screen. "Can you just fill me in later? I really need to get this done anyway."

"Yeah, no worries. I'll text you later." Taking my chances, I lean in and give her a peck on the cheek. She reddens slightly, but doesn't push me away. I feel like we really reconnected last night, which eased some of our tension, but it's going to take a little extra time—and some groveling on my part—to get completely into her good graces again.

"See you later, Angel," I murmur next to her, nipping her ear playfully and earning a little yelp in return. Her eyes are heated as I pull away.

I can wait, but I'm only human.

Grinning, I leave her house, taking a rideshare to the hotel to change and pick up my car before going to Twin Rinks. I feel better than I have in months. Hell, in years even.

"George!" I greet the contractor with a hearty handshake and clap on the shoulder when I enter the rinks. "Were you waiting long?"

"Not at all." He grins. "Are you ready to go over the contract and we can get things going once we get Ms. Hartwell's and the council's approval?"

"Let's do it, we can sit in the bleachers."

An hour later, I'm sitting in the Twin Rinks lobby as the sound of kids showing up for hockey practice fills the air, a stark reminder of why we're here, trying to save this place. George and I have gone through every revision and item that needs updating, and I take a copy to bring to Sophie and the council.

"Would you give this one to the council as well?" George asks, pulling a packet of papers from his bag.

"What is it?" My brow furrows in confusion as I take it from him.

"It's an alternate proposal that one of the council members asked for. He said it wouldn't pass, but he wanted to see it down in writing anyway."

I'm about to flip through the packet when he claps me on the shoulder. "Once we get both signatures, we can get started the next day. You just let me know."

"You got it, George." I smile at him as he walks away, and it finally feels like things are going well. I made headway with Sophie, the rinks are coming together, and still not a peep from Dad.

I find myself with my hands braced on the side of one of the rinks, staring out at the ice as one of the practices starts. The kids begin with warm-ups, skating laps around the rink. So many memories flash through my mind. Playing with my high school team, going skating with Sophie on the weekends, watching her games with her rec team...

"Carter, my man! How are you? It's been too long." My head turns to find a guy who looks vaguely familiar, all up in my space and smiling at me like we're best friends. My eyes narrow as I try to place him. His blonde hair is styled neatly, longer on the top and shorter on the sides. And while he seems like he might work out, he doesn't carry himself in a way that would suggest that he played sports in high school.

I definitely don't know him from hockey.

"Oscar Davis, from high school, remember?" He sticks his hand out, and I barely recall hearing that name from Sophie a couple of times back then. Well, more like Abbie and Gwen giggling about something and Sophie telling them to shut up.

"Hey, man, how are you?" I don't really care, but engaging seems like the fastest way to make this guy leave, so I shake his hand and step back to regain some of my much needed space.

"I'm good." He nods. "So, you and Sophie working on saving the rink, huh? Is the old team back together again?"

Shit, that's right. This is the little fucker who had a huge crush on Soph back in high school. Abbie and Gwen teased her relentlessly over it, and she always told them to leave it alone because he was harmless.

Despite the fact that he came to all of her hockey games and always tried to talk to her in the hallways, he was never a threat to our relationship so I left well enough alone. I only ever stepped in if she was uncomfortable, but I was never rude about it.

"Yeah, we're both working on the project to save the rec center." My answer is noncommittal, but how interested he is in the situation irks me.

"Sure, but have you... rekindled the old flame yet? Do you really think you and her will work this time? How long are you even planning on staying here? I doubt she'll put up with you abandoning her a *second* time."

What the hell is this guy playing at? He's acting way too familiar for my liking. And I definitely don't like the sound of her name on his lips.

Time for the "Golden-Boy" gloves to come off.

"I'm not sure that's really any of your business, Owen."

"It's Oscar." He narrows his eyes at me.

"Sure it is. Listen, Owen, I don't really like the way you're talking about Sophie and me." I fix him with a look that I've perfected during my years of dealing with reporters. "You're asking me a lot of personal questions, and it really isn't any of your business."

Oscar barks a sarcastic laugh. "Okay, fine. Just tell me, is it really weird seeing her again? I mean, especially after she's been with me."

What the actual fuck.

Even if she had been with him over the years, it's her business. Why the hell does he think that would matter? And why is he disrespecting her privacy like that?

I arch a cold brow. "Are you in the habit of discussing Sophie's private life with others? Because I might take offense to that."

Oscar takes a half-step back, and a glint of worry sparks in his eyes before he waves me off. "Forget it. Catch you later, Williams."

I don't respond. Fuck that guy.

I turn back towards the ice after Oscar slithers off, and a moment later, Benson Scott approaches me.

"Poor kid." He clicks his tongue. "I don't know if you remember, but his dad, Julian, used to be on the town council. He passed away from cancer last year. Oscar got elected to take over his seat."

"Yeah..." I scowl, watching Oscar's back disappear out the double doors of the rink. Shaking myself out of my funk, I turn towards Benson, who's looking at me with curiosity. "I just met with the contractor, and have a final proposal that just needs Sophie and the council's sign off, and then we can get started within a couple of days. We should start putting up signs now, warning the patrons we'll be closed for an undetermined amount of time. Have we confirmed with Willow Creek that their rink can accommodate all the teams that need to practice?" Willow Creek is the next town over and is only about a thirty minute drive from Ivy Glen.

Benson smiles. "Yep, heard back yesterday." He's quiet as he looks out at the rink. "You think Sophie will sign off on the changes?" he asks cautiously. "You know how much she cares about this place."

"I do." I nod solemnly, "With this proposal, the heart and soul of this place will stay intact. It'll just have a shinier casing."

Benson murmurs his approval and I feel the need to stop him before he leaves. "I hope you know, Benson," I take a breath as he focuses his gaze on me, "I care about the Twin Rinks immensely, but nobody, not even me, feels that as deeply as Sophie does. And I'm going to do everything in my power to make sure the new rebuild does her justice."

Benson only gives me a knowing smile. "Oh, I know, my boy. I know."

Chapter Seventeen

SOPHIE

It's Tuesday, my second day back since Mom banned me from the flower shop. It's a slow morning for once and I'm trying to put together a page for the look book on the computer.

It would be a lot easier if I could stop thinking about my night with Carter.

It was amazing. And the *connection*. The way he looked into my eyes as he made love—No. We didn't "make love". That would require actual love. And we're not there... right?

Right. We had sex. Totally hot, non-committal, mind blowing, passionate sex.

And I really, *really* hope it happens again. In a purely sexual-desire kind of way. Because we're not in love.

Abbie and I have been texting non-stop since that night. She hooked up with Jake, but insists they're both just having fun. If only I could figure out how to get my heart on the same page as hers.

Shit. I look at the page I just typed and realize I've been one off when going down the list for the arrangements, and every single one has the wrong picture next to it.

I sigh, erasing all my work from the last thirty minutes.

My mind goes back to Saturday night, to our conversation at the bar. He said he hadn't wanted to ghost me but had to because of his dad. I desperately want to know the entire story. What was so terrible that he felt like he had no choice but to leave me behind?

I'm scared of what it means if he tells me the entire story, and I agree with him that he had no choice. That I wasted nine years of my life being angry at him for something he had no control over. But I'm more scared of what it means if he tells me and it doesn't justify any of his actions.

It's like Schrodinger's cat.

Or in this case, Schrodinger's deep, dark secret.

We haven't really been able to talk about what happened between us yet. Sunday night, Hart's Flowers went into full on crisis mode when I received an email from our suppliers that we wouldn't be getting any of the trillium flowers we'd special ordered for a funeral happening today. Apparently, the refrigeration system in the truck went out, and all the flowers arrived on site wilted.

While not necessarily a flower for a funeral, they were the deceased's favorite flowers and their children were adamant that we acquire some for the service. I spent all of yesterday calling different flower shops to see if they had any, and drove halfway across the state to pick up some from a city on the border of Connecticut. I made it back to the shop at around ten at night and was up until one in the morning making the arrangements for them to be picked up today.

Now that we're out of crisis mode, Carter and I are supposed to meet for lunch today to talk about the plans the contractor drew up. Once he has my sign off, he'll take it to the council. It's important to me to meet with Carter to clarify a few things and go over the timeline before making anything final.

I check some entries for the books before my alarm goes off on my phone, telling me it's time to leave for lunch.

"I'll be back in an hour!" I call out to Kerry, who is in the back doing arrangements.

"Take your time!" she responds and I smile, loving that I can trust her to take care of the place while I'm gone.

When I get to Sal's, the man himself is behind the counter. He's pushing eighty now, but still loves running this place. He's in his normal uniform, red and white striped apron and all. "Hey there, Sophie!" he says from behind the register.

"Hi, Sal." I give him a warm smile. "I'm meeting Carter here. Has he come in yet?"

Sal smiles knowingly at me. "He's at your usual booth in the back."

Of course he is.

Butterflies flutter in my stomach at the sweet gesture, and I make my way to 'our' booth.

His hair is wet and pushed back like he's just stepped out of the shower. When I reach him, the scent of his body wash fills my nose, telling me he has, in fact, done just that. A tight blue t-shirt stretches across his pecs, making his icy eyes pop as they rise to meet mine.

I don't miss the girls in the opposite booth ogling him as I approach.

"Hey, Cart." I use his old nickname without thinking about it.

Carter stands up, looking at me up and down in a way that suggests he's evaluating my body language. Probably wondering if I'm freaking out since it's the first time we've seen each other since we... reconnected. I give him a small smile, communicating that I'm okay, before he sweeps me into a brief hug.

"Hey, Angel," he murmurs into my ear before pecking me on the cheek.

He slides back into the booth, and I'm still standing there, fingers pressed to where his lips touched my skin.

I need to snap out of it.

"You have the files?" Attempting to brush off the awkward

moment, and ignoring the dirty looks from the girls in the booth near us, I slide into the seat opposite of him. I need to talk about us, but I am too chicken to start there.

He looks at me another moment like he might not let me get away with the diversion, then nods. "I do," he confirms. "I've put sticky notes on the pages that you emailed me questions about so we can cover them easier."

"Thank you. Let's order, and then we can get started."

Our waitress comes over and takes our order. The food comes three pages in, and by the time we finish eating, he's answered all my questions, confirming that we can keep the original building itself. We do need to tear out the actual rinks, redo the piping underneath, and rebuild the ice rinks to be state of the art. The entire building needs to be rewired to be up to code since it hasn't been looked at since 1976. Then we just repaint, and add a few technological perks. Like new scoreboards, implementing a new POS system to include a monthly membership so people can scan their membership card when they come in. An updated security system rounds everything out.

We're just about to wrap up when someone entering the diner catches my eye. Is that...?

"*Shit*, Oscar's here," I mutter, wishing I could disappear into the cushion of the booth. He's been asking me out at least twice a month for the last six months and I haven't wanted to be rude, but I don't know how I can pull off a "dropped call" if we're talking in person.

"Oscar?" Carter asks, tensing slightly before turning around.

"No, don't turn—" Too late.

Oscar's eyes light up when he sees us and heads straight back to our table.

"Sophie, how are you? Long time, no see."

Taking a sip of my drink, I eye Oscar before answering, "I'm fine, Oscar. What's up?"

I'm not trying to be rude, but I haven't gone out with the guy in two years, if you could even call it that. We never even slept together.

"It's good to see your beautiful face in person. It's been so long. Do you finally have a free evening coming up?" His voice is light, but there's an undertone of annoyance.

Carter's eyes shift between the two of us, clearly deciding if he needs to step in. I've been handling Oscar myself for years now though.

"Nope, no free evenings coming up." I smile tightly. Can this guy not take a hint?

Carter looks about ready to ask him that very same question when Oscar grimaces. "Oh. Well, let me know." He turns his head towards Carter. "Williams. Good to see you again." He walks away before backtracking and turning to Carter like he forgot something. "Oh yeah, I just wanted to tell you what a great idea that rinks proposal was. I took a peek at it at last night's council meeting. I've got to say, tearing down a money pit like the rec center and replacing it with an NHL arena? Genius move."

My blood runs cold. An arena? That's not what we talked about. That's not what we just spent an entire lunch going over. When I glance at Carter, his brow is furrowed with confusion.

"What the fuck? I never—"

"Huh. I could have sworn that's what they said." Oscar shakes his head. "Anyway, enjoy your lunch, you two. Sophie, pencil me in when you get a free evening, okay? I'll cancel whatever plans I already have."

He walks away, leaving Carter and I alone at our table.

Has this whole thing been a lie? What was the point of putting together this proposal if he had one for an arena set up? Unless... was he planning on taking my signature from this contract and superimposing it over the other one?

"What was that, Carter?" My voice is cold.

"Honestly, I have no idea what he's talking about." His eyes seem sincere and a little confused.

"I don't believe you, and that's the problem." My voice is still hard. "Who else would try to bring an NHL team here?"

"The contractor gave me a second proposal to give to the council that I didn't look at. He said that one of the council members requested it. That must be what Oscar saw." He shakes his head. "Trust me, I don't have the clout it takes to convince a club to move."

I want to believe him. What he's saying... it makes sense.

Sitting back in my seat, I sigh. "I hate feeling like this, suspicious about everything. You never gave me any reason to distrust you while we were growing up..." I motion to him with my hand. "You need to give me something. Something true, Carter."

He rubs the back of his neck. "Yeah. I mean, yes, I can do that."

This is it. I'll finally know why he betrayed me all those years ago. "I want to know about the pictures I saw online."

He blanks. "What... what pictures?"

"The ones I saw posted on graduation day. It looked like you had just gotten done with practice and there was this girl... she was kissing you." The words burn coming out, but he genuinely looks like he doesn't know what I'm talking about.

Then a sudden realization crosses his face. "About the time of graduation?" he asks, leaning forward.

"Yes," I say, unable to meet his gaze. All the emotions from that day flood back to me. The confusion, the betrayal.

The devastation.

"I... shit, Soph. I think I know what you're talking about." He runs a hand through his hair. "I was out of it. I *missed* you. I couldn't stop thinking about you. Then Dad ambushed me with this press conference thing during a training he sent me to, and this girl came up to me. Before I even knew what was happening, she was laying one on me." His lip curls in disgust. "That's all those pictures were."

My heart stutters. He... he didn't cheat on me? "I... I thought..."

"I don't blame you," he says, his tone understanding. "It's not like I *didn't* ghost you after."

My gut twists at his words, at his acknowledgement of his behavior. "Will you tell me why? What went wrong? In your letter... you said we would make it work."

He lets out a sigh, and runs his hands over his face. "I don't know if you ever knew, or if you remember, Soph, but my dad is not a good man. For one, his helping me get into the NHL wasn't because he wanted me to follow my dreams." He shakes his head sadly, making my heart clench.

"On the drive to Notre Dame, he made it pretty clear I was just a meal ticket to him. An ATM machine that he'd be able to cash in on once I made it big. When I tried to tell him no, he... threatened Mom. I had only realized a few years beforehand the... extent of the abuse. He never left the bruises where anyone could see them, and he had always been so careful that I never knew.

"But once I pieced it together, it was like he didn't care anymore. He'd do it in front of me. I tried to stop him once, and that's the only time he ever hit me. Knocked me right out, and when I woke up, Mom was in worse shape than she would have been had I just left it alone. It was scary when he got like that. Sometimes," he swallows roughly, "sometimes I was afraid he wouldn't stop."

My heart clenches at his words. His dad threatened his mom? I knew he was a bit controlling and hard to get along with, but... he *hit* her?

"Dad moved to Indiana to keep an eye on me, threatening to take it out on her if I took a step out of line. As far as you..." He swallows, looking up at me nervously. "He told me if I didn't leave you behind, he would use his influence to make sure your parents' shop sank to the ground. That he would make sure you would never get into any college, or employed by any company." His voice cracks. "I just... I just wanted to keep you safe. So I had to stay away. He was always there, demanding money, holding everyone's well being over my head. I could never forgive myself if something happened to either one of you." Unshed tears glisten in his eyes. It's absolutely devastating to see Carter look so... defeated.

My voice is rough when I ask, "What changed?"

"He's disappeared. He'd been gone for longer and longer stretches of time before showing up again and demanding money, then a year ago, he just disappeared completely off the map. When we first went to Notre Dame, he sold the car dealership. Gave up his seat on the council. It didn't make any sense. At first, I thought I was just his source of income, but a few years later, I realized he had a gambling problem.

"The first time he called to demand money outside his agent salary was a year after I was drafted. It started with a couple thousand at a time, then the years went by and the demands became more frequent, the amounts he was asking for increased." His shoulders slump as he runs his hands over his face, like talking about all this is physically paining him.

"It wasn't until he dragged over a hundred thousand from me over the course of a month that I realized something was going on. Since being gone, he hasn't called to terrorize Mom, he hasn't knocked on my door for a dime, and he's not with any of his old friends. I hope to hell all his shady shit and gambling caught up to him. I just finally felt safe to come home. To you." He looks down, not meeting my eyes.

Why?

Is it shame? Or embarrassment? He deserves neither of those things.

"Why... why didn't you tell me?" My voice is quiet. I could have... done something. Well, maybe not, but at the very least, I wouldn't have been left with so many questions.

"Sophie." He sighs, meeting my eyes. "I know you. You would have tried to save me. You would have gotten involved, and he would have followed through on his threats. I couldn't let that happen."

My heart breaks for him. For the boy I knew, and what he had to go through. For what he had to watch his mom suffer, and be helpless to stop it. The thought of being under the thumb of his dad completely all these years and never having a choice in the matter makes me feel sick.

Abbie and Tom were right. All this time, *I* was the one angry at *him*. How could I have ever thought he would willingly leave me like that, ghost me like we meant nothing? How could I have thought the worst of him when he was *protecting* me? Logically, I know that I had no other information to go off of, but guilt eats away at me anyway.

"Carter." My voice chokes, holding back tears of grief. "I am *so* sorry." He looks up at me, his eyes glassy with emotion. "I wish..." I trail off, looking down and twiddling my thumbs. "I wish you hadn't had to go through all of that alone. But, you're right. I wouldn't have taken his threats seriously. I would have told you I didn't need a job or college as long as we're together, and for him to do his worst." A bitter laugh leaves me. "I would have jumped in headfirst to try to help, and would have just made the situation worse for both of us. And your mom."

Carter tentatively reaches across the table, covering my hand with his. When I don't pull away, he tightens his fingers around mine. "Let me take you out tonight. We can go out for an evening, just the two of us."

When I look up at him, his beautiful blue eyes are shining with hope, and it's easy to smile at him. Now that everything's out in the open, and I know that he really *didn't* have a choice, I want to know him again.

I want to hear about what's happened in the last nine years.

How he feels since accomplishing his dream of playing for the NHL.

I want to know if he still dips his fries into his milkshakes, or eats his carrot sticks with peanut butter.

Most of all, I think I want this, whatever *this* is, to go somewhere.

"I think I'd like that."

Chapter Eighteen

CARTER

Why am I nervous? This is Sophie we're talking about. The same Sophie I've been on countless dates with.

But it's not, is it?

I mean, she's still sweet and caring, but she's different now. Grown up. I can't just show up and expect her to automatically like the same things. But I've grown up too. I'm not the same eighteen year old kid coming by to pick Sophie up for burgers and a movie.

I'm Carter Fucking Williams. I can do this.

I can take a girl on a date. Not just any girl. *The* girl.

I can show her how well I can treat her.

The light of the setting sun casts Sophie's front door in a golden glow, and I take a moment to get my nerves under control. With a deep breath, I finally reach out and ring the doorbell to the townhome that she and Tom share.

Shit. I had thought that the flowers would be a good idea, but I hadn't wanted to risk running into her at the flower shop, so I got some from the grocery store. But now she's going to think I'd rather support Big Flora than their small business—

"Carter!" Jordan's eyes light up with glee when he opens the door and sees me.

"Jordan!" I mirror his enthusiasm, and we do the overly complicated handshake he spent a full hour teaching me at the rink the other day.

"Hey! I thought that was a you and me thing!" Tom calls out from behind Jordan in feigned offense.

"Sorry, Dad," Jordan shrugs grinning, "You told me Carter was like family though, right?"

"I did." Tom rolls his eyes, coming to stand next to his son. "Hey, man." He finally acknowledges me. "Lookin' sharp."

I glance down at my outfit, a light blue button down, and dark gray jeans. It's nothing particularly special, but I feel good about the outfit. Soph always used to tell me she liked me best in blue.

"Thanks." I grin, then glance behind him at the stairs. "Is she almost ready, or...?"

"We've been sent to distract you while Aunt Fee finishes putting her face on." Jordan supplies helpfully, and Tom lightly elbows him.

"Jordan, you weren't supposed to say that out loud. Now she's going to get mad at *me*."

"What? It's not like Carter thinks her eyelids are *naturally* gold!"

I know she already agreed to go on this date with me, but it makes me almost giddy that she's getting ready and cares about what I think. It's like she's giving me a real chance.

"It's fine, you guys," Sophie's voice calls from the top of the stairs. "I'm ready now."

Then, she descends, and my jaw nearly drops. She looks so beautiful.

Her auburn hair is barely curled and frames her face. Her makeup is done, and she does, in fact, have gold eyeshadow. But what really gets me is the dress.

The sleeves of the light green dress drape off her shoulders in a way that's innocent and sultry at the same time. The fabric scrunches around her waist before flaring out, hitting just at the knees. She has on these sexy little strappy heels that remind me just how amazing her legs are.

She's gorgeous.

Breathtaking.

And I wasn't lying when I told her nobody else has ever measured up.

"Soph," I get out once I'm no longer speechless, "you look amazing."

"Thank you." A soft pink blush colors her cheeks.

Jordan leans in close to me, whispering conspiratorially, "You *do* know they aren't actually gold, right?"

"He knows, Jordan," Tom chides, then gently ushers Jordan out of the way as Sophie makes her way down the stairs. Tom steps toward me, speaking low so only I can hear. "Listen... I know you had your reasons last time, and I know the way it happened was for the best, but just... don't hurt her again, okay?"

Swallowing roughly, I nod. "I don't plan on it."

He pats my back right as Sophie approaches. "Oh," she acts surprised and points between Tom and I, "were you actually taking *him* on the date?"

"No, that's next week." Tom winks at her and I roll my eyes.

"You wish, Hartwell." My tone is deadpan and Sophie laughs the light, sparkling laugh that I've missed so much. Smiling at the flowers, Sophie passes them off to Tom, before we bid the two of them goodbye and walk down the front steps of the porch, my hand on her lower back.

I hear the door click shut behind us and Sophie stops, looking at the vehicle on the curb. "That's not your car."

"You're right, it's not." I grin, taking her hand and leading her to the brand new red pickup truck I rented just for our date tonight. "Does it look familiar?"

"It's..." She looks up at me, her face shining with emotion, "it's just like the one you used to borrow from your dad when we'd go down to the lake. It's even the same color."

"It's about ten years newer, but I thought it would be nice."

"It's perfect." Her smile is bright, and I would do literally anything to keep that look on her face forever.

We ride to the restaurant in comfortable silence, and it takes me back to years ago, when I would drive us to the movies, or the lake, or whatever date we had planned. My fingers itch to reach for hers across the middle console, but I hold back. She's *just* opened back up to me and I don't want to come on too strong.

I pull the truck up to the front of the restaurant and roll down my window, while Sophie looks at me in confusion, "I don't think you can park here, Carter—"

She's cut off by the approach of the valet. "Mr. Williams! I can take your keys."

"Oh," she says quietly, shifting in her seat.

"Let me get the door for you," I hop out of the truck, passing my keys to the valet, and make my way around to the passenger side. Sophie places her hand in mine when I move to help her out, and we walk hand-in-hand into the restaurant.

We've made the relatively short drive to Willow Creek, home of the nicest restaurant in a fifty mile radius—The Elysian Table. Valet, a maitre d, and a months-long waiting list for a reservation. Unless, of course, you're an NHL hockey star.

"Mr. Williams," the maitre d greets us when we walk in, and Sophie stiffens slightly. "Miss." He nods at her. "Please allow me to take you two to your table."

"Thank you," I scan the nametag on his black vest, "Antonio."

Once we reach our table at the back, I pull out Sophie's seat and she gives me a tentative smile. Antonio hands us both menus, and I open mine, looking over our options. After tonight, she'll see that I can give her the best of what life has to offer. I can provide for her.

"Good evening, Mr. Williams." The waiter comes over and

pours us glasses of water. Sophie looks down nervously, her brow furrowing. "Would you care for some wine? Any appetizers?"

"I think we need just a moment, please," I say kindly, giving him an apologetic smile. I'm not planning on rushing Sophie's choices, I want to get her anything she wants.

"Take your time." The waiter nods his head and heads off to his next table, allowing us a longer opportunity to look at the menu.

Sophie seems tense tonight. Which is strange because up until we pulled up to the restaurant, she seemed at ease. Happy, even. Is she worried about something? Surely, she can't think I'd make her pay for half the check. That must be the issue.

"I'm not sure..." Sophie trails off, and she bites her lip the way she does when she's thinking.

"Don't look at the prices." The order comes out hard, so I quickly reach my hand across the table, caressing hers softly. "It's all on me tonight, Angel. Okay?"

"The appetizers cost what I pay Kerry for a half day at the shop." Her lips purse as her eyes briefly meet mine, but she doesn't pull her hand away. Was this a mistake, bringing her here? I know things aren't exactly luxurious for her, but I thought... I guess I thought she'd be impressed.

"I feel massively underdressed," Sophie mutters, eyeing the menu again.

"You look beautiful." I put my menu down and give her a look. "You're the most striking woman here."

Her cheeks flush again, "Thank you, but... that's not what I mean." She sighs at my confused expression and gently disentangles her hand from mine, motioning around the room. "I mean, this is a summer dress, Carter. Not a fancy-ass-restaurant-dress. There's a woman over there wearing an actual designer dress and pearls. Real pearls."

Yeah, okay. I fucked up. This clearly isn't a place Sophie is comfortable being, and I just got completely carried away trying to make myself look good for her.

I sigh, pushing up abruptly from the table and hold my hand out to Sophie. "Fuck it. I don't know why I'm so nervous trying to impress you. You've never cared about fancy stuff before, why would you start now?"

She lets out a small nervous laugh and glances around the room. "What are you doing?"

"Do you want to get out of here?" I'm sure I'm drawing stares from other patrons of the restaurant, but my gaze is firmly on Sophie.

Her shoulders relax as she finally takes my hand. That bright smile is lighting her face again as she stands up. "Hell, yeah."

Chapter Nineteen

CARTER

THE LAKE IS BEAUTIFUL TONIGHT. AFTER WE DITCHED The Elysian Table and came back to Ivy Glen, we picked up a couple of to-go orders from Sal's, took the truck to Ivy Glen Lake, and backed the truck in so the bed is facing the water. I'm glad I had the foresight to put some blankets in the storage container in the back of the truck because this April night is a little chilly. Now, we both have blankets wrapped around our shoulders, and one spread out in the bed. Our feet are dangling off the tailgate, and we're eating the best damn burgers in Massachusetts.

"So... what's it like?" she asks, continuing the conversation we're having, "playing hockey professionally. It was your dream."

I watch the reflection of the moon in the lake as I think about the question.

How do I tell her that the first few years are a blur because Dad was always threatening Mom and up in my ass about money? How the stress of it overrode any good memories I have?

"It... I'm not going to lie. Once the thrill of joining the NHL wore off, it quickly turned into... a job. It should have been more than that, it should have been everything, you know? Dad, well he... he had turned it into something so toxic, I forgot to love the sport. It was always about the next payday for him, the threat to Mom was always there, and I never got the chance to just... enjoy my reality."

She shifts a little closer to me so our thighs are pressed together and my heart rate picks up. "Now it's your choice. Do you know what team you want to sign with yet? I'm sure you have your pick." She turns her head to face me, her eyes shining with warmth.

"I don't know yet. Jake and I have talked about trying to get on the same team, and that might limit our options. In the end, I'll be happy just to get to play with him again, no matter what team we're on."

Just like that, I can see the walls building back up behind her eyes. She's telling herself to not get attached. Reminding herself that I'll be leaving as soon as hockey season starts. Shit. I have to slide in there and remind her that it doesn't *have* to end when the season starts. That we could make something work.

"What I do know, though..." my hand slides over hers, intertwining our fingers, "is that I will do everything I can to stay close to home." The words are quiet, but I hope she can tell how much I mean them. At this point, is hockey worth a life without her in it?

Her hand, while calloused from all her hard work, is soft compared to mine. Holding it brings me back to the days when she knew exactly how much she meant to me, before I fucked everything up. I hope she'll let me make it right again.

She smiles at the water before facing me again. "Yeah?"

My smile grows to match hers. "Yeah."

We say nothing, staring into each other's eyes. I could get lost in those pools of honey forever. Her cheeks tinge pink before she looks back out over the water, breaking our stare.

When her head tilts slightly and rests against my shoulder, it's like... shit. It's almost like I *have* her again. Like there's been a knot in my chest and this one act of vulnerability from her loosens it just a little.

There's still so much I don't know about her, though. I want... no, I *need* to know everything I missed when it comes to Sophie Hartwell.

"Soph?" I ask quietly, not wanting her to move from her spot on my shoulder.

"Yeah, Cart?"

"Tell me about *you*. I used to know you so well, and not knowing what you've been doing the last nine years feels like... like I'm missing a part of myself somehow."

She sighs against me. "Well, you know I help take care of Jordan. And that I help with the flower shop and manage the Twin Rinks..."

"Yeah, okay, but...." I take a deep breath and turn to face her, making her move her head from my shoulder as much as I want to stay just like that. Forever. "Is there anything you really enjoy doing? Like, if your parent's flower shop ran perfectly and business was booming, and the rec center was saved and everyone was taken care of... what would you want to do?"

She runs her teeth over her bottom lip and shrugs. "I like helping. Taking care of people in the town. It makes me happy."

I can see in her eyes that she means it. She wants to take care of everyone else, but what about her? There's nobody here to take care of Sophie while she runs herself into the ground, worrying about everyone else.

And it's my fault. I should have been with her. But maybe... maybe I can make it right—at least for tonight. She needs to get out of her own head. To not have room for anything else in that brilliant brain of hers except for the pleasure I can bring her.

"You're looking after the ones you love... will you let me take care of you, Angel?" I murmur, unable to help myself as I reach and tuck a strand of hair behind her ear.

Her sharp intake of breath and glance down to my mouth is all the invitation I need. My lips brush hers gently, and she melts into my touch.

A small moan escapes her when my hand cups the back of her neck as I deepen the kiss.

Our lips move sensuously as she fists the front of my shirt, trying to pull me closer. Her teeth nip at my lower lip, turning me borderline feral. I grip the back of her neck tighter, plundering her mouth and earning a soft whimper in response..

Her. All I need is her. Her sounds, and her taste, the feel of her body against me.

Breathing hard, I pull away, keeping my hand on the back of her neck and pressing our foreheads together. "Will you trust me to give you what you need?"

"Yes." Her voice is low and so fucking sexy.

"Good girl." I give her a single, slow kiss. "Get on your back."

She nods, and moves to lay further up the truck bed.

Crawling over, I can't help but revel in how goddamn gorgeous she looks with the moonlight illuminating her pale skin, her hair spread out underneath her head and her eyes looking at me, full of want.

My lips capture hers again, and I settle against her, kissing her breathless. Trailing down her neck, her dress moves easily when I pull it down, exposing her breasts.

My Angel went braless tonight. I smile against her skin as my lips move down to capture her nipple. She writhes against me as my tongue laves and sucks at the sensitive skin, and I reach one hand up to remove her underwear from beneath her dress.

"Ah, Carter," she cries out, her hands twinning in my hair to bring me closer to her delicious tits. Her legs move to help me remove her panties, and my hand immediately palms her pussy, causing a shaky moan to leave her at the pressure.

"More, please," she pants as I grind the heel of my hand against her clit.

"Shhh, Angel," I murmur, detaching my lips from her nipple. "You'll get what you need, I promise."

With one hand, I take both her wrists and move them above

her head. "These stay here until you come, okay? You move your hands, I stop."

When she nods, I remove my hand from her wrists and settle between her legs, pushing her dress up to her waist. My tongue runs through her folds and she shudders, but when I look up, her hands are still in place.

"Good girl," I say against her pussy lips before devouring her. My tongue wreaks havoc on her clit, tracing circles around it before biting it gently. A sharp cry leaves her as her back arches, and her hands shoot to my hair.

Immediately, I lift my head, raising my brow. "Only good girls get to come, Angel." I nip at the soft, milky flesh of her inner thigh. "And good girls do what they're told."

Pouting, she puts her hands back above her head, wiggling her hips closer to my face. "Don't be a brat, or I'll get the handcuffs next time." I growl, and she shivers at my words before I dive back in.

Fuck. I love how she tastes. Before long, her legs are shaking, she's panting my name, as she falls over the edge and into bliss. After her release, her arms come down, stroking my neck and hair.

"Fuck, your pussy is heaven. If I could only eat one meal for the rest of my life, my permanent seat would be on the floor with my head between your legs."

Her eyes blaze at my words, and I sit back on my knees, undoing my belt and shimmying my pants and boxers down so my dick is out.

"Spread your legs wider for me, Angel." I command, and she complies, allowing me to slide forward until my hard cock pushes against her pussy lips. "Are we still safe?" I ask, glancing down between us. The thought of another man even just touching her makes my blood boil, but I'm not trying to be presumptuous and scare her away by acting like she owes me anything.

"I am, are you?" She props herself up with her elbows and

looks at me with enough attitude that I want to spank her until her perfect ass glows pink.

We can do that another time, though.

"There is only you," I murmur in her ear before sliding my cock all the way inside her in one thrust. She keens, dropping down on her back again, and I pull away, then snap my hips forward again. "Only ever you, Sophie."

"Yes, yes," she chants, her hands running over my shoulders and biceps. I angle my thrusts upwards, hitting her g-spot and her panting grows harder.

I'm fucking her so hard into the bed of the truck I'm sure she'll have bruises.

Without removing myself from her, I flip us over so I'm laying on my back. She sits up to ride me, and I grip her hips firmly, setting the pace as she slides up and down my cock.

Using my heels as leverage, I thrust up from beneath her, and I can feel the way her body shudders against mine. "Touch yourself," I order her quietly. "Touch yourself while I fuck up into you."

"I—What?" She blinks at me, her cheeks pink, then shakes her head. "I've never done that in front of anyone before..."

"Fucking touch yourself, Angel. I want to see your fingers slide across that pretty pink clit while I make you fall apart." I say with more force, taking one of my hands and wrapping it around her neck. I squeeze gently, not enough to hurt, but enough to remind her who's in charge here. To ground her.

Her cheeks become even more pink before she bites her lip, tentatively moving her hand down to her pussy. "Good fucking girl," I growl, and her pupils blow at my words, lust evident as she stares at me, rubbing her clit in firm, short strokes. Watching her come undone by her own hand almost has me blowing my load before she comes, but soon her channel clenches around my cock, sending me over the edge as well.

My head falls back against the floor of the truck bed, and my chest rises and falls as I try to catch my breath. Her body collapses on top of mine, and we hold each other, both of our chests heaving.

Sophie is everything I've been missing. Her warmth, her touch, her beautiful heart. This moment... her in my arms, both of us half-naked, the stars in the sky, is one that will live in my mind for the rest of my life.

We lay together in silence for a bit, before she speaks.

"You're good at it too, you know," she says quietly.

"At what?" A yawn escapes me.

"Taking care of people."

Her words have me bringing her closer to my chest, pressing a kiss into her hair. Before long, her breathing turns shallow, and when I tilt my head to look at her, she's fast asleep.

I'll let myself rest for a few moments, and then I'll take her back to my hotel room so she can get some real sleep.

She doesn't stir when I fix her dress, covering her beautiful breasts once again. Nor when I lift her from the bed of the truck, tucking her into the passenger seat before making the short drive back. A small whimper escapes her when I carry her into my hotel room and place her in my bed.

"Carter?" she whispers, her eyes half closed as I shimmy her dress down her body, before replacing it with one of my shirts.

"Shhh, Angel. I'll take care of you." Getting up, I head to the bathroom and wet two washcloths, then bring them back to her. The first one I use to wipe her face, getting under her eyes where her makeup smudged and capture her lips in a swift kiss. The second one, I run between her legs, cleaning up the mess we made.

With that taken care of, I pull us both under the covers and she snuggles close to me.

Having her in my arms, thoroughly satisfied and boneless, is better than anything I could have dreamed. It's the missing piece of my life I've been chasing since Dad forced me away from Ivy Glen.

Now that I have her again, I'm never letting her go.

Chapter Twenty

SOPHIE

It's been a week since the night in the back of Carter's truck and things have been going... surprisingly well. We've spent the last seven days re-learning everything there is to know about each other, both in the bedroom and in our everyday lives. Carter hangs out with Jake or helps his mom with some home remodeling while I'm at work, and more than once, I've watched him on the ice with Jordan and his friends.

We haven't seen each other yet today, and I had planned to go over to his place for dinner. Then, I got his text an hour ago, and I thought I read it wrong. Silk scarves? What on earth could he want to do with those?

"He wants you to bring *what?*" The excitement in Abbie's voice coming through my phone makes me chuckle as I search the back of the closet.

"Silk scarves." I nearly blush at Abbie's squeal on the other line.

"Damn. Maybe Carter needs to give Jake some ideas because that is *hot*."

Chuckling, I grab a small stool from my room to stand on to

reach the top shelf. "Oh? I thought things were still exciting between you two."

"It's just sex," Abbie says almost defensively. "As long as I get a decent amount of orgasms at least two times a week, I'd say it's going fantastic."

Rolling my eyes, I grab the box from the back and nearly shout in victory. After pulling it down, I settle on the floor to pull out a few options.

"Hu uh. You're not fooling me. Don't forget I've known you since kindergarten and know all about your long-standing crush on Jake Ashford."

"No way, that was years ago," Abbie protests. "He hardly noticed me back then, and we even hung out in the same group of friends. Now, it's his turn to wish he had my heart."

Running the material through my fingers, I nearly shudder at the sensation of the fabric against my skin. Maybe Carter was onto something after all. "Well, if you guys ever decide to make it more than just sex, you could up that to five nights a week. Maybe Carter can give these to Jake next."

"You lucky bitch," Abbie mumbles. "Did you find any?"

My mouth goes dry, and all I think about is him binding my wrists together while I'm completely naked, utterly at his mercy.

"Uh huh," I choke out, licking my lips.

"Okay, call me tomorrow with all the dirty details!" She hangs up the phone, and I pull myself together enough to head to Carter's.

I feel almost ridiculous as I let myself into Carter's hotel room, a bag full of silk scarves on my arm.

"There you are." He wraps me in arms, kissing me breathless before the door shuts fully behind me. "Let me see what you brought. My cock's been hard since I texted you earlier." His eyes are like fire, burning straight through me.

Biting my lip, I step back and hand him the bag. "Will they..." I swallow as his face lights up looking through my bag. "Will they work?"

"Oh, they'll work just fine, Angel." His eyes darken as he looks from the bag to me. "I've been imagining you naked on my bed, wearing nothing but these wrapped around your pretty little wrists."

My thighs clench at his words. I've never been tied up before. Doing that with Carter sends a thrill through me.

Before I know it, I'm naked on the bed, one hand tied to each of the two top bed posts, and a scarf wrapped around my eyes like a blindfold.

"You look good enough to eat," he murmurs as the bed shifts, his weight coming next to me. "I might just have to have you for dinner."

"Don't make promises you can't keep." Carter has a dominant streak, and I know my words will taunt him, but I can't help it. The thought of having him lose control is too irresistible to ignore.

He releases a throaty chuckle near my ear before he takes my earlobe between his teeth. "Oh, Angel, I keep every promise I make."

His words have a shiver of anticipation running through me, and I let out a breathy moan. "Please, Carter."

His lips move down to my peaked nipples, kissing and laving attention on both of them, making me a panting mess. Without my sight, every sensation is heightened tenfold. That I'm at his mercy, his to use as he sees fit, lights fire in my veins.

"One day I'm going to fuck these perfect tits," he growls, gently dragging his teeth over my nipple. I cry out, the sensation of them scraping my skin sending me into overdrive.

His hand finds its way to my already soaking folds, running through them with deft fingers. They circle around my clit with precision, never quite touching where I need them most.

"Shit, Carter!" My voice rings out in the room, and he groans into my skin as he moves his mouth back up to my neck.

His touch finally lands on my clit, and the few small circles he rubs is all it takes before I'm screaming my release.

"That's it, Angel," he says into my neck. "I know you have more in you, and I want every single one. They're mine." His voice is sultry and possessive, sending a thrill through me. When I only moan in response, the bed shifts, then his weight settles over me as he puts his mouth right next to my ear.

"Say it. Tell me that every delicious orgasm that tears through this fucking perfect body belongs to me."

"They're yours," I pant, my heart hammering in my chest. "All of them."

"Good girl," he rumbles, dragging my earlobe through his teeth again and causing me to cry out. His weight moves back towards the bottom of the bed as he devours my pussy with the fervor of a starved man. My wrists pull at the silken scarfs binding them, and a sense of peace comes over me at the fact that I can't move, even if I wanted to.

I should feel trapped.

Instead, all I feel is... safety. Carter has me, and he's going to take care of everything.

My orgasm shatters me into a thousand pieces as he pulls my clit into his mouth and sucks.

Hard.

Before I've finished coming down from my high, he's untying the scarves from the bedpost, pulling me off the bed and to my knees. When I lick my lips in anticipation, still blindfolded, he chuckles lowly. "You want my cock, Angel?"

"Yes," I whisper, leaning forward.

He tsks at me, gripping the hair at the back of my neck. "Not so fast, you'll take what I give you like a good girl, won't you?"

Doing my best to nod, I let out a moan when he guides his tip to my mouth. Salty precum meets my tongue, and I swallow him down eagerly. "Tap my thigh if it's too much," he says, before drawing out and thrusting in, holding my head in place. He's not rough, withdrawing as soon as his head tickles the back of my throat.

"I can take more," I tell him when he withdraws again, earning a rumble from his chest as he slides back in, this time holding himself in place for a few seconds before sliding out. Then he looses control and fucks my face, hard. Tears stream down my cheeks. I feel myself dripping down my thighs as he uses my mouth. The obscene sounds he makes only turn me on more, knowing that I'm the one causing him to act this way.

Suddenly, he pulls out of my mouth with a pop and pulls me to my feet, turning me around and bending me over the side of the bed. Grabbing my long hair in a tight grip, he drives into me in one hard thrust, causing me to see stars as white-hot pleasure fills me. My fists grip the sheets tightly, and a wanton cry escapes me.

Everything is heightened since I can't see what's happening. Before long, I'm screaming his name as I clench and cum around him yet again, sending him to his own release as well.

He nearly collapses on top of me, but moves so he lands on the bed and removes my blindfold. Blinking at the light in the room, my focus is immediately drawn to Carter, who moves to kiss me gently.

"Thank you," he says softly, wrapping me in his arms. "For trusting me enough to let go."

It would be dangerously easy to get used to waking up like this. Slowly, with the soft rays of morning light peeking through the hotel room curtains and strong, warm arms wrapped around me. My arms aren't even sore from the restraints, and Carter's steady breathing tells me he's still asleep, so I close my eyes, basking in the feeling of being in his arms.

. . .

What we did last night flashes through my mind. I'm not sure I could ever let go like that with anyone else. With Carter, it feels so good to let him be in control. It's amazing, it's like he knows my body better than I do and can always give me just what I need in order to let go.

Plus, the man is amazing at aftercare. He washed my hair and body in the shower, then gave me a full body massage before feeding me Chinese food from my favorite restaurant.

It's clear that he never stopped caring about me, even if he had been powerless to do anything about it. Every time we're together, whether we're skating at the rink together, grabbing a bite to eat, or tumbling in bed, it's like a mix of apology and desperate need. Like he's trying to make up for every year we spent apart.

I can't afford to get too used to it. Before long, hockey season will start again and it's possible he'll sign with a team nowhere near here. He said he wanted to stay close to home, but I'm trying to be realistic. What are the chances of that actually happening?

But you know what? It doesn't even matter. Because we're not in a relationship. We're just two old friends reconnecting.

In every possible way.

As amazing as this week's been, this morning I'm stressed, anxiety turning in my gut.

Today is the press conference announcing the new plans for Twin Rinks. First, I'll need to present the new programs I thought of and list of ways to bring in business once the rebuild is done. Then, Carter will present the 3D model of the building he had the developers create as a sort of grand finale. The exact model I approved of. Not the one in the second proposal.

I remember how Carter had stormed into the last council meeting, demanding to know who had requested that proposal for an NHL arena. After exchanging glances and murmuring their ignorance, the entire table looked to Oscar, who was the only one who hadn't said anything. If his pale-as-a-sheet complexion was anything to go by, he hadn't told a single soul what he was doing.

"It was just... I was just curious," Oscar had stammered, looking to his fellow council members for support.

When none came, Oscar had blanched further, and we received an apology from Abbie's dad, Michael, about the confusion.

Sadly, the memory of that moment where Carter stood up for me does little to stifle my nerves about the presentation.

I've never been great at public speaking, and I'm nervous about talking in front of so many people. Addressing the board during a meeting while I'm in the audience? Not a big deal.

Being the one at the front of the room, addressing hundreds of people? In front of reporters and cameras. Very big deal.

Everything that could possibly go wrong runs through my head. What if everyone hates it and the town convinced the board the rinks are a lost cause after all? What if everyone loves it and it doesn't turn out how it's supposed to? What if I get up there and puke in front of everyone—

I almost stiffen as Carter's arms tighten around me, throwing me from my panicking thoughts. "Good morning, Angel," he rumbles into my ear.

"Hey, you." I try to sound unfazed by the scenarios running through my head. Or so I think.

He immediately senses something is off. Using his hands to roll me over, Cart scoots back and brings us face to face. He looks so beautiful like this. Mussed hair, sleepy smile, and an imprint on his cheek from the pillow.

"What are you thinking about?" he asks, his eyes searching my face.

"How do you know I'm thinking about anything?" I arch a brow, fighting the smile that wants to appear despite of my worries. I love that he reads me so well. When he first came back to town, it really pissed me off. Now though, I realize that it's a testament to how much he's always cared about me.

"Your voice did that thing it does when you're nervous about something. Like a little breathy twitch at the end of the word." His brows are furrowed like he's trying to figure something out. "What's making you anxious?"

There's no point in trying to hide it from him. "It's just... the press conference today. It has me a little on edge."

"It's going to go great," he reassures me, running his hand up and down my arm. "You're going to kick ass, and everyone's going to love it."

"Yeah, but what if—" My question is cut off by him pulling me closer and pressing a kiss to my lips.

"We can't have you attending the press conference all stressed," he murmurs against my lips, skimming his fingers down my collarbone and across my breasts, leaving goosebumps in his wake. "Let me take your mind off things."

I barely nod before his lips are on mine again, his hands trailing up and down my naked body until every touch has my nerve endings lighting up. His fingers skim over my thighs, coming over my ass and dangerously close to where I want him. Every second of his featherlight touch has me more aware of every sensation. When he comes around to my breasts again, he gently pinches my nipples, causing me to gasp into his mouth and press my legs together, desperate for friction.

Chest rumbling, he pushes me to my back and puts a knee between my legs. The feeling of his mouth on my neck as he lovingly massages and tweaks my nipples is pure heaven. When his hand moves down towards my aching pussy, I'm sure that one touch will have me falling over the edge.

He starts slowly though, his fingers moving languid circles, but they never move to my clit. His tongue laves at my nipples, his teeth teasing the flesh. My hips lift unconsciously, trying to push him in the right direction. When I grunt in frustration, he clicks his tongue at me.

"Patience, Soph," he says teasingly, torturing me a little longer. Everything is becoming too much, too sensitive.

"Touch me like you mean it," I whimper. "Please, Carter."

He moves his face back to mine and kisses me, catching my bottom lip between his teeth. "Okay," he breathes out, moving his fingers to my clit as his tongue licks a path up my neck.

Fuck yes.

This is what I need, the pads of his fingers brushing against my sensitive nub, sending jolts of electricity through me. A high pitched moan escapes me as his touch brings me higher and higher. Just when I'm about to fall over the edge... he stops.

"I—what?" I sputter, reaching for his hand. What the hell? I was so close.

He chuckles. "If I let you come, it's all over, and you'll go right back to worrying about the press conference." "

My mouth gapes open. "You're going to make me wait?"

"Just imagine," he says, bringing his hand back to my pussy and once again rubbing in agonizingly slow circles. "Being brought close to the edge, again and again, but never getting to come. And then," he nips my ear, "hours later, when you finally do get to, all that pleasure," his pace increases slightly, "that buildup that you went through, finally reaching it's peak and throwing you into the greatest fucking orgasm of your life."

His words are downright sinful. I keen, my back arching off the bed, and a cry escapes me. What would that be like, to have an orgasm like that?

His fingers still again.

"Carter!" I whine, nearly panting for release. I want to have what he talked about later, but holy shit, I *need* to come right now too.

But Carter's in control. He always seems to know exactly what I need.

"I think one more time will keep your mind off things long enough to get through the press conference" He grins wickedly at me, his fingers returning to my clit.

This time, when he stops, he kisses me tenderly before I can protest. "Later, when I have you falling apart all over my tongue, that can be your reward for kicking ass at the press conference."

Then he carries me to the shower and continues torturing me with his meticulous care as he washes my body and hair and gets me ready for the press conference.

By the time I'm fully dressed and ready to go, one thing is abundantly clear—he certainly did get mind off things, and if his distraction is just a taste of what reward awaits me, I'm going to blow this press conference out of the fucking water.

I'm nearly blinded by the flashing of cameras, and I suddenly wonder how Carter hasn't permanently lost his vision after dealing with things like this for years. We're standing in front of the Twin Rinks on a raised platform while reporters, the local TV news, and citizens of the town gather around. A text from my mom helped calm my nerves somewhat before we went in front of the cameras, but now the anxiety is back in full force.

> Mom: You're gonna knock 'em dead! BOTH of you! :)

The memory of her little emoji makes me smile though. It took her forever to learn how to do that.

Carter is currently standing at the podium, giving a speech about how we're going to restore the rec center to its "deserved glory", and showing the 3D model on the display screen behind him. He has his charming smile on, and the crowd is eating it up.

Thank goodness.

I had been decidedly less eloquent than Carter, but got through my notecards outlining our new rewards program and how we'll draw in customers from outside towns with recreational ice skating events on holiday weekends.

"And that, ladies and gentlemen, is what the jewel of Ivy Glen will look like." He smiles at the cameras, posing next to the screen as the area explodes in flashes of light, photographers taking the opportunity for the perfect shot.

"We are now open for questions," Carter announces.

"Mr. Williams, Mr Williams!" The reporters all call over one another, vying for his attention. Carter points to a reporter with a microphone that reads Channel 6 News.

The reporter, a man who looks to be in his early thirties, clears his throat before speaking. "Mr. Williams, is there any word on who you're going to be playing for this upcoming season?" He points the mic toward Carter, awaiting an answer.

Fucking hell.

We're here about the rec center, not Carter's hockey career. I know he can't control what questions they ask him, but shit. *Can we please focus on what's important?*

"Not yet, but hopefully, I'll be staying close to home so I can continue to support the rinks. Reviving the rec center has been a team effort, but Sophie Hartwell," he lifts a hand in my direction, "has really been the driving force behind the whole thing. Without her vision, love for the town, and commitment to keeping the heart of the rec center intact, we never would have gotten this far."

He turns his head towards me and smiles that brilliant smile, winking at me. At the motion, the cameras flash like crazy again, momentarily stunning me. My cheeks flush pink at the attention, and I do my best to not look like a love struck teenager.

My heart pounds and thighs clench at his public declaration. He's all but claiming me, in front of everyone.

I'm his.

This presentation needs to wrap the fuck up so I climb that man like a tree.

Six hours later, when I'm coming apart on his tongue in his hotel room, I realize one very important thing.

This reward was *so* worth the wait.

Chapter Twenty One

CARTER

I'VE GOTTEN USED TO WAKING UP NEXT TO SOPHIE. Coming into consciousness with her wrapped up in my arms has easily become one of the best parts of my day. Her soft hair in my face, the way she always smells amazing, the feel of her soft curves under my hands; not only is it enough to make my morning wood painfully hard, and we end up having slow, lazy morning sex more times than not, but it also makes it so easy to imagine waking up like this every day, for the rest of our lives.

She had to take Jordan to school this morning, so she went home last night to sleep in her own bed. She might've come to see me before work if she didn't have to open the flower shop this morning, but I guess Kerry had something important come up and couldn't do it. The hotel feels empty without Sophie here, making us both coffee that we sip together as we rest against the headboard.

Without her humming coming from the shower as she washes her hair.

Without the warmth of her very presence as she clicks through spreadsheets on her laptop, sitting on the bed in nothing but my t-shirt and underwear.

It was torture trying to say goodbye to her last night, trying and failing to resist the urge to kiss her senseless each time she told me, "Now I *really* have to go."

But... I *have* been taking up most of her free time, so I won't complain.

Even though I want to.

My running shoes in the closet catch my eye, and I might as well make the best of an otherwise shitty morning, since that's now what I consider every morning without my girl.

Shitty.

It's been a while since I've gone on a morning run, so I lace up my shoes and head out the door. Running has always been my go-to way to clear my mind. It pushes out all the noise and lets me have some semblance of peace. Back when Dad was still in my life, I'd run twice a day. There's something freeing about pushing my body to the limit, feeling the wind on my face and the pavement under my feet.

As I run, I go over what plans I have for the rest of the day when Jake texts.

Jake: Hey man, we still on for lunch today?

Me: Duh. Sals?

Jake: Duh. Smartass.

Jake: 12:30?

Me: See you then

He doesn't normally check to see if we're still meeting. Since he got back to town, Wednesdays are lunch at Sal's, and then we hit the rink or something. Maybe something's on his mind.

Just as I've run until my legs are sore, my phone dings again, this time with a text from mom.

Mom: Do you want to come over for breakfast after my therapy appointment? Dr. Monroe will be here in five minutes.

Me: Sounds great! Need me to bring anything?

Mom: Just yourself, sweetie. Love you.

Me: Love you. See you soon.

An hour and a hot shower later, I'm parking in Mom's driveway, ready to spend quality time with her before I meet Jake for lunch. Someone closes the front door behind them as I approach, and I come face to face with a small woman with red hair and a pair of large, square glasses.

"Mr. Williams." She smiles at me. "It's good to see you again."

"You as well, Dr. Monroe. I trust everything is going well?" Dr. Monroe has done wonders for Mom's mental health. I swear she smiles more and more every day.

"Since she's disclosed that I can speak to you regarding her progress, I can tell you that she's doing very well. I do think she would benefit from meeting other women who have been in her same situation though." She pulls a pamphlet from her shoulder bag. "I gave Vivianne one as well, but we have an all-women's domestic violence support group that my office heads up, and we have a retreat happening soon. She'd be gone for about three months, but I believe it would be groundbreaking for her."

Nodding my head, I flip through the pamphlet. It's at a hotel in Colorado. Spas, pools, massages, hiking, and various well known speakers are listed on the pages, as well as a section detailing how they'll break up into smaller groups to have more conductive conversations.

This is perfect. Mom has always done her best to take care of me. It's time I go beyond and give her what she needs.

Smiling, I hand the pamphlet back to her. "That's a great idea.

Set it up and send me the invoice, please. I'll make it a sort of surprise vacation for her. She deserves it."

"Yes, she does." Dr. Monroe smiles kindly at me as she puts the pamphlet back in her bag. "I'll have it set up by the end of the day."

Mom is in the living room when I come in, reading a book on the couch. She looks happier. More... lighthearted. The first few sessions she was always a mess after, but Dr. Monroe had said that it's a completely normal response to dredging up repressed emotions and painful memories. Now, she seems lighter and lighter every time.

"Hey, Mom." I bend down from behind the couch and press a kiss to her cheek before coming around and sitting on the opposite side from her.

"Hi, Sweetie." Mom puts her bookmark in her book before setting it on the cushion next to her and pulling off her reading glasses. "I have an egg casserole in the oven. It was frozen, so I popped it in when I texted you earlier. Should be ready any minute."

"Sounds good," I tell her, leaning back. "Everything go okay with your appointment?"

"Dr. Monroe is amazing. I feel so comfortable with her, and she's made me realize that nothing your father did is my fault."

Why would she think it's her fault? Have I ever made her feel that way? Ice crawls in my veins at the thought of Mom thinking I ever blamed her for anything Dad ever did.

"Did I..." I choke on my words, "Mom, have I ever made you feel that way?"

"Oh!" She scoots towards me on the couch, grasping my hand. "No, never, Carter, I swear. I just meant that on some level, I had always felt like it was my fault. But that was because every time he would..." she contorts her face, the words clearly hard for her to say, "*abuse* me, he made sure to tell me it was because of my actions. And when you hear the same thing every day for years, eventually it's just second nature to believe it. But Dr. Monroe is helping me see that there is nothing that I could have done to ever warrant such behavior. That the only one responsible for his actions is *him*."

Relief fills my chest at her words. I don't know if I could live with myself if I ever made her feel she deserved anything Dad gave her.

It's strange to hear Mom actually acknowledge the abuse. For years, she thought it was her job to make sure I was never subjected to the harsh reality that is my piece of shit father. If she had to refer to it at all, she would just say that stress got to him, or that he lost control of his temper.

I'm so fucking glad he's gone now, wherever the hell he ended up. Mom wouldn't have been able to make this kind of progress in her recovery if the threat of his presence still lingered.

An alarm goes off on her phone, and she smiles, patting me on the knee. "That'll be the casserole." I feel a faint smile on my face as I watch her go to the kitchen.

I hate that she went through what she did, but hearing her talk about it, acknowledging that even though it's something that happened *to* her, it's not something that happened *because* of her, gives me hope. Hope that with enough time and healing, Mom can be back to who she was before Dad's abuse started.

Well, maybe not the *exact* same, but she'll be resilient. She's a survivor, a warrior. My mom has seen the other side of hell and is crawling her way back topside step by step. She'll come out the other side reformed, reshaped, and stronger than ever, and fuck, I can't wait to see it when she does.

"Hey, man." Jake says when I slide into the booth across from him at Sal's. "How's it going?"

"Since yesterday?" I tease, since we see each other nearly every day. "It's going great. Though Soph didn't get to sleep over last night... shit, I missed her. I'm pretty sure I'm in love with her all over again."

Jake snorts. "No kidding. We don't get through a single conversation without you bringing her up at least once." His words are ribbing, but his tone is light, and I know he's happy for me.

"You're welcome to bring up Abbie at any time," I raise a brow, trying to get a read on him. He's been oddly cagey since they started hooking up. Usually, he's all about bragging about his conquests.

"Nah." Jake shrugs. "You know me. We're just having fun."

Unease fills me. I hope Abbie agrees. "Be careful, you know she's not your usual hookup—"

"Thank fuck," Jake mutters under his breath.

Ignoring him, I continue, "Just, make sure you're both on the same page about what you're doing, otherwise someone could end up hurt. By someone, I mean Abbie."

Jake rolls his eyes. "That's not—"

"I mean it Jake." This time my voice is serious. "If you end up hurting her, you know Sophie is going to be pissed. Those two are like fucking wolves when it comes to protecting each other."

If she thinks it's just sex as well, then great, but Jake's never been in any kind of relationship where he sleeps with a girl more than once. I don't think he realizes what that could do to Abbie's emotions if she's thinking they have something more than what it is.

"And let me guess, if it comes to picking sides, which it won't, by the way, you're standing by Sophie?" He raises a brow, already knowing what I'll say.

"I'm not trying to be a dick, but yeah." I shrug. He knows where I stand.

He shakes his head. "I know, man. I wouldn't ever dream of coming between you two."

"I didn't think you would. I just need to make sure I'm taking care of Sophie, and that extends to looking out for Abbie as well."

He chuckles. "You're too fucking noble for your own good, Carter."

Giving him my best shit-eating grin, I wink. "Only for Soph."

"And on that note... I have some interesting news that pertains to both of us."

Well, *that* piques my interest. "Oh yeah? What's up?"

"I've been in contact with the team manager of the Boston Reapers. They want to meet us. They should be calling you today."

My heart leaps into my chest. This is... it's like Jake walked in here and served me the answer to all my problems on a silver platter. A few more offers have come in since the press conference, all teams considerably closer to Ivy Glen than my previous offers, but none of them have felt *right*.

I can't help but think this is why. Boston is a dream come true.

"That's amazing!" I tell him. "Being in the same state as Sophie, and playing on a team with you? That's... shit, not to sound corny, but that's like a dream come true." I can't help the enthusiasm that permeates from my voice, but Jake looks less convinced.

"I don't know, I'm not sure I want to stay in the state with my family so close. You know I love them, but..." Jake trails off, his expression neutral.

He *does* love his family, but he feels like he's on the outside looking in sometimes. He's already insecure about his relationship with them without having to add family dinners and shit into the mix.

I'm just about to tell him that they love him too, when his expression dissolves, and he turns back into his usual laid-back self. "Regardless, they're asking if we can meet in three days. That good for you?"

"Yeah, set it up for whenever. We can drive together." I can't help the huge cheesy smile on my face. Damn. It's possible that I could have it all if this works out. The girl, the job... what's left after that?

I'm not going to tell Sophie about the meeting quite yet though. If everything happens how it needs to, I'll be able to make some sort of grand romantic gesture, showing her how much I want to be with her.

"If this works out, I'll probably live in the city and you can commute to the suburbs if you want to be near Sophie." His tone is teasing. "The 'married' life just isn't for me, man."

I chuckle at his comment, but... fuck, the thought of Sophie with a ring on her finger, one that *I've* given her, does something to me. Something primal and possessive surges into my chest at the image in my mind, and *shit*, I want that. I want a ring on her finger and a house in the suburbs with a white fence and a dog and even kids someday.

But... what if it doesn't work out? I can't help but worry about what will happen if they try to hand us a shitty contract they won't budge on. This meeting could be the ticket to having everything I've ever wanted. What I wouldn't give to get to stay with Sophie *and* play with Jake again.

My face must be reflecting my emotions because Jake looks at me with compassion. "Hey, it'll work out, Carter. They're getting a hell of a package deal if they sign both of us on." His expression morphs to a goofy grin. "They could call us 'Cake Willford', our NHL duo name." He seems so proud of his combination of our names, "Jake Ashford" and "Carter Williams".

"Fuck off," I chuckle, shaking my head. "You're right. We're two players with great stats, I'm sure the meeting will go well, and everything will work out."

I don't want to think about the possibility of it not working out. After all Sophie and I have been through, I can't stomach leaving her again.

Chapter Twenty Two

SOPHIE

"Willow Creek Community Rinks is going to be your new home for the next year," I tell the group of concerned parents in front of me from behind the front desk. "I've met with the manager personally, and she's assured me that everything will be ready for your kiddos by the start of June. It's a bit of a longer drive, and the rink is accommodating the currently scheduled practice times as well as they can. And it's not forever. This time next year, we'll all be back skating at the Twin Rinks."

That we could get something set up with Willow Creek has been a life saver, but parents understandably have some concerns and questions. Even *I'm* a little antsy about the whole thing, and I don't have any kids playing hockey. But, that's what happens when routine and familiarity are thrown out the window.

"Is it true that Carter Williams is paying for all the repairs on the center and paying the fees to the other rink so we can practice?" One mom in front of me asks, her eyes wide.

I smile. "It is. Mr. Williams has taken care of everything, including the contract with Willow Creek." Not too long ago, that statement would have burned like acid coming out, but now, I'm finding it somewhat of a relief that I have help. That he wants to do this because it matters to him and it's not just some PR stunt. Between the rinks, coaching, the flower shop, and helping Jordan, I hadn't realized how much I was drowning until Carter came and took some of the burden away.

"And the last day Twin Rinks is open is May 30th?" A dad asks, making notes on his phone. We scheduled closing to be right after the intramural hockey team championships, before the summer camps start so there's no interruption in playing for the kids.

"That's correct, in two weeks. Here are some flyers highlighting everything you need to know." My hand waves at the flyers stacked at the end of the front desk and then I check my watch. "Now, if you'll excuse me, ladies and gentlemen, I have a hockey team to coach." They all thank me and grab a flyer, allowing me to head to the rink where my team is practicing.

I start my girls off with warmups, skating across the ice in short sprints, and I can't help but remember being in their shoes. Well, skates. Being a teenager is hard, but having a team of girls that have your back makes it more bearable. Most of my old team, the Ivy Glen Thorns, have moved away since high school.

Being on the ice, in the exact same place where Carter and I spent so many evenings and weekends together, makes it all too easy to remember how it used to be like... as if it was only yesterday...

"You're gonna have to go faster than that if you want to catch up to me!" I taunt, turning my head so he can hear me. He's closer than I had thought, a devious smirk appearing on his face at my words.

Shit talking about who's the faster skater had turned into a race around the rink. It was free-skate time, but the rink closed in fifteen minutes and we were the only two left. Since my parents extended my curfew last year when we started high school, Carter and I spend a lot of evenings at the rink together.

He comes up next to me now, our pace even. I've had feelings for him for a while, so when his arms close around my waist, practically pulling me off my feet, my stomach swoops so violently I feel like I might be sick.

"Carter!" I shriek, stumbling in his hold. We both lose our balance, tumbling over, but he holds a hand to the back of my head, making sure I don't crack it on the ice. Shit, that's going to bruise tomorrow.

Before I know it, I'm laying with my back on the ice, breathing hard and looking up into Carter's endless blue eyes. He's panting heavily from skating, his hand still under my head. I might have imagined it, but I swear his eyes dart to my lips briefly.

His breath hitches right before I find my voice. "You fucking cheater!" Using all my strength, I push him off me, and his back hits the ice with an "oof".

"You said I'd have to go faster if I wanted to catch you." He smiles that blindingly charming smile that turns all the girls at our school into mush.

"I said, 'catch up to me', you buffoon." I laugh, shaking my head. My heart rate is finally slowing down, and when I look up, Carter has gotten up and is holding his hand out to me.

It's surprisingly warm as it surrounds mine, and as he pulls me to my feet, I find him staring at my face again, his eyes different than I've seen them. Darker, more heated. My heart pounds in my chest for an entirely different reason now. Is he getting closer? It doesn't even seem like he knows he's doing it.

I'm leaning in too, I realize, and he's just about to bend down when—

"Come on, Soph! Carter, do you need a ride home?" Tom bursts through the door, and we jump apart at the sound of his voice.

Tom gives Carter a ride home, the three of us squished into the cab of his pickup truck. It's a tight fit, but it's not like I can breathe right now anyway, with the feel of Carter's side pressed against mine, the backs of our hands resting against each other.

Does he feel it too? All I would need to do is move my hand a little and he'd be holding it. Was he really about to kiss me? Did I want him to?

Of course I did.

Maybe if I tell him how I feel, he'll feel the same way.

I smile to myself at the memory, then blow my whistle and direct my team to passing drills. I never got the chance to tell him how I felt first, he beat me to it. A few weeks later, when we were doing homework at his house, he confessed his feelings for me. From that point until the championship game our senior year, we had been inseparable in a different way.

When practice ends and my team is heading to the locker room, I spot Carter, Tom, and Jordan entering the rink.

"Hey, guys."

Carter's head snaps in my direction, and he meets me at the edge of the rink, halfway bending over the boards as he takes my face in his hands and kisses me breathless. Making me completely forget that we're in the company of both my brother and nephew.

I could get used to this kind of hello.

"Hey, now, not in front of the children," Tom chides, his footsteps getting closer.

Carter pulls away, his hands still on my face as he gives me a cheeky grin and kisses my nose. "Sorry, children." His wink makes insides do funny things, and then he turns back towards Tom and Jordan.

"'The children' didn't see anything," Jordan pipes up, walking past us to head to the locker room.

Tom and Carter bark a laugh, and my face warms in embarrassment as I swat Carter on the arm.

"No kissing me in front of them anymore." It's becoming harder and harder to rein in my feelings for Carter. I'm having to remind myself that we're just having fun, and it'll do me no good to catch feelings again and be heartbroken when he inevitably leaves at the start of hockey season.

I pointedly ignore the niggling in the back of my mind that's essentially screaming, *Who are you kidding? You already have feelings!*

Nope. No feelings. Just nostalgia and amazing orgasms.

Carter leans in close to my ear, whispering. "Then maybe you shouldn't tempt me by looking so fucking kissable. It makes it hard to keep my mouth off you." His words send heat straight to my core, especially at the image of his mouth on *other* parts of my body. I resist the urge to swat him again.

Luckily, Tom doesn't seem to realize what Carter just said to his little sister, and moves to put his equipment bag on the team bench. We trade places on the ice and I sit with Carter in the bleachers as we watch Tom coach his team. His hand is warm and comforting as it holds mine, keeping me warm in the cold air of the rink.

Jordan is probably pushing himself the hardest, followed closely by Bodhi and Theo. They glide across the ice doing passing drills, their eyes are hard and focused.

When they switch to a scrimmage, it's almost mesmerizing watching the three of them work together. It's like they anticipate each other's moves. The other team has possession of the puck, and Jordan uses his body to block a shot, allowing Theo to fly by and take possession, skating towards the opposing goal. Jordan catches up and protects Theo as he skates towards the goal by keeping himself as a barrier between him and the defense. Theo moves to take the shot, and thanks to a quick deflection by Bodhi, the puck soars into the net.

I take a video for my mom, who wishes she could attend every practice, but the arthritis in her hands gets too aggravated from the cold temperatures of the rink.

Me: Look at Jordy go!

Mom: He's amazing!

Watching them play brings me back to my memory from earlier, and I speak before I can think better of it.

"Hey, Carter?" I ask suddenly, turning my head towards him.

"What is it, Soph?" he murmurs before pressing a kiss into my hair.

"Do you remember... the day before our first kiss? How we were racing in this rink..."

"And I grabbed you and we fell onto the ice together?" He finishes my sentence so quickly a shocked giggle escapes me. "Yes, yes, I do. Why do you ask?"

I don't know why, but the fact he remembers that day just as well as I do makes something warm unfurl in my chest. "When we landed, and you were on top of me, were you...?"

I have no idea why I'm asking him this. What if his answer is no? I'll just feel stupid. It changes nothing now, and there's no point in me knowing. Quickly losing my nerve, I shake my head and face the ice rink again. "Nevermind, it doesn't matter."

A finger under my chin lifts my head back in his direction as he looks at me intensely. "If you were just about to ask if I had thought about kissing you, the answer is yes. Many, many times that day, and it wasn't the first time either. It was just the first time I thought you might have wanted to kiss me back."

My heart thrills, which is ridiculous. We've slept together just about every day for the last week and a half, and somehow, this little admission has my heart pounding harder than it has since he showed up back in Ivy Glen.

"I've told you before that my feelings started for you back in middle school." I whisper, this conversation seeming suddenly too intimate for the bleachers at a public ice rink.

"I didn't know back then though," he says, his eyes searching my face. "And you... I had thought you saw me as just a friend. But no matter who else wanted to date me, on some level, it was always you, Soph. Even then, you were it for me. Please don't doubt that."

Even then? Does that mean... that now...

His lips are almost touching mine again when Tom's whistle sounds, making us jump apart like we're teenagers who almost got caught making out by the teacher. The irony of it being Tom again, like it was that day, almost makes me laugh.

"Tom!" Carter stands and approaches the ice as Jordan's team heads back to the locker room. "I'm taking Sophie out. You good here?"

I'm so glad he said something because after that conversation we just had... I'm wanting some alone time with him too.

Tom looks over at us with a glint in his eye. "Yeah, I'm good. I got the boys for the sleepover tonight so I'll have plenty of help cleaning up."

It doesn't sit right with me to just *leave*. I stand and walk over to the edge of the rink. "I can stay and help clean up—"

Tom isn't having it. "Nope. You don't worry about a thing, Soph. I've got it. You two have a good time."

"Okay," I concede, "Thanks, Tom."

"Now," Carter puts his hands on my shoulders and turns me to face him, "why don't you go home and get changed and I'll pick you up in an hour."

My brow raises and I suppress a smile, my lip quirking slightly to the side. "You mean you don't want to take me out in a ratty shirt and my Twin Rinks hoodie?"

Carter presses a soft kiss to my lips and murmurs, "You would bring me to my knees wearing a fucking paper bag, Angel, but I have a feeling you'll want to get changed for our date."

"Okay." I swallow. "I'll see you in an hour?"

He flashes me that panty-melting smile he keeps in his arsenal. "I can't wait."

Chapter Twenty Three

SOPHIE

"WE'RE GOING TO LITTLE ITALY?" MY VOICE IS EXCITED as I look back and forth between Carter and the restaurant in front of us. I haven't been here in... years. It was always the family favorite for birthdays and special occasions, and Carter came with us more than once. It's in Willow Creek, so I haven't really had a reason to come out.

"Is that okay? I know it's kind of a tradition for your family," he asks, looking almost nervous.

"Of course it's okay," I tell him, unbuckling my seatbelt and opening my door. "I haven't been here in so long. If you listen closely, the Fettucini Alfredo is calling my name."

Carter laughs as he gets out of the car and comes to my side. As we walk into the restaurant, hand-in-hand, my heart fills with... something I don't want to name right now.

Once we've sat, Carter takes my hand across the table. "I should have taken you here on our first date, instead of that other restaurant."

"Don't worry about that any more." I smile reassuringly. "In case you don't remember, we ended up having a *very* good time that night." Memories of that night in the truck bed nearly lights my body on fire, and I'm wishing he had kept that rental.

"I know, but it's more than that." He sighs. "When I would come here with you guys, I always wished that I could take you here on a date."

My brow furrowed. "I'm confused. Why wouldn't you have been able to?" It couldn't have been a matter of money. My family was firmly middle class, but his family was on another level. He would have easily been able to afford to take me to a place like this.

"I guess I haven't fully gotten into what kind of pressure my dad had me under." He smiles grimly. "I wouldn't have been permitted to leave town lines with you, much less spend more than what it cost to go to Sal's or go see a movie. Dad knew it would look bad on him if I never paid for *anything*, but he was against me dating you enough to be petty about it."

Knowing what I do about his dad now, it really shouldn't surprise me that the abusive asshole hadn't been my biggest fan. Back when I first realized, it really bothered me, but good riddance. He doesn't deserve the space it takes in our minds to hate him.

"After all of that, this should have been the first place I took you, that's all I meant." He says, squeezing my hand before releasing it. "Anyway, enough about that asshole. You said you haven't been here in a long time. Why? Your family used to come here for everything."

"After the accident, Tom couldn't bear to come here without Sarah, so we just kind of stopped." It had been really hard, coming here for a birthday dinner for the first time after her death and seeing the raw pain in Tom's eyes. None of us had thought of it, and we turned around and went home.

We're interrupted by the waiter, whose eyes widen in recognition. "Can... can I take your order?" He shakes his head, "I mean, I'm sorry. Drinks. Can I get you something to drink, Mr. Williams? I mean—"

Carter lets out an easy smile, the same one I've seen on the poster in Jordan's room. "Call me Carter. What's your name?"

The waiter, now that I'm looking properly, can't be older than his late teens. "Joey, sir. I mean, Carter. Could you..." His cheeks flush as he rips a piece of paper from his pad, "Could you sign this for me please? I've been following your career since you signed with the Vultures."

"Of course." Carter takes his pen and signs the little sheet of paper, and the waiter looks like he might faint in excitement.

"Thank you so much," he stammers, pushing the piece of paper into the front pocket of his shirt. After that's out of the way, Joey seems to have an easier time around Carter, taking our drink order, and once he leaves, I chuckle, shaking my head.

"What?" Carter gives me a knowing look, surely betting I'm about to give him a hard time about our waiter's reaction to him.

"Do you ever get used to it?" I ask, gripping his hand across the table. "I know you as just... Carter. It's so strange seeing people fawn over you like that."

"It's... different." He smiles, shaking his head. "If they're sweet like that kid, it's nice. I can see how much they love the sport and I love that I feed into that somehow. But if they're pushy and demanding, which is more often than not, I'm not inclined to sign a single thing they own."

"You deserve to be recognized for what a great player you are. For how hard you work," I tell him truthfully. The next words catch in my throat with emotion—the knowledge that I should have said this way sooner. "I know I haven't said this since you've been back, but I'm so proud of you."

"Your opinion is the only one that matters to me, Soph," he says, his expression serious. "None of this is worth it if I don't have you at my back."

A shiver runs through me at his words. Does he really feel that way? I push that thought away quickly. Of course he does. This is Carter.

I'm thinking I might feel the same way.

After dinner, he won't tell me where we're going. We're clearly heading back to Ivy Glen, but then we pull into the parking lot of the rec center, and I still have no clue what's going on.

"Did you forget something here earlier?" I turn and look at him, and he shakes his head, smiling.

"Nope. Just thought you might be up for a rematch of our race, since the last one ended prematurely."

"It only ended prematurely because you knew you were going to lose and tackled me." I raise my brow.

"I think it's time to put your money where your mouth is, Hartwell." He smirks, a challenge in his voice.

"I'll put my *body* where your mouth is." I breathe, and he groans, leaning back.

"Fuck, Soph. I call sabotage. How am I supposed to win when I have a raging hard-on?"

"I'm sure you'll figure it out." I smirk, getting out of the car and heading across the parking lot, Carter following close behind me.

Twenty minutes later, we're on the ice, and I'm skating as hard as I can. Shit, he's fast. But more often than not, I'm doing sprints with my team so I'm not out of shape either. Adrenaline pumps through my veins, blood pounds in my ears. He's just behind me, and it's almost like he's the predator, and I'm his prey.

Then we're neck to neck, and I'm half wondering if he's going to pull the same move and grab me in his arms, but eventually, we both pass the goal we deemed the finish line, breathing hard.

For a minute, we just look at each other, panting from the exertion. "Tie?" he finally asks, and I nod before he pulls me in, crashing his lips to mine.

His hands in my hair, my fists twisted in his shirt, we collide like two waves in the ocean. Nipping at my lip, he picks me up bridal style and skates me off the ice. I'm so lost in him, that I don't realize that we're in the locker room until he breaks our kiss, setting me on the ground directly in front of the lockers. Without a word, he drops to his knees, unlacing my skates and pulling them off, before unbuttoning my pants and pushing them and my underwear down my legs and helping me step out of them.

I expect him to drop his pants and take me hard and fast, but instead, he stays on his knees, looks at me, and says, "You said you'd put your body where my mouth is." Then he pushes his head between my legs.

"Ohhhhh." A sigh of relief escapes me when his tongue swipes through my folds, and he groans at the sound, hiking one leg over his shoulder and settles in like he's about to eat his last meal. My back hits the lockers, the metal digging into me, and I don't care because the feel of his tongue on me is so fucking good.

My hands land on his head as his tongue circles my clit, making tingles run from my toes straight into my pussy. "Permanent fucking seat," he rumbles, referencing his words from our night by the lake.

"If I could only eat one meal for the rest of my life, my permanent seat would be on the floor with my head between your legs."

He knows just how to work me, one hand gripping my thigh that's propped on his shoulder, the other one digging into my hip as he holds me in place. "Fuck, Angel, forget the sitting. I could spend my whole life right here, worshipping at your altar on my knees."

With the attention he's lavishing on my needy clit, he may as well be worshiping.

My fingers twine through his hair and pull, earning a growl from him, the reverberations sending jolts of electricity through me, making me cry out. He works me with his mouth, periodically dipping his tongue inside of me and fucking me with it, before returning to my clit. "Come for me, Angel," he says into my pussy before he pulls my clit into his mouth and sucks *hard*, tipping me over the edge as I fall into blissful oblivion.

He looks up at me, eyes dark, before standing and claiming my mouth with his. Tasting my release on his lips is so fucking erotic that my hands move to his belt.

But he stops me, a wicked glint in his eye. "We need more privacy for all the things I want to do to you."

"But you're..." I pull back and motion to the clearly bulging erection in his pants.

"Blue balls are worth it now, if it means I get to have you exactly how I want you when we get back to the hotel." He smirks. "Don't think for one second that won't include your mouth on my dick." A thrill runs through me at his words, and I can't stop myself from kissing him again.

This whole night, the dinner, the race, and now this... he means it. He's done everything to show me how much he cares and how much he *did* care, even back then. The feelings that I swear I'm developing rise to the surface, but I push them down. This won't last forever.

"I agree, on one condition." I pull back, raising my brow.

"Oh? And what would that be?"

"I agree, but only if you never use the phrase 'blue balls' in a serious sentence ever again."

He chuckles and kisses me again. "Deal."

The ring of Carter's phone wakes me up. "Carter. Alarm." I grumble from beneath the blankets. When it keeps going off, I raise my head.

Why isn't he turning it off?

I look around, but he's not in bed. Then I hear the shower running.

Sighing, I crawl to his side of the bed to turn off the alarm, but at the sight of the screen, my blood runs cold.

The screen is filled with countless messages, all from a contact named "Nicole".

I've been stupid.

So, so stupid.

Bile rises in my throat as I scroll through them.

> Nicole: I miss you baby
>
> Nicole: Can't wait to see you
>
> Nicole: I need to feel your hands on me
>
> Nicole: I'll be there to see you soon

A selfie comes through of a model-thin blonde seductively biting her lip. I had thought it couldn't get any worse, but I was wrong.

I'm going to be sick, right here in this hotel bed. My vision swims. It's the same girl. The girl who was photographed kissing him right after he left.

He... he told me he didn't know what was happening when those pictures were taken. Had it all been a lie? Could it be that he's had *her* this whole time?

Betrayal turns in my gut. Why would he do this to me? Make me some kind side piece while he has someone else waiting for him? Make me fall in love with him all over again, when he hasn't meant a single word he's said?

I'm such an idiot. I can't believe I fell for it.

I need to leave. I can't be here one more second.

Not able to get my clothes on quick enough, I rip my shirt over my head and nearly trip and faceplant when I pull pants on, but luckily he's still in the shower when I slam the door behind me, marching out of Carter's life before he can take off from mine, yet again.

Chapter Twenty Four

CARTER

"Hey, Soph?" I call out, leaving the bathroom with a towel around my waist. "Have you seen my…" The room is empty.

"Sophie?" The sheets in the bed are tossed around, and Sophie's stuff is nowhere to be seen. Worry fills my chest. It's not like her to just take off without a word, but maybe she sent me a message.

My phone goes off on my nightstand, and relief fills me. That's probably her, telling me that there's an emergency at the flower shop or something. But when I pick it, rage fills me.

Damnit, damnit, damnit!

My phone is filled with messages, but they aren't from Sophie.

Fucking Nicole.

The most recent one is front and center.

> Nicole: Hope you're keeping the bed warm for me.

Sighing, I open the phone to read the rest of the messages.

> Nicole: I miss you baby

Nicole: Can't wait to see you

Nicole: I need to feel your hands on me

Nicole: I'll be there to see you soon

Then a fucking ridiculous selfie of her biting her lip.

The messages are misleading and overly familiar, and absolutely make it look like we have something going on. I immediately dial Sophie's number, but it goes straight to voicemail. *"Hi, you've reached Sophie Hartwell. If this is in regards to Hart's Flowers, please call—"*

Shit! I dial again.

"Hi, you've reached So—"

Fucking damnit!

I try again, but don't stay on past the "Hi". She must have turned her phone off. I don't think she was going through my phone, but if the sound of messages woke her up, I have no doubt she would have gone to turn off the volume and saw these messages instead. I shoot off a text that I hope she doesn't just ignore when she turns her phone back on.

Me: Sophie, I can explain. Please call me.

Me: I know that's what everyone says, but I mean it. There is NOTHING going on with anyone else. You're the only one.

The urge to chase her down and explain that Nicole is just a puck bunny that can't take no for an answer is nearly overwhelming, but I have to leave for that meeting in Boston with Jake, and if we miss that then *everything* will go to shit.

Gut churning, I hurry and get dressed, trying not to think about how devastated Sophie must feel. She thinks I betrayed her.

My phone pings again, and I swear, if it's another text from Nicole...

Jake: I'll meet you outside in ten minutes.

Exhaling through my nose, I toss my phone back on the bed and finish getting ready. I need to focus. If I can just get through this meeting and sign with Boston, I can ensure that I stay in state and be with Sophie. Then, I can apologize when I get back tonight.

It's not perfect, and not finding her right now is killing me, but if I want any chance of us being together long-term, I have to land this contract.

I'm nearly to my car when the sound of clacking high heels makes me look up.

Fucking Nicole.

Bleach blond hair, green eyes, and a body like a stick. She's in a skirt that's way too short, and she looks at me with heavily made up eyes in a way that I'm sure she thinks is sultry.

"Carter, baby, I missed you!" She approaches me with open arms and I take a step back.

"Nicole, what the *fuck* are you doing here?" I don't keep the venom from my voice.

"Where else would I be?" Her voice is sickly sweet as she tries to latch onto my arm. "I've been waiting for you," she coos, and my stomach drops. No woman besides Sophie should touch me like this.

My hand rips hers off my arm, and I ignore her sound of protest. "Lay off, Nicole. This is getting old. I've made it clear multiple times that I'm not interested and things are never going to happen between us again."

"But Carter..." She juts her lip out.

"No buts. You're entering stalker territory, and if you don't get the hell out of Ivy Glen, my lawyer will draw up a restraining order." It's a low blow, but I can't take it anymore. I've basically been running from this girl since a very drunken, stupid mistake in college my sophomore year.

Her face contorts in anger. "Don't worry, Carter. I know that I'm what you want. You'll see."

"Fucking delusional," I mutter, walking away right as Jake comes out to the parking lot. His eyes widen when he sees Nicole, but he ignores her as we get into my car and drive away, leaving her fuming.

"Shit." Jake lets out a breath. "What the fuck is Nicole doing here?"

"Fuck if I know, but she's already risking my chance at getting Sophie back for real." Just the memory of her finding those texts sends my stomach roiling again. I have to nail this meeting. If Boston offers us a shitty contract, I'm half-tempted to take it at this point just to stay with Sophie.

Jake shakes his head. "She's crazy. I bet she saw you on the news for the rec center and that's how she knew where you were. The number of games she showed up to last season alone was intense. We need to get her off your back for good."

Easier said than done. I'm going to file a restraining order first thing on Monday and hopefully, that will help. I'll block her number and even change mine if I have to.

"Yeah, man, I know." My white knuckle grip on the steering wheel eases when I sigh. Sophie *has* to believe me, but even I know that those texts look bad. I'll just have to make sure this meeting goes perfectly, and use the fact that I'm staying in state as a grand gesture of commitment.

Part of me feels like all the progress we've made over the last few weeks will have been erased, and she'll be right back to hating me.

I have to explain. If I learned anything from last time, it's that not telling her the whole truth will only fuck things up more.

"Mr. Williams, Mr. Ashford, it's a pleasure to meet you." The Reaper's GM shakes our hands, followed by Coach Lawson, the head coach. We're meeting in a spacious conference room that takes up much of the top floor of the office building we're in. The windows overlook the Boston skyline, giving a lovely view of the Hancock.

"Mr. Hanson," I greet the GM, nodding politely. "We're very excited to speak to all of you today."

"Likewise," the coach says, smiling wide. He looks to be about forty, with the slightest bit of gray at his temples. He had played for the Reapers for four years before being traded to the Ontario Coyotes in California. He came on as the Head Coach for Boston about five years ago.

Once we all take a seat at the conference table, Coach Lawson and Mr. Hanson get straight to business. "Now," Mr. Hanson says, steepling his fingers in front of him, "the purpose of this meeting is to get to know you two. We know the numbers and stats, but what about your character? Are you going to mesh well with the team? That sort of thing."

That's the bottom line. It doesn't matter how well Jake and I play if our personalities are like a hand grenade to the rapport the team has going on right now.

Jake and I exchange a look. "We're happy to tell you anything you want to know."

Coach Lawson nods. "Before we get to that, let me tell you what you can expect from me as a coach. My coaching style can vary slightly from season to season depending on what kind of team we have on the roster. What I will *always* emphasize, however, is team cohesion. The Reapers have each other's backs both on and off the ice." He looks between us with an assessing gaze. "Does that make sense? I don't stand for petty squabbles between teammates that will fuck us up during a game."

"Yes, sir," we say in unison, earning a smirk from the coach.

Mr. Hanson speaks up. "As I'm sure you've figured out by

now, we have two open spots. Our Left Wing retired, and our Center... well, according to official reports, he's taking a voluntary leave of absence to take care of some... family business. Between the four of us, though, he won't be returning."

What's the story with that? It's none of our business though, and as long as we sign a contract guaranteeing our spot, I really don't care.

"One thing," Coach Lawson says, tapping the table with a finger, "last season, we had some... issues between players. We're doing a summer skills camp in an attempt to team-build and get us to our best before the pre-season starts. It's our one non-negotiable as *all* players are required to attend. It'll be six weeks, we leave the first Monday of June."

Shit. We're only two weeks away from June. But if it's mandatory... and it means I can sign with Boston, play with James, *and* stay near Sophie...

"I don't have a problem with that," I tell him, glancing at Jake. "Neither do I."

"Great. Now that we have that out of the way," he grins, looking between the two of us, "let's learn a bit about you guys."

We spend some time talking about our interests and home life, what we like to do on the off season, and where we would plan on staying if we were to sign with the team. The conversation flows easily, and it really does just feel like they're trying to get to know us.

After about an hour, Mr. Hanson and Coach Lawson exchange a nod before standing to shake our hands. "Well, boys," Mr. Hanson says, "we'll be sending out your contracts by the end of the day. Take the rest of the week to look over them and if you have any revisions you'd like to request, we can talk it over on Monday."

"Holy shit, we did it!" I nearly shout when we're in the car. I can't wait to get home and tell Sophie.

"Fuck, we sure as hell did, man. I'm not super excited about having to do a summer camp." Jake sighs and lets his head fall on the headrest. "What are your plans for your living situation now that you're staying close to home? You can't live in that hotel forever. I wasn't joking when I said I didn't want to be too close to family. I think I'll get an apartment in the city and enjoy the single life."

Despite my excitement, a shrug finds its way to my shoulders. "When I imagine it, I see myself living with Sophie."

Coming home to Sophie, whether it's from practice or a road trip, sounds amazing. We could have a house together, just the two of us, and she could do whatever she wants. She would never have to work a day in her life again if she didn't want to. And hell, if she did want to, I'd move heaven and earth to ensure she gets to do exactly what she wants. "Maybe... shit. Maybe I can even buy a house for the two of us and surprise her with it. Something with a yard. Maybe a fence. Or we could get a fixer upper and do it together in the off-season so it's exactly how she wants it."

"Damn, Carter." Jake laughs. "I knew you always loved her, but a house? Are you sure? That's like... the rest of your fucking life you're talking about."

Jake's right on one thing, I never stopped loving Sophie. When I came back to town it hit me like a freight train and I don't think I'll ever be the same. The question "am I sure?" doesn't even take a blip of brain activity to answer.

"Yeah," I say, smiling to myself. "I don't think I've ever been more sure of anything in my life."

Chapter Twenty Five

SOPHIE

After I leave Carter's hotel room, the drive home is an angry blur.

My grip is white-knuckled on the steering wheel. When I pull up the house, Tom's car is already gone. Thank god he won't see me like this and make me answer a million questions when I'm trying to process everything.

Why did I believe Carter when he told me what happened when he left for college?

Why does he keep messing around with me if he has a woman like *that* waiting for him? Angry tears burn the back of my eyes as I make my way into the house. I don't know who I'm more mad at, Carter or myself. I had kept my guard up for a reason, and all it took were some pretty words and mind-blowing orgasms for me to turn into a gullible pile of goo.

After washing my hair so vigorously I'm sure that my scalp is raw, I changed into my work clothes and drive to the shop. I had thought that maybe having some time to think would help me cool down, but no. My anger is still like this ugly thing in my chest, consuming me from the inside out.

Kerry is helping a customer with an order when I storm in,

and I head straight to the back office, aggressively sitting in the chair at the computer desk.

Nicole. That's the name of the girl he cheated on me with back when he first left. I should have asked him. I should have waited for him to get out of the shower and made him tell me to my face what a lying, cheating, asshole he is before finding out by accident.

I need to talk to someone, to vent everything right now before my emotions bury me completely. After pulling my phone out of my purse, I type out a text to Abbie.

> Me: Are you coming for lunch today? Need to talk.

> Abbie: I'm so sorry, Soph, we're swamped today and I can't get away.

> Abbie: Everything okay?

> Me: It's fine. Talk to you later.

Sighing, I put my phone back in my purse, pointedly ignoring all the missed calls and texts from Carter. There were times when he was *my* Carter. My sweet, sensitive, caring Carter. That Carter wouldn't cheat on me. He wouldn't come back and lead me on only to crush me again.

As the day goes on, Carter and his betrayal plague my mind. Can it even be considered a betrayal when he was never loyal to me to begin with?

Part of me wants to believe Carter has a reasonable explanation. But another part of me doubts it all. Am I such a poor judge of character that I fell for lies and tricks? Because really, this puts into question everything that I've learned since he's been back. How am I supposed to trust anything he says?

Noon hits, and I come out to the front, knowing I can't hide in the back office forever. "Kerry, go ahead and take your lunch."

She looks over at me, surprised. No doubt she's been able to tell that something's been off all day. "You sure? I can stay and help."

Smiling tightly, I nod. "Yep, will you bring me back something though? You can take my card with you."

"You got it."

Kerry hasn't been out of the shop for five minutes when *she* walks in.

Nicole.

What the fuck is she doing here?

Okay, play it cool. It's not good for business to kick someone out if she doesn't even know who I am. But I can't bring myself to welcome her into my shop, so I do my best to ignore her, busying myself on the computer. She's probably just here to browse, she'll be in and out in no time.

Not so much.

"Sophie, right? Sophie Hartwell?" Her voice has a nasal quality to it, and I look up into green eyes that glitter with condescension. The fact that she knows my name and where to find me firmly points me away from my "she doesn't know who I am" theory.

"Yes. How can I help you?" I eye her warily. It's not like I'm afraid of her, but what could she possibly want?

"The first way that you can help me is by staying away from my man." Her voice turns venomous as she looks me up and down with a critical eye. Her words hit me like a punch in the gut.

"I'm sorry, what did you say?" I've seen plenty of movies with mean girls to recognize what's happening, but I didn't think conversations like this actually happened in real life.

I can't believe my ears. She's showing up at my flower shop because she feels threatened? Looking at her, I don't see how she can feel threatened by anyone. I mean, I've never felt self-conscious about my appearance, but Nicole looks and is dressed like she just stepped off a runway. Tall, thin body, designer clothes, perfectly styled blond hair...

"I'm *saying*, you're temporary. Carter always comes back to me. You're nothing but a bed warmer," she sneers, looking me up and down. "Carter and I have been together since college. You know, love at first sight." A dreamy look takes the place of her sneer for a moment before it returns. "You'll never be more than a hookup because he has the perfect package right here."

The blatant aggression and disdain in this woman's eyes is appalling. She legitimately hates me. She might think she has a good reason, but... if she really has been with him all this time, why would she put up with him sleeping with someone else to begin with? But then again, how can she be this possessive over him if there's nothing going on?

My mind turns in circles as Nicole stares me down, and I know one thing for sure. I don't deserve any of the hatred she's spitting at me and this woman needs to get the hell out of my store.

I finally find my voice. "Listen, Noelle, right?" Her eyes narrow at me and I continue. "Carter can make his own choices, and in the meantime, I am under no obligation to sit by idly while you spew this nonsense. If you don't mind, please get the fuck out of my shop."

With a huff, she turns and storms out.

What the hell just happened?

My hands are almost shaking as I stare at the door Nicole just left through.

Seeing the selfie she sent him, and then seeing her in person, I can't help but think of the night of graduation. I had been so upset by the pictures of him with Nicole and trying to reach him. I hadn't even noticed Tom and Sarah weren't in the stands with my parents until after the ceremony.

"Where's Tom and Sarah?" I ask my parents, worry turning in my gut. Tom would have never missed my graduation on purpose.

Mom, holding Jordan, shifts him on her hip as she checks her phone. "They didn't make it, but we haven't heard from them either, not even a text."

Dad puts an arm around me. "We're so proud of you, kiddo. I'm sure that whatever happened with Tom and Sarah couldn't be helped. They would never choose to miss your graduation."

I know he's right, but it still stings. On the ride home, Mom asks me what I want for dinner. I dangle a toy in front of Jordan while he sits in his car seat. Dad says Tom and Sarah will probably just meet us at the house when they're done.

When we finally arrive home, a police officer parked out front has Mom's face draining of all color.

"Mr. and Mrs. Hartford?" The officer asks when we're out of the car. Then everything happens so fast. The next thing I know, we're back in the car, heading to the hospital because Sarah and Tom were in an accident.

The car is silent until we reach the ER, my parents rushing ahead to talk to the nurses while I push Jordan's stroller.

Carter should be here. It's not right that he's so far away while our lives are being turned upside down. Wheeling Jordan to an empty corner of the waiting room, my fingers tremble as I call Carter. Despite the betrayal I feel at the sight of the pictures, I need him. I need him to be here for me, but more importantly, for Tom. It goes to voicemail.

"Carter... Tom and Sarah were in a car accident. We don't..." My voice chokes as I hold back a sob. "We don't know how bad it is yet, but please come home. We need you. I need you Carter... Tom needs you. If you don't come for me... please come for him."

He never called me back.

That was the night everything changed. The night I knew I had lost him for good. When I woke up that morning, we were still together. Twelve hours later, not only did I know he had cheated on me, but he couldn't even be bothered to answer a message telling him Tom was in the hospital.

Kerry brings back lunch, and I pick at it until I leave for the rinks, never really finishing.

By the time I've gone to the rinks, finished practice with my girls, and closed up the rec center, my stomach is roiling. I don't know if it's from hunger or anxiety.

"Sophie." The sound of my name has my head whipping around, my eyes landing straight on Carter. He's wearing a button up shirt and tie, the tie loosened and the sleeves rolled up. "I've been trying to get a hold of you—"

"Why? So you can feed me more lies?" The words explode out of me, all the anger and frustration pouring into my voice.

"I haven't lied—"

"I fucking saw the texts, Carter! I saw the texts from Nicole, saying that she misses you and will see you soon, and that selfie she sent! She's the same fucking girl you cheated on me with all those years ago!" Tears sting my eyes at Carter's dumbstruck expression. "She came to my work. She said you guys have been together since college. That means that the night of Tom's accident when I needed you, you were with her. You left me for *her*. After you *just* lied to my face, telling me that it was some kind of misunderstanding with those photos." I can't keep the hurt from my voice. "How am I supposed to trust anything you say right now?"

It's a question I desperately hope he has the answer to. I want to trust him, to believe that everything he told me wasn't a lie. But I don't see how that's possible.

"Sophie, I swear on my life, I didn't even realize it was the same girl until now!" His voice is desperate as he takes a step toward me. "She's a puck bunny—fucking crazy. Nicole has been following me around for years now, convinced that we're something that we're not." I swear on my life, Sophie, I am *not* with her."

Relief fills me at his words. I'm not some side chick, stealing someone else's man. She just... texted him. "But if you didn't ever date her, why is she showing up here, acting like she's your girlfriend?" My words come out strained, and Carter's face turns to one of regret.

I knew it, I knew it, I fucking *knew* it.

Carter winces, running a hand through his hair. "Once..." At my scoff, he quickly puts his hands up and walks closer to me. "I slept with her one time, sophomore year. But I was drunk, and lonely, and I knew you and I were over, which devastated me. It was a mistake, nothing more."

"Do you realize you're telling me not to worry about the girl who not only had her mouth all over you in photos while we were still together, but also fucking slept with you when you hadn't even given me the courtesy of an official break-up call?" The words are cold coming out, and I know that it's not the whole story, but my heart is cracking every second this conversation goes on.

"We weren't together though," Carter pleads, his eyes shining with unshed tears. "Tom told me you had moved on."

"I deserved to hear it from you, Carter! You owed me closure after everything! I know your dad said not to contact me, but don't try to tell me he wouldn't have at least let you call to end things, with how much he hates me."

"I was scared!" he shouts. "I didn't want to say goodbye. I couldn't bear it. I kept thinking that I would find a way for us to work out. But the more time that passed by, the harder it got. By the time I finally had an opportunity to reach out and explain, I was afraid it had been too long for a phone conversation. So I came back."

My head shakes. No. He came back for the twin rinks project. For the PR.

His voice holds steady as he tries to get me to meet his eyes. "I didn't come back for PR, or for the rinks. Not even for Tom. Do you think I would have wanted to put one foot in this town if you weren't in it? This whole time, I came back for *you*. Because I love you, Sophie, and I never stopped."

It doesn't add up. Nothing makes sense. How can he say he never stopped loving me but then keep secrets from me like this? He let me believe nothing happened with Nicole until I pushed the issue. Is he just saying he came back for me so I forgive him?

"I..." My voice chokes out, and I shake my head. "I need time.

Is this going to keep happening? How many more women are going to show up in my flower shop claiming to be in a relationship with you? Everyone you've ever slept with?"

"What?" he asks indignantly, "That's not going to happen, Soph."

"Did you think it would happen this time?" I counter, matching his ire, "I just don't think I can handle it if women keep crawling out of the woodwork claiming they're your girlfriend."

"Like I said, that's not going to happen. Nicole is nuts. There has been no one. No one special. No one of any meaning. There's only ever been you. " He sighs, rubbing a hand on the back of his head. "Listen. I wanted to surprise you, but... I'm going to sign with Boston, Soph. I want you. I want to build a life here in Ivy Glen with you."

My head shakes. "What? Build a life...? Carter, I don't even know if I can trust you right now." Does he think that staying in Ivy Glen will just magically fix the damage from the bomb that went off when I saw Nicole's texts this morning?

"God, Sophie!" His frustration bubbling to the surface. "What the fuck else am I supposed to do on top of everything else I've done since I got here to show you how serious I am?"

Right now, I don't have an answer. I'm not sure anything can fix this.

My arms cross, and my tone turns icy. "I understand why you left back then, Carter. I forgave you and accepted all the years we lost. But forgetting? Trusting you again? That's not so easy. I *know* why you stopped calling. It was a choice you made because it was too hard to say goodbye. But do you know where I was while you were putting off giving me closure? I was crying myself to sleep at night, wondering where I went wrong. Asking myself why I wasn't enough for you. Questioning if what we had was even *real*." I let out a shuddering breath. "I get it. I do. But it doesn't erase the years of self doubt. And it sure as hell doesn't make the pain go away. You didn't just break our relationship when you walked away... you broke *me*. I'm not the same Sophie anymore. And right now, I'm finding it really hard to brush it all away, just because you say so. " My head shakes as I take a step back. "I need some time to think."

I would have been ecstatic if I had this information twenty-four hours ago. But now? I can't even think about it.

His face falls. "You're right. Fuck, Sophie, I'm so fucking sorry. I wish I could change the past. Take back the mistakes I made that cost me you. But I can't. Have your time. I'll get rid of Nicole, I promise. She's fucking insane and means nothing. You can even ask Jake. But just so you know, I'm leaving for team building camp in two weeks. It's a requirement of the contract."

His words echo in my mind as we part ways, driving opposite directions as we leave the rink.

He's staying in town. He says it's for me.

But how can I get myself to believe him when it feels like history is about to repeat itself all over again?

Chapter Twenty Six

SOPHIE

JUNE PASSES IN A BLUR. IN THE TWO WEEKS BEFORE Carter left, my phone pinged at least once a day with a message from him. First, explaining further the situation with Nicole, how she's been to almost every game and always tries to get his attention. How he's never indulged her except the night of the "worst drunken mistake of my life".

I had to laugh at that.

Then he was updating me on communications from the contractor, letting me know the exact dates he'll be gone for summer training camp.

Now it's the beginning of July, and I'm definitely *not* counting down the days until he gets back.

Nope. Not me. Just like I haven't been obsessively rereading the texts he sent me before he left.

I should be sleeping. Instead, I'm laying in bed with my phone open, rereading the first text he sent me after I drove away from the rink's parking lot in a rage.

Carter: I've already told Nicole to GTFO of Ivy Glen or I'm getting a restraining order. I've also blocked her number. You need to know, my heart has always belonged to you, Soph.

The words had done nothing to soothe my anger at the time, but now I look to them for comfort, rereading the last eight words like they're the air I need to breathe

My heart has always belonged to you, Soph.

And I haven't seen Nicole since that day. Something tells me that if she were still in town, she's the kind of woman who would rub it in my face.

I scroll through the rest of the messages. Sometimes it's something useful like information on the rink construction, and sometimes it's something completely random, like how he thought of me when he went to Sal's for lunch. In one of his messages, the longest one he's sent, he talks about how he'll be back in August, and he's planning on staying in Ivy Glen and making the forty-five minute commute to the Garden every day.

The day he left, it was radio silence, and has been since.

I know I told him I need time, and he's respecting that. Which I appreciate.

I do, really.

It's not like I *care* if he texts me anyway.

Damn it, who am I kidding? I miss him. Terribly.

I hadn't realized it at the time, but part of why I fought so hard to keep him out was the fact I was afraid of getting hurt again. The moment there was even a kernel of doubt, I pushed him away. Demanding space and ignoring his attempts to fix things.

And now... now that he gave me that space, I miss him.

Still, one thought keeps nagging me. What if he *isn't* just respecting my need for space? What if this all became too much for him, and he's moving on?

That's what keeps me from texting him and telling him that I want him to come back. I don't think I'd be able to handle it if I were to reach out and get rejected.

It's better to wait until he comes back. If he comes back.

I shake my head. No. He will come back. He has to...

My eyes catch the corner of my screen. Shit. It's three in the morning. I shake my head and put my phone down on the nightstand. I'll only get four and a half hours of sleep at this point and I've already been feeling more tired than usual.

Tossing and turning for hours after with thoughts of Carter plaguing my mind does nothing to help me feel rested, and by the time I blink my eyes open in the morning to the sound of my alarm, my stomach drops.

It's nine thirty. It's been going off for over an hour. I've slept straight through it.

The flower shop opens at nine and Kerry can't make it in until noon.

Shit shit *shit*.

Scrambling out of bed, I don't bother with a shower like I normally would, and have to double my deodorant to avoid any chance of B.O. and pull my hair into an unwashed, messy bun. Five minutes later, I'm hightailing it out of the driveway like my ass on fire and make it to the shop by nine fifty.

I don't even want to think about how many customers I missed this morning. I can't believe I overslept. I *never* sleep in. But then I couldn't sleep last night, and I started looking at Carter's texts...

Sighing, I shake my head as I unlock the front door, making the little bell jingle. The sound grates on my nerves, as if it's announcing to everyone, *"Hey guys! Sophie finally decided to show up to work!"*

That might just be me though. Everything seems to set me off recently. This whole situation with Carter is really fucking with my emotions.

At least I don't have to worry about the rinks or picking

Jordan up. Twin Rinks closed for construction at the beginning of June, and with Tom off for the summer, he's been able to take Jordan, Theo, and Bhodi to summer camp. I'll have the house all to myself this weekend since Tom and Jordan are heading out on their annual father-son road trip. It's left me with a lot of free time, but I'm not sure I like it. I'm so used to going, going, going, and this summer has left me alone with my thoughts way too frequently for my liking.

Once I settle behind the front counter for the day and open the register, I see a note from Kerry on the counter.

Sophie,

I've pre-arranged the orders for pick up today and they are in the fridge. The front windows have been cleaned, the back's been swept, and all the shelves have been dusted.

The morning should be easy, relax and take a break ;)

Kerry

Shit. With the rink closed and not having to worry about Jordan, all I've *been* doing is taking a break. I know she means well, and she's trying to get me to relax, but how does she not realize by now that I *need* this? The work keeps me busy so my thoughts don't spiral, especially with Carter being gone.

Fine. If all the work for the shop is taken care of, I'll start a financial plan for the rinks once they reopen. Hell, while I'm at it, I'll run some numbers for expanding the flower shop's business like Kerry and I planned too.

I'm determined to not think about Carter one more second than I have to, and if I have to drown in numbers to achieve that, then so be it.

The sound of a knock on my door has me placing my laptop on the coffee table where I had been knee-deep in numbers for the rec center. Who's knocking on my door on a Sunday evening? I swear, if it's Mrs. Allan next door complaining about how I parked my car again—

"Abbie?" She has two containers of Chinese food in her hands, looking me up and down with an assessing gaze.

"Hey girl, I brought dinner—your favorite, Chen's Palace. I know Tom and Jordan are on their little father-son vacation and thought you could use some company." She holds the food up and grins, but there's a glimmer of concern in her eyes.

"You're the best." I give her a smile. "Sure, come on in." After shutting the door behind her, I walk to the couch and pick my laptop back up. "I'll join you as soon as I'm done working on this set of numbers."

"What is it?" Abbie asks as she settles into the couch next to me.

"Just some figures for the rink once it opens again. I want to be ready." No point in telling her that if my brain stops concentrating for too long, it goes straight to Carter. I'd just get an "I-told-you-so" look, and I don't want to deal with that right now.

"I don't know why you don't go into business for yourself, Soph. You know that the members of this town would much rather come to someone they know and trust than have their accounting handled by some suit in Boston." She passes out the containers of Chinese food, making sure I get my extra spring roll.

Ever since my date with Carter when he asked me what I would do if nobody needed me at the shop or the rinks, I thought about working for myself, putting my business degree to use on my own accounting business. The thought of it had always filled me with unease. I'm used to being the one helping, not the one needing help. Knowing how many people I have at my back, it doesn't seem so scary.

"Maybe... maybe I will." My smile is genuine, and I imagine

myself in a little office on main street, people that I've known for years coming to me for help with their taxes, finances, or even just budgeting advice.

"Really?" Abbie nearly squeals, sitting forward. "What changed? I've been trying to get you to do something for yourself for years."

"I don't know," I shrug, but I can't keep the smile off my face when I think of Carter's words. "Everyone is always telling me to do something for me. Kerry only needs a bit more training to take over the shop, and things with the rink are changing. They might need a full time manager after they reopen. I'm not sure I can commit to that. Plus, Jordan is getting older, and before long, he'll be too old for a babysitter."

"It just... finally feels like the right time."

My phone rings, and I pick it up from the coffee table, checking the caller ID. "Fucking Oscar," I mutter, promptly hitting the "ignore" button.

"Girl, he's still trying to get you to go out with him?" Abbie asks incredulously. "Guy's got some balls."

Tossing my phone on the couch next to me, I turn to her. "The calls have only gotten more frequent since Carter left. It's like he thinks I'll be into him without Carter here or something." I snort. "When in reality, every time Oscar calls, I miss Carter a little more."

Abbie gives me a sympathetic look. "You want me to tell him to fuck off for you?"

Shaking my head, I grab the container of honey sesame chicken in front of me. "No, he'll stop eventually. If you get involved, it might cause problems for your dad on the council. We don't know if Oscar is petty enough to bring it up."

This time, Abbie snorts. "I'm pretty sure he is, considering he's petty enough to try to call a council meeting about the rink just to see you."

A shiver runs through my body at that memory. He's always

been persistent, but he's really creeping me out now. Last week, Oscar attempted to call in an "emergency meeting" regarding "issues with the rink construction" that I know for a fact Carter already took care of. One call to George to verify was all I needed to refuse to attend. I wouldn't have felt comfortable without Carter there anyway, but at least I had the information George sent me in case he happened to concern other council members.

Pushing the frustrating memory away, I open the container of my favorite chicken from Chen's Palace, but instead of the mouth-watering, sweet, tangy smell I was expecting, I'm met with a sickly sweet stench that makes my stomach curdle. Bile rises in my throat, and next thing I know, I'm in the bathroom, on my knees in front of the toilet, heaving my guts out.

Hair gently lifts from my shoulders and I look up to see Abbie standing above me, with concern in eyes. "Holy shit, are you okay? Obviously, you just barfed, but have you been feeling sick other-wise?" She comes over and presses the back of her hand to my fore-head. "You look a little peaky."

"Yeah," I wipe my mouth, "I think maybe I'm just off, you know? Stress and all that. I slept terrible last night"

She eyes me carefully as I take a deep breath, waiting for my stomach to settle so I can stand up. Turning on the sink, I stick my mouth under the faucet and swish some water, trying to get rid of the taste of bile before getting out my toothbrush.

"So, I feel bad for kicking you out when you just puked your guts out, but like... I really need to pee," Abbie says, grabbing her purse and rummaging through it. "Shit, do you have a tampon? I left mine at home."

"I'm not sure, I haven't..." My blood runs cold, my heart pounding out of my chest. I haven't been paying nearly as much attention to my cycle since Carter's been gone.

Fuck. Fuck fuck *fuck*.

I'm late. I'm never late.

"Phone. I need my phone. A calendar." My hands pat my pockets for my phone, but come up empty.

"Use mine," Abbie says quickly, fishing hers out and handing it to me unlocked.

My heart pounds in my chest as I open her calendar app, desperately trying to remember the last time I had my period. Carter had bought me four different kinds of heating pads and two tubs of ice cream, and we sat on his bed watching movies all night.

That was... that was the day after he confronted the council about that alternate proposal for the NHL arena. The week before I saw the texts from Nicole.

Six fucking weeks ago.

Abbie's face turns pale as she registers the look on my face.

"Okay, it's okay. Don't panic. It's probably nothing. People have late periods all the time. But, okay," She takes a deep breath. "Let's make sure. All the pharmacies will be closed already, but I can run to my uncle's practice and grab some tests."

My head nods numbly as I stand there in shock, vaguely registering the sound of my front door opening and closing as Abbie leaves. I can't believe this is even a possibility. I'm on birth control. I take every pill religiously, right when I wake up. Except...

God fucking damn it.

I grab my current birth control pack from my purse and race up the stairs to my bedroom, wrenching open the bathroom door and digging in my trash.

Scraps of tissue and make-up remover pads litter half the floor before I find it.

Last month's birth control packet. The last date of the pills was a Tuesday...

And the first day of my new packet is a Thursday.

I skipped a day. And I'm ninety-nine percent sure I know exactly what day it happened. The morning that I stormed out of Carter's hotel room after seeing the texts from Nicole. I had been so angry and distracted that I didn't take my pill.

My stomach roils and I lurch for the toilet again, dry-heaving. What the hell am I going to do?

I can't have a baby.

I can't.

Carter and I aren't even... I don't know *what* we are right now. He hasn't reached out since he's been gone. I know I asked for time, but... for weeks, when he first got here, I wanted him to leave me alone and he wouldn't listen. *Now* he takes my request seriously?

Or... the thought of him just being done with me makes me sick to my stomach. I just don't know how I could have been so careless and stupid. Ten years of being on birth control and I never once miss a pill. I get emotional one time and screw everything up.

Abbie finds me in my bathroom, clutching the toilet bowl with trash all over my floor. "Oh, Soph..." There's pain for me in her voice as she comes up next to me and rubs large circles across my back. "It's going to be okay. No matter what the test says, I'm here for you."

Swallowing roughly, I hold my hand out for the tests, which she places gently into my palm.

She's right. I can do this. It's just peeing on a stick. That's the first step. What comes after...? We'll just see about that.

Ten minutes later, we're huddled in my bathroom, staring at the three positive pregnancy tests on my bathroom counter.

My breath quickens, my eyes burn, and I allow a moment to feel sorry for myself.

This is insane. I messed up *once*, and now my life is about to change forever. How is this fair? I'm already pulled in too many directions as it is, and now I get to add being knocked up on the list? I've already done part of the whole baby thing once. I know how much time and effort it takes, and I didn't even have the rink and flower shop to think about when I was helping Tom with Jordan. How am I going to manage this?

Fuck.

Take a deep breath, Sophie. The moment is over. Time for the real question. What do you do now?

Am I ready for a baby? I'm not sure.

Do I even want one with Carter? The cynical part of me isn't sure, but I need to tell him. If he leaves... if he decides he doesn't want me or the baby, then at least I gave him a fair shot.

He deserves the chance to be the kind of father that his never was.

I don't want to believe that he would leave, even if I haven't heard from him while he's been at training camp. He's the type of man that would stay, if only for his child. Not that I would want that to be the reason he stays, but deep down, I believe that he loves me. He would stay for me, and for the baby.

What would that look like? Me, him, and the baby together. Carter's onyx black hair, my honey brown eyes. My heart stutters. This imaginary child is the same child I've envisioned every time the thought of having a child someday would cross my mind.

I don't think I've ever seen myself with a child that wasn't his.

Despite everything over the last nine years, and because of everything in the last three *months*, I love him. I'm pretty sure I never stopped. That all my tried-and-failed, short lived relationships never worked out because they weren't *him*. I just never realized it.

Abbie grips my shoulder. "Holy shit, Soph. Are you going to tell him?"

Swallowing, I nod, and my voice is rough when I speak. "Yeah. I need to tell him. But... can you not say anything for now?"

"Of course!" She nods furiously with a look that says "As if you even have to ask!"

"Thanks." My eyes are focused on the two little pink lines of the test that have turned my life upside down. "Carter deserves to know first before anyone else finds out about this."

I'll tell him as soon as he's back. And maybe... we could make it work.

Make *us* work.

Chapter Twenty Seven

CARTER

I'M HOME.

Passing by the large, wooden road sign that reads "Welcome to Ivy Glen" makes my heart feel ten times lighter. Being in the same town as Sophie again settles something within me.

As much as I missed her while I was gone, the team building camp had been amazing. My muscles ached every grueling day, but for the first time in my life, I played without Dad's shadow looming over me. I had almost forgotten how much I *love* the sport. Jake and I meshed instantly with the rest of the team, and I'd be lying if I said playing for the fucking Boston Reapers didn't make me want to do a damn cartwheel.

Despite how great the last six weeks went, there's been an undercurrent of worry about how Sophie and I left things. I agreed to give her space, and didn't push after she ignored my texts for two weeks.

That ends now.

I need her more than I need to breathe. There's not a world that exists where Sophie and I aren't together. I refuse to let it be that way for another second.

As soon as I can hold her, kiss her, and make her understand she is the only one for me, everything will be right again.

Now that I know how hard it is to be apart from her, there's no question how tough it will be when I'm on the road during away games. But that just means that I'll have to make every second we *are* together count.

Mom's house is on the way to Sophie's, so I'll just drive by really quick and make sure everything is in order since Mom's on her trip and I've been gone a while. Then I can go surprise my girl. The things I want to do to her...

My mind is consumed by images of Sophie naked on a bed and waiting for me, but the sight of a beat up truck in the driveway, dented and scratched to hell jolts me out of my fantasy, sending a chill to my bones. A man tries to get into the front door of Mom's house, *my* childhood home.

What the fuck is he doing? Who is that asshole?

The man walks to a window, fogging up the glass as he peers inside the house. I'm just about to grab my phone and call the cops, when he turns around and I see the ugly sneer on his face, jolting with horrified recognition.

Dad.

His hair is grayer than when I last saw him, not to mention how much less of it there is. A beer-belly pokes out slightly from under his shirt, and his jeans have rips and stains.

Fuck.

Fuck fuck *fuck*.

My foot does not let off the gas as I pass the house, and I pull to the end of the street before flipping around and parking a few houses down on the other side of the road.

And just like that, I'm fifteen again, hyperventilating because Dad is going to be so mad when he sees me, and how we changed the house. He's going to take it out on Mom, and it's going to be all my fault.

Dammit. No. I need to get my shit together.

I'm not fifteen anymore, and he can't do anything to me. He can yell and sputter all he wants, but I'm a grown-ass man. Mom is away, safe from his wrath. But when she gets back... I swallow roughly. When she gets back, the stakes will change.

What the hell is he doing back in town anyway? He was gone. Not a peep from him in over a year and now he shows up back home? I thought... shit. It had crossed my mind more than once that he might be dead.

Or in jail.

I nearly bang my head on the steering wheel in frustration. It was so *stupid* to assume that just because I hadn't heard from him, he was gone. Thank fuck I sent Mom on that retreat and changed the locks, otherwise she might have had to deal with him. Shit. Mom. She gets back tomorrow. If he had come a day or two later, she would have had to see him again.

I've never been more thankful for the security windows I had installed than when I watch Dad try to pry the windows open. What the fuck should I do? Before I can spiral further, he finally gets into the beat up truck he's parked in the driveway and drives away.

I put my car back into drive and follow him. This is probably a terrible decision, but I need to see what he's up to. Maybe I'll get an idea of why he's back in town. The sooner I know why, the sooner I can figure out how to get rid of him.

Not knowing what else to do, I hit the button on my steering wheel to call Jake.

"Miss me already, hotshot?" Jake teases as his voice fills my car. "I know you love me, but don't be getting clingy—"

"Dude, shut up. I..." My heart pounds in my chest. I can't get the words out. Like if I say them out loud, it'll be even more real than it is already.

"Woah, Carter, what's wrong?" Jake's tone shifts instantly, concern filling his voice.

"My... fuck. My dad's here." I spit the words out, bitterness stinging my throat.

"What? I thought you said he was gone. Never coming back."

"That's what I fucking thought!" God damnit. This wasn't supposed to happen.

"Right, okay, chill out. I know you weren't expecting him to come back, but nothing is going to get fixed if you lose it." Jake may not take much of life seriously, but he knows what my dad is capable of. I only started confiding in him after we were both in college, but it didn't take long to catch him up.

A sigh leaves me. He's right, I need to get it together. "Shit, I'm sorry. I'm just freaking out over here. Whatever this is, it can't be good."

"No kidding. Are you going to talk to him?"

"I'm following him right now. We just got off the highway and we're on the outskirts of Willow Creek." Jake curses under his breath. "I can't let him near my mom. *Fuck*, I can't let him near Sophie. I swear, if he gets anywhere near her..."

"What are you going to do?"

"Fuck if I know. There's no way I'm letting him get his hooks back into me. I can't leave Mom here, he could get to her at any time." He already proved that much by trying to get into the house.

"Do you need me to stay in town until we figure out what's going on? I could help keep an eye on things." Jake's always been a great friend, offering to come and stay with me over holiday breaks to keep my dad off my back. He had wanted to go back to Canada as soon as possible and pack up his apartment before the season started. I need to as well, but I need to get things sorted out with Sophie first.

It wouldn't hurt to have an extra set of eyes looking out for Mom. "Maybe. I'll let you know. He just stopped at some shady-ass motel. I gotta go."

"Drop me your location and send me a proof-of-life text when you're done."

His words get a strangled laugh out of me. "Yeah, yeah."

The long, single-story building looks like it hasn't been repaired in the last twenty years. A half-burnt out sign reads "Willow Motel", most of the letters flicker like they might go out at any moment.

Is this where he's staying? Years ago, Dad wouldn't have been caught dead in a place like this. But now, his thinning gray head of hair disappears into one of the rooms, the curtains drawn tight.

How did he even know I was back in town? Is he even here for me?

I pull my car off the side of the road and let my head fall back against the seat. Shit. This is not good.

What the fuck am I going to do? What does he want? If he wants more money, he has my number. Why did he have to show up here? Should I send Mom away or take her and run?

We could go to Boston, and I could still honor my new team's contract. But if I'm on the team there, the chances of Dad finding us again are too high. My name would be plastered on every bit of news related to the team, not to mention press conferences after. I'd have to pay to break my contract and move to a completely different state. Maybe California or something. Mom's always talked about going to the beach there someday. We'll put everything under an alias and he'll never be able to find us again.

The thought of reneging on my contract and giving up hockey to move across the country makes my stomach sour... but for Mom? I would do anything to keep her safe, even if that means giving up the sport that I love.

Shit, what about Sophie? I would rather die than leave her again, but I have to think of her safety. Maybe I can ask her to come with us. No. I would never ask her to leave her family behind for a life on the run.

If I know dad, this isn't a one time thing. He'll keep coming, keep being a threat. I can't stay with her, but I can't let anything happen to her either. Dad may have been all threats ten years ago, but who knows what he would do now? The thought sends fire through my veins, anger lighting me up from the inside.

No.

He won't be touching Sophie, Mom, or me, ever again. I'll make damn sure of it.

Swallowing, I put the car in drive and turn around, heading back towards home. It's getting dark, and I need to talk to Sophie. She'll be done at the flower shop soon, and she needs to know why I'm leaving.

At least this time, we'll have a chance to say goodbye.

Chapter Twenty Eight

SOPHIE

Carter should be back any day now. If I'm counting right, it's been exactly six weeks and one day since he left for training camp. I hoped I might see or hear from him today, but the sun is almost completely set and he hasn't come by the shop at all.

The first two weeks of morning sickness were absolute hell, but I haven't been getting as sick since I've figured out what my triggers are. So far, I have to avoid Chinese food, Mexican food, pickles, and Ranch salad dressing. If I stay away from those, I don't ever actually throw up—I just *feel* like I'm going to. Which doesn't seem that much better, but if it keeps me from emptying my guts into the toilet every meal, I'll stay away from any food that makes my stomach feel funny.

My boobs hurt like hell too. I don't think I realized how many times a day I accidentally knock against them until each touch had me recoiling in pain. Leaning over the counter at work. Crossing my arms. Hell, I can't even sleep on my stomach anymore.

The hardest part has been not being able to tell anyone. Obviously, Abbie knows, so that helps, but I desperately want to tell Mom. Or even Tom. If only so that they can tell me that everything will be alright. So they can reassure me that Carter wouldn't ditch his own kid, and put my worries at ease. Tom surprised our parents with a cruise for their anniversary and they're currently out of town. Mom would know something was wrong in a heartbeat.

Carter deserves to know first.

My gut twists. I hate that I can't shake the distrust that's been manifesting over the years. I could have sworn he'd be back by now. In his text before he left, he said he'd come back as soon as he could. Is it really possible that he's done with me, and that's why he hasn't reached out?

Shaking my head, I try to clear my mind. No. I can't think like that, it's only going to stress me out. Taking a deep breath, I go over what I'm going to say to him in my head.

I'll start with the fact that I know it's horrible timing, and we aren't even *together* together, but I made a mistake on my birth control. And while I don't know what it means for us, I would love it if he wants to be in the baby's life.

But more eloquent than that.

When it's thirty minutes to closing, and I'm just about to close up shop, the bell over the front door rings.

Looking up, my heart pounds and all the air whooshes out of my chest.

Carter.

He's just as handsome as he was when he left two months ago, his black hair sexily disheveled like he's been running his hands through it. A blue t-shirt is tight across his muscled chest, and his jeans cling to his toned thighs.

Shit. This pregnancy must be making my hormones more out of sorts than I thought because all I can think about is moving around this counter and climbing the man in front of me like a tree.

"Hi," he says, almost like he's out of breath.

"Hi." My voice is just as breathy even though I've been sitting all day.

We just take each other in. His eyes trail up my body before landing on my face, but there's nothing sexual about his gaze. It's almost like he's checking to see if I'm okay. Like he has to see me with his own two eyes to confirm.

"I'm sorry, Sophie," he blurts out, "I'm so, so sorry, and I hope you're not still mad at me. Nicole and I... we're *nothing*, and have *never been* anything. She should be long gone by now."

I swallow roughly, my heart pounding. "I haven't seen her since that day. She hasn't shown her face since you've been gone."

"Good." His shoulders sag in visible relief. "You... you have to know, I've never seen myself living my life with anyone else but you."

My heart flutters. Could it be that he would stay and be *happy* about it?

"But," he continues, looking down, "I have to tell you something—"

All thoughts of the little speech I practiced go out the window. They fly away, leaving only two words in their wake. My mouth opens before I can stop myself and the words spill from my throat like ill-timed word-vomit.

"I'm pregnant."

His eyes widen, and his face stills.

His mouth gapes open, then closes, and then opens again, but no sound escapes him.

Dammit. That was... less than ideal. But moments pass, and he just continues to stare at me. What is he thinking? I know I wasn't eloquent with how I told him, but is he going to say *something*? Ask me how this happened? Or how long I've known? How we're going to make this work?

Unshed tears sting my eyes, as the seconds tick by, the heavy feeling of rejection settling over my bones like lead. This is Carter. We're supposed to be a team. I had practiced telling him he had a choice, but I don't think I thought he wouldn't want to be there. I have no contingency plan for if he leaves. If he rejects both me and his unborn child.

His eyes look at my face like he's expecting me to laugh and tell him it's a joke. Based on his reaction, I'm tempted to. At my silence, his expression morphs to one of devastation, fear almost. I need to say something, I know I do. But all I can do is stand there, trying to keep the tears at bay as I wait for him to say something.

Anything.

Blame me. Yell at me. Ask me how I could be so irresponsible. I'll take anything at this point if it fills the void of the silence that stretches between us. He says nothing, my lip wobbling and him frozen in place, staring at me in what I can only describe now as horror.

"Carter?" I choke out quietly. "I know it's a shock, but—" Before I can finish my sentence, and, without a single sound, he turns and walks out the door, the bell ringing in what feels like a mockery of the situation. A highlighted sound to let me know, "This is the exact moment everything went to hell".

My heart shatters.

What I feel now is a hundred times worse than what I had felt when I saw the texts from Nicole. At least then he had still been trying to explain. Right now, I am utterly alone.

He left. Again.

This time, he can't blame it on his Dad, or circumstances outside his control. He looked me straight in the eyes and walked away.

When I hear his car start and the tires squeal out of the parking lot, my feet carry me as fast as they can to the door. I twist the lock before turning around and dropping to the floor, sobbing into my knees.

I can't stay here. Carter's face is a tattoo in my mind, staring at me in shock and disbelief. But I am not in any condition to drive right now either.

Hiccuping between sobs, I pull my phone out and dial Abbie's number. "Hey Soph, what's—" she cuts off when another guttural cry leaves me. "Holy shit, what's wrong? Are you okay? Where are you?"

"At shop..." *hiccup*, "told Carter..." *hiccup*, "about baby..." *hiccup*, "he left!" I finally get out, rubbing my face to wipe the snot away from my nose.

"Oh, fuck no," Abbie spits, "You just hold on, Sophie. I'm coming to get you. That asshole thinks he can just leave? Uh uh. I'm on my way babe, I'll be right there."

She stays on the phone with me the entire time, my sniffling and hiccuping the only sound as she makes the short drive from her house to the flower shop.

Knocking on the door sometime later lets me know she's here. Abbie waits while I stand up and unlock it, then sweeps me into a bracing hug.

"He's an asshole if he thinks that's the right move," Abbie says as she holds me close.

"He didn't say *anything*. He just stared at me like I was an alien or something for like three minutes before turning around and leaving."

"Hmm." Abbie lets go of me, only to grab my purse and turn off the shop lights. "That doesn't really sound like Carter. It's possible he was just in shock and reacted poorly." She ushers me out the door and digs my keys out my purse, locking the shop up for me.

Shit. I am so lucky to have a friend like her.

My head shakes in disagreement. "You didn't see him, Abbie. He looked... like... I don't even know. Like I just gave him the worst news possible." Which, okay, fair enough. I didn't exactly have the best reaction when I found out either. But to just leave? Without a word? Deep down, I never saw this as a possible outcome. Where do I go from here? Do I wait and see if he comes around? Do I accept that he's not going to be a part of our lives and move on?

"We'll figure it out, Soph. With or without Carter." Abbie unlocks her car and I climb into the front seat, immediately pulling some tissues from the center console.

We drive in silence back to her house, and when we pull into her driveway, I'm not sure I want to get out yet. The tears are still coming, a fresh wave rearing its head every time I relive the way he just walked away, but at least with Abbie here, I don't feel so alone.

"Thank you, Abbie. For coming to get me." My voice is wobbly, and it's hard to get out the words between breaths.

"Of course, Sophie. I'm always here for you." She takes my hand, and looks at me with tears in her own eyes. "I'm just so sorry you have to go through this right now. But even if you don't have Carter, you do have so many people who love you and want to help. Me, your parents, Tom, and this whole damn town who loves you so much."

"I know," I sniffle. "And I love you too." Squeezing her hand in mine, I send her a sad smile.

"Okay," she declares, wiping her eyes and throwing her door open. "Enough sad stuff. I have a freezer full of ice cream and an empty couch calling our names. We can watch rom-coms or I can search the internet for a movie where the girl and her bestie off the ex-boyfriend and get away with it."

That has me barking a laugh. "Maybe we can just do a straight up comedy." I pull a face. "As long as it's not 'Knocked Up'."

As Abbie and I stuff our faces full of ice cream, I can't even pay attention to the movie. The shock of what happened has left me in a constant state of disbelief. My mind just won't shut off.

How could he do this to me? How could I *let* him do this to me, again? What am I going to do now?

I could be a single mom. What would that look like? I could take some maternity leave after the baby is born, and when I'm ready to go back to work, I'm sure my parents would help out with the little one. Would I need to move out of Tom's house? I doubt he wants to go through the newborn phase again, but maybe he wouldn't mind if it's for his little niece or nephew.

My hand unconsciously wanders down to my belly even though it's still flat, something that's been happening more and more recently. One thing I do know, is that no matter what, I'm going to love this little one so much that they will never feel a shortage of it. Whether or not I'm a single mom, this baby will never feel the sting of rejection from Carter Williams like I have.

I'll make sure of it.

Chapter Twenty Nine

CARTER

Holy shit.

Sophie's pregnant

How the fuck is she pregnant? She's on the pill. This shouldn't have happened.

I've never seen myself being a father. Hell, I don't think I've ever *wanted* to be one. Guys on my hockey team would bring their kids to games, and all I could see were small, fragile, malleable lives that could be fucked up so easily.

Just like mine was.

How could I let a child go through anything similar to the life I had growing up? Realistically, I understand that I'm nothing like my dad. But... was he always the way he is? Or did he start out a decent guy, slowly morphing into the man he is over time? What if the same thing happens to me?

The thought of being anything like Dad makes me feel like I'm going to be sick. I mean, it's not like I had a great example of what a dad should be growing up.

And I have no idea what to do.

What I do know is I need to keep that piece of shit away from Sophie, our unborn baby, and Mom. I need to figure something out to keep everyone safe.

I don't even know how long he's been in the area. Has he already seen Sophie and me together? Is he going to hold her safety over my head all over again?

I don't want to leave her behind again, but I would do it. To keep her safe. Keep my child safe.

I'll give him whatever the hell he wants as long as he stays far the fuck away from Ivy Glen. Will that be enough though? Will anything ever be enough?

There's only one way to find out. I need to talk to him.

Simply leaving with them isn't an option anymore. There's no telling how far he would go to track me down, and I refuse to raise a child that needs to live in fear like I did.

For the last eight hours, I've been wide awake, replaying last night in my mind, wishing I could have reacted differently. Not let my panic control me. To tell her what threat lies in wait for us.

When she told me, my mind went blank of everything but the word "pregnant." It echoed through me like I was in some kind of horror movie. One more life for Dad to threaten. Another thing he can hold over my head.

Words had failed me, and I had fled with only one thought on my mind.

I need to protect my family.

I couldn't go back to Mom's house. The last thing I need is for Dad to come by again and think I'm living with her. So I spent the night practically wearing a hole in the carpet of my hotel room from pacing so much. Thoughts of Sophie, the baby, and how I'm going to keep everyone safe racing through my mind.

He needs to go. He can't know about Sophie, or the baby, or the life I'm planning on building with her. If I can get him to leave for good, we'll all be safe. I just need to figure out what the hell he wants. Mom gets back later today, and I'd rather stick rusty nails in my fingers than make her see him again.

Which is why I'm here now. At five a.m., standing outside

Dad's motel room, summoning the courage to meet the beast head on. But I keep thinking about Sophie, and the tears that welled in her eyes as I stared at her.

I love her. I love her so damn much.

Fuck, I shouldn't have just left like that, but I panicked. Fucking froze like a coward, and then left. I'm not going to freeze now. Taking a deep breath, I reach my hand out and knock on the door.

There's a sound of shuffling around and some mumbled cursing coming from inside before the door swings open.

"It's too damn early for housekeeping—" The gravelly, gruff voice cuts off when he sees me. His eyes widen slightly, but that's the only indication I get that he's surprised to see me. "Well, well. Mister Big Shot has come to pay Dad a visit."

He looks even worse up close.

Wearing only a white t-shirt and boxers, the man stands before me scratching his belly, with a cigarette hanging from his lips. His face is worn with wrinkles that weren't there a year ago, and his skin is sallow, showing just how poorly he's been taking care of himself.

There's nothing of the man I remember looking back at me, who always dressed impeccably, making sure to keep up a perfect image. His voice is the same, though. It still makes my heart pound, bringing back too many memories.

Him yelling at mom, yelling at me. Threatening those I love. For so many years I just rolled over and gave him what he wanted.

But no more.

I keep my voice even, never breaking eye contact. "I saw you at Mom's house yesterday."

An ugly sneer makes its way to his face. "Yeah, what of it? I paid that fucking mortgage for years. I have a right to everything in it, including your sorry excuse of a mother. If I want to go to my own home, I will. Especially when I haven't seen a dime from my ungrateful son in over a year." He doesn't even bother hiding the threat in his voice or recalling the fact that the house isn't technically his.

"You vanished off the face of the earth for a year. You can't hold that over me." My words are strong, even as I try to keep my hands from shaking. I hate that I can't help but feel like a small, petulant child arguing with his father.

He scoffs at me. "I don't want your excuses, Carter. You know my accounts, you could have sent something over. That's why I'm here."

"So you want more money." My anger comes through now, causing him to narrow his eyes at me.

"What I want, *you ungrateful little shit*, is what I'm due. What I'm owed. You wouldn't have gotten picked up by the NHL if it wasn't for me. *I'm* the reason you got into Notre Dame in the first place. I want half your salary for the team you signed with this year." The venom in his words is nothing new, but half my salary? It's more than he's ever asked for. But maybe, if I can get him to leave town...

"If I give it to you," a heavy sigh leaves me, "that's it. And you have to leave Ivy Glen for good."

"Yeah, yeah sure. As long as you send me half your check every month, I'll leave this shitty town alone." Relief hits me, but it's short lived. "But I'm not leaving unless I have $500K *in hand* by the end of the week."

Five hundred thousand dollars? By the end of the week? It's not like I don't have the money, but that's a lot to just get ahold of in five days. Not to mention, do I even want to give it to him?

Do I have a choice?

"Fine," I bite out, "I'll be back by the end of week with your money. But if I get wind of you even breathing the same air as Mom while you're here, you won't get a fucking dime. Understand?"

"Don't fucking threaten me," he growls.

"I'm not threatening you," I counter, "I'm informing you of what will happen if you go near Mom."

Dad grunts. "If you don't get me that money, I'll make sure to stick around a good long while."

He slams the door closed in my face, and I stare at it, blinking. Did I just... negotiate with Dad?

I... I stood up to him. Now I'm walking to my car filled with the possibility of hope. This is what I came here to do, but leaving somewhat victorious from a standoff with Dad is an unfamiliar feeling.

It feels too easy. But maybe... this could work. Maybe he'll take the money and leave. Sophie and I can live out our lives together happily raising our baby.

Shutting the car door behind me, my fingers grip the steering wheel as I breathe for the first time since I saw him yesterday. Motion from behind the window next to Dad's door catches my attention. A curtain moving, then Dad's snide face looks at me before disappearing entirely.

My stomach sinks. It dawns on me—he thinks he's won.

Of course he does. There's absolutely nothing that can make him keep his word to stay away. The bastard's said what he felt he had to for now, so I'd give him the money without a fuss.

I pull away from the motel, driving back towards town. The pit in my stomach returns as I realize *nothing* will ever be enough to keep him away for good.

Chapter Thirty

CARTER

"Carter, sweetie, I missed you!" Mom wraps her arms around me before I can take her luggage and put it in the trunk. My car is parked along the curb at the airport, the area filled with the sounds of people reuniting with their loved ones after being away.

"I missed you too, Mom." I press a kiss to her hair before lobbing her bags into the car and shutting the door.

After leaving Dad, I drove around aimlessly, my mind running in circles. What if he doesn't actually leave? I have nothing to force him to hold on to his end of the bargain.

My only consolation is that he doesn't seem to know about Sophie and me yet. If he did, he would have threatened her as well. He probably only arrived in the last couple of days, and if I get him the money, he'll be able to take off like he was never here.

What then, though? Do I tell Mom he came back so she can constantly live in fear again? What about Sophie and the baby? A part of me hoped that if I figured out how to get rid of him, I could stay. But, he won't be gone forever and will continue using any leverage he can against me. Maybe I should still leave. If he never finds out Sophie's child is mine, I'll be able to keep both of them out of this. Keep them safe. Yet the idea of leaving them behind, never being in my child's life, is gut wrenching.

She rambles excitedly as I pull onto the highway to get back to Ivy Glen, filling me in on all the details of her stay. My shoulders relax when she doesn't sense anything is wrong. "I got all my girls' phone numbers so we can keep in touch." She smiles proudly. "Evelyn, the one who was in the room next to mine, she works as a librarian in Willow Creek! We can get together all the time."

"That's great, Mom." My grin is genuine. It's been so long since I've seen her so happy.

"It was everything I didn't know I needed, Carter. We went on hikes nearly every day and—oh my, the spa! So incredibly relaxing. You can gift me a spa visit for Mother's Day next year." She winks. "And every year after that."

She tells me about the small group sessions and workshops, as well as the one-on-one therapy every attendee received twice a week.

She seems so happy and full of life, I see no reason to bring up Dad. As long as I get him the money, she doesn't need to know... I don't want to bring her back down to where she was before she left.

We pull up to the house and I shudder at the memory of Dad trying to get in. It's fine. He'll be gone by the end of the week.

"I got it, Mom." I pull her bags out of the trunk and take them to the front door as she unlocks it. Fuck, I am exhausted. The thought of going back to my hotel and crashing the rest of the day sounds like heaven at this point. Guilt churns in my gut. I should really go see Sophie, but what if I end up leaving? What will I say to her?

Once she gets the door open and takes one of her bags inside, I follow, lugging the rest behind me. "Do you need me to take them upstairs?"

"Oh, no I can do that." She waves me off. "It's good to be home, isn't it?"

Home. Sophie's face flashes in my mind at the word, and I do my best not to buckle under the grief leaving them will cause me.

"If you don't need any help, I think I'm going to take off. It's been a crazy couple of weeks, and I could use some sleep." My tone is apologetic, but before I can move back out the door, Mom grabs my arm.

"Wait," she says, her eyes shining with… excitement? "Can I show you something first?" She starts going through her luggage in search of something. Whatever this is, it must be important, so I walk the few steps into the living room and make myself comfortable on the couch.

"Here." She comes over, placing a tablet in my hand. On it is what looks like the cover of a children's book, an illustration of a child laughing while riding a bike. The words on the image read, "Little Carter Joins the Race".

…What?

I scroll to the next image, this time the illustration is of a little girl tying ice skates. "Little Sophie Takes the Ice".

"Mom… what is this?" I ask as I continue scrolling, each title with the name of someone I know, Jordan, Tom, Jake…

She shrugs, looking at me with determination in her eyes. "Since you left for college, I know I've been too scared to even leave the house, but I'm tired of hiding, Carter. Of being afraid of what anyone thinks of me. This is what I've been doing in my spare time. For years, actually." I stare at the image currently on the tablet. It's an illustration of a little girl peeking out of the front door of her house with the title "Little Vivianne Faces the World".

Mom moves closer to me, before reaching over and scrolling down on the tablet in my hands, instead swiping across like I was doing. That's when realization dawns on me. These are stories. And this one, the one I'm looking at now, is about my mom. About Vivianne.

My eyes graze the first few paragraphs, and I can hear Mom's voice in the words.

"I've been illustrating and writing children's books for a while now, but I never had the courage to tell anyone about it, let alone publish them." She gives me a soft smile. "This retreat that you sent me on... the people I met... I know now that the strength I need has always been there. Your dad did his best to squash it, and strip it from me entirely." She gets up and starts pacing, like she can't get the words out if she's sitting still. "No more, Carter. Nothing and no one is going to do that to me again. I'm going to start living my life the way I want. The first step is publishing these books. And every single one will be dedicated to *you*."

My heart stutters in my chest. Me? But I failed her so many times. I couldn't keep her safe. My head shakes, "No, Mom, I—"

"Don't you dare tell me you don't deserve it, Carter Williams." She interrupts me with conviction in her voice. "It was *you* who saved *me*. You've helped me realize that I don't need to be afraid anymore. You pushed me to get the help I need to live my life freely for the first time in almost thirty years." She stops pacing, takes a deep breath, and faces me. "I will not be a doormat anymore. This is me finding my strength again."

Swallowing, I nod, tears welling in my eyes.

She looks at me softly, coming over and sitting next to me again. "Do you want to read them?"

When I nod again, she takes the tablet from me, scrolling back to the first book, "Little Carter Joins the Race".

And so I read them. I go through every single one, sometimes laughing out loud at the antics these kids get up to, and always feeling pride for Mom when the story reaches its conclusion, a life lesson learned. Smiling faces, eyes full of joy are illustrated beautifully on the screen.

"How..." I trail off after I read the last one, the one with Mom's own name that she said she wrote while at the retreat. "How can you see so much good in childhood when our story is anything but?"

At that, she grasps my hand, and looks me in the eyes. "I know that your childhood was not as happy as it could have been. I should have left your father a long time ago. I am so sorry, Carter. I was the adult and you were the child; I should have protected you. Instead, it was you who protected me. The guilt from my lack of action used to feel worse than any pain he inflicted. But now I've had the chance to heal. To be inspired. To learn. I realize that it was never my fault, just like it was never yours. It was only your father's. He was the only one at fault for his actions. He's had both of us in his trap for too long, and I refuse to give that man anymore power over our lives. So, despite our history, and the way our lives have played out... I choose to hope. And just because mistakes were made in the past, that doesn't mean that the future can't be bright."

The future. Sophie. Our *baby*.

"Mom..." I choke out, my chest tightening. Will she be disappointed with how I reacted? Will she think that I'll be just like Dad and fuck it all up? I have to tell her everything. She's stronger now, she can handle it. And she needs to know about Sophie, about Dad... all of it.

She senses my shift in demeanor and looks at me with concern in her eyes. "What is it, sweetie?"

"Sophie... she's pregnant," Mom lets out a little sound that is a mix between shock and excitement, but doesn't say anything, letting me continue, "and I'm scared. When she told me... I freaked out. What if I'm just like Dad? I don't want the baby to have the same childhood that I had." Then I swallow, trying to get the next words out with a strong, steady voice. "And... he's back. He wants more money, and if I know Dad... it won't stop at this. If we let this continue, one way or another, he may end up with every penny. Right now, he wants five hundred thousand and half my salary for the next year. I have no idea how to keep you and Sophie safe, *and* handle dad at the same time?"

Mom is silent, looking down at the floor. I expect tears or

panic, Hell, I half worry that all the work she's accomplished over the last three months will be undone.

"You can't." She finally looks at me.

"I... what?" I let out a shocked laugh. It's not funny, but... what the hell?

"You can't do it all, Carter. Because your father will never stop. Not unless he's taken down once and for all. And I'm going to help you." She nods with finality and stands. "Come with me."

Dumbstruck, I follow her up the stairs as she moves with purpose, pausing when we get to the door to the attic. She pulls it down and heads up the ladder, me trailing behind her.

"What are we doing up here?" I ask, coughing at the dust swirling around as Mom starts moving boxes.

"Back when you were in high school," Mom calls out from between a stack of them, "your father had me managing some paperwork for the car dealership and sometimes he would bring paperwork home from the council. If I would come across anything that seemed suspicious—numbers or transactions that didn't quite add up, or vehicle loan interest rates that didn't match the paperwork from the lender—I would make a copy and store it up here. Aha!" She cries in victory, pulling out a gray, unassuming box from the bottom of a stack of old belongings. "Here," she says, pushing the box towards me and motioning for me to open it.

In it are stacks and stacks of invoices, audits, and ledgers.

"What exactly am I looking at here??" I ask, thumbing through a chunk of the documents I had picked up.

"Embezzlement, false financial reporting, and predatory lending at the dealership," she says proudly. "Finally my business administration degree is paying off.

"I had been too afraid to say anything," she continues, "I thought he might hurt me, or worse, you, and so I kept quiet. But I'm not scared anymore." She pushes the box towards me. "Take it to the police station, and see if they can do anything with it."

"I'll take it tomorrow morning." I nod at the box. "We'll make sure he pays for everything he's done."

"Good." She smiles, and it's a smile I don't think I've ever seen on her. Not a hint of hesitancy or fear. "And Carter?"

"Yeah, Mom?" I put the lid back on the box and tuck it under my arm.

"You can't let him take anything else from you. Don't worry about me, I'm not afraid of him anymore." She gives me a rueful smile. "Let him come, I'll call the cops. I'm finally ready to do what I should have done when you were younger, and stand up to that bastard. And in the meantime..." she levels me with an understanding but firm look, "Sophie knows what kind of man you are. You just need to explain why you reacted how you did. We both know that she's the only one who's ever held your heart."

She places a hand on my cheek. "No one will be a better father than you. You are nothing like *him*. Just look at the compassion you've shown over the years. For Tom, how you've sent him money around the holidays because you wanted to help him even when you couldn't be there. For Sophie, making the ultimate sacrifice in pushing her away to keep her safe from your dad. Hell, even for the Twin Rinks, which wouldn't have gotten the full makeover it needs if it weren't for you. Carter Theodore Williams, you are everything that is good and strong in this world, and this child will be lucky to have a father like you."

Her words hit me hard. If Mom, who's seen every ugly and fucked up part of Dad, can look at me and tell me I'm nothing like him? I'm having a little bit of an easier time believing it.

I can't leave them. I *won't*. And more importantly, *I* can protect them.

With the information Mom has on him... this *gift* that she's given us, we have a chance to live a life without ever having to live in fear of Dad again.

Now, I just need to get my head out of my ass and fight for my family.

Chapter Thirty One

CARTER

This is my second morning in a row standing in front of a door I'm too nervous to knock on. Thankfully, it's Tom's house this time, not that shitty motel Dad is at.

Briefly, I'm brought back to the couple of months ago when I stared at this same door, nervous about my date with Sophie.

How different things are now. What if she hates me? What if she thinks I can't be a good dad because of how I reacted, or thinks I don't want her anymore?

If the roles were reversed, and she just walked out after revealing some life-changing news, I know I'd be questioning everything I know about her, considering I don't think she'd be capable of doing something like that.

A heavy sigh leaves me. The only thing I can do is knock. My knuckles rap the door, and my heart pounds as I wait. I just need to see her face. Hear her voice. Drop to my knees and apologize.

The sound of the door unlocking has my heart pounding harder, and when it cracks open, I'm ready to see Sophie's beautiful face, only to be met with Tom.

"Hey, Carter, I'm assuming you're looking for Sophie?" He rubs his eyes like I woke him up.

"Um... yeah." I scratch the back of my neck. "Is she here?"

"No, she's not." He levels me with a look. "Listen, I don't know any details. But Sophie was *really* upset the other night and has been at Abbie's since." Shit.

"Fuck, okay. I'll head that way." I run a hand over my face.

"Do you want to tell me what's going on?" Tom asks, leaning against the doorframe. His expression is curious, and a little guarded, like he's not sure if he should be pissed at me or not.

He should be.

"Not yet, but after I talk to Sophie, you'll get all the details. Promise." That's not really a conversation I'm looking forward to. He may be my best friend, but he's also Sophie's brother. He tries to toe the line between being there for me and taking care of his sister, but if a choice was necessary, he would choose her. Fuck, if I was him, I'd punch me in the face.

With that, I hop in my car and ten minutes later, I'm ringing Abbie's doorbell. It's too early for her to be at the flower shop, so she has to be here. When nothing happens for a few minutes, I double check the car in the driveway, thinking I might have the wrong house. But nope, that's her car in the driveway.

This time I knock, my knuckles pounding on the door as I pray Sophie will talk to me. "Sophie! Tom told me you're here!" I don't even care how desperate my voice sounds. "Please talk to me!"

Finally, the door cracks open, and I'm met with a *very* pissed off Abbie. She's dressed in scrubs and has a bag over her shoulder, like she's about to leave for the day.

Sighing, she looks me up and down. I'm sure I look like a fucking a mess. My hair is tousled, my shirt is wrinkled, and in the last 48 hours, I've barely slept, so I won't be surprised if I have bags under my eyes.

"I'm going to work," she tells me before I can say a word. "You need to get your shit together and fix this."

Swallowing roughly, I nod. "I will."

"Good. She's on the couch." With that, she glides past me, getting into her car and driving off. Entering and shutting the door behind me, I peer around the corner and see Sophie sitting curled up in a pile of blankets, eyes red and puffy, and nose chapped with a pile of tissues around her. Auburn hair is piled high on her head in a messy bun, but even in her haphazard state, she's still the most beautiful woman I've ever seen.

The urge to take her into my lap and comfort her is overwhelming, but I haven't earned that back yet. For now, I'll keep contact minimal until she decides she's ready to forgive me.

"What are you doing here?" she chokes out, wiping her eyes furiously.

My mouth opens and closes, all the fear and panic rushing back into me. What if I fucked everything up so astronomically she never forgives me?

"Get out, Carter." Her words are quiet as she looks down at her hands.

"I can't," I choke out, "I—" My words cut off as my feet move toward her on their own, and before I know it, I'm on my knees in front of her, taking her hands in mine. "Sophie." Her name leaves my lips in a plea.

Her honey-brown eyes are glassy and red rimmed as they take me in, appraising me, but she says nothing. She doesn't pull her hands away from me, though.

I deserve the silence. I also deserve for her to scream at me. But I just need her to listen to what I have to say, so maybe it's a good thing she's not speaking, considering our history of how me trying to explain myself has gone.

"I shouldn't have left. It was so, *so* wrong of me. You have every right to be furious. I was a complete and total asshole. I don't deserve your forgiveness for my reaction, but I'm going to beg for it anyway. You need to know what happened that day." I swallow roughly, attempting to get the next words out.

She doesn't move. She doesn't acknowledge me in any way, her face practically void of any emotion. But I know that look. That's her trying-not-to-cry look. Hopefully, I won't be the cause of any more tears.

"Last night, before I came to see you, I drove past Mom's house and I saw...Dad." She stiffens as her eyes widen, but I keep going. "He was trying to break into Mom's house and thank fuck she was still away at her retreat, otherwise I don't know what could have happened. I was terrified, Soph. I couldn't stop thinking about what he could do to you if he found out about us or questioning why the hell he was even in the area. No matter what, I knew it couldn't be good. I was going to take Mom and run. Get her out before he could make our lives hell again. I wanted to ask you to come, but I couldn't expect you to uproot your life with no guarantee of safety. When I came to you, I was going to say goodbye."

A little sound of protest escapes her, and I don't miss the new tears in her eyes as she studies me, listening to my every word. So I continue, "But then you told me about... about this little life growing inside of you, and all I could see was how my dad could rip everything away. How can I keep a child safe when I can't even..." I choke on my words. "When I can't even keep you, my mom, or myself safe? When I can't escape the one man who could absolutely ruin everything for us? I shouldn't have run, I know that. But all I could think about was that I needed to figure out how to protect my family. And I needed to do it right away.

"So I left to do just that, not even realizing I didn't utter a single word. Then, I started to think of every possibility of how I could fuck it up. How I don't know how to be a good dad, and I got scared. It was like a siren going off in my head, warning me that I would only cause harm to the baby. That Dad was the only example of a father I had growing up, and I'll become just like him." My words are wobbly, but it's not in fear anymore. No, it's in barely restrained anger at *him*.

"Carter, no. You're *nothing* like him," she says fiercely, her eyes burning with determination.

"I'm coming to realize that." I give her a sad smile, squeezing her hands, before I tell her the rest. "I knew that I had to get him as far away from Ivy Glen as possible for that to happen. I went and saw him, thinking maybe, if I figure out what he wants, I can give it to him and keep him away from all of us. He wants... well, almost everything. Half my yearly salary, plus five hundred thousand dollars by the end of the week. He says if I give it to him, he'll leave Ivy Glen and stay away."

"Do you think he actually would?" she asks, sniffling slightly.

"I don't know. If I know my dad, it would get him to stay away for maybe a year, tops. But then he'd come back. He always does. I know that now. I thought maybe just giving him the money and leaving anyway would be best. If he never knew the baby was mine, he'd have no reason to come after you." Sophie's eyes light up in anger, but before she can rip me a new one, I keep going. "But... then I talked to Mom. She made me realize how wrong I've been about everything."

Taking a deep breath, I look straight into her shining honey-brown eyes. "Mom was the one who helped me find the strength I needed to stand up to Dad. She made me see how I am nothing like him, and I never will be. And then..." I shake my head, a small laugh leaving me. "Then she handed over all the evidence we would ever need to put him in prison. She's been collecting it for years. All the proof we need to get the cops on him is sitting in a box in my hotel room right now."

She looks like she's about to speak again, but I need to get all of this out.

"I love you so, so much." My voice wavers, needing her to know just how much I mean it. "I was a coward. I had decided that leaving would be better than putting you in danger, when really, I was taking away your choice in the matter. I made all these decisions that affect your life... without you. I was trying to keep you safe, but all I did was push you away. All I want is to protect you and the baby. I want... no, I *need* to be with you Sophie. You are it for me. I am completely, unashamedly, unconditionally, in love with you and our child.."

She almost knocks me over when she throws herself at me, wrapping her arms around my neck and nuzzling close. My heart stutters as she wraps her legs around my waist and I situate us so I'm sitting on the floor, holding her close.

Feeling her against me for the first time in over six weeks is like finally being able to breathe again. Like a piece I didn't even realize was missing locks into place. My arms wrap around her middle like I want to keep her there permanently. We just sit there, her wrapped around me like a koala and me, breathing her in, reveling in the feel of her.

She feels like home.

"I love you too," she murmurs into my ear, not moving from her position. "And I'm sorry I didn't believe you about Nicole. I know you wouldn't hurt me like that. But I saw her texts, and it was like reliving graduation night. I wish I had answered your texts before you left, or even agreed to see you, but it was easier for me to fall back into self-preservation mode. I shouldn't have done that though, you've more than proven yourself when it comes to me, and you deserved more. Whatever comes next, we'll face it together. But," she pulls back, her hands on my shoulders as she looks me in the eyes, "don't ever pull shit like that again. If we're going to be together, we need to be a team. That means no sacrificing yourself for the greater good, no just deciding we'd be safer without you, and *telling* me when something like this happens."

Swallowing roughly, I nod "I know. I'm sorry."

"I mean it, Carter. I know it's a default mode for you, but you're going to have to get past it if you want to keep me around.

"I'm never going to disappear on you again." My hands grip her waist. "And from now on, I'm telling you everything as it happens."

"Good." She sighs. "I promise to listen to what you have to say instead of immediately going on the defensive and running away. And…" she looks at me and raises a brow, "I'm going to the police station with you. I want to see you take that bastard down."

Her eyes are no longer glassy, instead shining with a fierceness that I've seen so many times. She looks so damn beautiful that I can't help but stare at her, wondering how I got so lucky.

She's going to be an amazing mother. Her heart, her protectiveness, her loyalty, her determination. How she pours all of herself into everything she does—this baby is going to be the most loved child on the planet.

"What?" she asks, her expression softening when she realizes I'm not saying anything.

Smiling, I shrug. "Just thinking about how lucky I am. How I get to have the love of my life *and* have a baby with her."

She smiles blindingly at me, and then her eyes dart to my mouth. I don't know who moves first, but one second, we're staring at each other, and the next, we're crashing together in a soul-consuming kiss.

Every emotion that I have for her pours into the kiss as our tongues dance together. Her soft lips on mine light my skin on fire, and I pull back, breathing hard. She lays her head on my shoulder, her chest moving up and down as she catches her breath.

"You're tired," I note, running a hand through her hair.

"Moreso in the last couple of weeks. Baby needs a lot of energy," she murmurs into my shirt.

"Can I get you some food, and we can go back to my hotel?" I ask hopefully, continuing to run my fingers through her hair.

"Mmmm. As long as you keep doing that."

A soft chuckle leaves me. "I promise. Whatever comes next, we'll face it together. It's you and me, Soph."

Once we're back in my hotel room, snuggled on the bed after eating some breakfast, I feel like I need to tell her what happened on graduation night. "About that night..."

"Which one?" she asks sleepily.

"The night of Tom's accident." I admit, and feel her head shift so she could look at me. She must see the pain on my face because she tries to sit up, but I keep my arms around her so she stays in place.

"You don't have to talk about it. I don't know what happened, but now that I know how your dad was..."

I shake my head. "No, I need to get this out. It's good if you know exactly what we're dealing with." I let out a shaky exhale. "Dad and I were in the locker room at the rink. He had me running extra drills, even after practice had ended so we were the only two there. He was berating me, listing off all my mistakes, and I glanced at your text about missing me at graduation."

My eyes shut tight and I swallow, remembering the way my heart dropped when I never got an answer from him.

"Then your phone call came through, and I tried to answer it. Dad... doesn't like when he feels like I'm ignoring him. He snatched the phone from me, and... well, the situation ended with him beating the absolute shit out of me." She stiffens underneath me, and I run my hands soothingly up her back, even though the memories are making me angry as fuck. "After he decided I had enough, he threatened to do twice the damage to Mom if I picked up the phone again. And *that's* when I realized just how much power he held over me. I didn't hear your voicemail, or find out about the accident until the next day. So I texted Tom, explaining everything but begged him not to tell you. I knew that if he did, you would try to get involved and help me, and I couldn't risk that. The only way to keep you safe was to keep you out."

"Carter..." When she says my name, it's full of compassion and regret. Regret for me, and the situation Dad had me in. "You did the right thing. You were only eighteen, what more could you have done? You kept me safe, and while I'm so thankful for that... no more running. I can't lose you, I don't know if I... if *we* would survive it."

"You're the only one who's ever had my heart, Soph. And this time, not even the devil himself could make me walk away. Remember, it's you and me. And that little bean growing inside you."

As we drift off to sleep together, I try to prepare my mind for tomorrow. Going to the police station, telling them everything I know. Anything to keep my family safe.

That's what Sophie, and the life she's growing are. My family.

If anyone ever threatens my family again... let's just say Dad is lucky I'm not going to risk jail time to give him what he deserves.

After what he's done to Mom, to me, and by extension, to Sophie, he deserves the worst kind of torture that I would happily give him if it didn't mean ripping my family apart.

Tomorrow... it's the first step in ensuring that none of us will ever have to live in fear again.

Chapter Thirty Two

CARTER

Dad's going to know what we're doing.

That's all I can think as I grasp Sophie's hand across the center console while we drive to the police station. Each car we pass, my eyes dart to the driver, wondering if it's Dad, come to make good on his promise early.

Sophie squeezes my hand. "It's going to work out." She nods her head confidently. "It has to be." The last bit is quieter, like it's more to herself than to me.

The box of documents from Mom sits in the backseat, the seat belt buckled around it to keep it in place. When I'm not staring down oncoming cars, my eyes dart to the rearview mirror to make sure it's still there. Like it will randomly disappear and along with it, our chance of taking down Dad.

Nodding, I squeeze her hand back. "I know." Everything will be okay as long as I have her by my side.

By the time we pull up to the police station, my nerves have settled, and Sophie's hand in mine serves as an anchor, keeping me grounded in reality. We walk into the station hand-in-hand, the box of evidence tucked under my free arm.

There's a uniformed officer behind the front desk, rifling

through some papers when we come in. He looks up at us, his features forming a curious expression as he takes in the box under my arm.

"You folks need some assistance?" the officer asks as we approach. I place the box on the counter, and pat the top. "I have some information about Jeremy Williams I thought you all might be interested in."

His eyes widen, and he looks back and forth between me and the box before asking, "You're Carter Williams, right?"

My smile is grim. "Guilty."

He nods. "I'll be right back."

Sophie and I exchange a glance. Maybe the hockey fame will have an actual practical purpose for once.

"That's a good sign, right?" Sophie asks quietly. "They didn't just take the box and dismiss us. Maybe they already have a reason to be suspicious of him."

"I think you're right." I smile down at her and kiss the top of her head. Having her here with me soothes something in my soul. Not having to bear the weight of this alone, like I've done for so many years, is like finally being able to breathe again. I hadn't realized how much of a toll it was taking until now.

"Carter Williams?" A voice catches my attention, and I turn to see a man approaching us. He's not wearing the standard officer blues, but is in a pair of dress slacks, a button up shirt with a tie, and a shoulder holster. He looks to be somewhere in his fifties, with fine lines around his eyes, and gray at the temples of his otherwise jet black hair.

"Yes, sir." I nod, before holding out my hand.

"Detective Scott Peterson," he gives my hand a firm shake before releasing it and holding it out to Sophie, "Miss...?"

"Sophie Hartwell," Sophie says, shaking his hand as well.

"Of Hart's Flowers!" he says with a smile that crinkles his eyes, "Your shop has definitely saved my ass once or twice when I needed flowers to apologize for working so much. And you two did some great work saving the rec center how you did."

Sophie gives him a smile. "Thank you."

He turns back to me. "I understand you have some information on your father? Let's go to the back and have a chat. We can chat in one of the interview rooms for some privacy." Detective Peterson leads us to one of the back rooms, set up with a small rectangular table and a few chairs. "Do you mind if I go through the files you brought?" he asks, gesturing to the box under my arm.

"Not at all." I place the box on the table, and he rifles through the contents as Sophie and I get situated in the seats at the other side of the table. Her hand lands on my thigh, her thumb rubbing soothing circles on the side of my leg.

"This is..." Detective Peterson shakes his head, "This is exactly what we need."

"For what, exactly?" I ask, my brows furrowed.

"To carry on with the case. I've been trying to nail down Jeremy Williams for years." I shouldn't be shocked, but some part of me is. I'd known my dad was into some shady shit, but to think that the police were actively trying to take him down... I wish I had known. Maybe I could have helped in some way. All the years he extorted me for money, all the threats against Mom... I swallow roughly.

"Do you remember the board member, Julian Davis?" The detective asks, looking between us.

"Oscar's dad," Sophie says quietly, nodding.

"He came to us around fifteen years ago with some proof against Jeremy for embezzlement of town funds. He covered his tracks so thoroughly, however, there wasn't ever quite enough proof to arrest him." The detective runs a hand through his hair as if he's reliving the infuriating days of knowing someone is guilty and not being able to do anything about it. "But then, he left the board and the town. For years, there was no further evidence, which in itself points to Jeremy being the one responsible. Then, Julian got his cancer diagnosis about five years ago and didn't know how much time he had left, so he let me know that he told Michael Wixx to keep an eye on things and to tell me if saw anything suspicious. Michael was also on the board at the time and Julian felt he was the only one he could trust."

Michael Wixx... that's Abbie's dad, and he's still a board member. Sophie looks at me with wide eyes. I know what she's thinking—that this goes so much deeper than either of us thought.

"Julian passed three years later, so I started working with Michael, and about ten months ago, Michael started finding discrepancies in the numbers again. Any time there would be votes on local tax changes and funds would start coming into the town accounts, bits and pieces were disappearing. The allocation amounts weren't lining up. I, of course, had my suspicions. But with Jeremy Williams being gone for so many years, I knew someone else either took over what he started, or Williams was still involved somehow. My hunch told me it was Williams, so I followed it. I put out a call to the precincts in surrounding states, and it didn't take long to get a call back. He's been one state over this entire time. I don't believe in coincidence, and if you ask me, that's a damn good one."

Holy shit. This... I'm not an expert on elected officials embezzling taxpayer dollars, but that would have to put him away for a long time, right?

"So... what that means now..." Detective Peterson looks between the two of us, tenting his fingers in front of him. "This information that you brought in is great. It's enough to arrest him and have him face a trial. But it only covers what happened over ten years ago. What we need is to get proof of those involved now, and confirm that includes him. With Jeremy not being on the board for close to ten years, any new evidence won't point diarcitly to him."

"He's back in town... well, Willow Creek. Told me that if I give him five hundred thousand and half my yearly salary, he'll leave Ivy

Glen for good. He's been extorting money from me for years, holding my mom's safety over my head. I've only known about the abuse since I was in high school, but I know it's been going on longer. Mental *and* physical. I'll help you catch the fucker in whatever way I can."

The detective's eyes harden in a way that tells me exactly what he thinks of a man hitting his wife.

"Would she be willing to testify to that in court?" he asks, "I understand if it's too hard, but we need whatever we can get to show his character and then we could possibly bring up separate charges of domestic abuse. We can also bring up charges for extortion. With all of this combined, we may be able to have him locked up for the rest of his sorry life."

A few months ago, I wouldn't have even asked Mom to stand before a room and relive her trauma. But after yesterday, seeing her resolve and newfound strength, I think she might want to. She deserves to have the world know just how much of a piece of shit he is. "I'll ask her and let you know."

"Good." He nods. "Would you be willing to wear a wire? If you're supposed to meet up with him to 'hand over the money,'" he uses air quotes, "we could set up a sting and possibly get him talking. Maybe even get a confession. I would hate to arrest him for his crimes from over ten years ago alone, for a judge to throw out the case due to outdated paperwork and no proof beyond that."

"Whatever you need." My voice rings with conviction.

"Great." He places the lid back on the box. "I'm going to come up with a plan and look at this evidence in more detail. I'll give you a call in the next couple of days."

"Looking forward to it." We each shake his hand again before we leave the room, escorted out by another officer.

I *am* looking forward to it.

Knowing that by next week, Dad could be sitting behind bars awaiting trial, and no longer a threat to my family, has a sense of rightness settling into my bones. We could finally be free of him, once and for all.

"She can't just close the store for an hour for her lunch?" I frown, holding the passenger side door of my car open for Sophie as she hops out.

"No," she shakes her head, "I'm not going to lose an hour of business for no reason, that's just silly. I'm pregnant, not an invalid, Carter. I can still do my job. Also, I told Kerry she could take the afternoon off."

"I know, I just..." A sigh leaves me as I grab her around the waist. "Don't think that I don't know how ridiculous I'm being, but I don't even want you on your feet. You're carrying precious cargo."

There's been a shift inside of me since talking to Sophie this morning. After our conversation, a ferocious sense of protection reared its head, and I just want to wrap her up in a layer of bubble wrap and never let anything from the outside world touch her or our baby again. It's my job to keep her and the little life inside her safe.

She lets out a small laugh as she rolls her eyes, and her thumb reaches up to smooth out the crease between my brows. "It's good for me to keep my mind busy. As much as I would love nothing more than to just nap in bed with you all day, I need the routine."

"Who said anything about napping?" The corner of my mouth quirks up and she laughs again before wrapping her arms around my neck and kissing me.

"You're insatiable," she murmurs against my lips.

"Fine, fine." I relent after she pulls away. "I have some stuff to do for my mom anyway, but I want you to stay at my hotel with me tonight."

"I'll meet you there after work," she agrees, burying her face in my chest as I hug her against me. Something about the simple domesticity of the exchange has my heart fluttering in my chest. It's both old and new at the same time. Sure, we were in love back then, but now it's deeper, more complex. There's more layers than there were before, as well as a deeper understanding of what it means to love someone with your whole heart and to do everything in your power to protect them.

Another quick goodbye kiss later, and I'm in my car driving again. Though... I may have told a little lie. I'm not going to Mom's. Instead, I make my way to John Kayne's office, the local realtor. I'm going to find us the perfect house as soon as possible. I want a life with Sophie. That starts with finding a place for us to both call home.

Being in a hotel takes away from the reality that this time, I'm here to stay, and nothing could drag me away from Sophie ever again.

It's time to start building our future.

00
15

Chapter Thirty Three

SOPHIE

"How about... Marjorie, if it's a girl?" I ask after swallowing a mouth full of pizza.

"Do you want our baby to be born an old lady?" Carter laughs as he tosses a napkin at me. His black hair is sexily tousled from our lounging, his broad shoulders laying back against the fluffy pillows of the bed.

We're back in the hotel room for the evening, sitting on the bed with a pizza box between us as we go through possible baby names. The evening has been lighthearted, the impending threat of Carter's dad tucked away in a little box until we want to face reality again.

I got comfortable as soon as I arrived, hopping in the shower to rinse off my day of work and emerging in only one of his t-shirts, the hem falling around mid-thigh.

"I think it's cute," I pout, but then realize I know of at least two old ladies named Marjorie. "Do you have any better names up your sleeve?"

"Hmmm..." He places a finger on his chin in faux thought. "I've always liked the name Hunter for a boy. And for a girl... Jessica."

My nose wrinkles. "Nuh uh. One of the girls that always fawned over you during high school hockey games was named Jessica. I like Hunter though."

"Was she the one with blonde hair and braces?" He looks at me quizzically.

"No, she had brown hair and always had it in two buns on top of her head. She tried to make her own jersey with your name on it." I scowl. It was just a t-shirt that she had used fabric markers to put his name and number on the back.

He bursts out a laugh. "You were so patient. If any guy looked at you for too long, I saw red. How did you not shank a bitch repeatedly?"

"I knew you were mine." A small smile appears on his face. "I was the only one you wanted, I knew that. Let the other girls look, you made it clear to everyone that you belonged to me." He never looked twice at the ones who would dress provocatively to get his attention. And when we were next to each other, he always had an arm around me or found other small ways to touch me and stake his claim.

"Belong," he says, looking at me with that grin on his face.

"What?" I blink, jarred from my thoughts of the past.

"You said that I *belonged* to you. Past tense. I still belong to you, Angel. I'm all yours. "

My heart stutters in my chest. This is still new... kind of. Sure we were together for years back then. But we only admitted that we still love each other when he got back from training camp. This is different from love in high school. Back then, we had no real grasp on what true, hard commitment looked like. Now, everything means more.

"I know." I smile, my heart full of love for the man next to me. "But I'm still not naming our baby Jessica."

He barks a laugh, and offers an alternative. "How about Hazel?"

"Love it. Let's make a list." I pull out my phone and start a list on the notes app. We spitball names back and forth, only putting ones we both agree on. Then I have a thought.

"Carter..." I trail off, still looking down at my phone. "What do you think about Vivianne? If it's a girl." My bottom lip gets caught under my teeth, and I meet his eyes.

They shine with warmth, and he looks at me in awe. "You would be willing to name our baby after my mom?"

"I love your mom. And she's been through so much, and came out stronger on the other side. She's a survivor, and she raised the love of my life, turning him into the sweet, kind, loyal man he is. What better way to honor her?" Carter told me all about the retreat that his mom went on and how she's practically a different person now, and all about the children's books she's been writing.

"I think," Carter leans over, placing a gentle kiss on my lips, "that you're the most amazing woman I've ever met, and she would be over the moon if we did that."

I smile against his lips. "I love you."

"I love you too, Angel." He pulls back and tucks a strand of hair behind my ear. "Are you feeling okay? Nauseous or anything? Tired?"

His concern is so sweet, but I can already tell I'm going to feel smothered before long if he keeps it up. "I'm fine, mother hen," I tease.

"I'm not being a mother hen," he protests. "You were on your feet at the shop, and then you had to pick up Jordan..."

"Being on my feet won't be an issue for too much longer. It might please you to know..." I trail off, not sure how to say it. I haven't told anyone else this yet, but since Abbie and I talked about it the day I found out I'm pregnant, I've been thinking about putting my future career plans into action. "I've been thinking about our conversation that night at the lake, and I'm going to do something that I want to do. I'm going to open my own small accounting firm in town."

His face lights up with a smile brighter than any one that I've seen from him today. "Sophie! That's great!"

I can't help my smile at his happiness for me. "Yeah?"

"Fuck yeah!" He does a little arm pump that makes me giggle. "God, I'm so fucking proud of you. You're amazing, you know that? Do you need help finding an office space? Or like, shit, an assistant or something? Anything you need, I'm here. We'll make it happen."

"You've always known how to push me to be my best. And I think this is how I do that. Kerry loves the flower shop, and it's time I hire a few more girls and make her the manager. Who knows, maybe my parents will even let her buy it if she wants." A shrug leaves me. The flower shop, while I've had a good time working there for the most part, was never my dream. At least with Kerry, I know it'll be in good hands. "I'm not sure what the time-line on that would look like though or what your schedule will look like."

"Practices will start in September, and the baby will most likely be born sometime in March, right?" I nod my head in answer to his question. I haven't had my first doctor's appointment yet, but the online calculator estimated somewhere around March 22nd. "So, the season will still be going on, but I'll have to let the team manager and coach know that a contract change will have to be made because there's no way in hell I'm missing the birth of my child. I can ask for no away games after you hit thirty five weeks."

My brow furrows. "But Carter, this is your *dream*, and if you do that, you'll get significantly less play time—"

"You are, and have always been, more important to me than hockey," he says sternly, moving the pizza box to the side table and then bringing me closer to his side.

Snuggling in closer to him, my fingers dance lazily across his chest, drawing a little shudder out. "Did you ever imagine that we would be like this again?" I ask quietly.

"I'm pretty sure I always wanted to end up back here, with

you," he murmurs before pressing a kiss to my hair. "I would avoid thinking of a future outside of hockey because when I did, I imagined how our life might have been different if Dad hadn't ruined everything. That just filled me with so much regret and sadness, I didn't want to dwell on it."

Shit, I'd done the same thing over the past nine years. Buried myself in work and did everything for everyone because if I stopped to take a breath and think about what I truly wanted, it would have included Carter.

Never did I imagine that it would be a possibility again.

Before I can say anything, Carter's phone rings.He picks it up, checking the caller ID. "I think it's the police station." He answers, and I can't hear the other side of the conversation, but Carter tenses slightly before relaxing again. He listens intently, and at the end of the call says, "Yes, sir. I can do that. I'll see you then."

"What's going on?" I pull back and prop myself on my elbow looking at him.

"It was Detective Peterson. They have a plan for me to help bring down Dad."

My heart stutters. It's really happening. Once this is done, we won't have to worry about him ever again, and we can live our lives in peace.

"They'll put a protective detail on Mom at the house. They want me to call him and say I have the $500k and pick a location to meet," he says, his gaze studying me for my reaction. I keep a straight face even though the thought of him walking into a metaphorical wolves' den to face his father has my stomach in knots. "I'll wear a wire, and see if I can goad him into some sort of confession. Then, Detective Peterson's team will move in and arrest him regardless. One way or another, Soph, two days from now, things will be over with him for good."

My heart hammers in my chest and my bottom lip tucks between my teeth. Isn't there another way? Carter should never have to deal with his dad again, with what he's put him through. Not to mention the danger he could possibly be in...

"Soph?" Carter asks, reaching over with this thumb to release my lip and run his thumb over the sensitive skin. "You okay?"

Swallowing, I nod. "I wish you didn't have to do this. We're *finally* together, no more misunderstandings between us. I hate the idea of you facing him again... who knows what he could do if he gets even more desperate?" A sigh escapes me and I run a hand over his cheek. "But I understand. I don't like it one bit, but if this is what we have to do..."

His eyes shine with understanding as he leans towards me. "I just got you back, Angel. No way in hell is my old man going to tear us apart again."

With that, his lips capture mine in a slow, deliberate kiss. I sit up, leaning into his touch. I grip his arm as his hand comes up to cup my cheek tenderly. Gently, still kissing me, he pulls me onto his lap so I'm straddling him while he sits up against the pillows. The kiss is almost chaste at first, but then his hands run down my back before reaching my ass. "No underwear, Angel?"

"Thought they might get in the way." I say breathily, my hands gripping his arms. The next second, his tongue seeks entrance into my mouth, and I let him in greedily, basking in the feeling of being in his embrace again.

There's a tenderness between us that wasn't there before. Or perhaps it was, but hidden beneath the layers of defense I had put up to keep our relationship casual. One hand moves from my ass to my front as he gently caresses the thin material over my sensitive breasts. A small moan escapes into his mouth, and he swallows it hungrily, reaching under my shirt to run his rough hands over my quickly pebbling flesh.

Holy ever-loving shit. This is the first time we've been intimate in a little over two months, and it's like every sensation is heightened.

His lips move from mine and down across my jaw, leaving

open mouth kisses as he goes. He takes his time as he massages my breast, suckling and licking his way down the column of my throat until he reaches my collar bone. The sensation is divine, his gentle but erotic touch making me forget about how sore they've been lately. "I've missed you so much," he murmurs into my skin. "Every day I thought of you and wished I could take you into my arms."

Lifting the hem of my shirt, he moves to pull it off me and then takes my sensitive nipple into his mouth. His hot tongue swirls around, and my head falls back in bliss. "I must have read your texts at least twenty times," I admit on a gasp. "I should have answered you, I just—"

"I know, Soph," he cuts me off, reaching his hand to the back of my neck to pull my face toward him in a sweet kiss. "You needed time to think. As much as I hated to give it to you at the time, I understood."

His blue eyes shine with warmth as he pulls away, gently pushing my hair behind my ear. "I love you." My voice shakes with emotion as my fingers thread through his hair. "So damn much."

This time, when our lips meet, there's a desperation there. Not for the way our bodies are physically together, but for the connection we'd been lacking the last nine years. Even when we were sleeping together before, there was never any promise of a future behind it. Now, I pour every ounce of love and devotion into this one kiss.

He moans into my mouth, one of his arms snaking around my middle and the other reaching down between us.

His fingers find my pussy, and he hums in appreciation when he feels that I'm already soaking and ready for him. Spreading my wetness around my clit, he rubs small circles that light my body on fire.

"Oh, fuck! Carter!" I can't stop the cry that escapes as euphoria washes over me, shamelessly riding his hand until I come down from my high. My head drops onto his chest as he removes his arm from between us, my gasping breaths filling the air between us.

His shirt is soft against my cheek, but I hate the barrier separating us.

My hands move from his arms to the hem of the offending fabric, sliding my fingers underneath and running them over his lower stomach in a way I know makes his toes curl. He shivers, and I bite back a grin, lifting his shirt to reveal the hard planes of muscle underneath.

He really is a masterpiece.

After helping me remove his shirt completely, I move off him, staying on the bed, and watch as he shimmies his sweatpants down until his magnificent cock springs free. I look down, licking my lips at the sight of it, but Carter has other ideas.

Sitting up away from the pillows, he lifts me by my hips, settling my entrance right over his erection. His icy blue gaze never leaves mine, lowering me onto his throbbing length. We both groan, my hands settling on his shoulders to steady myself.

And then he's moving.

I may be on top, but Carter is definitely the one still in control as he fucks up into me, firmly gripping my hips. He stares into my eyes as he thrusts upwards, each time he bottoms out sending waves of pleasure throughout my body. Physically, we're obviously as close as we can possibly be. But, it's so much more than that. His very soul connects to mine through our eyes, the steadfast devotion he feels for me clear as day behind his pools of blue.

"Fuck, I love you," he says before pulling my mouth to him. His lips and tongue move with mine like two pieces of a puzzle fitting together. Like he wants to claim me, consume me whole.

I would let him.

My hands roam the muscles of his chest, his mountainous shoulders, and his strong back as we move together. Fire pools low in my belly as I feel another orgasm rising within me, this one more of a slow growing tidal wave than the whirlwind of pleasure the first one was. One of his hands moves from my hips back to my clit and his touch shoots a jolt of electricity straight to my core, launching me over the edge.

My scream of pleasure is swallowed by his mouth, and before I can register what's happening, he's flipped us over so he hovers over me, still seated inside my pulsing heat.

Moving on top of me, he hikes one of my knees over his arm as he pushes all the way in, again and again, reaching deeper than he has this entire time. Each thrust sends an electric jolt through my over-sensitive body, and my fingernails claw at his back as the sensation nearly overwhelms me.

"Sophie, Sophie, Sophie," he mutters against my lips like a prayer as his hips stutter. He finds his release and sends me over the edge one final time.

Instead of collapsing on top of me, he falls to his side, flipping me to my side to face him, and holding me close. We catch our breaths together, a sweaty heap of limbs tangled together in the best way.

When he gets up, pulling me with him, I don't question it. He leads me to the bathroom, and turns the shower on to scalding, just how I like it. After he's washed every inch of me and dried me off, he pulls me back to bed, wrapping himself around me. We drift off together like this, keeping each other close, the beating of his heart in my ear the sweetest sound I've ever heard.

Chapter Thirty Four

CARTER

Gravel crunches under my feet as I approach the chain link fence walling off the Twin Rinks construction site from the rest of the town. George didn't ask questions when I texted him this morning, asking him to leave the padlock off the gate. It pushes open easily, allowing me to slip inside.

I almost jump when Detective Peterson's voice sounds in my ear, jolting me back to reality. "Keep walking, straight ahead towards that light pole. It gives us the best visual to make sure the situation doesn't get out of hand."

I don't risk nodding in acknowledgement, and opt to simply follow his orders. My heart is pounding so hard I wouldn't be surprised if they pick it up through the wire I'm wearing. Everything hinges on tonight. This confession is the key to make sure my piece of shit father rots in jail for the rest of his worthless life.

The only thing that keeps me focused is I know exactly where Sophie and mom are. Sophie decided to wait it out with Abbie at her dad's house, since he's the one who's been working with the detective until now. Mom is safe with a police detail guarding her house. Out of sight of course, so Dad doesn't get suspicious if he drives by, but knowing they're there lets me focus on the task at hand, instead of worrying about my family.

The weight of the bag of cash in my hand is like a physical representation of the burden I've been under the last nine years. Quickly checking my watch, which shows 8:55 p.m., my gut churns in anticipation, knowing that my final confrontation with my dad is only five minutes away.

"You ready, Carter?" the detective asks.

"As ready as I can be," I mutter under my breath... I have to be ready.

Now, if only I could get my damn heart to stop racing.

The sound of a truck rattling closer puts my sense on high alert, and it takes everything in me to act calm and casual. What if he realizes what's happening? What if he catches on and bolts before they can arrest him?

"Williams spotted, pulling up in a brown pick up," another voice says in my ear. "The team is in position." I'm not sure exactly where they are, but there's plenty of cover with the construction equipment and work trucks parked nearby.

"Ten-four," Detective Peterson says. "Remember, Carter, if there's a hint of danger, you get out of there. My men are ready in case things go sideways, but you can never be too careful."

Before I can make any move of acknowledgement, the slamming of a car door has my eyes drawing towards my dad. The street lights illuminate his triumphant sneer. Cocky bastard.

Little does he know he's already lost. I can't wait to see that look wiped from his face when the cops put him on the ground and cuff him.

He's dressed up more than he has been since he's been back, in a worn out suit and tie, like this is some kind of grand moment for him instead of him extorting his only son for money. He walks through the opening I left in the gate, looking around the area to make sure we're alone.

"Dad," I greet, keeping my voice even.

"You got the cash?" His voice is rough as he approaches.

"Clearly." I hold the bag up. "But I want you to answer some questions first."

He stops, his eyes narrowing. "You think you can give me fucking orders? You wanted me to leave, so give me the damn cash."

I keep my face blank, playing the part of the confident, co-conspirator. "I know, but I think I know what you've been doing... and I want in."

Dad will never confess to me unless he has something to gain from it. A textbook narcissist will only respond to one thing.

Stroking his ego.

"Oh yeah? What is it you think I'm doing, Mr. Big Shot?" He eyes me, stepping closer, his seemingly permanent sneer still present.

"You haven't needed any extra money from me for the last year because you've been getting it from somewhere else, right? I'm not going to be a hockey player forever. I need to make sure I'm set long after I retire. Whatever you've got going on, bring me in on it."

Dad's expression quickly morphs from one of surprise to a cocky grin. "You want to know how your old man makes the big bucks, huh?" He lets out a low chuckle. "I never took you for a kid who would stray from the straight and narrow. Too high and mighty."

"I'll do what I have to do." I give a noncommittal shrug. "Fuck everyone else. I need to look out for *me*." The words burn coming out, and Dad looks taken aback for a second. Shit. Did I lay it on too thick?

"I've never heard you talk like that before," he says, his tone indecipherable as looks me over with an assessing gaze.

Dammit. He's catching on. I'm acting too out of character to be believable.

I stay silent, trying to keep my shoulders from tensing, hoping he's not about to say fuck it and leave.

"Hm..." My heart pounds in my chest, waiting for him to question me. I wonder how I'm going to get us back on the right track. "I guess you aren't quite the fuck up I thought you were. As long as you look out for your old man as well."

It's everything I can do to not sigh in relief. "The Twin Rinks are set to make big bucks once they reopen." I offer, my throat burning at the words. "And I've ensured I never loose access to their POS system we're installing. We can both be set for life." I really hope I'm selling this because every word I speak makes my skin crawl in revulsion.

Dad considers me. He seems to accept my sudden turn towards financial crimes, and chuckles darkly as he takes a step toward me. "Okay, son." Wow. He has never called me "son" in my life. It would be kind of nice if he wasn't such a fucking asshole. "There's only one problem. I have... an inside man. If you want in, you'll have to get rid of him."

"Get rid?" I startle. We just jumped the long gap from extortion to murder. "Get rid of him how?"

Dad smirks. "I don't really give a shit as long as he doesn't ever show back up here, looking for money."

"Tell him you'll do it, but you have to know what the operation is first." Detective Peterson sounds in my ear.

"Okay..." I say slowly, shifting on my feet. "I'll figure it out, but not before you tell me what the whole operation is about. I need to know if it's worth it."

"Oh, it's worth it," Dad says, shaking his head. "You'll be swimming in so much cash you'll be drowning. Think of it as an... initiation. As soon as you get rid of my insider, you can take his spot on the council, then I'll fill you in on what you need to do."

His place... on the council? Shit. His inside man is a council member?

"Keep him talking," Detective Peterson mutters. We're so *close.*

"I want you to bring me in *now*." I say, more confident than I feel. "If you want in on the rinks, you'll tell me now, and then I'll make a decision. Why would I do all the work to get rid of your inside man without my cash in hand?"

Dad is silent, his gaze going steely as he looks at me.

Stroking the ego isn't getting us far enough, so it's time to go the other direction.

I bark a laugh."Who am I kidding? Maybe I need to approach the other guy since he's probably the mastermind behind the whole thing."

Dad's vein pops in his head and his face turns red. "Don't test me, you little shit. I've been taking what I'm owed from the town of Ivy Glen since before you even hit fucking puberty."

A swoop of victory goes through my stomach, but I know we need more. He needs to admit to every foul thing.

"Oh yeah? Then why do you even need this guy if you can do it all on your own?" My words are a taunt. An invitation to spill all his dirty little secrets. Now, he just needs to take it.

"I don't *need* Oscar Davis," he sneers. "I was able to funnel out money for years before I had a little helper." Shit. Oscar is who's been helping him? I can't really say I'm surprised, but it lights a fire in my veins knowing he's been pursuing Sophie while tangled up in my dads business.

"Keep going," Detective Peterson says, more to himself than to me, an edge in his voice.

"Why *Oscar*?" I ask, letting true disdain drip from my voice, letting him think it's about the perceived incompetence of his choice rather than the fact I just fucking hate the guy.

Dad smirks. "He knows exactly what to do and how to do it. He found the files his useless father kept all those years ago, and reached out, hoping to get in on it since he doesn't know how to do it alone. How could I resist?" He chuckles. "The best part is, I didn't even have to be here this time around. Then the contract year came around, and I was already coming back to find you.

When I saw you on the TV, promoting this useless project," he motions to the spot where only the bare structure of the ring now stands, "you told me exactly where you were. Now, I can clear my gambling debts, make even more money, and not worry about avoiding Ivy Glen anymore because the only person who had a clue what I was doing is dead and gone."

Fucking bingo.

"Got him." Detective Peterson hisses. "Move in."

"Ten-four." The other voice in my ear confirms.

I did it. I got him to confess.

"Thanks for the help, Dad." I can't keep the smug grin of my face as the armed officers descend from their hiding places. "You're never going to touch Mom, or anyone else I love, ever again."

Dad's eyes widen at my words as reality sinks in. His face contorts in rage that is so, so sweet to see. He's finally getting what he deserves. "You fucking rat! You set me up?!" He shouts, reaching a hand into his jacket. "I own you, you fucking piece of shit! If I'm going down, I'm taking you with me!" I'm so busy reveling in the rage on Dad's face that I don't even register the flash of metal as he pulls something from his hip.

"Suspect has a gun!" Peterson shouts into my ear, and then everything happens in slow motion.

I'm frozen in place as Dad's arm raises, and two shots ring out, almost at the same time. Shock fills his face, a second before a sharp pain lances my arm.

"Fuck!" he screams out, the gun dropping from his hand as an officer tackles him to the ground, pinning his hands behind his back. Blood seeps through the material of his pant leg as he squirms, screaming obscenities.

I touch my hand to the spot on my arm that's screaming in pain, and when I pull it away, it's covered in blood.

My dad shot me.

Shit. Even I didn't realize he had it in him to try to kill his own son. I stare at my hand in shock as the sound of a siren approaches, red and white lights going off in my peripheral. Paramedics pop out of the ambulances that park outside the gate, rushing a gurney to my dad.

"You good?" Detective Peterson comes up next to me, his eyes on my dad as the EMTs load him onto the gurney.

I grimace, showing my bloodied hand to the detective. He quickly inspects my arm. "It's just a graze, but there's a second ambulance coming to check you out."

Swallowing, I nod. "I need to see him taken away first."

The paramedics wheel the gurney past us, and I look coldly at the man who doesn't deserve to call himself a father. Cuffed to the handrail and still bleeding from the bullet in his leg that took him down, he looks like nothing more than the scum at the bottom of my shoe. A miserable waste of space. Looking him dead in the eyes, I feel nothing but relief. "If you believed that I would really try to be a part of your pathetic scheme," I tell him, "you obviously don't know me at all."

"You fucking piece of shit!" Dad screams, spit flying out of his mouth and his arms thrashing in rage. "I'll fucking kill you! And that bitch you call a mother! I'll end her and make you watch, you pathetic, useless—"

His ranting is cut off by the paramedics closing the doors after loading him in.

Detective Peterson sighs. "Don't worry. With the information we got and threats like that recorded, plus the additional evidence you found for shady dealings at the car dealership, not to mention the attempted murder we all just witnessed, he should have enough years racked up in his sentence to be behind the bars for the rest of his life."

Attempted murder charge. Shit. A part of me is still shocked that Dad tried to fucking kill me. But I can't find myself to be hurt by his actions. Emotionally at least. Physically, the graze from the bullet fucking hurts. Otherwise, I'm just so fucking grateful it's all finally over and because of that, I can't be sorry about how this all happened. I would do it all over again if it meant keeping Sophie, the baby, and my mom safe.

Despite the pain in my arm, and the pounding in my heart as I watch the man who raised me being taken away in an ambulance, I feel like I can finally breathe.

It's over.

He's never going to hurt us again.

I'M GOING TO WEAR A HOLE IN ABBIE'S DAD'S CARPET IF I'm not careful.

When we learned everything Detective Peterson had to tell us about Carter's dad, I had been nervous. I reached out to Abbie's dad, Michael, since he was the one who had been working with the detective since Julian Davis died.

He assured me that Detective Peterson is a good man, as well as an exceptional detective, and if anyone could get Carter through this unscathed, it's him.

"Soph, everything will be fine," Abbie says gently from her place on the couch, her chocolate brown eyes watching me intently. Her brown, shoulder length hair is pulled back, and she looks as almost as tense as I feel as she picks at a thread in her leggings. "Carter's a big boy, and the police are there in case anything crazy happens."

The words do little to comfort me because the reality is Carter, the love of my life and father of my unborn child, is in a potentially dangerous situation, and I'm helpless to do anything about it. My elbow clips the large wooden cabinet that holds a million different mugs when I pass by, the sound of the ceramic cups jostling on the glass shelves setting my nerves even more on edge.

"I know." I sigh, wringing my hands as I continue my path back and forth across the living room, opting to pass between the overstuffed chairs so I don't bruise my elbow again. "I still don't like it though." I wrap my arms around my stomach and take a big breath, trying to calm down by inhaling Carter's scent. Wearing his T-shirt and hoodie today was a comfort I couldn't deny myself.

"Detective Peterson will make sure he's safe," Michael says, sitting next to his daughter. His hair grew in gray when we were in teens, but it's a full head of it. He's in a polo and jeans, looking calm and collected as I internally lose my shit. "This is an opportunity to get him out of all of our lives for good. Carter is the only one he might confess to."

They aren't telling me things I don't already know. It doesn't make it any easier. "I'll just feel better when I hear from him." The thought of anything happening to Carter makes my insides feel like they're going to fall out of my chest.

I wish I had told my parents what was going on, but they don't return from their cruise until tomorrow morning and nobody else knows about tonight except Jake and Tom, who's at home with Jordan.

"The detective said he'd call me with an update as soon as everything gets wrapped up." Michael's voice is calming, his experience raising Abbie as a single dad evident in the way he speaks evenly, never insinuating that I'm overreacting. Only a man who raised a teenage girl single handedly could achieve that, especially considering the level of hormonal mess I'm at right now.

My phone ringing jolts me out of my thoughts. "Hello?" I don't recognize the number, but put it on speaker in case it's the detective calling.

"Yes, hello, is this Sophie Hartwell?" The voice is chipper, like the customer service voice I use when I answer the phone at the flower shop.

"It is..." I answer cautiously. I swear, if this is someone trying to sell me something when I'm waiting to hear from Carter—

"My name is Jackie, I'm a nurse here at Ivy Glen General Hospital. I'm calling on behalf of Carter Williams. He was just brought in—"

Suddenly, my heart is pounding so hard in my chest, the nurse's voice is drowned out by the sound of my blood rushing in my ears.

The hospital. I need to get to him.

My phone drops out of my hand and I rush out of the door, Abbie's voice calling after me.

Is he dying? Did his dad attack him? Or did things turn violent and he got caught in the crossfire? I try to tamp down the irrational anger rising in my chest. They assured me that he would be safe. He's obviously not safe if he had to go to the damn hospital.

I can't breathe. Why can't I fucking breathe?

My heart pounds harder as I yank on the door to my car. Why won't this thing open? Despite logic telling me that if the first three times I tried to open it didn't work, it's probably locked, my hand continues to pull on the handle, desperate to get into the goddamn car so I can get to Carter.

He's probably wondering where I am—

"Sophie!" Abbie's voice cuts through my frantic thoughts as her hand lands on my shoulder. I shudder, gasping in a breath and letting my forehead fall to the glass of the window.

"The car won't open!" I hardly recognize the voice that comes out of me.

"Sophie, babe, look at me." Abbie's hands grasp both my shoulders and turn me around. "None of that," she tsks, taking her thumbs and swiping them across my cheeks. Have I been crying? "Take a deep breath," she orders, and I struggle to follow her directions.

"I... can't!" I gasp out, holding onto her forearms for support.

"You can, and you will." Abbie says firmly. "This stress isn't good for the baby, Soph. Take a deep breath."

The baby. Think of the baby.

Closing my eyes, I take a deep breath.

"That's it," she murmurs, rubbing circles on my shoulders with her thumb. "Deep breaths."

I take one, then two more, and feel my heart rate slowing down. My eyes open, and I'm met with Abbie's concerned gaze. "Now *you're* crying." I point out, and she releases me, wiping under her eyes.

"I'll drive," she says, grabbing her car keys from her back pocket.

Swallowing, I nod, and move to Abbie's car as she gets into the driver's side. The drive to the hospital is tense, and I spend most of it concentrating on taking deep, measured breaths. Just like that, I'm back in the car on the way to the hospital when Sarah and Tom had their accident. Will this turn out the same way? Am I walking into a room where the love of my life is dying? Or worse... already dead?

As soon as we pull into the visitor lot of the hospital my panic spikes. Carter is here, in this building, and he could be dying. I fly out of the car a second before Abbie even puts the car in park. The automatic doors slide open for me and I'm greeted by the flickering fluorescent lights of the ER waiting room.

There's a nurse station straight ahead and I charge towards it. "Excuse me," I gasp out, catching my breath from running. "I'm here to see Carter Williams. I don't know if he's in trauma or what, but a nurse called me—"

"Ah, Miss Hartwell." The nurse smiles kindly. "That was me. I can take you to his room now."

"Thank you," I nod, following after her as she walks down the hallway. Fluorescent lights illuminate the stark white hallways as we pass by another nurse's station where a few of them are gathered around a computer. How can everything be so calm when my heart is pounding so hard I'm surprised it's not making an imprint in my chest?

"Here we are," she says, opening the door and walking in first. "Mr. Williams, you have a visitor." She steps aside, and my steps falter when I'm met with...

Carter, looking completely fine. His phone is in his hand, and he hits a button and lays it on the bed when he sees me, a genuine lighting up his face.

"Angel! I've been trying to call you, but your phone just keeps ringing." There's a nurse on his other side, wrapping his arm in bandages. "I got a little bullet graze, but they stitched me up and I'll be good as new soon enough. They already said they can discharge me tonight."

I'm rushing him and throwing my arms around his neck, quiet sobs wracking my body.

"Oof!" He lets out a grunt, wrapping one arm around me.

"Careful," the nurse, who just finished wrapping his arm, chides.

Her words do nothing to loosen my grasp on him. He scared the shit out of me. I can already feel my sobs turn into gasping breaths again.

"Whoa, whoa, whoa, Soph. It's okay, I'm okay," he murmurs into my hair. My breathing doesn't slow though. I could have lost him. I just got him back, and he could have been ripped from my life, leaving me to raise our child by myself.

Black spots cloud my vision, and my head feels light. "I feel like I'm going to... faint..." I manage to choke out, my hands fisting his shirt.

"Shit, Soph, okay, breathe," he says in my ear as he hauls me into his lap and starts speaking to the nurse. "She thinks she might pass out. She's pregnant, and I can't imagine this is good for the baby. Is there anything we can do to make sure everything is okay?"

I don't catch the response but I feel him nod as he continues to rub circles on my back with his good arm. "I'm okay, Angel, I just got a couple of stitches."

"What happened?" I manage to get out between gasping breaths.

A slight kiss against my hair settles me slightly. Carter tells me everything his dad said. How Carter made him think he wanted in on his scheme and got him to confess. How the shooting happened and how they hauled his dad off to prison. The steady timbre of his voice combined with his touch on my back have me settling, my breathing evening out as I listen to him talk. I'm not sure how long we lay there together, but I'm almost completely calm when Carter gets to the part where his dad outed Oscar Davis.

I sit up with a jolt. "Wait, Oscar was the one helping him this time? Shit, I knew something wasn't right with him." Thinking back on it, I'm not one bit surprised. He always acted like a nice enough guy, but there had been some sort of... ick underneath it all. Like he was trying too hard to be nice.

"Yep. Before Detective Peterson shut the door to the ambulance, he told me that he'd be paying dear old Oscar a visit." Carter sighs wistfully. "Wouldn't be surprised if he's in handcuffs right now."

Before I can answer, a voice calls out from the direction of the door.

"Ms. Hartwell, would you mind taking a seat in this bed?" I turn and look as the nurse who wrapped Carter's arm pushes a second hospital bed into the room. Behind her, someone else is wheeling in what looks to be an ultrasound machine.

I guess being a hotshot hockey star in a small-town hospital has its perks.

Nodding shakily, I stand, and situate myself in the bed they've placed next to Carter. The nurse secures and then inflates a blood pressure cuff around my arm so hard it almost hurts, and then releases the pressure. "One-seventeen over seventy five," she says, "which is in the normal range. Our attending OB-GYN, will take a look at the baby and make sure everything is okay."

With that, a kind looking older lady with glasses perched on her nose and graying hair enters the room. "I'm Doctor Roberts. It's nice to meet you Sophie. How many weeks are you?" she asks, situating the machine closer to my bed.

"My first OB appointment is in a couple of days, but if my math is right, I should be about eight weeks." My voice is stronger now, my panic having subsided with Carter's help. "You're actually the doctor I have my appointment with."

She nods, smiling. "If you've already filled out your paperwork online, I don't see why we can't just do this portion of the appointment now. We can try the external ultrasound first then, and see if we can get a view of the fetus."

"Thank you." I swallow, and settle back into the bed as she raises it to a half-sitting position and moves my shirt up, pulling out a bottle of gel. A small gasp leaves me at the coldness of it hitting my bare stomach. Feeling Carter grasping my hand, I notice he's gotten up from his bed, and is staring lovingly at me as the doctor puts the wand to my lower stomach.

She moves the wand over my belly, spreading the gel around. I gnaw on my bottom lip, and Carter gives my hand a reassuring squeeze.

"Hmmm..." Doctor Roberts' eyes are on the screen in front of her. "Perhaps we should try the transvaginal—" Her words are cut off by the sudden sound of whooshing. "Ah. There we go." She smiles, holding the wand in place and using her other hand to turn the screen towards us.

My heart leaps into my throat and Carter's breath catches. The picture is fuzzy, but the shape of a head attached to a little body is evident. I can't believe it. We're having a baby. I've known for weeks, but to be able to see what they look like as they grow inside of me brings a whole new level of understanding.

It's real. This is all real.

"Is that..." Carter chokes out, tears welling in his eyes.

"Your baby," the doctor says proudly, before moving the mouse around, clicking it a couple of times. "And you were right about the timeline. Baby is measuring at about ten weeks."

"Oh my god," I choke out, my eyes fixed on the tiny body on the screen. "How big is it?"

"A common comparison used at this stage is that of a kumquat." The doctor smiles, "Or, about this big," she holds her fingers about two inches apart, "if you're like me and have never actually held a kumquat."

A shocked laugh leaves me. A baby. We're really having a baby. Carter's laugh joins mine as he leans over, capturing my lips in a fierce kiss. "We're having a baby," he whispers against my lips before pulling back and giving me the most blindly handsome smile I have ever seen on him. Hmm, if we weren't having a baby, that smile would certainly make me want to keep trying.

The doctor clicks a couple more times, then there's a whirring sound at the bottom of the machine followed by a ripping. "Here are a couple of pictures for you two." She hands them over, then wipes my belly off and helps me adjust my shirt. "I'll leave you two alone for a moment."

Doctor Roberts and the nurse who took my blood pressure head out the door, the latter wheeling out the second bed and making a note to get me some paperwork to fill out before I leave. Carter and I settle into his hospital bed, me between his legs and resting my head on his chest, staring at the ultrasound pictures. His hands come around to cup my belly. "I..." The words choke in my throat as tears fill my eyes. "I can't believe it. We're having a baby."

"I know how you feel," he says, pressing a kiss to the side of my head. "I wonder how many weeks until they're the size of a hockey puck."

I laugh. "Why is that?"

He shrugs, a small smile on his face. "Then we can refer to the baby as 'Little Biscuit'"

"What do you think, hm?" I look down at my belly, rubbing my hand over the spot where the ultrasound wand was minutes ago. "Do you want to be Little Biscuit?" Turning my head, I place a gentle kiss on Carter's lips. "I think we can call them that now."

"Alright, Little Biscuit." Carter says, moving one of his hands over mine. "Mommy and Daddy already love you so much. We'll always take care of you, no matter what." There's an emotion in his words I can't quite place, but part of me realizes it's his promise to Little Biscuit to be nothing like his father.

Taking his hand, he grips my chin, tilting my head towards him. His lips capture mine, slowly and full of love as a contented sigh leaves me. "That goes for you too, Angel. Nothing in this world will ever separate us again, I promise."

His words settle over me in a reassurance I didn't know I needed, and I can feel the truth of them. His dad is gone, and we won't need to live our lives looking over our shoulders. Nothing can stand between us and a future of love and happiness. We've been through so much already, I know we can face down anything as long as we're together.

Chapter Thirty Six

SOPHIE

Shortly after the ultrasound, Abbie found us, letting me know her dad drove my car here for me. She'll take him home. She hands me the phone I left on her dad's living room floor and my purse. "I'm so glad you're okay, Carter," she says, nodding at him.

Tears well in her eyes, and I hold my arms out to her, dropping the ultrasound face down next to me. "Oh, come here, you big softie."

She throws herself at me, laying her head on my shoulder and wrapping her arms around both of us. "My dad got filled in by Detective Peterson. I hope you don't mind, but I called Jake. I thought he'd want to know and be here."

"Thanks, Abbie," Carter says warmly, patting her head like a puppy. She snorts, and stands up, wiping at her eyes right in time for Jake to show up.

His eyes fly to the bandage on Carter's arm, looking shocked. "Holy shit, man, are you okay?" he asks, still standing in the doorway, running a hand through his messy brown hair

"I meant to call you, but then I couldn't get a hold of Sophie.

It's just a graze, though," he says, shooting his friend a guilty smile. Jake's features relax as his blue eyes light up in relief.

"Thanks for calling me, Abbs," he murmurs into Abbie's ear, pressing a kiss to her hair before coming around to Carter's other side. Blushing, Abbie looks taken aback at his public display of affection, but she recovers quickly, shrugging. "He's your best friend."

Jake looks to Carter, eyeing his bandage. "Fuck, he actually shot you. But... it's over? He's really...?"

"Detective Peterson says that between the financial crimes and the attempted murder charge, we won't ever have to see him again." I pick the ultrasound photos back up, thankful we're all safe.

"Thank fuck," Jake mutters, suppressing a shiver. "That guy always gave me the creeps." His eyes slide from Carter to me, and then to the ultrasound picture in my hand, his jaw dropping. "Is that...?"

My cheeks hurt from how hard I'm smiling. "Uncle Jake, Auntie Abbie, meet Little Biscuit." A small squeal leaves Abbie as she goes to stand next to Jake, both of them looking at the photo.

"It's like a little bean..." Jake mutters, his eyes wide.

"A kumquat," I supply helpfully, snuggling back into Carter's chest and watching their expressions.

"So tiny," Abbie coos, wiggling her finger in front of the photo like it's the actual baby.

"I'm so happy for you guys," Jake says, gently grasping Carter's shoulder. "You deserve all the happiness in the world."

"I think he just told me he loves me," Carter stage-whispers, mock surprise on his face.

"Oh, shut up, dickhead," Jake laughs. "You know I do."

"Little Biscuit..." Abbie chuckles and shakes her head before taking the photos from Jake. Pure adoration lights them as she trails a finger over the little blip where the heartbeat is, then seems to snap out of it and whips a hand towards Carter. "*You're* not allowed to pick baby names anymore." We dissolve into a fit of giggles while Carter and Jake chuckle and shake their heads.

For the first time in a long time, I'm no longer carrying the weight of years of regret on my shoulders.

I've never felt more free.

"You ready?" Carter asks, tightening his arm around my shoulder as we prepare to leave his hotel room the next day. By the time they had discharged him from the hospital, it was one in the morning, and I drove us both back to his room before we collapsed in the bed, exhausted as hell.

"So ready." I nod, grasping his hand. He looks as delicious as ever in dark wash jeans and a green t-shirt that hugs his muscular chest and shoulders. I'm itching to peel it off him and run my tongue between his pecs.

My train of thought startles me. It must be the hormones. Ignoring my newfound urge to lick Carter, at the most inconvenient times, I shoot him a smile. "It felt strange keeping it from them. Now that the threat of your dad is gone, and things are finally settled between you and me, I want to tell them in person."

He brushes some of my long, curled, auburn hair from my face before pressing a kiss to my temple and handing me my phone. "Let's do this then."

The drive to my parents house is short, but that doesn't stop me from being weirdly nervous about telling my family. Carter tightens his hand around mine, stopping me from compulsively brushing down the skirt of my sundress. "You're killing me in that outfit, Angel. If you keep drawing attention to the skirt of your dress, I might just have to pull over and remove the whole thing for you." The heat in his voice sends a jolt of need straight through me, and I'm half tempted to do it again, just to see if he follows through.

Shit, these hormones are out of control.

The words distract me, and before I know it we're inside the house, stuffed on the couch.

Mom and Jordan are on the couch next to us, and Dad and Tom stand by them, their postures relaxed.

"What happened to your arm, Carter?" Jordan asks, his eyes wide. "Are you okay?"

"Oh, I'm fine, bud." Carter grins without missing a beat. "Got an injury at hockey camp." I'm so grateful we asked Tom to not mention what happened at the stake out and the real reason for Carter's injury. I hate lying to them, but Jordan doesn't need to know all the gory details. Besides, this moment is about Little Biscuit. We won't let the actions of Jeremy Williams ruin the joy of the day.

"So," I take a deep breath. "We have some news."

I have no idea why I'm so nervous. I don't think they'll be mad. Hell, it's not like this is some kind of teenage pregnancy. I'm twenty-eight years old for fuck's sake. Why do I feel so jittery?

"If you're going to tell us you're back together again, I think we already knew that." Tom hedges, looking between Carter and me.

"That's definitely part of it..." I bite my bottom lip. "But there's more." When I can't find the words, I grab the set of ultrasound photos from my purse in my lap and hold them out to Mom. "Carter and I are together, but we're adding... a Little Biscuit."

A shocked squeal escapes Mom, and I find that all my worrying was for nothing. Mom is lighting up like a damn Christmas tree, on her feet and hopping up and down with joy. Dad is just staring at me, with a small smile on his face and tears welling in his eyes. "My little girl..." he murmurs fondly.

They're taking it way better than I had imagined. No questions about how it happened, or even if it was an accident. Just pure, unadulterated joy.

Jordan stands and looks between us and my mom, a look of confusion on his face. "What is it? What's going on?"

"Carter and Sophie are having a baby!" Mom all but shouts, a huge smile on her face.

"That little blob is going to be my cousin?" Jordan asks incredulously, peering at the photos, before smiling widely.

"It sure is," Dad smiles, patting Jordan's back.

Tom's the only one who hasn't said anything.

"Tom...?" I ask cautiously, taking in the blank look on his face. He shakes his head like he was lost in thought, before clearing his throat.

"You guys mind giving us the room?" Carter asks Mom and Dad, who nod their agreement.

They usher Jordan out of the room, Mom whispering something to dad about "beautiful grandchildren".

Tom walks over and sits on the now empty couch. "Listen, I'm not going to pretend that it's not weird learning that my best friend knocked up my sister—"

"Tom!" I gasp indignantly. He can not be serious. He's never cared about that.

"I'm *joking*," he says rolling his eyes "Honestly, though, I am happy for you Soph. And you too, Carter."

An internal sigh of relief escapes me. "Thanks, Tom." My voice is soft, almost quiet. I hadn't realized just how much his reaction would mean to me.

"That means a lot," Carter admits, his voice thick with emotion.

"Really, I couldn't be happier for the two of you. Without you Sophie..." He looks away, blinking furiously. "I don't know what Jordan and I would have done if we didn't have you after Sarah." He shakes his head, looking back at us, his eyes glassy. "After all you've both been through, you deserve every happiness there is in the world. I've had a front row seat to the love and devotion you show everyone around you. Your child will be the luckiest baby in the world. Plus, having a kid of your own? That's a whole new level of joy." He looks between the two of us with a softness I haven't seen in a long time.

I sigh, leaning my head on Carter's shoulder. "Love you, big brother."

"I love you too, Soph." Tom smiles, looking between us. "Both of you." Then his expression turns serious, his blue eyes hardening. "But Carter?"

"Yeah?" Carter's voice is hesitant.

"You're my best friend. I've been able to separate myself from the history of your relationship all these years because you weren't here. But if you ever hurt my sister again or make her cry, I *will* punch you in the fucking throat."

A startled laugh escapes me at the intensity of his words, but Carter looks serious as Tom continues. "No more mistakes, no more fuck ups. Got it?"

Carter nods. "I'll come to you myself for it if I ever hurt her again."

"Good to hear," Tom says, bracing his hands on his knees before standing up and turning back towards Carter. "Now that *that's* out of the way, I know you're probably anxious to fill your mom in on everything."

Carter nods in agreement, and a few hugs and goodbyes later, we're back in the car heading for Carter's mom's house.

Carter hadn't seen any point in causing his mom undue stress by telling her about the plan to take down his dad. Now that everything is over, though, he wants to see the look on her face when he tells her Jeremy Williams is gone for good.

Parking the car in his mom's driveway, I instantly notice the figure standing there. A tall, slender, super-model type figure with long blonde hair and a short skirt. Nicole.

Oh, *hell* no. This bitch is delusional if she thinks she has any leg to stand on when it comes to Carter Williams. That man is *mine*.

"Nicole!" Carter nearly roars, slamming the car door behind him. "What the *fuck* are you doing here?"

I'm out of the car before he can even think of opening the door for me, and I join him in front of the car, linking his hand in mine as we go to confront the beast.

"Carter, baby," she simpers, closing the distance between all of us with a few steps as we approach the driveway. She eyes our linked hands before her gaze travels to the bandage on Carter's arm and tries to grab his free hand. "Are you okay? I can't believe *that girl* you're slumming it with got you hurt."

Carter wrenches his arm away, shooting her a steely look before gently releasing my hand and stepping in front of me. Shielding me. Is it bad that the sight of him protecting me from his psycho stalker makes my panties wet?

"Leave. Now," he grinds out, his hands flexing in anger.

"But Carter!" she whines, stepping towards us again.

That's it. I've had *enough*.

Stepping out from behind him, I point a finger at her. "Stop acting desperate. How did you even find out where his mom lives, you fucking stalker?" I snap, venom dripping from every syllable. This chick needs a wake up call. "This is disgusting. He doesn't want you."

Her eyes narrow as Carter puts a protective arm around me and pulls me closer. "She's not just 'that girl'," he snarls, "Sophie is my fiance, and the love of my life."

Fiance? My heart flutters. I can't believe he just said that. I mean, we've said that we're together forever now... but I didn't realize how much I want him to actually propose..

Nicole's face contorts in rage. She stamps her foot like a petulant child. "No!" she shrieks, "You're mine, Carter Williams! I'm not letting this... this bumpkin take you from me! We belong together!"

Before either of us can say a word, the front door opens, and Vivianne steps out, looking as fierce and protective as a mama bear. There's an apron tied around her neck and a spatula in her hand as she turns her fury on Nicole.

"If you don't get off my property this instant, you... you... two-cent ho, you will see a side of me you *really* don't want. Get the hell out of here." Her voice is laced with anger, and Nicole's eyes widen at the threat.

"I'm not... I don't..." she stammers, taking a step back.

"I would listen to her," I tell her in a stage-whisper. "Mama V's pretty scary when she's mad." I may be embellishing a little, seeing as I'm not sure Vivianne knows what part Nicole had in mine and Carter's issues, but Nicole pales slightly, before hurrying away from the front porch.

"Keep an eye out for that restraining order! If I catch you around me or my family again, I'll have you arrested," Carter shouts after her, before he grins, looking at his mom with respect. "Way to go, Mom."

Vivianne looks between us before pulling me into a tight hug. "Nobody is going to mess with my future daughter in law... or future grandbaby."

We all chuckle at that, and Carter turns to me, eyebrow raised. "Mama V?"

"It seemed fitting." I grin at them. "She came out in mama bear mode." Vivianne gives me a warm smile, before she spots the bandage on Carter's arm.

"Carter, what happened? Are you okay?" She fusses over him, looking at his arm.

"That would be Dad," Carter admits, then quickly adds, "But it's okay. He's gone for good this time."

Her eyes light up. "Tell me everything." We head inside, my eyes widening up at how they've redone the place. The walls are painted a light cream color with teal accents. New lighting fixtures brighten up the space further, turning Carter's once dreary childhood home into a home I can see our baby running around, visiting with their Grandma. I can't wait to see the rest of the house.

Carter leads his mom into the living room and has her sit in one one of the new teal armchairs, before proceeding to tell her all about the set up, and how he got his dad to confess to all of his crimes.

"The detective asked if you'd be a character witness if necessary," Carter says carefully, trying to gauge his moms reaction.

She doesn't even hesitate. "Yes. Anything to get that bastard put away for as long as possible." I wouldn't have blamed her if she never wanted to even hear his name again, but she's determined to see him pay for his actions. Carter sweeps her into a hug right as my phone rings.

"Hey, Abbs," I answer. "What's up?"

"Hey, Soph. Just checking in and seeing how you guys are doing. Dad made one final statement at the station today to help close out the details of the case, and I went with him," she says with pride. "We're just leaving now."

Carter gives me a questioning look as he pulls away from his mom.

"One second," I tell her, then put the phone on mute. "It's Abbie. She's with her dad, who just made a final statement at the station."

"I don't know how I'll ever be able to repay him if he had any part in putting Jeremy behind bars where he belongs." Vivianne says to Carter, then her face lights up as an idea strikes her. "Oh! Do they want to come for dinner?"

Carter shrugs, motioning to me.

I unmute the phone. "Sorry, we're just at Carter's mom's for dinner. She wants you to join us so she can thank your dad for all he's done."

"Hold on, let me check." I hear shuffling on the other line before Abbie's sounds again in my ear. "We would love that!"

Abbie says excitedly. Her voice lowers conspiratorially. "Dad just said he's going to change into something 'more appropriate' for dinner and he never does that. I think he's excited."

Not even a half hour later, the five of us sit around the dining room table, have a wonderful dinner together as Michael tells everyone how he's been working with Detective Peterson for years. Dinner comes to a close on a light note, with laughter, easy conversation, and talk of baby names.

The way that Vivianne and Michael lean towards each other while talking, how she laughs at his jokes, and the stars in both of their eyes when they look at each other has me smiling.

"Am I imagining things?" I lean over and whisper to Abbie, who seems to have noticed the same thing I have.

"Definitely not," Abbie rounds her eyes and shakes her head slightly. "I haven't seen him like this in... ever." By the look on her face, she's overjoyed that he's having this connection with Vivianne.

I smile, grasping Carter's hand under the table. Maybe we aren't the only two who are getting a second chance at love.

Chapter Thirty Seven

SOPHIE

"Cart, you missed the turn," I tell him when he goes past the hotel. While dinner was amazing, it's been a really long day and all I want to do now is snuggle up in bed. A detour was not in my plans.

"Nope," he says, smirking at me. "I know exactly where we're going."

When I try to push for more information, he only makes a zipping motion across his lips. I recognize the area we're in now, a new section of houses built in the last ten years.

"You may notice we're still in the Ivy Glen school district," he says lightly, glancing at me. "You also may notice we're right in between my mom's and your parent's house."

Now that he mentions it...

We pull up in front of a beautiful, white, two-story home with a wraparound porch, a trellis wrapped in ivy on the side, and sky blue shutters.

"Carter..." I ask slowly, looking at him. "Where are we?"

He only grins, and gets out of the car before opening my door and taking my hand.

He didn't.

Did he?

"Carter..." I ask again, turning towards him when we reach the little stone walkway that leads to the porch. "Whose house is this?" My heart is pounding in my chest, and he shocks me by getting down on one knee.

"Sophie. I love you so much. You had every reason not to let me back in, but you did anyway. You gave me another chance, and I want to spend the rest of my life giving you everything my heart has to offer." I gape. Is he...?

"Now," he continues, fishing around his pocket. "I may not have a ring, but..." he pulls out a small keychain. "I have a key. Sophie Hartwell, will you make me the happiest man alive, and marry me?"

I can't believe the one thing I've always wanted is right in front of me. Carter. The boy I fell in love with, and the man who made me love again. Both of them look back at me through the crystal blue eyes of the strong, loyal, protective man on his knees in front of me.

I let out a shocked laugh. "You never do things by halves, do you?" I sniff, and he smiles up at me, unshed tears in his eyes. "Of course. Of course I'll marry you."

He goes to stand, but before he's even fully on his feet, I throw myself into his arms, wrapping my legs around his waist as he catches me and kisses me breathless.

"Do you want to see inside?" he says against my lips.

I only nod, kissing him again as he walks us to the front door. He breaks the kiss to unlock it with the key, and carries me into the kitchen.

"Before the grand tour..." he rumbles, "there may not be a bedroom set up yet, but there is plenty of space on this counter for me to ravage you on, and I am *starving*."

A shocked gasp leaves me as he places me on the kitchen island,

and I don't even get a good look at the interior of the house before he's wiggling me out of my jeans and underwear, kissing down the exposed flesh as he goes. The granite is cold on my ass, but I forget all about it when Carter tosses my clothes to the side and steps between my open legs, devouring my mouth, his fingers teasing my entrance.

I shiver flows through me at the brush of calloused skin against my own, his mouth moving from mine down to my neck. "We'll start in the kitchen, but after we move in, I want to fuck you on *every single surface* of this house."

"Don't threaten me with a good time." I gasp as he bites my neck just how I like it— gently, not hard enough to hurt, but enough to keep me in place as he slips two fingers into me. The feel of his teeth on my skin has my pussy clenching in need and he chuckles darkly as he removes them and licks them clean.

"It's a promise, Angel." His voice is husky as his fingers plunge back inside me, this time in hard, determined thrusts. I moan at the sensation, and he keeps pumping in and out of me, curling his digits up to hit my g-spot. "

A keening sound leaves me, my hips trying to push upwards, wanting his fingers deeper. More. I need *more.* "Carter please!" I whine, clutching his shirt desperately.

"I've got you, beautiful. For the rest of our lives. I love you so damn much." His fingers never leave my pussy as he uses his other hand to push against my shoulder, a ghost of kiss brushing over my lips before he lowers me until I'm laying flat on my back like his own personal buffet.

"I love you too, Carter," my voice is breathless as he now towers over me, taking me in.

The heat of his gaze lights my body on fire, his thighs pushing my legs apart so I'm wide open for him.

Lowering himself to his knees, he presses a kiss to my mound. "Shit, you're so perfect, Sophie. My Angel. My *future wife.* " He then nips at my inner thigh before his tongue finds me, licking circles around my clit as he continues fucking me with his hand. Ice travels down to my toes as he lavishes my pussy in attention, licking and sucking and kissing, until I'm a needy, panting mess.

"Use my face, Angel," he orders, pulling back slightly. "Fuck my mouth with this perfect pussy. I want to taste how desperate you are for me." His words release something inside of me, and when he returns his mouth to my dripping center, my hands tangle in his hair, desperate to hold him close.

I'm under no illusion that I'm in charge. The only reason I'm able to hold him tightly, bucking up into his mouth, is because he's *letting* me. And fuck, if that doesn't turn me on even more.

"Please! Carter, I'm so close!" My words make him double down on his efforts, his tongue honing in on my clit as he licks in short, firm strokes, and his fingers curling up to hit my g-spot *just right*.

"I got you, Angel. I'll always have you. Let go and come for me." Then he pulls my clit into his mouth and sucks *hard*, I'm done for.

I come with his name on my lips, stars bursting across my vision as my pussy clenches around his fingers, my fingers tightening in his hair. He laves at my clit through the aftershocks of my orgasm, slowly removing his fingers, and when he sits up to kiss me, I wrap my arms around his neck, planning on never letting him go.

Years ago, I never would have thought I'd not only have Carter back by my side, but a baby on the way as well. This house that we'll make a home in—with our family, friends, and love—is something I never knew I was missing. A place to raise Little Biscuit as well as any other children we might have. A sanctuary we can call our own. A place to build new memories together, for the rest of our lives. The gift Carter's given me means more than he'll ever know.

While I wish we never had to be apart to begin with, I now realize I wouldn't have had it any other way. The struggles we went through to get here, the lessons we learned, and the people we have become, that's what has made our love stronger than ever. And that love is... everything.

It's Sophie and Carter. Forever.

Epilogue

SOPHIE

June – Ten Months Later

"Oh, Sophie, sweetie, you look absolutely breathtaking," Dad says, looking at me with tears in his eyes.

I *do* feel beautiful.

My hair is done in an elegant updo, and my dress, complete with lace appliques and pearl embellishments, hugs every curve perfectly. It's the perfect wedding dress.

We're standing outside the double doors to the ice rink of the newly opened Twin Rinks, waiting for my cue to walk down the aisle. I had debated on an indoor or outdoor wedding, since it's June and the weather is gorgeous, but when I saw the idea online for a "wedding on ice" I just knew we had to do it. There's a large sheet of plexi-glass covering the ice so the ceremony can proceed without everyone slipping around. The grand opening of the rinks isn't until next week, so tonight we're free to use it as we please.

It only seemed fitting to have the wedding here, since it's the place that brought us together again.

"Thanks, Dad." I smile, desperate not to tear up and ruin my professionally-done makeup.

"He's right, babe." Abbie says, adjusting my veil. "Carter's gonna have a heart attack when he sees you." She takes her role as Maid of Honor very seriously, and is determined to make sure not a hair is out of place for the ceremony.

Tom, as Carter's Co-Best Man, has surprisingly been equally fussy about Carter, making sure he got his haircut and picked out the right tux. While Jake, his Other Best Man, did what Jake does best... plan the bachelor part. All I know is that whatever happened that night pissed Abbie off to no end.

"There's Mama!" Vivianne's voice calls as she walks down the hall, pushing a stroller, followed by Abbie's dad, Michael. After dinner all those months ago, the two of them started dating, and I've never seen Mama V look more alive.

"How's my little man?" I coo, peering into the stroller at the littlest love of my life. Chase has his daddy's black hair, and my honey brown eyes. He coos at me as I let him grab my finger. "You look so handsome in your dapper ring-bearer outfit." He's too cute for words in his little white button up, suspenders and bowtie.

"You look gorgeous, dear," Vivianne says to me, smiling and pulling me into a hug, unshed tears shining in her bright blue eyes. She's looking so much more alive than she did only a year ago, her slightly graying black hair swept up in a chignon and a long, flowing navy blue dress wrapped around. She pulls away and dabs at her eyes. "We'll get him inside so Jordan can push him down the aisle."

Jordan, while claiming he was too old to be a ring bearer, had jumped at the chance to be a part of the wedding and push his little cousin down the aisle.

Dad steps aside to talk to Michael before Jake pokes his head out the doors. "We're on in five, folks." He shoots a wink to Abbie, who bites her lip, before disappearing.

I look between the now closed door and Abbie before asking, for probably the millionth time, "So, what's *actually* going on with you and Jake?"

Abbie shrugs as she moves a tendril of hair near my face. "Nothing really. But holy hell, is that man looking fine today. And it *is* a wedding after all, so I'll definitely be getting laid tonight."

I laugh and shake my head. At least she's over whatever happened at that bachelor party. They've had a sort of on again-off again fling the last ten months, but I can never get her to give me a straight answer on how she actually feels about the guy.

He lives in Boston near the Garden since both he and Carter are playing for the Reapers now, but I know that they always spend at least one night together whenever he *is* in town. Now that the season is over, he's been in town more often than not, staying in the guest room of our house when he comes to visit.

They had a great first season, the team making it to the play-offs, and almost winning the Stanley Cup. After Carter came home from their last game and completely ravaged me, he admitted that once this contract is over, he's thinking he's only going to sign for one more season.

After I had started to protest that this is his *dream*, he shushed me with a kiss. "I miss you guys too much when I'm gone. I want to be home more, be with Chase, and help you manage the rinks."

"Anyone can help manage the rinks." I had rolled my eyes.

"Anyone can. But I want to. You need it now that your business is taking off."

He was right. Starting my financial advising company was slow going at first, but once word spread that town local Sophie Hartwell was open for business, people that I've known for years started coming to me for their taxes and even estate planning.

It's been a lot of hard work, especially with a newborn, but I'm finally doing something I love, and Carter has been supportive every step of the way.

But my company clearly wasn't the only reason for Carter's change of heart. "Besides," he had said, "I refuse to miss any moments of our kids growing up."

"Our kids? You do realize we only have one right?" I'd questioned.

"For now. I want a hockey team's worth with you, Angel." I had laughed when he said it, but in the back of my mind, I wouldn't be opposed to having at least two more. He had kissed me slowly after that, the act filling me with so much love and devotion, I couldn't even argue.

If that was what he wanted, who am I to stand in the way?

"Oh, it's time!" Abbie whispers, peeking through the doors and bringing me back to the present.

"Ready, Pumpkin?" Dad asks, coming over and holding his elbow out to me.

Smiling, I nod, and loop my arm through his.

I am.

Ready to officially start the rest of our lives, with Carter, Chase, and my family by my side.

Turn the page for a Back on Ice bonus scene!

Bonus Chapter One

ABBIE

ABBIE AND JAKE'S FIRST NIGHT

"Do you want to get out here?" Jake's voice rumbles low as he dances behind me, the heat of his words sending a stream of warmth through my veins that has nothing to do with the shot I downed not too long ago. The feel of his strong hands gripping my hips and his hard chest at my back only add fuel to the fire.

He's the last person I'd thought I'd see tonight, but it is by no means an unwelcome sight. He's so close his breath is hot in my ear, and I can only imagine how good that would feel in *other* places.

I suppress a shiver at the thought.

How many times had I dreamed of this in high school? Of Jake, finally seeing me as more than just a friend of the group? Of him realizing that I was *right fucking there*, and how perfect we'd be together?

Too damn long. And now that he wants me? I'm going to enjoy this delicious moment for as long as I can.

"I don't know," I keep my voice light, pretending his voice in my ear alone *didn't* just make my panties wet. "That guy over there's been making eyes at me all night. Maybe I'll go home with him."

I'm not even sure if that's true. I haven't noticed anyone else this whole night, but Jake's never pursued a woman who didn't instantly get on her knees for him. Not that I *won't* do that...but he needs to work for this, at least a little bit.

His hands tighten on my waist. "I doubt you'll keep that option open when I tell you all the dirty things I want to do to this fucking sinful body."

His voice is low and gravelly, almost like a growl. Shit. Why is that so hot?

"Oh?" Bending forward slightly as we move, I make sure my ass presses against the crotch of his jeans, teasing him. "Like what?"

I know I'm playing with fire here, but I want to see how far I can push him before he finally loses control.

"Like," he murmurs before spinning me around to face him. "Me burying my head between your thighs and letting you ride my face until you see stars."

"Is that right?" I ask breathlessly, his words rolling through my mind.

Pulling me close, my hands rest upon his muscular, broad chest as his hard cock presses against my stomach. The evidence of his arousal is enough to make me clench my thighs with desire as his dark blue eyes flash with heat before he lowers his head next to mine. "Yes, that's right. I want to bend you over every surface of my hotel room and fuck you so hard your voice is hoarse from screaming my name and I've ruined you for anyone else. Can you handle that?"

My mouth goes dry, and he pulls back, looking at me with one cocky brow raised.

Shit. Game *on*.

"Can I handle that?" I shrug with a smirk, taking a step back, baiting him. "Can you prove that you're worth my time?"

His smirk disappears, and he glances to where Sophie and Carter are standing off to the side, talking. Sophie, for once not looking at Carter like she wants to rip out his throat.

Hopefully, they'll fuck it out.

Jake's dark blue eyes land back on mine with a new intensity, and in the next moment, he's grabbed hold of my hand and is dragging me off the dance floor. The action surprises me enough that I just go with it, and before I have a chance to wonder where the hell he's taking us, we break through the small crowd, entering the narrow hallway with two private bathrooms.

"What are you doing?" I ask, my eyes wide and my heart pounding in exhilaration.

"Fucking proving it," he says, before opening one of the doors and pulling me inside.

The speed at which he locks the door, shimmies down my jumpsuit, and lifts me onto the sink counter makes me question how often he does bar bathroom hookups. But the second he bends over, spreads my thighs open and sucks my clit through the fabric of my thong, I find that I don't really care. The feeling of his hot, wet mouth on me with only a layer of lace between us is one of the most erotic things I've ever experienced.

"Holy shit," I cry out, spreading my legs wider and bracing my hands on the edge of the counter.

He only chuckles and stands up, pressing a dirty, open-mouth kiss to my neck before moving my thong to the side, slipping two fingers inside of me. "Look at you, playing hard to get," he tuts, pulling his face back slightly and pumping his digits in and out as I writhe under his touch, "when you're so wet from just dancing with me."

"Yeah?" I gasp as his other hand dips into my bra and swipes at my stiff peak. "Don't pretend you didn't have your hard cock pressed against me two minutes ago."

He gently tweaks my nipple, sending a bolt of need down straight to my clit. "The only one pretending here is you, Abbie." His fingers never leave my channel as he drops to his knees and pulls my thong completely to the side, burying his face in my aching pussy. He licks and sucks with such intensity that I'm holding on to the edges of the counter for dear life.

Damn. Has he taken a class on how to make a girl come apart in less than five minutes? Because that's what it feels like.

I've had my fair share of hook-ups over the years, but none of them were ever this fucking *good*.

The fingers of his free hand dig into my thighs in the most delicious way. It seems so unreal that the guy I was head over heels for in high school, the one who never saw me as anything more than a platonic friend, is so desperate for me that he's on his knees in a bar bathroom eating my pussy like his life depends on it.

The thought has my head spinning.

His teeth graze me ever so slightly, and my toes curl as one of my hands reaches for the mop of hair I love so much.

"Shit! Jake!" I scream when he sucks my clit into his mouth at the same time he curls his fingers upward and hits my g-spot perfectly.

I shatter on his tongue, my thighs shaking uncontrollably as my orgasm overtakes me. I come so hard white spots cloud my vision, and my heart is damn near pounding out of my chest.

Panting, my eyes are wide as I take in Jake on the floor in front of me, pulling away with that fucking cocky smirk as he wipes the back of his hand over his mouth. "So...do you want to get out of here? Or do I need to keep proving how much I want you?"

Swallowing thickly, I reach and grab the collar of his shirt, pulling him up to me. His mouth meets mine in a fervent kiss. The taste of myself on his lips has me nearly moaning, the well of need within me growing even though I just came apart moments ago.

His tongue tangles with mine, his desire and pure *want* as evident as the still hard bulge pressing against my center. Pulling back, we're both breathing hard when I look into his ocean-deep blue eyes. "Your place, or mine?"

***

The door to Jake's hotel room slams behind us as he backs me against the wall, devouring my mouth. My hands reach for his belt buckle, and in the next instant, we're ripping off each other's clothes, all illusions of his cool, calm, and collected attitude thrown out the window.

Once we're both completely naked, we stare at each other for a split second, taking in each other's bodies. I might as well be looking at a statue of a Greek god. Hard planes of muscle make up his chest and abdomen. His thighs are so thick, I have no doubt the force of this man slamming his deliciously large, throbbing cock into me would leave me walking funny for days.

His dark gaze roams over my bare breasts, his eyes filling with hunger as they travel down my body and back up to my face. With how he looks at me...shit. I'm ignoring the fluttering of my heart because that's fucking *dangerous*. I shove away the feeling deep down into the recesses of my mind.

The way my nipples tighten and heat fills my belly, though? I know exactly what to do with that.

I've barely taken a step towards him when he scoops me up, hiking my legs around his waist and digging his fingers into my ass cheeks as he carries me to the bed. "Should I eat this pretty pussy again?" he asks, moving one of his hands to quickly swipe at my aching center.

"No," I shake my head, grinding my pussy against the underside of his shaft and letting out a small whimper. "I want you inside me. Now."

"Fuck, Abbie," he groans and shudders at the feeling of my nails digging into his shoulders. "You're a damn siren, you know that?"

He tosses me onto the bed, my back pouncing against the

mattress as a squeal escapes me. "Mmm. Am I luring you to your doom?"

He chuckles as he reaches into the bedside drawer and pulls out a condom. "That's right, Abbs. Now that I've had a taste, I'd fucking chase you across the ocean just to take this body how I want."

A shudder runs through me at the thought of him *chasing* me, and his gaze snags on my lower lip as I bite it.

"You like that don't you?" he asks, his voice low as he crawls onto the bed, moving toward me and looking every bit the predator. "You want me to hunt you down, rip every piece of clothing from your body and *take* you?"

"Oh, *fuck*," I moan at his words as he grips my hips and flips me over so I'm on my stomach. Then he presses my hips forward, lifting them so my ass is in the air. His tip swipes through my folds, brushing my clit, the simple touch making my toes tingle.

In one smooth move, he thrusts into me, and I cry out, my hands fisting the bed sheets.

"It wouldn't matter how far or fast you ran," he pulls out almost completely on a groan, his fingers digging into my waist, before slamming back in, "I'd catch you, and give you exactly what you deserve."

I gasp, fighting the cry that wants to slip out of me at his continued thrusts. "And what do I deserve?"

"I guess you'll have to find out," he grunts, as he pounds into me, hitting my g-spot with every snap of his hips, dragging ragged breaths from my throat. When he wraps an arm around my middle and pulls me up so my back is flush against his chest, I can't help the loud moan of sheer want that escapes me. His cock hits me even deeper than before. Reaching up behind me, I twine my fingers through the hair at the base of his neck as his fingers find my clit and he licks, sucks, and nibbles at my neck.

White hot fire consumes me, and I cry out at the explosion of my release, my body shaking and clenching around him.

"Fucking hell," he gasps, releasing me so his cock slips out and flipping me onto my back again. "When you came, you squeezed me so hard I thought I might blow my load early."

"Would that have been a bad thing?" I ask, still breathing hard from my orgasm.

"No, but I want to be able to see your pretty mouth open in pure ecstasy by the time I'm done." With that, he lifts both my legs against his chest before sliding back into me.

"Shiiiit!" I cry at the sensation of being suddenly so full again.

"Just like that," he grinds out, dragging his thumb across my bottom lip. The way my tongue darts out and licks his thumb is pure reaction. "Shit, you really are a siren."

He braces his hands against the bed, leaning forward until I'm almost bent in half. This angle is even better than the last one, and I don't try to stifle the filthy, wanton sounds coming out of my mouth.

"Oh, Fuck! Jake! Yes!" The next orgasm sweeps me away like a hurricane, and when I feel his movements stutter and his cock pulse inside me, the groan of his release is one of the sexiest sounds I've ever heard.

"Shit...Abbie...*fuck*." He collapses next me, our chests heaving as we try to catch our breath. We lie there in silence for a few minutes. The only sound in the room is our ragged breathing as we both stare at the ceiling.

It's not until I sit up, leaning back on my hands that I catch his smirk as he stares at me. "Bet you're glad you didn't go home with that other guy now."

I choke on a laugh before simply shrugging. "Meh. I've had better." I let out a small shriek when he launches himself at me, tackling me to the bed.

"I guess we'll just have to remedy that." His eyes are full of playfulness, and I realize *this* is my cue.

It's easy to slip out from under him, and I ignore the look of surprise that etches into his features. He watches, dumbstruck as I shimmy my clothes back on and grab my stuff. "You can remedy that another time. Thanks for the fun, Jake."

His mouth hangs slightly open as I walk to the door of the hotel room. "Yeah..." he clears his throat. "Will I...will I see you again? While I'm in town?"

I give a noncommittal shrug. "Guess you'll just have to find out."

My heart pounds as I exit the room, heading down the hallway that leads to the lobby. I may have fallen for Jake in high school, but I'm not that girl anymore. He's a player through-and-through, and it's time someone beat him at his own game.

After all, the chase is the best part.

Bonus Chapter Two

SOPHIE

CHASE'S BIRTH

Being forty-one weeks pregnant *sucks*.

I'm sore, tired, my back always hurts, my ankles are swollen and I'm hot all the time. I'm ready to send this baby an eviction notice and escort them off the premises. Carter's hand lovingly rubs the large swell of my belly as we relax in bed together. His black hair is pushed out of his face, giving me a clear view of the love in his eyes as he looks at me.

One more week and Doctor Roberts will induce me. I can't wait that long, though. I need him *out*. As soon as possible.

Shifting against the mountain of pillows at my back, I pull out my phone and search "Natural ways to induce labor."

"Hmm..." I murmur, running my free hand over my exposed belly. "Ow!" I yelp as Little Biscuit's knee, or elbow, or *something*, jams into my ribs.

"I think I saw that." Carter winces before putting his face close to my belly. "Little Biscuit, save the elbows for the brawls on the rink, got it?" He then moves so that he's pressed against me, our faces sharing the phone screen. "Find anything?"

I make a face. "It says if I take castor oil, that could move things along."

"Castor oil?" His brows raise. "Is that something people just have in their homes already?"

"People used to think it was some kind of cure-all." I continue scrolling through the list.

Exercise? Ugh, I can hardly get out of bed. The thought of leaving the house and going for a walk fills me with dread. No thank you.

Spicy food...my heartburn is already out of control without adding that to the mix.

"Herbal remedies...oh wait!" Carter exclaims excitedly, having read ahead of me on the list. He gives me a wolfish grin and his blue eyes twinkle with mischief as he points to the last two bullet points.

Nipple stimulation, and sex.

Now *that*, I can get behind.

Before I can even agree, his mouth is on my neck, his hand coming up to my breast and gently massaging.

"Shiiit," I moan, my head dropping back against the pillows as I let my phone fall to the bed. God, I've missed his hands. His mouth.

It's only been a few days since we've had sex, but since my belly's started getting on the larger side, he's been too gentle. It's like he thinks he could hurt me if he really lets go.

"Carter!" I gasp as his hand moves under my shirt and brushes against my nipple. Everything is so sensitive, even the slightest touch has me arching my back and begging for more.

"Do you know how hard it is to not ravage you every single time I see you walking your sexy ass around this house, belly swollen with my baby?" He groans against my neck as fingers swipe my stiff peak again. "How hard *I've* been?"

I let out a keening sound as he moves his mouth from my neck, lifting up my shirt to lick flat across my nipple. My hand tangles in his hair as he licks and sucks the sensitive flesh, and I rub my thighs together, suddenly desperate for friction.

"I got you, Angel," Carter murmurs, my nipple popping out his mouth. His hand slides under the band of my sleep shorts and panties, groaning when he finds my already wet folds.

"Fuck, Soph." His fingers circle my clit. "So wet for me already."

A moan escapes me as he returns his attention back to my breasts, taking the other one between his lips this time. The hot sensation of his tongue on my skin combined with the expert precision of his fingers has me unravelling in seconds. My toes tingle and my vision turns white as the orgasm overtakes me, his name on my lips.

His fingers ease me through the aftershocks, then he slides them out of me and moves up to press a kiss to my lips. "You're so damn beautiful, Soph. So strong. I love you so fucking much."

"I love you, too." I kiss him back. "Now let's get this baby out of me."

Carter barks a laugh as he scoots us down the bed, removing both my shorts and his sweatpants before settling behind me like a big spoon. He tucks his arm under my head so I use his bicep like a pillow while I grab an actual pillow and stuff it under my baby belly. This has been a common position for us since I started getting bigger, seeing as I can't lay flat on my back anymore and riding him hurts my back too much.

His cock teases my entrance for just a moment. "Carter..." I whine, needing him in me right fucking now, and he kisses my neck before he slides in.

All the way in.

A small cry leaves me. "You feel like heaven," he groans as he slowly thrusts into me, his cock rubbing against my inner walls. "So damn tight."

"Ohhhh," I moan, arching my back to push him in further.

His movements are agonizingly slow and measured as he slides in and out. It feels good, but he's being too gentle. I need *more*.

"Harder," I gasp.

His movements falter for a moment. "But..."

"Stop holding back," I snap. "I'm not going to break."

"I don't want to be too rough—"

"I swear to fucking god Carter, if you don't drive that perfect cock into me with everything you have right now, I will—"

My rant is cut off by him hooking his arm under my leg and bucking up so hard into me I see stars.

It's perfect.

He's braced one of his feet against the bed, providing him the leverage he needs to give me exactly what I want.

When his free hand comes up and loosely grasps my throat as he drives into me, my eyes nearly roll into the back of my head.

This. I've missed this side of him so damn much.

"Are you happy now?" he asks breathlessly as he thrusts up at a punishing pace. "Happy that I'm going to destroy this perfect pussy until you come all over my cock?"

"So damn happy," I groan, my hands tightening on the bed sheets next to me.

He's hitting my g-spot so perfectly, his grunts feeding something primal in me. There's something about knowing that even when I'm roughly the size of a house, swollen and puffy, he still wants me like this.

"Carter!" I'm sure the neighbors can hear every single scream right now, but I can't bring myself to care. There's fire in my veins as my walls clamp down on his cock, my second orgasm washing over me like a tidal wave. My loud, keening cry at my release has his movement stuttering, and he groans as he empties himself inside of me.

"Fuck. *Fuck*. Sophie..." His hand drops from my neck, and his other arm releases my leg. I feel a kiss pressed to my shoulder as he catches his breath. "Do you think that did anything?"

"I…" I shake my head, panting heavily as a breathy laugh leaves me. Shit, if this doesn't put me into labor, nothing will. "I'm not sure. But I have to pee."

He gets out of bed and helps me up, slapping my ass as I waddle to the bathroom.

Shit, my back hurts without the support of the pillow under my stomach.

After emptying my bladder, I wash my hands and walk back to the bedroom, where Carter is sitting with his back against the headboard as he scrolls through his phone.

He looks up when I approach the bed, furrowing his brow with concern.

"Nothing?"

"Not yet, but we could always try for round two." I grin cheekily at him.

He scrambles towards me before standing on his knees at the edge of the bed, pulling me close to him. "I can get behind that."

His lips devour mine in a hungry kiss, and I wrap my arms around his neck. I wouldn't mind a continual sex marathon until Little Biscuit decides to make his appearance.

I'm so lost in him that I almost don't notice the trickle of wetness running down my leg. When it registers, I startle, breaking our kiss.

Did I just wet myself?

No, I literally just peed. But that means—

"Are you okay?" Carter asks, that worried look back in his eyes.

I take a step back, shaking my head. "I think—"

The movement has liquid gushing out of me, and our eyes both fly to the river of fluid that lands on the hardwood floor below me.

I swallow. "I think my water just broke."

Carter jumps into action, grabbing a towel for me to wipe off my legs before he throws on his clothes, and tosses random articles from my dresser at me.

"We need to get the hospital bag. Is the car seat installed in the car?" He shakes his head. "Right. Of course it is. We need to call the doctor, and our parents, and Abbie, and Tom..." He disappears out of the room in search of the bag with everything we're taking to the hospital with us, still listing off all the things we need to do.

I have just enough time to get dressed before the first contraction hits me. Cramping in my lower belly has me bracing myself against the dresser, trying to remember how they taught us to breathe in lamaze class.

Carter rushes back into the room, immediately coming to my side. "It's okay Angel. Remember, hee-hee-hoo, hee-hee-hoo." He models the breathing for me while rubbing my back, and the contraction passes, causing me to let out a sigh of relief.

He has my boots and jacket under his arm and holds them out to me. "Are you ready to go meet Little Biscuit?"

This is it. It's finally happening. Soon I'll meet the little man who has already turned our lives upside down in the best possible way.

"With you, I'm ready for anything."

Want to know how Carter and Sophie's story started?
Turn the page for a sneak peek of Left On Ice!

About Left on Ice

He was my everything and I was his…or so I thought.

Carter Williams has always been my everything—my first crush, my first kiss, my first love.

Growing up together in our small town, we bonded over ice hockey and became inseparable.

Now, it's senior year, and with his final high school hockey game approaching, I'm ready to take our relationship to the next level. After all, Carter's always been a star on the ice, and I've saved the last piece of myself for him.

After that, we'll face college together, wherever life takes us.

But as graduation nears and our futures unfold, one question haunts me: Is Carter ready to commit to the forever I'm dreaming of?

Or am I about to risk it all for a boy who might not be mine forever?

Our future is on the line, and so is my heart.

About the Author

Visit my website to stay up to date on all things Noelle Stone!
www.noellestoneauthor.com

AUTHOR BIO:

She's the literary architect of dashing billionaires and sassy, sweet heroines, adding heart-pounding twists and turns to every tale.

Her castle is filled with her loyal husband and the feline rockstar, Freddie Mercury Jr.

When she's not conjuring love stories, you'll catch her conquering the waves with her dragon boat crew, turning every adventure into a page-turner!